Blazing Hot COWBOY

KIM REDFORD

Published by Sourcebooks Casablanca, an imprint of Sourcebooks, Inc.
P.O. Box 4410, Naperville, Illinois 60567-4410
(630) 961-3900
Fax: (630) 961-2168
www.sourcebooks.com

Printed and bound in Canada.
MBP 10 9 8 7 6 5 4 3 2 1

Chapter 1

Up on Cougar Lane, the Wildcat Bluff Fire-Rescue Station's front door banged open. A half-naked man stepped into the open doorway and peered outside, drying his sable-brown hair with a white towel.

Lauren Sheridan stepped back in surprise to make room for him, not wanting to be run over by so much muscle mass. She'd been about to grasp the stainless steel handle of the metal entry door and walk inside. Now she simply gazed in appreciation at the hot body of a guy who belonged as the centerfold of a firefighter calendar. He could definitely claim the blazing month of August, particularly since he wore nothing but faded, ripped-in-the-knees blue jeans that he'd zipped up but hadn't buttoned so he'd left a slightly gaping fly. Eye candy.

"You seen Hedy?" He flicked a glance in Lauren's direction before he studied the parking lot while he used the towel to rough up his thick hair. "She must've slipped out while I took a shower."

Lauren felt his husky voice strike a deep chord within her, causing a memory—tantalizing by the feel of it—to swim up from the depths of her subconscious and hover on the edge of her conscious. Yet the memory eluded her until she caught the spicy, musky, with a hint of leather scent that was all his own. And just like that, she fell headlong back into the memory of that hot, steamy summer of love when she was just sixteen.

She jerked her gaze upward to look at the guy's face and felt her mouth go dry. Kent Duval, as she lived and breathed. She knew this man. At least, she'd known him as a boy. He'd once been her everything. And she'd shared wild kisses with him in the bed of his blue pickup up on Lovers Leap overlooking the Red River just north of their hometown of Wildcat Bluff.

He'd grown taller and wider in the shoulders, carved of muscle upon muscle with long, powerful legs. Once his sun-bronzed skin had been smooth, but now lines radiated outward from the corners of his eyes as if he laughed a lot or squinted in the sun. Maybe both. The planes of his face were sharper and more angular with high cheekbones and a square jaw. But his eyes were still the same fascinating hazel mix of brown, gold, and green.

Back then, they'd been head-over-heels in love and totally immersed in each other till one fateful day. She still felt the sting of her personal loss when her parents had told her that her daddy had a great new job. They were moving from Wildcat Bluff, Texas, to Stamford, Connecticut. And just like that, she'd been torn from Kent's arms. They'd been too young to fight the separation, although they'd stayed in touch for a while. Soon distance and college had drawn them into separate worlds. And she'd stuffed away her Kent-fueled, sweet-sixteen memories.

Now he was back in raw, vibrant color. As a boy he'd been irresistible. As a man he was the stuff of hot, sweaty dreams. She must have made some sound deep in her throat because he looked back, focused on her, then his eyebrows shot up in surprise.

"Lauren?" He dropped the towel—as if forgotten—and reached toward her with long, strong fingers outstretched as if they'd scoop her up like ice cream for a sweet, delicious treat.

"Yes." She smiled, feeling warmth for him uncurl in her depths just like the old days. "It's been a long time, hasn't it?"

"Way too long—thirteen years too long." Kent grinned, revealing straight white teeth and a deep dimple in each cheek.

She felt the past tug hard at her. Those dimples had once made him look like a naughty imp when he'd made suggestions that had pushed her limits. He'd always walked a bit on the wild side, and she'd always tried to pull him onto the straight and narrow. They'd seesawed back and forth, teasing and tormenting until they'd made everything come out right in the heat of their love and passion.

She'd been well aware that he'd featured in the fantasies of many a starstruck girl back in high school, what with Kent being a rodeo and football star as well as a smart and popular student. Still, he'd only had eyes for her till she'd moved away. Now she bet he had a well-deserved reputation with the ladies. Who could possibly resist him? Not that it mattered to her anymore. She'd sworn off guys, particularly heartbreakers.

She heard the soft, lilting, birdlike voice of Dolly Parton singing her famous song, "Jolene," drift outside from a radio somewhere in the station. The song jolted Lauren back to reality. No point in begging a woman to leave your man alone if he was bound to wander like Jeffrey, her player of a former husband. Burned once.

Twice shy. She wasn't ever treading that dangerous territory again.

Even so, she wouldn't walk away from Kent's friendship. She was glad to see him—a lot of him. She grasped his hand and matter-of-factly shook it.

He chuckled as he rubbed his rough thumb across the smooth flesh of her palm. "When were we ever on a hand-shaking basis?" He jerked her against his hard, damp chest, then wrapped her in his strong arms and gave her a big bear hug.

"Stop! You're squeezing the life out of me." And truth be told, she could hardly catch her breath—maybe from the crush but maybe from the fact that the sheer masculine power of Kent was causing her to lose her breath.

"Got to make up for lost time, don't I?" Despite his words, he set her back but kept his hands on her shoulders. "How'd you stop the clock? You look better than ever. And that's saying a lot."

When he followed those words with a flash of his dimples, she felt a telltale blush that she hadn't felt in years warm her cheeks.

He grinned even bigger at that display of how he was affecting her and planted a hot kiss on her forehead before he dropped his hands. "Hope you're back in town for more than a short visit."

She nodded, getting her feet under her now that he wasn't scrambling her brain and body with his touch. "I came to see Aunt Hedy."

"Join the crowd. I swear she gets around just as fast in that motorized wheelchair as she ever did on two legs."

Lauren smiled fondly, knowing what he meant. Hedy

Murray was a former rodeo queen, current backbone of the volunteer fire-rescue department, and owner of Adelia's Delights, a popular gift shop in Wildcat Bluff's touristy Old Town. Hedy was pushing seventy, and she'd never let anything in life slow her down. At least, not till lately.

Kent pushed long fingers through his damp hair in agitation, glanced around the parking lot again, and then gave Lauren a concerned look. "I don't mean to alarm you, but you ought to know upfront about Hedy."

"What?" She felt her breath catch in her throat, wondering if he knew something about her aunt that she didn't.

As if stalling, he reached down, picked up the towel, and twisted it in his strong hands, bronze skin in stark contrast to the white towel. "Last six months or so, Hedy hasn't been herself. It's as if she's got some kind of secret."

"Thanks for the heads-up," Lauren said on a sigh of relief that nothing new had come up, "but Ruby already told me." Lauren didn't mention it, but she'd always stayed in touch with Ruby Jobson, a longtime family friend and owner of Twin Oaks Bed & Breakfast where volunteer firefighters met to plan fund-raisers and other events.

"You've been in touch with her?" He slung the towel around his neck, letting the ends hang over the front of his shoulders. "She never said a word about it."

"I'm the closest thing Aunt Hedy's got to a daughter since she doesn't have kids of her own." Lauren didn't share her own little secret that she'd asked Ruby not to mention to anybody in town that she might return.

Gossip had wings in Wildcat Bluff, and she hadn't wanted Hedy—or anybody else—to be disappointed if she hadn't been able to come to town. And truth be told, she'd tried not to think about Kent at all because she'd locked those memories tight and thrown away the key. And now here he was in the flesh, holding that very key in his large hand.

"That's not strictly true and you know it. We all belong to her."

Lauren smiled, agreeing with his sentiment because Hedy had taught math in high school and rodeo in the arena. She'd always been a nurturing presence—like a second mother—in local kids' lives. "Mom wanted me to check on her, too. You remember they're sisters, don't you?"

"Yeah. But Connecticut's a long way from Texas."

"My parents still live there, but I was fairly close by."

"How close?" He took a step toward her as his eyebrows came together in a frown. "I thought you were back East."

"Houston. I finished up college in Texas."

"You've been in the state that long?"

She let a simple nod be her answer, not wanting to hear any recriminations, although she didn't really expect them. Still, he looked unhappy that she hadn't contacted him when she'd returned to Texas.

"You could've said something. Let me know you were back."

"We'd both moved on with our lives." She shrugged, feeling surprised that he'd still been interested enough that he'd wanted her to contact him. "Besides, I'd heard you were engaged to a Dallas model."

He shook his head as he gazed out into the distance, expression suddenly shuttered, then focused on Lauren again. "Yeah. But you should've also heard that's long over."

She nodded again, not sure if she should offer condolences or congratulations. He was giving her no clue as to how he felt about his former fiancée. She wouldn't be surprised if he still carried a torch for the beautiful gal who'd broken his heart and left him at the altar.

"Anyhow," he finally said. "I wish you'd have let me know."

"I'm here now. I drove in today."

"If you'd told me you were coming, I'd have flown down and driven you up here myself. I don't like to think about you coming all that way alone."

She cleared her throat, not wanting to get this personal with him so quickly but not knowing how to back out. He'd know the truth soon enough anyway. "I wasn't alone."

"Oh hell, don't tell me you brought a boyfriend."

"No."

"Girlfriend. Good. Best you don't take chances crossing Texas alone."

"I've been taking care of myself for a long time now." She smiled to take the sting from her words and at the notion that he still felt protective of her. Most likely his reaction was nothing personal, but just his cowboy way to respect and help ladies.

He gave her a rueful grin, revealing his dimples. "I'm sure you can. Guess old habits die hard."

"Thanks for the concern." She hesitated, not sure how

he'd react to her important news. "Naturally, Hannah came with me."

"Hannah?" He cocked his head to one side as he looked at Lauren in confusion. "Am I supposed to know her?"

"She's my daughter."

He froze in place, staring at her with eyes gone wide in surprise.

"Hannah is four years old now." Lauren babbled and knew it, but she desperately wanted to override Kent's shocked silence. "She's got her heart set on being a cowgirl."

"Kids." He spoke the one word on a wistful note. "I remember when we talked about having some of our own."

"That was a long time ago."

He nodded in agreement. "Congratulations. You beat me to the punch. I wish—" He shook his head as if driving away thoughts of what could've been. "Bet she's a doll, if she takes after you at all."

"Maybe too much. Sometimes she's a handful." Lauren chuckled, feeling relieved that the awkward moment with him had passed so easily. Once she'd thought he'd be the father of her children, but that was just a teenager's unrealistic dream. She'd always thought he'd make a great dad and was surprised he didn't have half a dozen kids already. She wished Jeffrey had been a family man, but that'd been beyond him. Even so, she'd always be grateful to him for Hannah, the most precious gift in her life.

"Guess your husband is with you."

She shook her head in the negative, feeling the usual

sadness at what could have been and what never would be now. Sometimes there were no second chances or good choices in life. Most times you did the best you could with the cards you'd been dealt. "He's no longer with us."

Kent raised an eyebrow, looking surprised at her words. "I don't mean to be nosey, but I'd like to know why not."

She took a deep breath before she spoke. Maybe she'd only need to share this information once, and then it'd be all over town. "Jeffrey died instantly in a small plane accident."

"Lauren, I'm so sorry."

"It's okay," she said in a stilted voice. Jeffrey had been her friend and Hannah's father, even if not a good husband. She wasn't sure she'd ever loved him—not like she should've. Hannah had been on the way and they'd decided to marry for her sake. But it couldn't last. She'd been talking with an attorney about divorce at the time of Jeffrey's fatal accident. Yet she still felt the shocking loss, and Hannah still missed a father figure in her life. A traditional family was over for them, but they were getting along just fine. Maybe she'd tell Kent about those years someday, but right now she could tell he didn't want to talk about his former fiancée any more than she wanted to talk about her former husband. She guessed painful memories had that effect on a person.

Kent stepped close and tilted up her chin with long fingers as he gazed into her eyes. "Are you still hurting from the loss?"

She shook her head in denial, but she could tell

he didn't believe her because he wrapped her tightly in his arms. This time, she gave into the temptation to be comforted and to feel cherished—if only for a moment. She laid her head against his bare chest, felt the dampness from his shower, smelled his heady scent, and listened to the strong beat of his heart that matched her own elevated heart rate.

When he stroked up her back with his strong hands, she felt his body grow hotter. She felt an answering response in her own tingling awareness. He spiked long fingers into her short hair and tilted back her head so she had to look up at him. What she saw in the depths of his eyes was all too familiar from those long-ago days. She hoped he didn't see something similar in her eyes. After Jeffrey, she didn't want a rekindling of what she'd shared with Kent. She'd run from involvement with guys after Jeffrey. Passion—even a man's love—were in her past, not her future. Kent was an old flame turned old friend. And she intended to keep it that way.

She gently cupped his face with one hand, gave another negative shake of her head to let him know they shouldn't go any further, and watched his gaze shutter in response. She felt a last caress of her shoulders, and then she was free and stepping back out of his reach. No words were spoken. No words were needed. And yet she felt as if she'd lost something special.

"Friends?" he asked in a voice husky with repressed emotion.

She smiled in response, feeling relieved that he'd bridged the gap before it'd had a chance to widen between them. "Always."

"Where are you staying?" He grasped the ends of the

towel in his fists—as if to control his impulse to reach for her again—while he gazed at her.

"Twin Oaks B&B." She spoke crisply to prove she could be just as matter-of-fact as he after their hot embrace. "I checked in before I came over here. I left Hannah trying on Ruby's red cowgirl boots."

"Sounds about right." He chuckled at the image, flashing his dimples again. "Y'all aren't staying with Hedy?"

"Hannah can have a lot of energy. I didn't want her to disturb Aunt Hedy's life." Lauren felt renewed worry at the thought of her adorable child. Hannah hadn't been the same outgoing little girl since the loss of her father, even if Jeffery hadn't made much effort to be a dad. Now Hannah seemed more cautious—as if life wasn't completely trustworthy. Lauren had tried to mend that wound in a variety of ways, but so far nothing had worked. She hoped Wildcat Bluff was a step in the right direction to heal her daughter.

"I bet she's like the wild child you were."

Lauren smiled, only too glad to be pulled out of her internal worry. She put her hands on her hips in mock annoyance. "Like you weren't in the middle of it all?"

He laughed, shaking his head at the memories. "If there was trouble, we could find it."

"Or make it." She joined his laughter.

"Weren't we lucky to be raised in Wildcat Bluff?"

"That's what I want for Hannah." She grew serious, letting her laughter die away. "I'm raising a free-range child."

He appeared confused by her words. "Is that what they're calling kids nowadays?"

"That's what they're calling children raised the way we were in this county."

"Oh, I thought somehow we were wandering into free-range eggs, chickens, or cattle territory."

She chuckled, enjoying his lighthearted banter.

"Are you back in Wildcat Bluff to stay?"

"I'm here for Aunt Hedy and to see how it goes with Hannah."

"Maybe you'll figure out you belong here—with all of us."

She smiled in response, knowing they were both skirting around the truth that the old sparks were blazing between them. But they were older and wiser now. They'd already been down that path and moved beyond it.

She was back in town for Hannah and Hedy. She wouldn't let whatever she personally might want or not want play a part in her decisions.

Chapter 2

Kent Duval's mind whirled as he tried to reconcile his teenage love with the young widow and mother standing before him. Lauren had the same honey-blond hair, chocolate-brown eyes, and to-die-for body that had distracted him from his studies in high school. Now she was so much more. And every last bit of her was setting him ablaze in a way he hadn't felt in a long time.

Why did she have to wear a sweet little hot-pink sundress with spaghetti straps that revealed her tanned, toned arms and her long, luscious legs? She wore flip-flops—a sandal he considered dangerous to anybody's safety—that revealed her pretty, high-arched feet with toenails painted a peachy color. She'd cut her beautiful hair that had once almost reached her waist to a short and sassy style that grazed her shoulders. He couldn't twine her long locks around his hands anymore to bind her to him, but her hair was still soft to the touch.

He was glad to see her—just how glad was evident in the hard pressure he felt exerting on the zipper of his jeans. He quickly dropped a hand to the waistband and slipped the critical top button into place before he accidentally exposed a whole lot more than his chest. He couldn't deny she was causing him to get hotter than a firecracker on the Fourth of July.

To cool down, he turned his thoughts to the Blue Norther that had dumped ice and snow all over Wildcat

Bluff County last Christmas Eve, but his body was having none of it. Spring was coming on strong and Lauren was standing before him, so there was no getting around the earthly renewal of the birds and the bees. Cold weather was giving way to that perfect time of year when a young man's fancy turned to—Lauren.

Still and all, he was a fool to get caught up in the past. Lauren was now a city gal. She had a precious little girl to raise and the memory of a lost love to fill her heart. There was no way a living guy with all his flaws could compete with a guy who'd been rendered perfect by his instant removal from the Earth. Best not toy with bad mojo. And yet, this was Lauren—*his* former sweetheart—and she stood before him looking wistful and smart and delectable. Just like the old days.

He resisted the urge to take her in his arms again to comfort her or head down a path that was dangerous to his heart. He'd thought for years that what they'd had between them was well and truly done and gone, nothing but raging teenage hormones. Now he wasn't so sure.

Maybe she'd caught him by surprise. Maybe he was still on the rebound. Maybe he'd lost his good sense. Last thing he wanted or needed in his life was a hot gal with a sad past. His former fiancée had cured him of a cowboy firefighter's desire to rescue every woman who washed up on his shore. Not everybody needed help, particularly flashy city gals named Charlene who—in the end—disdained country guys.

About the time he balled his hands into fists to keep from reaching for his old flame, he saw Ash, the station cat, saunter up, wearing a spring-green bow around his neck. He sat down in front of Lauren, looked up with bright, silver eyes in his handsome gray face, and yowled an imperative greeting. Kent just shook his head. Ash was a sucker for all the gals, and they adored him in return.

"What a pretty kitty." Lauren immediately crouched down, held out her fingers to be sniffed, and then petted Ash's broad face with gentle strokes.

"That's Ash." Kent watched the cat turn his head and give Kent a slit-eyed look of pleasure while Lauren stroked down his back to the end of his long tail. Typical Ash. He always got more than his fair share of attention from the ladies. Kent wished he could trade places with the cat and feel Lauren's soft hand stroke across his own body.

"You're such a handsome boy, aren't you?" Lauren crooned while Ash arched his back against her hand. "And where did you get that pretty bow?"

"That's Hedy's doing," Kent said. "He gets a special bow to celebrate the seasons and holidays."

"And he doesn't rip them off?"

"Are you kidding? This is Hedy we're talking about. You know how animals will do just about anything she wants."

"So true." Lauren chuckled, throwing Kent a warm glance as she continued to stroke Ash's back. "Kids, too."

He laughed with her. "I'd say that goes for all of us." He looked down at Ash. "Where's Hedy?" He didn't expect an answer from the cat, but not much got by Ash's super senses.

Ash yowled in reply, gave Lauren's hand a thank-you swipe with his long pink tongue, and then bounded through the open doorway into the station.

"Maybe he knows something we don't," Lauren said as she stood up.

"I bet he knows lots of stuff we don't, but he's not saying." Kent chuckled as he gestured after Ash. "Let's go inside and see if we can run down Hedy."

"Sounds good to me." She glanced up at the building, then back at him. "This station is new, isn't it?"

He looked at the fire station with its bright-red metal roof, five bay doors, and the regular door in front of them. "Yep. We still use the original station for the older rigs, but we really needed to update and add room for our new apparatus."

"How did Wildcat Bluff County afford it?"

"Remember when we volunteered in high school? We're all still doing the same thing. Donations. Fundraisers. Grants. Took us five years to put together enough dough, but we did it."

"Impressive. I can't wait to see inside." She gave him a soft smile before she stepped through the open doorway.

Kent hesitated, glancing at the horizon. The sun was going down in the west, casting long streaks of crimson and orange across the clear blue sky. He felt a cool breeze spring up, rustling the leaves of the live oaks. He wanted to find Hedy before it got dark, but most likely she was running errands and he'd gotten het up over nothing. Still, she just wasn't her usual feisty self of late.

He followed Lauren and Ash inside the small lobby with pale-gray walls, letting the door swing shut behind him.

Ash leaped up and sat in the middle of the simple gunmetal desk and gave Kent an intense stare.

Across from the desk, two shockingly bright-orange chairs that had to date from the late sixties rose in all their glory from the dark-gray vinyl floor. The matching chairs had been donated by a generous patron, but Kent had yet to see anybody sit in them. They appeared more Midcentury Modern eclectic than firehouse practical. But you never looked a gift horse in the mouth.

He tossed his towel on the back of the desk's practical office chair. He snatched his bright-yellow Wildcat Bluff Fire-Rescue T-shirt with a crimson firefighter-EMT logo from the top of the desk where he'd dropped it while drying off and looking for Hedy. He pulled on the T-shirt, tucked it inside the waistband of his jeans, and glanced over at Lauren.

She stood with her hands clasped behind her back as she studied the arrangement of colorful firefighter photographs in simple black frames hanging on the wall. "These are wonderful."

"Thanks. Hedy had them framed and put up."

"You took them?" She cocked her head as if in consideration. "Of course you did. I'd forgotten how you used to snap us with your camera."

"Got the bug and never lost it."

"I'm so glad. Great drama and heroics in your photos."

"I do my best, but it's just a hobby." He felt a rush of satisfaction at her compliment, but she'd always been supportive of anything he'd done.

"It's more than that and you know it."

"Lots of fine selfies out there nowadays." He shrugged, not about to blow his own horn. "Anyway, Hedy said we had to do something to coordinate with the orange chairs."

"She's right." Lauren laughed as she looked from the

photographs to the chairs and back again. "The bright-tangerine chairs do match the orange in the fires."

He just shook his head in response as he walked over to the desk, not about to get into decoration with anybody—particularly a woman. He'd always come out on the short end of that stick.

Ash looked up and yowled, holding down a yellow sticky note with writing on it with his front paws.

"What've you got there?" As Kent picked up the note, he heard the phone ring in the watch office next door, so he hurried in there. He picked up the receiver from the multiline phone on top of the gray laminate work surface that stretched across one side of the room. "Wildcat Bluff Fire-Rescue. How may I help you?"

"Kent, it's Hedy."

"Where are you? I've been looking for you."

"Didn't you get my note?"

Kent looked down at the yellow sticky note in his hand. "Just now."

"I called to you in the shower, but I left the note in case you didn't hear me."

"Are you okay?" He quickly reached over and turned down the knob on the radio, another donation in the form of a miniature 1930 reproduction wood radio with a big, bronze Superman "S" on the front. He didn't know if the giver thought firefighters were superheroes or had an ironic sense of humor. It didn't matter because the radio worked just fine—nondigital and all—since the sound was connected on a system throughout the station.

"Why do you ask?" Hedy said on an impatient note.

"It's just—"

"No matter. I'm over here in Sure-Shot at a fire site."

"How bad? What do you need?" Kent glanced up to see Lauren standing in the doorway with a concerned look on her face. He nodded to let her know he was taking care of the issue.

"Hold your horses. Billye Jo called me. She thinks it's just vandalism, but she'd like the fire on record."

"Okay. Thanks for getting right over there, but if you'd waited a minute I'd have been out of my shower."

"Think I'm not up to checking on a fire, deciding what needs to be done, and calling in volunteers after I've made my determination?"

Kent swallowed down his knee-jerk response to throw her words back at her. Everybody respected Hedy and she had to know it. She just wasn't herself. He was doubly glad Lauren was back in town because maybe she could find out if Hedy had a secret that was gnawing at her. "Hedy, you know I trust you. Now, what rig do you need me to bring out there?"

"Booster is plenty. The fire is behind the old gas station."

"Sinclair?"

"That's the one."

"I'm on my way."

"Thanks."

Kent hung up, feeling uneasy in the pit of his stomach. Fires always made him edgy. He glanced at Lauren. "Remember how to fight a fire?"

"As if anybody actually let us fight a fire back then."

"Right. But Hedy taught us the basics."

Lauren nodded in agreement. "I doubt I've forgotten anything she taught me."

"That's what I thought." He hesitated, remembering Lauren wasn't a carefree girl any longer. "There's a small fire behind that Sinclair station in Sure-Shot. I'm going to run over there and make sure it's contained so it doesn't spread. I'll take our new booster. It's got a three-hundred-GPM pump capacity and two-hundred-gallon water tank."

"Sounds impressive."

"It'll do the trick. You want to come along and help?"

She glanced down at her dress, then back up at him.

"You can find spare jeans and a T-shirt in the day room. Just in case you might need it, I'll toss in an extra set of firefighter gear for you, too."

She smiled, brown eyes lighting up with interest. "Sure-Shot. That little community still exists?"

"You bet. And they still breed the finest horses around here."

"Let me call Ruby. I doubt she'll mind taking care of Hannah a little bit longer."

"Just tell her you're going on a booster run and she'll more than understand the need." He crushed the sticky note and lobbed it into a trash can beside the filing cabinets. "Look, I can call Sydney or Trey to help if you don't want to leave your daughter the first day back in Wildcat Bluff. I probably don't need any help at all. Hedy's there."

Lauren put her hands on her hips and leaned toward him. "I appreciate the thought, but you're not going to get rid of me that easy. Do you actually think I'm going to pass up an opportunity to go to Sure-Shot, ride in the booster, and put out a fire?"

He grinned, liking her can-do attitude that was so much like the girl he'd known so well. "Now, if you'd added 'and spend a little quality time with Kent Duval,' I'd think that list couldn't be better."

She laughed, turning toward the lobby, and then glanced back. "Okay. You're on the list. But I'll expect a reward."

He stilled, feeling his heart pick up speed as images of hot, naked bodies tangled in the cool, soft sheets of his king-size bed flooded his mind. But no, they weren't going down that path. "Barbeque?"

"From the Chuckwagon Café?"

"Where else?"

"Perfect! It's been too long since I've eaten the best barbeque in Texas." She stepped into the lobby, and then called back to him. "And once I put on a Wildcat Bluff Fire-Rescue T-shirt to match yours, I'm never giving it back."

He followed, chuckling at her sassy words. "You know, that'll make you a fire-rescue volunteer for sure."

She stopped, put a hand on her waist, and thrust out her hip like she had in her younger days. "Guess that'll make me a cowgirl firefighter."

"Oh yeah." He figured she was the only one who could put out the wildfire she'd ignited in him.

Chapter 3

Lauren rode shotgun in the bright-red booster with *Wildcat Bluff Fire-Rescue* emblazoned on the outside doors. She felt a little guilty for leaving Hannah longer at Twin Oaks, but her daughter had been having a great time baking chocolate chip cookies with Ruby when Lauren had called them on her cell phone. Ruby had insisted they were fine and to take care of the fire.

Hannah needed to experience a wider circle of friends, particularly those who could teach her about country life where she would feel safe to spread her wings. And maybe Lauren needed to ease up on her own self so she could live life more fully and enjoyably after being so intently focused on her daughter and work in Houston.

She felt a familiar sense of loss at the thought of her former job in a Houston hospital. She'd enjoyed her work there as a physical therapist until the department had been closed for cost reduction. With just a little help, support, and encouragement, rehabilitation could work wonders on the body and psyche of folks recovering from injuries and surgery.

With nothing to hold her in Houston—like school for Hannah or work for her—she had decided to use her savings to take a chance on Wildcat Bluff. She could stay in touch with her friends and coworkers by phone and Internet. She hoped she could find a way to build a new life in a familiar and supportive environment, but only time would tell if that was possible. At the least, she could help Hedy in her store and in her life until she made sure her aunt was back to her old self.

Lauren plucked at the faded denim of the too-big jeans and sighed to herself. She'd taken special care with her appearance for her first day back in Wildcat Bluff, and here she was wearing borrowed clothes. At least she had a fine yellow fire-rescue T-shirt to go with her rose-colored flip-flops and straw handbag. She might as well give up trying to look stylish and go for efficient.

She swallowed a chuckle, knowing her concern about her appearance was laughable when compared to putting out a fire. She glanced at Kent. Nothing comical about him. He wore basically the same thing she wore, but he made his attire look hot and trendy. She noticed the easy way he handled the steering wheel with his big hands. She well remembered his roaming fingers on her bare flesh, a little rough from rodeo and oh-so-strong. Yet gentle, too. She clamped down on her mind that was veering off like a dodgy steer trying to outmaneuver a rope. She needed to focus on the here and now.

She glanced out her window at the view along Wildcat Road that had originally been known back in the late eighteen hundreds as Wildcat Trail. The rutted old wagon trail had been paved in the modern era and was now the major highway to and from Wildcat Bluff, unwinding its leisurely way through the prairie grasslands and rolling hills dotted with black and red cattle chewing their cud. Occasional thick stands of trees provided a little shade for the animals under the outspread canopies of pale-green leaves just unfurling in early spring.

When a pickup passed on the other side of the road, the driver raised a forefinger in acknowledgment and Kent returned the greeting. She'd forgotten how friendly everyone was in this county, but most likely they all knew each other. She relaxed into the comfort of familiarity.

"I doubt much has changed around here in the last thirteen years," Kent said. "You remember the history, don't you?"

"How could I forget our proud roots?" She smiled as she glanced at him, recalling the spiel they'd learned in school. They'd practically had to memorize a section of the local history book, and she'd never forget it. "Wildcat Bluff overlooks the Red River Valley. The Bluff was originally founded as a ferry terminus so folks could cross the Red River between Texas and Indian Territory, or Oklahoma now. Delaware Bend and Preston Bend were wild ferry towns, too, but they were flooded to make Lake Texoma, so they no longer exist except in memory and tall tales."

"Good to know you haven't forgotten the most important thing you learned in school." He chuckled as he gave her a mischievous grin.

She joined his laughter at the shared memory. "I might be a little bit Connecticut now, but I'm still mostly Texan."

"Glad to hear it."

"I've missed the Cross Timbers." She gestured out the window at the land around them. They were traveling down the north-south corridor of prairie that spanned horizon to horizon and seemed to go on forever, although it was in actuality only about ten miles wide here. The

Cross Timbers could narrow to three miles or roll out as wide as thirty miles. In Wildcat Bluff County, each side of the prairie was still densely bordered by stout post oak, flowering cedar elm, hard-as-nails bois d'arc, blossoming dogwood, Virginia creeper, and thorny blackberry. Unfortunately, the original old growth that had stretched from Kansas to Central Texas was now mostly gone—cut down to make way for pasture, farms, and housing developments.

"Don't you mean the Comancheria?" Kent chuckled as he glanced over at her.

"You're right. I've missed this little bit of Comanche Earth." She smiled back at him, thinking of all the local folks who were descended from the Comanche whose empire had once ranged from central Kansas to Mexico. In the old days, there'd been a brush fire every year, and the tree line that made up the border of the Cross Timbers would grow back too dense to penetrate. Comanche warriors had used the prairie between the two tree lines as a secret passage so that enemies couldn't see or attack them.

"We're still protecting thousands of acres just like always, but we keep the wildfires under control now so the thicket line doesn't grow as dense."

"I remember that from school. And it's so beautiful here." She glanced at Kent's strong profile that proclaimed his heritage. She could easily imagine him in a long line of colorful Comanche warriors on horseback wearing breechclouts and carrying bows and arrows as they rode down the prairie to protect their people and homeland.

"Special, too," he added in a thoughtful tone.

"I can see that most of the original growth is still here."

"You know how it is in this county. Nobody's selling to strangers if they have kids around here. From one generation to the next we keep riding herd on the land." He glanced over at her. "That includes your family. You're a descendant of Republic of Texas pioneers."

"But my parents left."

"Hedy is still here." He reached over and squeezed Lauren's hand. "And you're back."

When he wrapped his fingers back around the steering wheel, she felt the loss much the way she'd felt it when she'd gone from Texas to Connecticut. She realized now just how much she'd missed Kent, as well as the Cross Timbers. Wildcat Bluff County was sandwiched between the dry West and the wet East, so they got the best of both worlds. And the timber kept rainwater deep in the soil.

Kent had gone quiet, so she turned her attention from the land to the man beside her. "Are you working Cougar Ranch now?"

He glanced at her, then back at the road. "Guess we've got a lot to catch up on, don't we?"

She smiled, realizing that she suddenly hungered to know what he'd been doing with his life. "I don't mean to pry, but—"

"That's okay. I want to know about you, too."

"Long or short version?"

"Long."

"That'll take time."

"Let's plan on making the time."

She felt a little thrill at his words, but she tamped down on the feeling. They were just old friends catching up.

"As far as me," he continued, "I'm working Cougar

Ranch and I'm working with Cuz Trey on Wildcat Ranch next door so we get the best from all our herds. You remember the two Duval family ranches used to be one sprawling spread, don't you?"

"Not really. I wasn't too interested in business back then."

"Yeah." He chuckled, giving her a quick glance. "We all had our minds on more important matters, didn't we?"

"Rodeo and—"

"Us."

She didn't want to go there, not in the close confines of the truck with his familiar scent and nearness setting off too many sensual memories. "Did you go on to Texas A&M in College Station like you planned to do?"

"Yep." He tossed a grin her way. "If you like, you can call me Dr. Duval now."

She gasped out loud and turned to face him. "You got a doctorate degree?"

"Thought I might as well while I was at it."

"In what?"

He laughed as if he could hardly believe it himself. "Animal husbandry. What else? Not poetry."

She joined his laughter. "Remember how we had to memorize Chaucer and recite sections in class?"

He groaned, shaking his head. "Don't remind me. I can still speak those Old English words—with a Texas drawl."

She laughed even harder. "One thing for a fact, Wildcat Bluff made sure we all got a good education."

"And it helped me get through college." He gestured at the cattle out in a pasture. "Nowadays, a smart rancher needs to know animal husbandry. Gotta make the most of our resources and take good care of our animals."

"I can see your point. Is your family still raising buffalo?"

"Yes. Fact of the matter, Trey and I are looking for ways to increase our herds. There's a lot of demand out there for bison meat now 'cause everybody wants to eat lean and stay healthy. Bison's a superfood."

"I didn't know that."

"True enough. Turns out the Comanche and other native nations knew how to eat right—buffalo, wild plants, and berries." He gave her a mischievous look with his hazel eyes. "All this talk is makin' me hungry."

She nodded in agreement. "I just like to see those big, shaggy animals on the range. They're so beautiful."

"There used to be millions. It's sad so few are left, but they're making a comeback."

"And you're helping do it."

"I'm doing my best." He turned west onto U.S. Highway 82. "What about you? Didn't you always want to help others?"

"I'm a physical therapist, but the hospital where I worked closed the PT department to cut costs."

"Ouch. Bet that's hard on folks."

She clasped her hands together. "We'll all find a way to make it. My friends are looking for work and our patients are finding other physical therapists."

"Good." He nodded in understanding. "So now you're footloose and fancy-free?"

She smiled at the image. "That's one way to put it. Actually, I'm taking advantage of the opportunity to see about Aunt Hedy and figure out if Hannah might like living here."

"What about you? Don't you want to be back in Wildcat Bluff?"

She hesitated, not quite sure how to answer him because she'd been putting herself last for a long time.

"You've got lots of old friends here."

"I'm glad to be back. I guess I just don't want to be disappointed if nothing is quite as good as it seems in hindsight."

He reached over and squeezed her hand. "How about we make new memories even better than the old ones?"

She felt the familiar heat surge between them with just that single touch. She took a deep breath, not sure if she wanted to stop where her feelings were taking her. It'd been so long since she'd allowed her emotions free rein. Now was probably not the best time—and yet she felt a deep ache that belied her thoughts.

"How about it?" He squeezed her hand before he took hold of the steering wheel again.

She glanced over at his strong profile, shaking her head. He didn't have to do anything except exist to set her on fire. She didn't need to reach Sure-Shot to feel the heat of a blaze. Kent was creating one inside her right at this very moment, and she was losing her ability to resist.

He looked her way and their gazes caught, held, and merged in a building inferno. "Hell, you've got no idea how much I've missed you." And he clenched the steering wheel with his fists.

She felt tears blur her eyes at his words, conjuring up those deepest emotions she thought she'd locked away forever. "Yes," she heard herself say in a sultry voice not quite her own. "Let's make new memories."

Chapter 4

On the drive to Sure-Shot, Lauren turned her mind from Kent to the land around her. A touch of green here and there was beginning to sprout in the dry, golden grass of the prairie. She couldn't help but contrast this area with the lush, almost tropical beauty of Houston, near the Gulf, which never experienced sharp contrasts in temperature.

She felt a special place in her heart for both parts of the Lone Star State, but she realized now that Wildcat Bluff County resonated deep within her. She glanced at Kent's strong profile as he easily handled the big booster the way volunteer firefighters were trained to do. Perhaps she'd left more of her heart in the Cross Timbers than she'd realized, and not just in the land, but in the people as well.

Once more she determinedly turned her thoughts away from Kent to focus on her surroundings. She knew she'd traveled from cattle country to horse country when she saw the fence lines that stretched along both sides of the highway change from barbwire to white round pipe or four-slat wooden enclosures. She watched as one horse ranch after another flashed by, announcing their names—from whimsical to practical—in black sheet metal cutouts or burned into wood arches that towered over the entrances to sprawling houses, red barns, and metal corrals.

Thoroughbred horses with rich chestnut coats in a variety of shades grazed in some pastures, while in others, brown-and-white painted ponies sought shelter from the sun under the spreading limbs of green live oak trees.

Soon Kent turned south at a sign with Western-style letters that read, "Sure as Shootin' You're in Sure-Shot!" under the black-and-white silhouette of a smoking Colt .45 revolver.

Lauren had always liked the idea that Sure-Shot had been named for Annie Oakley, the famous sharpshooter and exhibition shooter who'd been called "Little Miss Sure Shot" on the Wild West show circuit.

No doubt about it, North Texas folks still gave Annie Oakley her due and took their horses, cattle, land, and safety a tad on the serious side. Everybody knew it and acted accordingly, so there wasn't much trouble of any kind. That made the fire surprising, but the old wooden frame buildings had to be vulnerable to a stray spark or other fire hazard.

Kent followed the asphalt two-lane road that turned into Sure-Shot's Main Street. The small town nestled at the once vital and vibrant intersection of an old cattle drive trail that ran north to south and the railway line that ran east to west.

Lauren had almost forgotten how Sure-Shot looked like the set of an Old West film. Old Town in Wildcat Bluff was built of brick and stone, while Sure-Shot had a classic wooden false front commercial district. A line of single-story businesses connected by a boardwalk, covered porticos, and tall facade parapets extending above the roofs were individually painted in green, blue, or yellow with white trim. Small clapboard houses with wide front porches and fancy double-wides fanned out around the downtown area.

Once upon a time, Sure-Shot had catered to cowboys on their cattle drives from Texas to Kansas and back again. Lively dance halls and noisy saloons, along with the mercantile, café, blacksmith shop, livery stable, bathhouse, bank, and freight depot had all done a brisk business just like the same type of stores had in Wildcat Bluff.

Lauren felt almost as if she'd stepped back in time. A few pickups and Jeeps were parked in front of the businesses, but a couple of saddle horses with their reins wrapped around the hitching post in front of the Bluebonnet Café switched their tails at flies in the afternoon heat. She bet their riders wore hats, boots, and spurs while they waited for takeout or sat down for an early supper inside the café. She chuckled at the idea of riding a horse to a restaurant for a meal in Houston. That simply wouldn't happen—not anymore.

"Smoke!" Kent pointed toward the end of Main Street where black smoke spiraled upward from the back of a building.

"Bad?" She leaned forward as he sped up, and felt her heart accelerate with the booster. She was glad they were the only ones headed down the street—so unlike busy city traffic. She couldn't see the fire, but she worried that it could easily spread to engulf the other structures.

"Hope not. I think we're in time."

As they drew close to the old Sinclair gas station, she could see the building was separated by several lots from the flammable downtown businesses. If the fire got out of control, that separation would help save the entire area. But she didn't doubt for a moment that Wildcat Bluff Fire-Rescue—as in Kent Duval—would find a way to contain the blaze. And she'd help all she could to do it.

As he wheeled the booster to a stop in front of the station, she noticed two dusty pickups and a van with a handicap license plate had parked across the street. She felt a burst of excitement at the sight because that had to be Aunt Hedy's hand-controlled van.

And then she saw her aunt sitting in her power wheelchair near the van, appearing so dearly familiar with her thick silver hair in a single, long plait lying over one shoulder of her turquoise pearl-snap shirt. A tall, lanky man wearing a cowboy hat and overalls stood beside a short, blond-haired woman dressed in faded jeans, a green shirt, and pointy-toe black boots. All three quickly started across the street.

Kent leaped out of the booster while Lauren set her purse aside, jerked off her flip-flops, and slipped on a pair of rubber boots. She stepped down from the vehicle and slammed the door behind her as she took off for her aunt. In the middle of the street, she threw wide her arms, laughing as Hedy gave a big whoop and holler when she caught sight of her niece. Lauren fell to her knees and hugged her aunt, feeling tears sting her eyes in happiness. Their separation had been way too long.

"Lauren!" Hedy gasped. "I'm so happy to see you. But what are you doing here?"

She leaned back, grinning as she took the low-key tack so typical of Texans to defuse highly charged situations. "Fighting a fire. What else is there to do out here in the sticks?"

Hedy laughed hard, following Lauren's verbal lead. "That's right. Nothing at all to do out here in the boonies." She motioned toward her friends, who were also laughing at Lauren's obviously ridiculous—so particularly funny—statement. "Real quick, I'd like you to meet my friends, Tom Barker and Billye Jo Simmons. This is my niece, Lauren Sheridan, come all the way from Houston."

"Pleased to meet you both." Lauren quickly got to her feet and shook their work-worn hands, figuring they had to be horse people.

"Likewise," Billye Jo said.

"Hey!" Kent called as he shut a booster door. "Think we could catch up on old times after we see to the fire?"

Lauren glanced over her shoulder. Kent stood with a big fire extinguisher hanging from a wide strap over each shoulder. He'd gone from old friend to firefighter ready for trouble in a matter of seconds.

"Kent's right." Hedy gave him a wave as she zipped across the street. "Folks, let's get this show on the road!"

Lauren brought up the rear as they all headed toward Kent. Now that she had a moment to reflect, she felt a chill run up her spine. Ruby and Kent were exactly right. Hedy simply didn't look her usual self. She had a paleness of skin and a lack of luster in her normally bright, brown eyes so like Lauren's own eye color. Her aunt had always hugged with vim and vigor and solid upper body strength, but not today. Was age or illness catching up with Hedy? She hoped her aunt wasn't hiding some terrible secret.

For now Lauren had to turn her mind to the more immediate problem of the fire, so she took a good look at the Sinclair gas station.

The structure appeared as if it had originally been

set up in what might have been a livery stable or other business connected to the downtown. It had the facade parapet extending high above the roof. Two sets of three hinged doors—once a bright green but now chipped and faded—would have opened to make wide automobile bays. The white paint on the false front with a large "SINCLAIR" sign in green had been worn down by time and weather.

As she followed the others around the side of the building, she noticed corrugated tin covered the building around a wooden window that still had a few intact windowpanes, but the paint had completely worn away to reveal the dry wood underneath.

She stopped beside Kent when they reached the back of the building. Three green barrels with "Sinclair Greases" printed on a red background above a big green dinosaur that was the oil company's symbol had been knocked over so that black sludge had spilled and run across the gravel that made up the yard. The old motor oil now burned hot, giving off a foul smell as black smoke rose into the sky.

"We're lucky," Kent said. "If those barrels had dumped their contents any closer to the building, it'd be long gone by now."

"And our entire downtown might have gone up in flames," Billye Jo added in a tight voice.

"That's right." Kent set down one fire extinguisher near Lauren's feet. He pointed the nozzle of the other can toward the grease that was closest to the station. He sprayed the outer edge, staying back from the roiling heat and pungent fumes.

"Can I do anything to help?" Lauren felt acrid smoke

burn her nostrils. She quickly stepped back, realizing there was no telling what kind of pollutants were being released into the air.

"I've got it," Kent said. "I'll contain the area with chemical spray and let the sludge burn out."

"Good," Hedy agreed. "That's what we figured would be best. But just in case, we wanted you to bring the booster."

Tom pointed toward the burning grease. "And we wanted you to see the problem. Now I'm thinking we ought to get some big fire extinguishers like that to keep on hand."

"It's chemical ABC." Kent sprayed halfway around the fire.

"If you like, I can put in an order for the same type of fire extinguishers that we use at the station and run them over to you." Hedy glanced from Billye Jo to Tom.

"Right neighborly of you," Tom agreed.

"I'll get on it as soon as I get back to the station."

"Thanks," Billye Jo said.

Kent emptied one fire extinguisher, set it down beside Lauren, picked up the full can, and then continued spraying around the fire. "It's best to let all this old grease burn up. That way it won't be a potential fire hazard any longer."

"Thanks," Billye Jo said. "Guess it doesn't look like it, but we've been working on this place. Serena, my daughter, is finishing cosmetology school. She's always loved makeup and clothes and hairstyles. She still plaits horses' manes for shows. And now she plans to turn this old filling station that was once run by her great-grandparents into the Sure-Shot Beauty Station."

"That's clever." Lauren glanced from the fire back toward the building, trying to see the station with fresh eyes. She was looking at more faded green and white paint. The back door's busted-out glass had been replaced with plywood. Two windows in the same condition filled out the picture. It wasn't a pretty one, but she could see the potential.

"High school graduates have trouble finding local jobs, so they end up going to Dallas and other big cities. Of course, some go on to college, but that's not for everybody," Billye Jo explained. "I'd do about anything to keep Serena or any young folks in town."

"I know what you mean," Lauren agreed as she imagined new paint, clean windows, and a bright interior. "This station could be really cute. I bet Serena would get plenty of business so folks didn't have to go into Wildcat Bluff or Sherman or elsewhere."

"It'd give us an option. She's got youth and energy on her side. Besides, this is her heritage and it means something special to her."

"I like her vision." Lauren nodded in agreement. "I've been living in Houston, but I grew up in Wildcat Bluff and I missed it."

"That's what Serena says about staying here. She's been driving all over and going online to find vintage Sinclair items. That's how we ended up with these grease barrels. She found a neon Sinclair Dino the Dinosaur sign that she's going to put in a window. She's got her eye on one of the green-and-white gas pumps with the round lighted globe on top with the big green dinosaur."

"Sounds like fun for your entire family." Lauren liked the idea more all the time.

"As long as you keep it safe," Kent added. "I'd say no more grease barrels."

Billye Jo nodded in agreement. "Here I am running on about my daughter's dreams when we need to be talking about the fire."

"I wonder how the barrels got knocked over." Kent finished his containment spray, stepped back, and set the can beside the other empty one. "Raccoons? Maybe big dogs played around back here and caused trouble. But it still wouldn't explain how the fire got started."

"That's the long and short of it." Tom lifted his cowboy hat and ran a hand through his thick, white hair. "Being fire-rescue like you are, I figure you're way ahead of me. But I can tell you right now these fires didn't start on their lonesome."

"You think they were set?" Lauren felt a chill run up her spine.

"Sure do." Tom gave her a grim look. "And they aren't the first ones we've had in Sure-Shot."

Chapter 5

Lauren caught her breath in shock at Tom's announcement and glanced at Kent to get his reaction.

"What other fires?" Kent stepped back from the barrels as he turned toward Tom and Billye Jo.

Tom scuffed the sole of his right boot over the gravel, looking a little sheepish. "Truth is we've had half a dozen small fires set around here since the first of the year."

"*What!*" Kent rubbed the back of his neck, glanced up at the sky, then back at Tom as if holding in his temper. "Why didn't you call sooner?"

Lauren didn't say anything as she realized the situation was much more serious than a few old barrels with their sludge burning up. She wasn't part of Wildcat Bluff Fire-Rescue, at least not yet, so she had no voice in the matter. But she couldn't help but worry about Sure-Shot.

Tom cleared his throat, glanced at Billye Jo, then back at Kent. "You know how cotton-picking independent we are here. We thought we could figure out the fires and get them stopped by our lonesome, but we're having no such luck."

"And we didn't want to be a bother," Billye Jo added. "Anyhow, we figured maybe kids were just letting off steam."

"It's been small stuff." Tom took off his hat and

gestured toward downtown. "It looks like somebody's setting fires in dumpsters behind the businesses. So far nothing's gotten out of hand, but now—"

"The culprit, or several of them, have gone too far." Billye Jo put her hands on her hips.

"We figure we've got a firebug on our hands." Tom squinted into the late-afternoon sun in the west. "That's bad news no matter which way you slice it."

"Downright scary, too." Hedy drummed her fingertips on the arms of her wheelchair. "The whole downtown could go up fast and furious. I doubt we could get here in time to save all the buildings."

"Maybe none of them," Kent added.

"Bottom line, we need to catch the culprit before somebody gets hurt," Tom said.

"I wish you'd called us sooner." Kent glanced around the area, as if calculating danger. "Firebugs usually escalate their actions."

"That's why we finally called out the big guns of Wildcat Bluff," Billye Jo said with a slight chuckle.

Hedy smiled at the term. "I wouldn't call us the big guns, but our fire-rescue will definitely want to stay on top of these fires and help you any way we can. That's what neighbors do."

"I don't suppose there's been any incriminating evidence left at the scenes, has there?" Lauren wondered out loud as she glanced around, but she couldn't tell what was normal or not.

"Good question," Tom said. "Believe you me, we've searched every site, but it's all been left clean as a whistle."

"You sure you didn't spot anything out of the ordinary?" Kent asked.

"Never," Billye Jo said. "It's frustrating as all get-out."

"Okay." Kent gave them a curt nod. "Be on the lookout. If anything like this happens again, call us right away."

"We will," Billye Jo agreed.

"And I'll get photos of this entire area before I leave so we'll have a record of the damage."

"That's good." Lauren glanced up at the Sinclair station, then back at the group. "Do you think y'all might want somebody on guard at night?"

"That's not a bad idea either." Billye Jo turned toward Tom. "We've discussed it around here, but didn't follow up. Now we'd better be proactive and defensive. I'll talk with the other downtown merchants."

Tom nodded in agreement.

"And I'll talk with Sheriff Calhoun," Kent added. "He'll want to know about your trouble and check out the fire sites. I imagine he'll send a deputy over more often to keep an eye on Sure-Shot."

"Thanks. I'll follow up with a call to him, too." Billye Jo said.

"Don't forget that we're not far away." Hedy gave Billye Jo a stern look. "Please call us at the first sign of trouble."

"We'll do it." Tom bumped a barrel with the toe of his boot. "Fire's about gone, but we'll stay here till it is cold."

"That's good." Hedy smiled at her friends. "Guess that's about all we can do for now, so we might as well get back to the station."

"Lauren, don't be a stranger in Sure-Shot," Billye Jo said with a twinkle in her eyes. "And when you decide to get a horse, keep us in mind. We've got the best of the best."

"I'll do that." Lauren agreed, liking these two plain-spoken, salt-of-the-Earth folks.

"We'll be looking for you." Billye Jo leaned down, gave Hedy a quick hug, and stepped back.

As Lauren walked around the side of the house beside her aunt, she gave a silent sigh of pleasure. All had gone well and she'd met new and interesting people. Maybe life in Wildcat Bluff County could be as good as she'd imagined down in Houston—if there weren't any more problems.

As she stopped in front of the station with Kent and Hedy, she felt her stomach knot in anxiety. She could tell each one expected her to ride back in their vehicle. She didn't know what to do because she wanted to be with both of them. And she certainly didn't want to reject either of them.

Hedy looked from Lauren to Kent, then back again. She gave them a big grin, as if knowing something they didn't know. "Lauren, why don't you ride with Kent? I'm sure you have a lot of catching up to do. Anyway, how many times in your life do you get to ride in a fancy booster?"

Lauren laughed, suddenly transported back in time when Hedy had been so supportive of them. "We've got a lot of catching up to do, too, Aunt Hedy, but Kent did promise me barbeque."

"Did he now?" Hedy threw back her head and laughed out loud. "Now there's a guy who knows how to make things right."

"If you'll meet us at Twin Oaks later, we'll bring enough barbeque for everybody," Kent said.

"I'd never pass up an offer like that," Hedy agreed. "Now don't lollygag. I'll see you back in town."

Lauren watched as Hedy zoomed over to her hand-controlled van, rolled inside, waved at them, and then sped down the road.

"Quite a gal," Tom said.

"I've really missed her. We've stayed in touch by phone and text, but it's not the same. Being here reminds me of so much I'd thought long gone."

Kent clasped her hand. "Not gone at all."

She felt the touch of his hand and the sound of his voice strike deep, making her feel molten from the inside out. He was getting to her. It felt almost like the old days when they'd been desperate to find times and places to be alone together. Hedy had seen them then and she'd seen them now. Maybe her aunt understood something Lauren didn't want to admit or refused to acknowledge. Either way, she was way past experiencing those heady days again.

Kent tugged Lauren toward the booster, and then opened the passenger door wide. "Come on. Can't let Hedy get too far ahead or she'll call us slowpokes."

Lauren chuckled at his words as she stepped up into the cab. "She'll probably call us slowpokes anyway."

"Let me take a few photos and we'll be on our way." He shut her door, walked around to the driver's side, opened the back door, picked up his camera, and jogged back to the station.

While she waited, she let the swirl of events settle into place. She hadn't realized that when she returned she'd step back into life here as if she'd never been gone. She felt almost dizzy from the rapid readjustment. And yet, it all felt so right.

She saw Kent round the side of the Sinclair station, smiling at her. She felt warmth expand from her heart outward again. No doubt about it, he had a powerful effect on her.

He opened the driver's side door, sat down in the seat, and placed his camera in the center console. He glanced over at her. "About Hedy. I know you want to spend time with her, but I'm selfish. I want you all to myself a little longer."

She felt her breath catch in her throat at the longing in his hazel eyes. She'd seen that look when he'd been what she'd wanted most in life. She felt a blaze of heat deep inside where she'd been cold for so long. She'd poured all her love into Hannah for a long time. She'd convinced herself that she didn't need or want a guy in her life. Had she been right?

"Lauren, tell me you're okay about Hedy. And us."

At Kent's words, she felt a surge of tenderness toward him. He'd always been attuned to her, and obviously that hadn't gone away. She reached over and placed her hand against his cheek, thinking about his adorable dimples. She felt a slight roughness and saw the telltale shadow that revealed he needed a shave—just another sign that while she'd been gone he'd become a man.

Kent turned his head and placed a warm kiss against her palm. "I missed you."

She nodded, unable to speak for the sudden lump in her throat. She sat back in her seat and crossed her arms over her stomach as if in protection because she suddenly felt emotionally vulnerable. Kent was reviving too many old memories and feelings that were catching her off guard.

"Lauren?"

She tossed him a smile, straining to make it look real. She felt a building heat, a growing need, a deepening desire for the one who'd once been her everything. And never could be again. "I'll have plenty of time to talk with Aunt Hedy later. Let's go home."

"Home sounds good." He grinned, revealing white teeth and deep dimples.

She couldn't help but notice that he looked a little predatory, as if he was ready and willing to do whatever it took to get what he wanted in life. A little shiver ran through her. She'd known the boy, but she didn't know the man. She needed to be careful not to get drawn back into a world that could lead to heartbreak. Home didn't need to mean Kent.

He switched on the booster's engine, gave her a quick smile, and then headed out of Sure-Shot.

She glanced back at the Sinclair station, but she no longer saw black smoke spiraling into the sky. Fortunately, this time the fire had been containable, so nothing was hurt and no one was endangered because of it. But she'd keep the knowledge in mind that life wasn't always perfect in this county.

Satisfied all was well for the moment, she exchanged the fire-rescue boots for her cool, comfortable flip-flops. She felt chilly now that the warmth of the day was slipping away and realized that up here in North Texas she'd need to set aside her flip-flops and sundresses for warmer clothing. She leaned her head back against the seat as she listened to the deep, powerful growl of the truck's engine.

And she resisted the feeling that she'd come home—in this moment at this place with this man.

Chapter 6

As Kent headed toward Wildcat Bluff, he felt relieved that for the moment all was well in Sure-Shot. But the small town definitely had a problem that could spin out of control. He glanced over at Lauren. If he wasn't careful, he might spin out of control about her.

He gripped the steering wheel, using hands made strong from dealing with recalcitrant thousand-pound animals like horses and cattle. He was thick with muscle all over, and that extended clear to his well-corded wrists. Point of fact, he had to be strong to be a cowboy firefighter, but the right gal could make a guy feel weak as a newborn calf with no respect for size or strength.

He personally knew better than to get sucked into a hot gal's planetary orbit. He'd been there once with his former fiancée. She'd kept him whirling around her till she'd found somebody who'd inflated her ego like a helium balloon, and then she'd kicked Kent right out of her closed system like he was nothing but cosmic trash.

Still, he figured he was lucky she'd cut him loose before kids had been added to her erratic orbit and they'd all gotten hurt. But her actions still rankled like a cocklebur under a saddle blanket. He'd been left gun-shy, but hopefully a whole lot smarter about the fairer sex.

He clenched the wheel harder. He should've seen

Charlene's rejection coming, but maybe he'd been too dazzled by her stacked, toned body that'd seen more time in the gym than in his king-size bed. He'd tried to make her happy. He'd bought her little blue boxes of pretty jewelry and he'd taken her to Paris—France, not Texas. Now he knew he'd sooner travel by his lonesome down the road a ways to see the miniature Eiffel Tower sporting a big, red cowboy hat than go halfway across the country and the big pond to take photos of Charlene posing in front of the original edifice.

"You okay?" Lauren asked with a note of concern in her voice.

"Sure." He guessed she'd noticed his grip on the steering wheel. He eased up before he broke the thing in frustration.

Once he got the booster to the station, he'd get back in his own truck that had caused Charlene to turn up her nose. But he knew a good vehicle when he had one. The F-150 was just getting broken in proper, the way a serviceable pickup ought to be. Quality, not flash.

He slanted another quick glance at Lauren. Could a guy lose a gal over a five-year-old truck? Maybe he ought to get a new one or a big SUV. No, he'd just wash his pickup and maybe add a little wax for shine. He might even take a vacuum to the inside, but that seemed like a lot of trouble for something that wouldn't last long. On the other hand, gals liked clean and pretty.

He drummed his fingertips on the steering wheel. *Pretty* was never high on his agenda of what needed to get done. First order of business had to be fire-rescue calls for immediate help, then ranch chores like feeding cattle and bison, riding horses, maintaining equipment, brush-hogging pasture, or bailing hay. The list was endless. Now that he thought about all he had to do, maybe he wouldn't wash his truck after all. It'd just get dirty again.

Anyway, if a woman was worth her salt, she'd appreciate something long-lasting and dependable instead of new and flashy. But that could be his own self he was thinking about instead of his favorite vehicle. Lauren had lived back East and down in Houston. Like Charlene, she most likely preferred spike heels with red soles instead of well-worn, re-soled cowgirl boots.

Somehow or other, his PhD didn't appear to translate to an understanding of the female brain. He wanted a practical, no-nonsense gal who'd like him for who he was and not try to change him into who she wanted him to be. Seemed simple enough. But he felt like he was in grade school where women were concerned nowadays. He hadn't always felt that way. But Charlene had made him question his own good sense.

Lately he'd been as edgy as a cat in a roomful of rocking chairs where the fairer sex was concerned, but Lauren had reminded him of what it'd once been like before he'd gotten burned by a hungry gal. Maybe his teenage sweetheart made him feel young again, as if anything was still possible, or maybe his hot response was simply a reaction to Lauren herself. Either way, he might as well enjoy the ride as far as it'd take him, but he'd keep a lock on his heart.

When he hit Wildcat Road heading north, he felt as if he was coming home in a lot of ways, not the least of which was due to Lauren by his side. Soon he started the climb up the bluff, passing gnarled trees, dense shrubs, and sandstone outcrops on either side. Puffy white clouds in a deep blue sky provided the perfect canopy over the vast land.

"No matter how many times I come up to Wildcat Bluff on this stretch of road," Lauren said as she broke the silence, "I feel as if I'm going back in time."

He chuckled, nodding. "I know what you mean."

"Imagine all the cowboys and Indians, outlaws and lawmen, ladies and ladies of the evening who made this trek back in the day." She gestured out the front window at the landscape around them.

"Plenty of times. Only we're getting to town a whole lot faster and easier than in a buckboard or on horseback."

"I'm glad for modern travel conveniences." She lapsed into silence again as she gazed right and left.

He didn't disturb her, knowing she was getting a feel for the area again. She'd been gone a long time. She might've changed a lot, but not much around here had succumbed to the world's faster pace. He was glad. They might update their farm and ranch practices, get their businesses set up on computers, and communicate via email and cell phone, but at heart they lived small-town and country lifestyles that depended on family and neighbors.

As the road continued to wind upward, he relaxed into the comfort of the booster. Fortunately, the fire in Sure-Shot had been fairly contained from the get-go, but the bigger issue of a firebug plaguing that area would continue to be a concern for Wildcat Bluff Fire-Rescue. He needed to alert the other volunteers about the issue, but Hedy might be ahead of him on that one. He'd check later to make sure everybody was on the same page regarding Sure-Shot.

He heard the booster's engine growl a little louder and work a little harder on the upward climb through the rugged, untamed land. A variety of bushes and ancient trees with spreading limbs sheltered tall, golden stalks of dry grass. The plains that stretched north to Canada had once been a sea of buffalo grass as tall as a horse's belly that provided food for millions of buffalo that kept the ground broken up with their sharp hooves so the grass grew wild and plentiful. Most of that grass was long gone due to sodbusters and town planners.

Several black-and-white buzzards with long necks and rotund bodies suddenly launched into the air from the side of the road, flapping long wings in their struggle to gain altitude ahead of the booster. He slowed down to give the birds a chance to get into the sky. Out of the corner of his eye, he noticed the white tail of a rabbit scampering to safety in the underbrush. As the birds gradually disappeared into the distance, he continued his slow pace so Lauren could look at the scenery.

"I'd almost forgotten all the varied wildlife that lives up here." She pointed out her side window. "Did you see that cute rabbit?"

"Yep. Check out the low limb on that pecan tree. A squirrel is shaking his tail at us for disturbing him. Pesky critters." Kent pointed toward the tree, and then refocused on the road. If they got a chance, the squirrels would strip green pecans from the trees in August so the delicious nuts never had a chance to ripen. There was no keeping squirrels from their goals once they'd set their minds on a particular pecan tree. He sighed at that ongoing nuisance.

Lauren laughed a tinkling peal of happiness that resounded in the cab. "They're so cute."

"Bet you fed them in Houston."

"Guilty. If you feed the birds, you feed the squirrels." She laughed harder.

He joined her with a chuckle of his own, feeling more lighthearted than he had in a long time despite thinking about thieving squirrels. "Animals never pass up an easy meal."

"Smart critters."

"True enough." He picked up speed again, feeling as if he kept moving back in time—not just to the Old West but to those hot, steamy summer days with luscious Lauren.

Near the summit of the bluff, he slowed until he almost brought them to a complete stop in the middle of the highway. Up ahead, the road dead-ended in front of a wild, natural growth of twisted trees, dense shrubs, and entwined vines. The living wall was green, brown, and thorny just like the original, impenetrable Cross Timbers.

"Independent cusses settled Wildcat Bluff," he said, reminding her of their shared past.

She nodded at him, eyes bright with happiness. "I know. They wanted safety from all the frontier dangers. And they got it."

"Wildcat Bluff still has its special, hidden entrance."

She grinned, flashing white teeth. "I was relieved to see it on my way into town earlier."

"Not likely we'd tear it out."

"Good. Heritage is important."

"And tourists love it."

He turned the steering wheel sharply to the right, and then maneuvered the booster back left. Now he could see a gap wide enough for trucks or campers, two or three abreast. If he hadn't known about the entrance, or seen it on a map, he'd never have guessed its existence. Back in the day, there'd been plenty of space to drive horses and wagons through the hidden entry into town.

He followed the wide road upward. When he reached the summit, sunlight bathed Wildcat Bluff in a golden glow. An Old West town with a long row of one- and two-story buildings built of rock and brick nestled behind a white portico covering a long boardwalk. Sunlight glinted off the shop windows. Everything appeared as fresh as if it'd been constructed yesterday.

"I didn't have time to stop and look at Old Town when I arrived earlier," Lauren said. "I'd almost forgotten how beautiful it is."

"We can thank the Italians our founders hired to build Wildcat Bluff. I still wonder how they knew master masons were working as coal miners for the Choctaw Nation in Indian Territory."

"Maybe everybody knew back then." She gestured at the town that spread out ahead of them. "Aren't we the lucky ones with this fine legacy?"

Kent drove into Old Town, turned onto Main Street, and saw the impressive Wildcat Hotel, a redbrick two-story building with a second-floor balcony enclosed with a stone balustrade supported by fancy columns. He found an empty parking place and pulled to a stop in front of the hotel's grand entrance. Cream brick keystones and brass planters with trimmed rosemary bushes welcomed the esteemed guests of the fanciest hotel in town.

Next door rose another two-story business with "SALOON" painted in tall yellow letters near the roofline. He glanced at the plate-glass windows with the words "Lone Star Saloon" hand-painted with gold in old-fashioned curlicue script. A wooden cigar store Indian stood at one side of the batwing doors and held flags of the Lone Star State and the United States.

"Old Town doesn't look like it's changed much since I lived here," Lauren said as she pointed down the row of businesses.

He chuckled. "Guess not much since the 1880s. Food. Drinks. Dance hall. Live country bands on weekends."

"Sounds like fun."

"You bet. We get a lot of tourists during Wild West Days wanting to experience a bit of the Old West like they do in Tombstone, Arizona." He glanced at Lauren, realizing he wanted her to like Wildcat Bluff again. He didn't need to push the town on her. She'd stay or she wouldn't. Still, she was rekindling old feelings that made him want more of everything, including her.

"Old Town looks as good as Tombstone. Maybe better."

"We're wall-to-wall folks during Wild West Days. They like to see our reenactment of the shoot-out between the Hellions and the Ruffians for control of the town."

"Is it anything like the shoot-out at the OK Corral in Tombstone?"

"Similar. Our shoot-out takes place in front of the Lone Star, but the ladies in their white pinafores turned the tide." He pointed at the batwing doors, and then turned to her. "You'd look good dressed up as a dance-hall darling."

"If I'm here in the summer, maybe you can persuade me to join in the fun." She chuckled, pushing back a golden lock of hair from her face.

"Christmas in the Country is fun, too. We get lots of out-of-towners for the event. I think you'd like it."

"I'd enjoy seeing it."

He leaned toward her, thinking how much fun it'd be to squire her about two of his favorite events of the year. But like a trick pony, he had to be smart nowadays about gals. "Come on. Let's go grab some grub. I need to get the booster back to the station pretty quick."

"Suits me. I'm starving." She opened her door. "Look! Adelia's Delights hasn't changed a bit. I can't wait to go to the tearoom and shop for gifts."

Kent stepped out of the booster, but before he had a chance to walk around and open Lauren's door, she'd joined him on the boardwalk. He looked in the front window of Adelia's and saw a big, fluffy, long-haired tortoiseshell cat lounging in the midst of blue crystal birds in the large Bluebird of Happiness display.

"Is that Rosie?" Lauren wiggled her fingers at the lounging cat.

"Sure is. She's still Queen of Adelia's, even if she's getting a little long in the tooth."

"I'm so happy to see her again. Look at those huge paws. I'd almost forgotten about Wildcat Bluff's polydactyl cats with the extra dewclaws. They're like the kitty cats at the Hemingway House in Key West."

"You've traveled some since I saw you last."

"A bit."

"You know how we prize our cats in Wildcat Bluff. They protect our businesses from unwanted vermin—"

"And provide lots of love and companionship." She glanced up at him, cocking her head as if remembering those long-ago days.

"Yeah." He felt his heart speed up as he looked deeper into her eyes, feeling as if he were plunging into a vat of the richest chocolate candy—Godiva's or See's came to mind. He broadened his gaze, taking in the smooth surface of her skin as he moved from the rich, dark chocolate of her eyes to the creamy, white chocolate of her face. She'd taste just as good as she looked. He had no doubt about that fact.

For a long moment, time spiraled outward as if no longer tethered to reality as he sensed the past slip into the present. She was setting his temperature on high, and he wanted to drag her into the boiling caldron with him. When her skin turned a pale pink, he knew a sense of satisfaction. He doubted he was the only one feeling the heat in their personal kitchen.

He cleared his throat to cover the pause that seemed to go on forever between them. He'd bet hard-earned money on the fact that neither of them was thinking about cats anymore—not while fireworks worthy of a Fourth of July celebration were exploding between them.

Chapter 7

LAUREN FELT AS IF SHE AND KENT WERE WRAPPED IN their own star-studded universe even though they stood in the middle of Old Town. Somehow, their personal world seemed to have been transported from when she was sweet sixteen to the present time and place.

She could easily lose herself in the depths of his hazel eyes that were still so changeable with the shift in his moods and thoughts. Right now the concentric circles of brown, green, and gold reminded her of a lush forest that lured her ever deeper to a crackling campfire.

She caught Kent's heat, as if his campfire had turned into a wildfire that had jumped boundaries to ignite her dry timber brought on by years of drought. She flushed with a needy ache. In a bid for control, she inhaled sharply, but that only caused her to drag his scent deeper into her lungs and make her even hotter. She wanted his lips, his hands, his body all over her as he brought her to completion with a passion that she now realized she hadn't experienced since those heady nights on the old, tattered quilts in the back of his pickup when they'd gazed up at a dark night sky and wished upon falling stars to love each other forever.

She traced the contours of his face with her gaze, wanting to touch him with her fingertips as if to make sure he was actually real. His skin was bronzed from the sun and stretched tightly across the strong planes of his face. She knew from past experience how a kiss from his full, sensual lips would ignite a raging fire inside her.

Now she couldn't help but compare her late husband Jeffrey to Kent, which she'd tried really hard not to do during her marriage. Maybe she'd been on the rebound from the moment she'd left Kent, or maybe she'd always been trying to find him in another guy, or maybe Kent's specter had always stood between her and any other man.

Yet she couldn't help but wonder how they'd lost each other so long ago. She knew and still she didn't know. Yes, she'd gone back East with her parents. Yes, she'd finished high school and gone to college. Yes, she'd married and had a child. But Kent had always been in her heart. Maybe she'd needed or thought she'd needed to prove to herself that she could make it on her own without the support of Kent Duval or Wildcat Bluff. Maybe time had simply spiraled outward, luring her away with glimpses of excitement that had never quite lived up to expectations. Except for Hannah. Everything she'd done and experienced was worth it for her darling daughter.

"You still hungry?" Kent asked, nodding toward the café without breaking eye contact.

"Are you?"

"I'm starved…parched…desperate for—"

"I know." She cut off his next words because she didn't want him to give voice to what she was feeling inside or what he was communicating with the heat of his body.

"Food isn't what I want," he continued, eyes turning dark with meaning, "but it's what we need."

"Yes. Absolutely. Right." She knew she was talking to cover up the emotions that were cascading through her and the feelings she was picking up from him.

She abruptly looked away, breaking the power of his gaze, and walked to the front of Adelia's Delights. She stopped to look at the play of light across the clear blue glass of the Bluebird of Happiness display. Rosie opened her eyes, gave Lauren a considering stare, and went back to sleep.

"Kent, look here." She leaned closer to the big display window and felt concern run through her. She tapped on the glass with the tip of her peach-tinted fingernail.

He stepped up beside her. "What is it?"

"I'm not sure, but didn't Aunt Hedy always keep her store full of unusual gifts?"

"I remember you and the other girls loved to go there and spend time."

"Look now." Lauren tapped the glass again. "There are sections of empty space in the display. She hasn't restocked the bluebirds that were sold. And look at the other shelves. There are gaps without merchandise."

"You're right."

"That means she hasn't been going to the gift market in Dallas or ordering from catalogs."

"Maybe she has more in the back and hasn't unpacked yet."

"That's possible. But why not get the merchandise out as quickly as possible? Like Aunt Hedy always said, 'You can't sell what's not on the shelf.' She never left empty space on her shelves." Lauren felt a sinking sensation in the pit of her stomach.

"What can I say? She's just not herself."

"And this is another upsetting example." Lauren walked the few steps to Morning's Glory next door. She peered in the display windows, but all the shelves appeared fully stocked with apothecary, beauty, health, and gift items.

"Everything looks okay here." Kent shaded his eyes with his right hand as he leaned in close to the window.

"Morning Glory is Hedy's good friend. Has she said anything about my aunt?"

"No. But I've been busy on the ranch and in the fire-rescue station. I haven't seen much of Morning Glory. I doubt if she'd tell me personal stuff anyway."

"True enough." Lauren thought a moment. "They've always been best friends and helped each other with their stores. If Aunt Hedy had boxes to unpack, I'd expect Morning Glory to help do it."

"Maybe. Maybe not. Hedy's got a powerful sense of independence. Morning Glory wouldn't want to make Hedy appear weak or incapable to herself or anybody else in town."

"You're right." Lauren scratched her head in frustration. "I can't come to town after all these years and stick my nose into other people's business. Imagine how that'd go over around here."

"You're family. Nobody'd blink an eye if you helped your aunt. Fact of the matter, folks would expect it."

"That's good to know." She glanced back at Adelia's Delights. "I'll do my best not to come on too strong or make Aunt Hedy feel uncomfortable."

"Sounds like the way to go."

Lauren nodded thoughtfully as she turned to look at the lavender-and-white display of luxurious bathrobes, bath salts, lotions, shampoos, and facial products. All of it appeared wonderfully decadent for a spa day of complete relaxation. A long-haired ginger cat that lay curled up in the folds of a white bathrobe opened one eye, gave a slit-eyed look, and returned to sleep.

"I wish we could solve the problem of Hedy right here and now," Kent said. "It seems like maybe she's got some kind of secret."

"If so, I'll try to find out what."

"Thanks. For now, best thing we can do is get barbeque and take it to her."

Lauren glanced up at him, saw his concern, and nodded in agreement. "You're right. Besides, I want to get back to Hannah."

"And I want to meet her."

Everything in Lauren went still as she looked away from him, suddenly wondering how he'd feel about another man's child. "Do you really?"

"Why wouldn't I?"

She heard the surprise and almost hurt tone in his voice. She quickly tried to read what was in his darkened eyes. "It's just—"

"She's your daughter. Nothing else matters."

"Hannah means everything to me."

He smiled, flashing his dimples. "Of course she does. I wouldn't expect anything else."

She returned his smile, feeling a warm tenderness toward him uncurl deep within her. She'd almost forgotten how that feeling had combined with desire to forge their connection so long ago.

"Let's get some grub." He gestured toward the café.

She was glad he'd broken the direction of her

thoughts. The past was the past. "I can smell delicious barbeque from here."

"You bet."

She gave the cat a little wave before she looked up and read "Chuckwagon Café" on the carved wooden sign painted in red and white that hung from hooks above the boardwalk, squeaking slightly as it swayed in the breeze. Red-and-white checked curtains filled the lower half of the large, front windows set in redbrick walls.

"Familiar?" Kent asked as he reached for the doorknob.

"It hasn't changed a bit." She smiled at a sudden thought. "You don't still work here on weekends, do you?"

He laughed, shaking his head. "Not lately. But Granny Duval still rules the family roost and the Chuckwagon Café. If she says jump, everybody asks how high."

Lauren chuckled, too, as she remembered the silver-haired, iron-willed, honey-sweet grandmother. "I've never forgotten the great food."

"How about the tidbits I used to bring you after I got off work?"

Lauren felt her mouth go dry as she slipped back in time again. Kent would drive her up to Lovers Leap where they could be alone, sitting close together in the bed of his blue pickup. He'd feed her tasty morsels one by one from his long fingers and whisper sweet endearments in her ears until all her senses ratcheted into overdrive. Soon other hungers would propel them down onto the old, soft quilts and into each other's arms.

"Remember?" Kent asked again.

"Oh yes."

She jerked her mind back from the past, remembering all too well. She felt hot and bothered just like in the old days when he knew exactly how much she wanted him and she knew how much he wanted her. *Young love.* She doubted it could ever arrive unscathed in the here and now, but she felt just as hot and achy right now in Kent's presence. But she needed to keep those feelings as echoes of the past and not something that was in the present, or risk heartache again. Even more, she now had a daughter to consider above all else.

Kent opened the café's front door and she stepped inside, hearing bells jingle against the door as it closed behind them. She looked around the long room, noting the high ceilings covered in pressed tin squares and the smooth oak floors. Wagon-wheel chandeliers—old lantern-type globes attached to the outer spokes of horizontally hanging wooden wheels—cast soft light over round tables covered in red-and-white-checked tablecloths. A tiger oak bar with enough dings and scratches to testify to its age stretched across the back of the room with battered oak bar stools in front and a cash register on one end. A window behind the bar revealed a kitchen updated with chrome appliances.

She heard her stomach rumble with hunger as she smelled the delicious scents of the café.

Kent chuckled at the sound. "I feel the same way."

She smiled in acknowledgment of the fact that he'd always known how she was feeling or what she was wanting. And he'd always done his best to help her achieve her goals. This time it was food.

A group of local folks seated at a nearby table glanced up, then nodded in greeting as they got up and headed for the front door. She didn't recognize any of them, but that didn't mean she might not have known them in the past. People could change appearance with new hairdos and clothes or as time passed and they grew older.

"Hold your horses!" a man hollered in a deep, rough voice from the back of the café. "I'll be out in a minute."

"If I didn't know better, I'd think we were back in high school," she said in amazement as she glanced around the almost empty café.

"I told you the place hadn't changed one iota."

"I'm glad. There was no way to improve it."

At the only occupied table, Lauren's attention was caught by the sight of a young woman with strawberry blond hair and a six-year-old with a mane of wild, ginger-colored hair that by looks alone had to be the woman's daughter. Lauren immediately thought of Hannah and felt sudden anxiety at being away from her own daughter for so long. But she'd soon be taking her great food.

"Lauren?" the woman called as she stood up, revealing her tall, willowy body.

"Sydney!" Lauren didn't know any other beautiful Valkyrie types except her old friend the basketball player and rodeo star.

Sydney took several long strides toward Lauren.

The little girl, dressed in blue jeans, a red pearl-snap shirt, and a wide, flashy, rhinestone-studded belt with a large buckle, leaped out of her chair and ran across the café.

"Uncle Kent!" She flung her small, muscular arms around his legs, grinning up at him.

"If it isn't my favorite cousin named Storm." He leaned down and gave her a big hug.

"I'm your *only* cousin named Storm!" She giggled as she stepped back.

As Lauren watched, she felt her heart swell with longing at the sight of the gentle man with the little girl. They obviously had a close, loving relationship. She wanted that for Hannah, but her father was completely out of the picture now, so that would never be true for her own child.

When Sydney grabbed Lauren in a big bear hug, she felt grateful for the distraction. She was getting too maudlin, particularly when she was just back in town and all was going well. She hugged Sydney, and then she moved back so she could look at her old friend.

"As I live and breathe, I'd heard you were back in town, but couldn't quite believe it." Sydney smiled at Lauren before she gave Kent a sharp glance with her hazel eyes. "I see my cousin has you in tow again."

"We went to Sure-Shot to check on a fire," Lauren said.

"Bad?" Sydney asked on a sharp intake of breath.

"No." Kent shook his head in denial. "But they wanted us to check it out."

"Aunt Hedy was there, so I was anxious to see her right away."

"Bet she's thrilled you're home." Sydney grinned, revealing bright-white teeth.

Lauren nodded as she glanced at the little girl who clung to Kent's hand as she danced around him in turquoise cowgirl boots.

"What am I thinking?" Sydney said. "Lauren, I want you to meet my daughter Storm."

Lauren quickly crouched down to be at the same eye level as the little girl. "Hey there. I'm glad to meet you. My daughter is about your age. Maybe you could be friends."

"You've got a daughter, too?" Sydney asked, sounding delighted with the news.

"Sure do." Lauren kept her gaze on the little girl.

"That's great!" Sydney said.

Storm dropped Kent's hand and stepped close to Lauren. "Is she a cowgirl?"

"No. I'm afraid not."

Storm shook her head with a disappointed look in her big eyes. "Too bad. My friends all ride horses."

"She's got her heart set on being a cowgirl. Does that count?"

Storm cocked her head to one side, as if considering the question. "Does she need help learning the ropes?"

"Oh yes. Do you suppose you'd have time to give her a few pointers?"

Storm narrowed her eyes in thought. "Best she doesn't learn any bad habits like sloppy riding or roughhousing with horses." She gave a quick, decisive nod. "Best I take her in tow pretty quick."

"That's a good idea." Kent smiled big enough to show his dimples.

"Thanks. Generous, too." Lauren grinned at the adorable girl who she hoped would be Hannah's new BFF.

Sydney chuckled. "You've got no idea. Storm's ready to teach or tell others what's best at the drop of a hat."

Storm put one hand on her narrow hip and used the other to point at her big belt buckle. "Hey, I'm wearing my credentials right here. All-Around Champion."

"That's exactly right," Kent said. "You're a winner."

Storm threw back her small shoulders and grinned, revealing a missing tooth. "Bring on your greenhorn. I'm up to the challenge."

"I'll introduce you soon." Lauren smiled in appreciation at Storm's supreme confidence. She'd be so good for Hannah.

She glanced from Sydney to Kent. Time seemed to stand still in the old café where they'd hung out when they were young. Now they were passing on their hopes and dreams and heritage to Wildcat Bluff's next generation. And it felt exactly right.

Chapter 8

"Why don't you two join us?" Sydney gestured at her table topped with two red plastic baskets, two red plastic glasses, and crumpled white paper napkins. "We were just finishing up, but we'd be happy to stay and talk."

"But not for long." Storm threw her hands out to each side. "I promised Roxy a big, juicy carrot before I go to sleep."

"Roxy is her horse." Kent glanced at Lauren as he explained the name, feeling as if they'd stepped back in time to their old, familiar ways in their old, favorite haunt. "And she's partial to carrots. Right?"

"Right on one count," Storm agreed, flipping her long hair over one shoulder. "But Roxy's a pony. Mom says I'm too little for a big horse."

"That's true." Kent quickly agreed with Sydney.

"You always agree with her." Storm pouted, but then she brightened as she cast a calculating look at Lauren. "I bet I could get you on my side of things. Your daughter—what's her name?"

"Hannah."

"If we had a big enough horse, Hannah and I could ride double."

Kent couldn't help but laugh at his conniving little cousin. She always had an answer for everything, particularly since she'd been raised mostly around adults and had sort of skipped over kid-speak.

"How do you think Roxy would feel about you throwing her over for a big, flashy horse?" Sydney asked.

Storm put both hands over her heart. "She knows I'd never do that. No doubt about it, I need *two* mounts."

At those words, Lauren, Kent, and Sydney laughed hard, shaking their heads at Storm's audacity.

"Hey, what's going on out there?" a big, deep voice boomed as a tall man limped out of the kitchen. "Sounds like I'm missing out on all the fun."

"Slade Steele!" Lauren called out, surprise in her voice. "You still work here?"

"What else would a bull rider with a catch in his get-along do besides cook for the ritziest place in Texas?" Slade grabbed Lauren in a big hug, adjusted his stance to favor his right leg, then lifted her off her feet and whirled her around in a circle.

Kent chuckled at the sight, then abruptly stopped laughing. Slade had cut a wide swathe with the gals for years. His cousin was well over six feet of solid muscle with a thick crop of ginger hair, sharp hazel eyes, and a contagious laugh. A barbwire tattoo circled his right bicep, while a rope tattoo circled the other. Scuffed brown cowboy boots led to faded jeans that led to a tight white T-shirt. But the machismo stopped there. He'd tied a red-and-white checked and ruffled apron with "Lula Mae" embroidered on the pocket around his waist.

When Slade finally set Lauren on her feet, she stepped back, and glanced at his apron. "Hey, Lula Mae, long time no see. I wouldn't have recognized you without your name tag."

Slade guffawed even as he shook his head. "Like I haven't heard that one before. I told Granny not to get me aprons with my name on them cause I wasn't gonna be working here long."

"And six months later, my dear brother has earned something of a reputation as a fine chef—or at least a good cook." Sydney walked over and linked arms with him. "You've increased business so much I doubt Granny will ever let you go."

"Don't say it." Slade rolled his eyes in mock horror. "Take a tumble from a bull, bust some stuff, and end up back at the café. I can guarantee you this wasn't on my life trajectory plan."

"Uncle Slade, there's nothing better than good food—unless its horses." Storm wrapped her arms around his legs in an obvious effort to comfort him.

Slade picked her up and gave a slight wince before he took a wider stance and set her high on his shoulder. "That's right. Who'd be crazy enough to want to ride a wild bull anyway?"

"Exactly." Storm giggled as she patted him on top of his head. "Let's ride, horsey!"

"This isn't play time," Sydney said, interrupting the antics. "Your uncle is working right now."

"Go, Uncle Slade, go!" Storm pretended to snap reins.

As Kent watched, he felt a yawning chasm open up under his feet. By now he thought he'd be the one carrying his own giggling little daughter around on his shoulder while her mother looked on with such love and devotion. He glanced at Lauren and saw the same adoring look in her eyes. If he wasn't careful, he was going to be struck by the green-eyed imp of jealousy.

He'd thought he was on the path to family happiness with Charlene, but that notion was blown to hell and gone. He'd thought he'd let his disappointment and resentment go, but here it was back again in spades. He had a lot in life, but he wanted so much more in the way of love and family. But that was a priceless commodity, and it wasn't something a guy could go out and rope.

"Lauren's got a little girl, too." Sydney held up a hand to her daughter, obviously determined to switch Storm's mind from fun and games.

"Is that right?" Slade turned toward Lauren in surprise.

"Yes." Lauren gave him a big smile. "Hannah is four going on five."

"Congratulations." Slade carefully set Storm on the floor and eased her toward her mother. "Did your daughter's dad come along with you?"

"No." Lauren hesitated, as if searching for the right words to explain her situation.

"Lauren's husband isn't around anymore." Kent stepped in to help ease this information to the family. "Small plane accident."

"I'm right sorry to hear it." Slade shook his head in concern. "Accidents happen to the best of us."

"Thank you," Lauren said quietly.

Sydney stepped forward and squeezed Lauren's hand. "You aren't the only one with that type of loss."

"You too?" Lauren turned to look at Sydney in surprise.

Storm grasped Lauren's other hand. "Daddy's gone to Heaven. Do you think Hannah's daddy is there with him?"

Lauren knelt and clasped Storm in her arms. "Sweetie, I don't know, but I hope so."

Storm patted Lauren's back. "Don't be sad. Mommy says folks that love us watch us from Heaven. I'm riding hard so Daddy'll be proud of me. I'll teach Hannah to do the same—if you like."

"I'd like that very much. And I think Hannah would as well."

Storm gave Lauren a quick kiss on her cheek before she tiptoed back over to her uncle.

Slade clapped his hands together. "Sounds like a plan. Let's celebrate Lauren's return to town. Blackberry cobbler with vanilla ice cream all around."

"Yum!" Storm grabbed Slade's apron and swayed back and forth.

"Sounds good, but I've got to return the booster to the station," Kent said. "We just stopped by to pick up barbeque on our way to Ruby's place. Hedy and Hannah are waiting for us there."

"Rain check?" Lauren asked, smiling around at the group.

"Only if Hannah can come." Storm gave everyone a big, bright grin.

"You bet," Kent agreed.

"Okay then, that's a plan, so we'll be on our way." Sydney started for the front door with Storm by her side. As she opened the door, she glanced back. "Lauren, when you get settled in, call and we can get the girls together for a play day."

"I'll give Lauren your number later," Kent said.

"Perfect!" Sydney shooed Storm out the front door.

"I'm looking forward to catching up while the girls get to know each other," Lauren called as she waved good-bye.

"Soon!" Sydney gave a little wave before she shut the door with a solid click behind her.

"Guess we better get on our way soon, too." Kent turned to look at Lauren. She was making all kinds of plans with others when he wanted to keep her for himself. But that was the way of a small town where everybody knew everybody. Maybe he'd better plan a trip up to Lovers Leap like the old days where they could be alone.

"What kind of barbeque do you want?" Slade grabbed a plastic menu off a nearby table and held it out to Lauren.

She held up her hands in mock surrender. "No choices for me. I want everything!"

Slade guffawed as he tossed the menu back on the table.

"I haven't eaten food from the Chuckwagon Café in so long that I've got to have it all." Lauren joined his laughter.

Kent couldn't help but smile at her happiness, even as he wished she wasn't looking quite so interested in Slade.

"You got it," Slade said. "I'll pack up a variety of meats. Coleslaw, potato salad, and baked beans sound good?"

"Wonderful!" Lauren clapped her hands together in delight.

"You're taking food to Hedy, too?" Slade turned toward Kent with a slight frown on his face.

Kent nodded, wondering why Slade was making a point of it.

"Truth of the matter, Hedy's been coming in when she's working at her store and ordering her usual. I don't know if it's my cooking or not, but she's been leaving most of her food on her plate." Slade shook his head, obviously concerned about Hedy.

"Do you mean she's not eating right?" Lauren appeared worried about her aunt.

"Maybe Hedy eats more at home." Slade cocked his head to one side. "But I kind of doubt it. She's always been bantam weight and now she's getting downright skinny."

"Something's just not right with her," Kent agreed.

"Lauren, I'm glad you're back in town for lots of reasons." Slade stepped close to her. "We'll all trust you to get to the bottom of what's going on."

"I'll do my best." Lauren nodded as she emphasized her words. "First of all, we'll make sure she cleans her plate tonight."

Kent smiled at the old saying that every child had heard a million times growing up in Wildcat Bluff, but he wasn't amused at all. Too many people were noticing too many things that didn't bode well for Hedy.

"Tell you what," Slade said, "one thing that seems to tickle Hedy's fancy are my pies. I've been making sure to give her extra big pieces."

"And she eats them?" Lauren asked.

"Some better than others," Slade explained. "I've been trying different pie recipes that are in Granny's old recipe book. I think some of them go all the way back to her grandma. Anyway, I'm doing my best to tempt her with something she'll eat."

"Thank you." Lauren reached out and squeezed his arm.

"I made a rhubarb-blackberry pie today with her in mind. I'll send it with you."

"Just a piece will do," Lauren said. "I don't want to take a whole pie that you could serve to others."

Slade grinned, revealing white teeth against his tanned skin. "I can make more. Anyway, what else have I got to do while I heal—if I ever do."

"You'll heal," Kent cut in, feeling lower than a snake

at his earlier jealousy. Slade was hurting all the time, not just from his injuries but from losing the life he'd loved since high school. Kent ought to be glad for anything that'd perk up his cousin. If making delicious pies would do the trick, he and every other member of the family would happily eat them.

"I really appreciate what everyone is doing for Aunt Hedy," Lauren said. "I was concerned before I got here, but now I'm flat-out worried about her."

"Hedy belongs to us all," Kent said. "We'll do anything to help her."

"If she'll let us help her. That's the big bugaboo," Slade added, shaking his head. "You know she's got an independent streak a mile wide."

"We'll find a way," Lauren insisted. "Just give me a little time to figure out what's going on."

"You got it," Slade agreed as he turned toward the kitchen. "Now let me box up your vittles."

On a sigh, Lauren turned to Kent. "Nobody's life is perfect, is it?"

"Not by a long shot, but with close family and good friends, we can make it through the hard times together."

"Thanks." She pressed a soft kiss to his cheek. "For everything."

And in that moment, he felt as if he'd come home—and he hadn't even known he'd been gone.

Chapter 9

A LITTLE LATER, LAUREN SAT WITH KENT IN THE booster. She'd wedged two brown paper bags filled with Chuckwagon Café goodies between her feet. She could feel heat from the food containers against the bare skin of her feet. Soon the tantalizing aroma of barbeque had her stomach growling in anticipation.

"Hungry?" Kent glanced her way, then back at Main Street as he drove toward the fire-rescue station.

She patted her tummy. "Guess I'm ready for the best food in Wildcat Bluff County."

"Or anywhere?"

"I wouldn't deny it, not with a Duval sitting this close to me."

"Smart gal." He chuckled as he turned right onto Cougar Lane and slowed to a crawl.

"Something wrong?" She felt a little twist of alarm run through her because he drove so slowly. Was there a problem with the booster?

"Yes and no." He eased into the station's parking lot, stopped under a bare-leafed mimosa, and put the vehicle into park. He turned to face her.

"Kent?" Now she doubted if the problem was with the booster. She didn't look at him, not sure if she wanted to see what was in his eyes or learn what was on his mind.

He sighed as he rubbed a hand across his beard stubble. "Today's brought back all kinds of memories."

"Good ones?"

"Yeah. I feel like I'm eighteen again and trying to get you alone."

She smiled as she saw his sincerity and remembered only too well what he meant. "Lots of friends and family around here. Aunt Hedy used to help us make excuses to get away."

"We ought to be grown up enough now not to need help, don't you think?"

She sighed, knowing she should tell him they didn't need to be alone, but she felt heat rising up and flooding her body. He was making her hot like he'd always done. But that was then. And now was now. They were well beyond such youthful fancies. Yet her thoughts didn't douse the fire that was building inside her, making her feel damp and achy in the deepest, most sensitive part of her. It wouldn't do. Not anymore. She tried to cool down with thoughts of ice cream, but that was too much of a sweet reminder of Kent. A snowstorm like she'd experienced in Connecticut was better for putting out fires.

"Others are waiting to spend time with you, but before I give you back I want to let you know that I'd like for us to find time to be together."

She swallowed hard at his words. Did she dare go down that dangerous-to-her-heart path again?

"Am I asking too much?"

"No," she heard herself say, even as she tried to come up with a good reason to stay away from him.

He clasped her hand and raised it to his lips. He kissed each fingertip before he placed a warm kiss on her palm. "You still have the softest hands."

"Kent, I'm not sure—" But her words caught in her

throat as he gently tugged her toward him, leaned forward, and nuzzled her cheek with his face. She could feel the scratch of his afternoon shadow against her skin, smell his scent, and feel the heat of his body. All were more tantalizing to her senses than the rich smell of barbeque.

"Can we go back up to Lovers Leap?"

She shivered even as he stoked her like a fire, driving her flames higher and higher. When he captured her shoulders with his large hands and caught her lips with his mouth, she felt smart reason and good intentions fly out the window. Instead, she leaned into him, feeling the hard muscles of his chest against her soft breasts. She moaned softly as he gently traced her lips with his tongue, as if tasting her again. When she nipped his lips in return, he deepened the sensual kiss.

And she reeled back in time to those heady days of youth when hormones ran wild. She grasped his shoulders, pulling him closer, needing his heat, his strength, and his desire in a way she'd thought long gone. She kissed him back, harder, longer, stronger as she reached up to dig her fingers into his thick hair and hold on against the rising risk of losing him all over again.

When he thrust back the seat, picked her up, and set her across his lap, she could feel the hardness of his desire for her, and that sensation drove her even wilder. He tore his mouth from hers and rained kisses across her face, down her neck, up to her ear where he lingered, teasing with his tongue as he obviously remembered her sensitivity. He stoked her flames just as she ignited his fire, and he brought her closer to fulfillment than she'd been in years.

Suddenly, he jerked his face away, breathing hard. He looked out across the parking lot at the fire station.

"Hell," he said in a low, rough voice, "we're acting like a couple of teenagers. Anybody could see us. We don't want to put on a show for the entire town to hear about."

She inhaled sharply as she tried to catch her breath and regain her composure, but it wasn't easy.

"Sorry. I started that and I'm out of line. But—"

"You had some help." She placed a soft kiss on his cheek, knowing he was right to consider their location. She eased off his lap and scooted close to the passenger door. She folded her arms over her stomach, feeling defensive at all the emotions that were cascading through her. Hot. Cold. And oh so very achy.

"I apologize."

"There's no need."

"Yes, there is. I didn't mean to come on so strong. It's just that—"

"It's been a long time."

"Hell yeah."

"Let's not rush into anything." She tried to sound cool and reasonable, even thought she was burning up inside and wanting so much more of him. "I just got back into town today."

"My lucky day." He leaned forward and put the booster into drive, then glanced over at her with eyes still dark with desire. "You always did know how to get under my skin. Guess you still do."

"I'm not immune to your charms either."

"Good thing." He focused on the station again. "We'd better get back to business—"

"Before the barbeque gets cold and Aunt Hedy comes looking for us."

"Right."

Still, he hesitated, and then glanced at her. "Can I have a rain check on Lovers Leap?"

She smiled despite herself. "Only if there are old, soft quilts and the Chuckwagon Café food, too."

"You mean I'm not enough?"

"You're more than enough." She knew she was getting in deeper by the moment, but she didn't have the will to stop. "That's just the trouble."

He grinned, flashing white teeth and deep dimples. "Maybe a little trouble is what we've both been needing in our lives."

She couldn't help but smile as he sent the booster forward with a sudden burst of speed. He was definitely Trouble with a capital T.

Kent pulled up in front of a station bay and picked up the remote control from the dashboard.

She glanced down the line of empty parking spaces. She recognized Hedy's van next to a blue pickup that looked like it needed help. Her own white SUV that had a light coating of dust from the trip was where she'd left it several spots down from the other two vehicles.

"Do you think Aunt Hedy called a tow for that truck?"

"Tow? Why would you say that?"

"Look at it. Not only is it covered in mud and dirt, it's got several big dints that I can see from here. It's probably got bald tires and has a flat."

"It looks like a perfectly reasonable work vehicle to me. Stuff happens out on ranches."

"Stuff?"

He gave a big sigh as he used the remote control to open a bay door of the station. "Why don't you grab the barbeque and I'll meet you at Ruby's."

"Wait!" She turned to look at him. He appeared a little hot, or uncomfortable, under the collar. "Oh no!" She quickly swiveled her head to gaze at the vehicle then back at him. "That's not your pickup, is it?"

He rolled his eyes in exaggerated annoyance, but the hint of a smile lurked about his lips. "That big dent came from a hardheaded bull bent on revenge. And the tires aren't bald. I've never been known to drive an unsafe vehicle."

She felt a sudden attack of giggles coming on because she'd just insulted his ride. And guys were notoriously sensitive about their vehicles. It shouldn't have struck her as funny, but it did. She put a hand over her mouth to try to stop the laugh that threatened to erupt, but pretty soon she choked, then chortled as her shoulder shook with mirth and a giggle rolled out.

"Go ahead and laugh," he grumbled as he pointed to her vehicle. "I suppose that pristine little prissy SUV belongs to you."

"I'm sorry," she managed before she laughed harder, feeling her eyes burn with moisture. She tried to stop, honestly, but she felt as if something had broken inside of her or had been let loose after so many years of pent-up tension and worry. She hadn't laughed this hard since the last time she'd been with Kent all those years ago. And the laughter felt wonderful.

"For your information, everything about my truck is in fine working order."

"Except the outside?"

"Not important." He looked at her, turning serious. "If I wash my truck, it'll just get dirty again. If I get that dint fixed, some other critter will take into his head to butt it again. Why bother?"

"You make a good point." She took a deep breath, tamping down the humor of the situation, because she could see he was serious about his vehicle. She might even be hurting his feelings, but he'd always played fast and loose with stuff. It just didn't matter to him.

"If it offends you, I can wash the truck."

"Oh no, it's fine. I remember now that you never did much care what was on the outside of anything."

"It's what's on the inside that counts." He reached over and took her hand. As he rubbed a rough thumb over her soft palm, he gazed into her eyes. "Lauren, you've always been beautiful. Everybody knows that. But it's your inner beauty that's always shone through that's nigh on irresistible."

"Oh, Kent, you big silly." She felt his words go straight to her heart, and now she felt like crying with the sheer tenderness and sincerity of his words.

"It's the truth."

"You've got a big heart that sees the best in everybody. Kent, I—"

A loud knock on the passenger door made Lauren jump, so she quickly looked out the window.

Hedy grinned at her. "Hey, let's get this show on the road!"

Lauren smiled back as she lowered her window. "I take it you're hungry."

"And I'm anxious to meet that little tyke of yours."

"She's going to love you." Lauren glanced back at Kent. "Guess Aunt Hedy's right. We need to get a move on."

"Go ahead and take the barbeque. I'll park the booster and close up here."

"We can wait for you," Hedy said.

"No need. I'll be at Ruby's pretty quick."

"Thanks." Lauren realized he was still holding her hand, so she squeezed his fingers and let go. "I'm sorry about being unappreciative of your truck."

"Don't worry." He chuckled, boyish dimples flashing with the mischief in his eyes. "I'll get you back for it."

"No doubt." She chuckled at his warm look that promised plenty of delicious trouble—just like the old days. "I'd better run inside and change clothes first."

"Go ahead like you are. I'll bring your dress."

"You sure?"

"Yes."

"Thanks. I'll wash the jeans and bring them back to the station. But I'm keeping the T-shirt."

"You sure you don't want to give it back to me?" He grinned even bigger. "I'd take it home."

She rolled her eyes at him, imagining taking his fire-rescue shirt away from him and snuggling against the softness and the smell of him in her lonesome bed. But she pushed those thoughts aside and turned her attention to Hedy, who was grinning up at them. "You hear all that?"

"Sure did. I'm not touching any of it with a ten-foot pole." She appeared delighted with them. "Let Kent lock up and we can be on our way."

"Okay." Lauren picked up the two heavy sacks of barbeque, then hesitated as she glanced at Kent. "It's good to be home."

He nodded, but his eyes were still alight with mischief. "Sure, that's what you say now. Wait till everybody's got you working on some project or other."

"I think I can handle whatever Wildcat Bluff throws at me."

He grinned even bigger. "Sure?"

"You two can bicker later," Hedy interrupted, chuckling. "We're burning daylight here."

"I'll see you at Twin Oaks." She gave him a quick smile, opened the door, stepped down, and watched him drive into the fire station.

Kent was certainly turning her world upside down, and she was starting to like it. She turned back to Hedy, tried to look serious, but couldn't keep the grin from her face.

"You look like the cat that ate the cream," Hedy said with a knowing glint in her brown eyes. "And I haven't seen that boy look so happy in a month of Sundays."

Lauren nodded as she pulled a key ring out of her purse. "I'm feeling pretty happy myself."

Chapter 10

As Lauren followed Hedy's van down Cougar Lane, she glanced at the houses on either side of the road. She liked the idea that so far she hadn't seen many changes in Wildcat Bluff, so the town was still familiar and full of wonderful memories. Most of the homes along here were large and set back from the street on an acre or two. She admired a Spanish hacienda with a red-tile roof, a white antebellum with columns soaring from the portico up to the second story, a pink-brick single-story ranch with a silver metal roof, and a multicolored pastel Victorian. Each house was beautiful in its own way.

She was ready to get to Ruby's and make sure Hannah was still enjoying Twin Oaks. Most folks considered the estate special because former Seabee Jake Jobson had spent his retirement years building the amazing place for his wife Gladys. Now their daughter ran Twin Oaks as a bed-and-breakfast that catered to weddings, reunions, and getaways.

When Lauren reached the top of Cougar Knoll, she caught her first sight of the estate. Jake had created a spectacular fence out of all the rocks he'd dug up, washed, and sized from the ten-acre property. She slowly drove past the amazing fence scalloped from rock post to rock post.

She noticed that the two thousand trees, mostly pine, which Jake had planted in perfect rows, had now grown tall enough to cast shadows over the neatly mowed and manicured acreage. She couldn't see it from the road, but she knew he'd also built a brick-and-wood bench beside the small pond so he could sit, watch frogs leap from lily pad to lily pad, and listen to the wind whisper through the pine trees. He'd been a special man and she'd always miss him, along with Gladys.

As she drove up to the B&B's entrance, she saw an arched black metal sign overhead that read "Twin Oaks" entwined with the silhouettes of two oak trees. She eased on her brakes as she watched Hedy continue down the road so she could park in front of the house and use the ramp for her wheelchair. Lauren would park in the visitor's area to leave room in front of the house.

She turned in past twin rock buttresses that curved outward from the fence on either side of the estate's entry. She drove across dry grass to a white four-board fence that enclosed a horse pasture behind a traditional red barn. She stopped her SUV and opened the door. For a moment she simply sat still as she listened to the wind in the pines, just as Jake had once done. She glanced around the area, remembering how there was always plenty to do for fun in season at Twin Oaks such as basketball, tennis, swimming, and golf.

She looked over at the imposing home that rose in planes, angles, and sharp rooflines. Red brick. Green trim. Slate-gray shingles. Three-car garage. Extra parking for guests by the tennis court. Jake's design of a multilevel Midcentury Modern house built in the 1980s was absolutely beautiful in its stark simplicity and welcoming ambiance.

Lauren was glad Twin Oaks remained pretty much

untouched by time. That was due to Ruby's appreciation, respect, and love for her parents' wonderful home. They were gone now, but their legacy lived on. Lauren couldn't be happier that she had such a great friend in Ruby and a good place to stay for Hannah's first few days in Wildcat Bluff.

She smiled at thoughts of her daughter and quickly slung her purse over her shoulder, picked up the sacks of barbeque, and stepped out of her SUV. Fortunately, she'd already carried her luggage inside and unpacked in one of the guest suites on the top level of the house.

After she locked her vehicle, not strictly required in the area but a leftover habit from big-city living, she walked across the grass, which was beginning to turn green in the early spring weather. She stopped beside a two-story pergola that had a picnic table on each level. Jake had built the brick pergola as a viewing stand for the nearby tennis court enclosed by a high chain-link fence.

She crossed the tennis court and reached the front of the house where Hedy had parked her van outside the three-car garage. She noticed trimmed rose bushes in a redbrick planter at the front edge of a covered porch that shaded a bank of sliding glass doors leading into the sunroom.

She hesitated a moment, enjoying the peaceful quiet. Hedy must have already zipped up the ramp and entered the kitchen. Kent hadn't arrived yet, so she figured he was still finishing up at the station. She took a moment to walk over to the huge oak tree.

Lauren patted the trunk as she looked up. "Hey, Big John. How're you doing? I do believe you've put on a little weight around the middle. It looks good on you." She chuckled at her words, still enjoying the fact that

Jake had named Twin Oaks after two huge trees that he'd also given names.

She glanced up over the roof and saw Big Bertha rising high into the sky on the other side of the house. Jake once explained that he'd built between the two ancient oaks so if lightning struck, it'd hit the trees and not the house. That'd turned out to be a good idea because Big John's center trunk was gray, lightning blasted, but new limbs had grown out around the damage.

She patted Big John's rough trunk again, then turned and walked to the front of the house. She slid open a door and stepped onto the terra-cotta tile of the enclosed breezeway, quickly shutting the door behind her. The garden room extended across the house to another wall of glass with sliding doors. She could see a redbrick gazebo with one side built around the trunk of Big Bertha.

Lauren felt air from a ceiling fan swirl across her face as she took a moment to study a colorful poster of a woman on horseback framed in gray barnwood that read "National Cowgirl Hall of Fame, Fort Worth, Texas." She knew a number of gals from Wildcat Bluff County were featured in the famous museum.

When she heard a meow, she glanced toward the sound. Temple lay nestled in one of three white cushions on the seat of a hanging wooden swing. He had bright, almost iridescent white fur, pale-blue eyes, and a black mark across his nose.

She smiled, acknowledging that Temple ruled the roost at Twin Oaks and everybody loved him. "Excuse me for not saying hello the moment I walked inside, but I didn't see you. White fur against white cushion. I'm sure you understand."

Temple yawned, revealing white dagger teeth and a long, pink tongue. He stood up, stretched, arching his back, and nudged one of her sacks of barbeque with the tip of his nose.

"Hungry?" She chuckled as she watched him leap down and walk with great dignity to the inside front door where he glanced impatiently back at her. "You're so spoiled. Everybody knows you love Chuckwagon Café's barbeque, and they bring you treats all the time."

He yowled, as if in agreement, and looked up at the doorknob.

"Can't wait, can you?"

She turned the knob and he strolled inside. The delicious scent of cookies wafted outward and enveloped her in the aroma of rich chocolate. She smiled in delight. Now this was her kind of treat, if not on Temple's list of favorites.

After she shut the door, Temple led her across the oak wood floor of a large living area. She caught her breath at the beauty as she glanced around the room. The slatted-wood ceiling soared upward to the roofline in a dramatic A-line design. A long balcony on the second floor gave a wonderful view out an upstairs window and across the area below. She particularly admired the redbrick fireplace that dominated one corner of the room and extended to the ceiling in another dramatic effect. Ruby had chosen contemporary furniture with upholstery in geometric patterns of green, burgundy, and gold to complement the house's design. A red half-brick wall and short staircase separated the living room from the kitchen and dining area above.

She glanced up at the bright, yellow kitchen, hoping to hear Hannah's voice. When she didn't, she felt a little worry bubble up. Ruby's trademark loud guffaw was followed by Hedy's deep chuckles. Temple took the three steps upward and she followed right behind him.

"Hey," she called. "Is anybody besides Temple ready for barbeque?"

"Be still my heart." Ruby pointed toward the white with gold swirls laminate countertop. "Set it right there where I can have at it." Ruby wore jeans, a red top, and black cowgirl boots. She'd styled her dark-brown hair in a simple, efficient blunt cut at her shoulders.

Hedy sat in her wheelchair at one end of Ruby's 1940s enamel, tin-top pie table with its wooden Art Deco-design base painted in yellow and orange.

Lauren gave her aunt a quick kiss on her cheek and then set the sacks of barbeque on the counter. "Where's Hannah?"

"That little apple of your eye is upstairs taking a nap. She got all tuckered out from baking a batch of chocolate chip cookies."

"I'm anxious to meet her." Hedy gave Lauren a big grin. "I'm hoping she's a chip off the old block."

"If she's anything like you, Hedy, we're all in trouble." Ruby guffawed again.

Lauren joined their laughter. She was so glad to be with these country Texas women with their humorous talk and down-home ribbing. She might meet a few like them in Houston, but here in the countryside, most of the women were like Ruby and Hedy. Straight talkers. Hard workers. Salt of the Earth. They had a generosity of spirit that never turned anyone hungry away from the table. Lauren knew she and Hannah couldn't be in better hands.

"We'd best feed Temple first, or we'll all be in trouble." Lauren pointed down at him.

"So true," Hedy agreed, reaching to stroke Temple's short, thick fur.

"And with those sacks you plopped down in my kitchen, we've now got a war on our hands." Ruby glanced at Lauren with a twinkle in her eyes.

"What do you mean?" Lauren asked as she pulled out a sturdy wooden chair with a yellow cushion and sat down beside her aunt.

"The smell of barbeque is in competition with the scent of fresh-baked cookies," Ruby replied with a dry tone in her understated Texas way.

"If you think that's bad," Lauren said as she absent-mindedly adjusted a stack of white paper napkins on the tabletop, "there's going to be an even bigger battle when I pull out the pie Slade baked and sent home for us."

"Yum!" Hedy looked at the sacks from the Chuckwagon Café. "What flavor?"

"Rhubarb-blackberry," Lauren said. "I think he's using us as guinea pigs for the new recipes he's trying out."

"I've been helping him out as his pie-taster." Hedy glanced around the kitchen, smiling mischievously. "Something about pies just suits me of late."

"I'm glad something does," Ruby said. "You've been eating like a bird."

Hedy just shrugged in response.

Lauren caught Ruby's gaze and received a nod of understanding in return. Maybe tonight, between pie, cookies, and barbeque, they could get Hedy to eat well for a change.

Temple yowled in an impatient tone.

"I'd best get that boy a plate before he decides to leap up on the counter and dig in all on his lonesome."

Ruby reached into a sack, pulled out a plastic container, opened the top, and selected a slice of beef. She broke the meat into bite-size pieces and set them in a blue china bowl the exact color of Temple's eyes.

"Is that for me or the cat?" Hedy chuckled as she pointed at Ruby's preparations.

"What do you think?" Ruby laughed as she set the plate under the wide bar that extended to the sink and around one side of the kitchen.

"I figure in this town humans eat on paper plates while cats get the best china." Hedy continued to chuckle as she pointed at Temple, who delicately sniffed the meat, then chomped a piece between his teeth.

Lauren joined their laughter, knowing Hedy's words weren't far from the truth. Folks had always loved and valued their cats in Wildcat Bluff. Thinking about love, she wanted to get upstairs to see her own little girl, but she didn't want to wake her just yet.

Suddenly she felt her child nearby, in the way mothers so often do, and glanced up at the short staircase that led to the top floor.

Hannah stood with her hand on the railing, looking like a sleepy blond-haired angel with big, brown eyes. She wore her favorite pink, long-sleeve T-shirt with rhinestones in the outline of a horse and matching leggings. She held up a too-big red cowgirl hat with one small hand so she could see out from under it.

"Mommy, I made cookies today!"

And Lauren felt her heart go out to the love of her life.

Chapter 11

"Sweetie, I can't wait to try them." Lauren pulled out the chair beside her and patted the cushion. "Why don't you join us?"

Hannah took a step downward, then stopped and sat on a carpeted stair. She shyly peeked out from under the brim of the large hat, brown eyes wide as she looked back and forth between Lauren and Hedy.

"I want you to meet someone special." Lauren kept her voice soft so as to reassure her daughter, since Hannah had become reticent around strangers.

"Aunt Ruby's special," Hannah said in a soft, sweet voice.

"Thank you." Ruby gave her an encouraging smile. "You're mighty special, too."

Hannah shyly ducked her head to study her bare toes. "You make good cookies. And you're a cowgirl."

"Not lately." Ruby chuckled as she set food containers on the countertop. "But I still know my way around a horse. Fact of the matter, lots of folks who hail from Wildcat Bluff won championships in their time."

"That's so true." Lauren gestured toward her aunt. "Hannah, I want you to meet your great-aunt Hedy. She's a former rodeo star, too." Lauren wished her daughter was as outgoing and trusting as she had been before the loss of her father. Somehow she was going to find a way to get her daughter back to that positive place.

Hannah stood up, took another step downward, and stopped again. She cocked her head to the side and grabbed her hat as it slid off her head. She held the big hat against her small chest. "How do you get to be a great-aunt?"

Lauren smiled, feeling intense love. "She's your grandmother's sister, so she's your great-aunt and my aunt."

"Ruby's my aunt, too."

"I'm a friend-aunt," Ruby quickly explained. "Hedy's your family-aunt."

"I like aunts." Hannah took the rest of the stairs down and stopped beside the table. She looked at Hedy's wheelchair. "Mommy fixes folks. Maybe she can fix you so you can ride a horse again."

Lauren inhaled sharply, wishing she'd explained about Hedy's wheelchair before Hannah had seen it. And just like an innocent child, she went straight to the heart of the matter.

Hedy chuckled, shaking her head. "Wish that were possible, but I'm not fixable. Anyway, I've got something better than legs." She demonstrated a few quick moves with her power wheelchair.

Hannah's eyes grew wide. "Bet you can go fast as a horse."

"Almost," Hedy agreed. "I hear you've got your heart set on being a cowgirl."

Hannah nodded as she held up one finger. "One, I need a pony." She held up two fingers. "Two, I need a hat and boots."

"Those are doable." Hedy leaned forward, hands resting on the arms of her wheelchair.

Hannah glanced at Lauren. "Mommy says 'first things first.' What's first?"

"I'll be happy to teach you," Hedy said with a twinkle in her brown eyes so much like Hannah's own. "Now that you're in Wildcat Bluff, all sorts of folks will be happy to help you become a cowgirl."

Hannah set the cowgirl hat on top of the bar. "That's Aunt Ruby's hat. Maybe one in my size is better." She looked hopefully from Hedy to Ruby to Lauren.

"Sounds like there's a trip to Old Town and Gene's Boot Hospital in our future," Ruby said. "We might all need a new hat or some other fancy thing just for the fun of it."

"True enough." Hedy grinned, perking up. "A gal's got to keep up appearances, doesn't she?"

Hannah nodded as she gave a big sigh. "I like aunts—and mommies." She clasped her middle with both arms and twisted back and forth. "I like daddies a lot, but sometimes they go away."

"Oh, sweetie." Lauren felt concerned, as she always did nowadays, at her daughter's sadness.

"That's why," Hannah continued in a stronger voice, "it's good we've got aunties and great-aunties and mommies."

"And plenty of them," Hedy quickly agreed.

Hannah flipped back a strand of long blond hair as she looked at Hedy. "I always give Granny a bear hug. She says it heals most anything. Do you want a hug?"

Hedy grinned as she held out her arms. "I can always use a hug, particularly one from my very own great-niece."

Lauren sniffed, holding back the tears that were filling her eyes. She couldn't be prouder of her daughter for being so generous with a stranger. Maybe love was what was missing from her aunt's life. If so, she and Hannah had plenty to give. And it wasn't a one-way street. They needed love, too.

Time seemed to stand still as she watched her daughter and aunt hug each other. She could've sworn it was only yesterday that Hedy had enclosed her in strong arms and helped make everything right in her younger years. Now it was Lauren's turn to help her aunt get her through to the other side of whatever was adversely affecting her life.

Hannah patted Hedy's face with her small hand, then stepped back and clapped her hands. "I know! Cookies first. Barbeque second." She glanced from one surprised face to another.

Ruby broke out in laughter and the others quickly followed her lead. "You've got a good point." She picked up a large cookie jar in the shape of a white cat and set it in the center of the table.

Hannah peeked under the counter at Temple. "Cookie?"

"I think he's biding his time for more beef," Ruby said. "Most likely he's napping between courses."

Hannah nodded sagely, then sat down at the table and reached for the cookie jar. But her arm wasn't long enough.

"Here, let me help." Lauren took off the lid and the delicious aroma of chocolate chip cookies wafted into the air. She picked up the cookie jar and held it out to Hedy first.

"Yum!" Hedy picked up a napkin, selected a cookie, took a big bite, and rolled her eyes in delight.

Ruby took the next cookie and made happy noises as she chewed her sweet treat.

Next Lauren offered the jar to Hannah, expecting her to grab a cookie or even two.

"Mommy, you're next." And then Hannah appeared confused by her own words. "Is that right, like you taught me?"

"Yes, sweetie, that's socially very polite." Lauren selected a cookie and waited for Hannah to pick one before she set down the jar.

Hannah held her cookie in two hands as she watched Lauren. "Go ahead, Mommy. It's good."

Lauren took a big bite and moaned in delight. As soon as she swallowed, she smiled at her daughter. "That's a delicious cookie. I'm proud of you."

Hannah shyly glanced down, then looked over at Ruby. "I had help."

"You did the hard work," Ruby said. "And I'll expect your help from now on out."

With a big grin on her face, Hannah took a bite of her own cookie. "Sweets first!"

"This time, yes," Lauren said. "Our special day deserves a special treat."

"You bet," Hedy agreed, finishing her cookie with gusto.

Lauren was glad to see her aunt enjoy the food. Maybe Hannah's presence in Hedy's life would make a positive difference. Still, she needed to have a heart-to-heart talk with her aunt and hopefully Hedy would open up to her.

"Okay, folks, looks like we're all set to go." Ruby dusted her hands over the sink and then lifted the last Chuckwagon Café container out of a sack. She rose up on tiptoe, reached into a cabinet, and pulled out a stack of plates that she set on the breakfast bar. "We're using Mom's Plainsman prairie green plates tonight in honor of the occasion." She reached into the cabinet again and selected matching green glasses that she set on the table.

"Are you sure about the Frankoma pottery?" Lauren asked. "I wouldn't want anything to happen to it, being vintage and special and all."

"Mom always said to use it all because saving it for a better day might never come." Ruby set Slade's delicious-looking pie with the browned-to-perfection crust on one of the plates. She pulled flatware from a drawer and set it beside the stack of plates. "And we're using Grandma's Duchess silver. It's about a hundred years old now and better than ever."

"Gladys always was a wise one," Hedy agreed, smiling as she looked at the pottery.

"So true." Ruby opened the refrigerator door and put her hand against a prairie green pitcher of sweet tea. "Cold enough. Now all we need is our man of the hour."

"What's that?" Hannah asked as she crumpled a napkin in her hands.

"That would be Kent Duval," Ruby explained.

"He and your mom used to—" Hedy said.

Lauren quickly cleared her throat to interrupt her aunt. "He's one of the local kids I grew up with."

"Oh." Hannah looked disappointed. "I hoped that was the name of a horse."

When everyone burst out laughing, Lauren looked at her daughter in amazement. Sometimes Hannah was just too cute for words, and other times she revealed wisdom beyond her years.

"Man of the hour better get here quick or I'm raiding the cookie jar." Hannah gave them a mischievous grin.

Temple yowled from under the counter, voicing his displeasure that supper was being held up.

Lauren laughed harder with Hedy and Ruby, realizing

that she hadn't laughed so much in ages, till she arrived in Wildcat Bluff. If laughter truly was the best medicine, she was in the right place to get lots of it.

"I'm all for breaking out Slade's pie." Hedy glanced up on the countertop. "May we at least see his latest culinary delight?"

"Hannah, I think you started something," Ruby said. "Dessert first."

"Yay!" Hannah bounced in her chair. "Barbeque second."

"If he doesn't get here soon, I'm for letting him eat leftovers." Lauren chuckled as she glanced out the front window, knowing none of them would ever do such a rude thing. The sun was low in the west and night was coming on fast, but still no Kent. She felt a little bit of worry blossom inside her, but surely he was okay. Maybe she just anticipated trouble so she could try to avoid it. Jeffrey's sudden demise hadn't helped her belief that only good things happened to good people. She'd found life had a funny way of taking unexpected turns.

"Manners," Hedy reminded Hannah.

"Right," Hannah quickly agreed. "Even if he isn't a horse, we ought to be polite."

Once more, Lauren surrendered to laughter and realized how much she'd missed the easy closeness of longtime friends and family. She felt doubly blessed that she'd been able to bring Hannah to Wildcat Bluff.

"If he'd gotten called out, he'd have let us know," Hedy said. "I bet he's just tidying up and switching the phones to the police department so there's always somebody available to take fire or other 9-1-1 calls."

“How long can that take?” Ruby asked, glancing out the kitchen window.

“Who knows,” Hedy said. “He got hung-up, that’s all. If I don’t miss my guess, he’ll be here soon.”

And about that time, Lauren looked out the window again and saw a pickup pull up in front beside Hedy’s van. She did a double take as Kent stepped out of his vehicle because she hadn’t recognized the truck as the one she’d seen earlier. This one had a Texas Firefighter license plate, but the main difference was that she could see the shiny, dark-blue exterior of what had earlier been covered in dirt and mud. He’d washed his pickup? Surely he didn’t do it just to please her.

“Kent’s here,” Hedy called as she wheeled over to the windows. “Ruby, would you look at that! He washed his truck.”

Ruby walked over to the windows and glanced outside. “As I live and breathe, he got a burr under his saddle for some reason or he’d never, and I mean not in a million years, have wasted a moment of his time at a car wash.”

Lauren cleared her throat. “I guess I did mention something about his truck being a little on the dirty side earlier. But I didn’t think—”

Hedy and Ruby turned toward her as one, looking beyond shocked as they laughed together.

“I doubt it has anything to do with me.”

“Oh sure,” Hedy teased as she wheeled back to the table. “I’m not saying a word about it. Not one single word.”

“Me neither.” Ruby hurried back to the kitchen. “Best pretend we didn’t notice or it’ll be another five years before he washes his truck again.”

"Mom washes our car all the time," Hannah said helpfully.

Hedy and Ruby laughed even harder.

Lauren felt obliged to defend her innocence again, but she stopped in shock the moment the door opened and Kent stepped inside.

He jerked off his big cowboy hat as he scuffed the soles of his mud-splashed cowboy boots on the yellow doormat. His faded jeans and T-shirt were dark with water, but that only served to emphasize the hard, sculpted muscles of his chest and thighs.

Immediately, he sought out Lauren and glared at her with hazel eyes gone dark. "There's a good reason for a guy not to wash his truck." He looked down at his wet jeans and muddy boots.

Hedy and Ruby snorted, choked, and finally burst into laughter while Lauren determinedly pinched her lips together.

"Not funny," Kent grumbled. "At least I had the sense not to vacuum out the inside. Otherwise, I might not ever have gotten here."

Hedy crossed her arms on the table and put her head down, but her shoulders still shook with her muffled laughter.

Ruby didn't even bother to hide her mirth. "Good thing. We're mighty hungry."

Hannah stood up, obviously not getting what was funny, and walked cautiously over to Kent. She stopped and examined him from the tips of his boots to the hat in his hands. Finally, she craned her neck, looked up at his face, and threw her small arms around his legs.

"Cowboy Daddy!"

Chapter 12

"HUH?" KENT LOOKED DOWN IN CONFUSION AT THE top of the blond head of a little girl clinging to his legs.

"Cowboy Daddy!" She grasped his legs harder.

He tried to dislodge her gently by moving his legs a little, but she stuck to him like a tick on a cow. He wouldn't think such a little bit of a girl would have so much strength. All he wanted was to do sit down and eat barbeque while he dried off from his trip to the car wash. Teach him to try to impress a gal. Pickups were meant to be dirty or they weren't doing their job.

If he could get hold of the girl's arms he might be able to pull her off him, but she looked too delicate to manhandle. He figured one good jerk and she might come apart. Slade would know what to do, because he was used to being an adoring uncle who knew how to play with kids. Kent knew how to rope and wrangle and hog-tie animals. Somehow, he didn't figure those skills were going to do him much good here and now.

"There now, li'l dogie." He patted the top of her blond head like he would reassure a calf, but he wasn't at all sure if it'd work on a kid.

She looked up and gave a big grin, revealing tiny white teeth. "Oh!" She threw out her arms and wheeled around several times. "Cowboy Daddy gave me my very own cowgirl name. He's the best!"

He stepped back. That wasn't the result he'd expected,

but he guessed the pat on her head had done some good. He walked over to Ruby in the kitchen who looked like an ally. But she wasn't paying him any attention. She stared at the little girl with her eyes wide in surprise. He glanced back.

The front of the kid's top was wet and muddy from her run-in with him. The mess wasn't his fault. He'd been blindsided the moment he'd walked in the door. But now he was under the microscope of Ruby, Hedy, and Lauren. They'd probably blame him.

"Sorry about that." Kent looked out the front windows longingly at his truck. He supposed he couldn't just leave and go fix fence or something else completely under his control.

"That's okay. Kids and messes go together," Lauren said, chuckling. "Kent, I'd like you to meet my daughter Hannah. Sweetie, this is Kent Duval."

"Hey, Hannah." He should've realized from the first moment that this little whirlwind had to be Lauren's daughter, but he'd had his mind on his truck and been caught by surprise.

Hannah gave him a big grin, grabbed his hand, and tugged him toward the table. "Cowboy Daddy, we got cookies. And I made them with Aunt Ruby's help."

"That's good."

"You can have one."

"Maybe later."

"Mommy and aunties like them."

He hesitated, hearing the hurt in her voice. What had he said that could cause such a reaction? He glanced down her. Were those tears in her eyes? Over cookies? He looked from Ruby to Hedy to Lauren.

They appeared to be holding their breaths as to what would happen next.

"They're real good, I think," Hannah said, voice dropping downward.

He caught the hesitation in her voice that hadn't been there before and he silently kicked himself for making her doubt her own abilities. Chalk it up to a clueless cowboy. "On second thought." He nodded at Lauren to let her know that he was getting the message. "I can't wait to try your cookies."

"Yay!" Hannah hurried over to the table and struggled to pull out the chair across from Lauren, but it was too heavy for her.

He set his hat on the bar beside Ruby's, then walked over and pulled the chair back from the table for her.

"Cowboy Daddy, this one, too." Hannah pointed at the chair next to the one she'd designated for him.

He pulled that chair out, but not as far. As he watched, she sat down and smiled up at him, looking just as pleased as punch about the whole deal.

"Better sit." Hannah patted the chair seat beside her.

He cast a look around the room, but he could see that he wasn't going to get any help from the ones who probably had a clue. They were backing the girl's play with supportive silence.

"Join us?" Hannah patted the cushion on the chair again.

He felt as if he'd stumbled into a little girl's tea party where she knew all the correct, polite, ladylike rules and he knew none of them. But he sat down anyway, even though he felt like a bull in a china shop on top of being wet and grumpy from washing his truck.

"Can you wait for your cookie?" Hannah asked in her high, lilting voice. "You missed sweets first."

"Yep." He refused to commit himself any further when he didn't know what she was talking about. Besides which, he could wait till the cows came home for a cookie. Now, barbeque? That was a whole other matter.

"Mommy, please put the lid on the cookie jar." Hannah said. "Cowboy Daddy loves my cookies so much he'll fuss if he has to smell them and not get one."

Kent didn't say a word, but he cocked his head at Lauren as if to inquire about the situation. All she did was smile and put a lid on the cookie jar.

"Thank you," Hannah said in a polite voice as she turned toward Kent. "Cowboy Daddy, are you hungry?"

"I could eat." He decided to remain noncommittal till he got the lay of this land, if he ever did.

"Barbeque?" Hannah asked sweetly.

"Yeah." He thought about the section of fence that needed a little attention as something he could wrap his head around. He started to count the number of U-nails he thought he'd need, but a small hand on his arm brought his mind back to the present.

"You're tired after a long day in the saddle, aren't you?" Hannah nodded at him in understanding with big, dark eyes.

For a moment she reminded him so much of the old Lauren that he felt like he'd stepped back in time. She'd been a handful. Guess her daughter was chip off the old block. And a cute one at that.

"He took care of a fire in Sure-Shot." Lauren finally joined the conversation, as if Kent had passed some type of initiation. "He's a cowboy firefighter."

"And Cowboy Daddy," Hannah insisted with a determined nod of her blond head.

"Why don't we all chow down on barbeque?" Ruby moved the two cowboy hats out of the way and then lined up the barbequed beef, potato salad, baked beans, and coleslaw in their open containers. She finished off the row of food with Slade's pie. "We're eatin' easy tonight—buffet style." She took the pitcher of tea out of the refrigerator, filled the glasses, and set it on the tabletop.

"Hannah, I'll fix you a plate," Lauren said.

"Thank you, Mommy, but—" Hannah gave Kent a sweet smile. "Cowboy Daddy wants to do that, don't you?"

Kent swallowed hard, glanced at Lauren, and got a nod in return. "Yeah, sure. What do you like?"

"I like what you like," Hannah said.

He quickly stood up as he glanced down at Hedy. "What can I get you? Looks like I'm fixing plates around here."

"Man of the hour." Hedy chuckled, shaking her head. "Think I'll just save my appetite for pie."

"Auntie Hedy," Hannah piped up. "Remember, sweets second."

Hedy laughed. "Okay. I guess I'm outnumbered. Bring me a little bit of it all."

"Good choice." Lauren gave Kent a warm smile.

He felt that smile all the way to his gut with a little zing along the way. Life had sure been easier in high school. Maybe he was doing okay with the womenfolk after all. But he sure as hell wouldn't get cocky.

After they maneuvered around the bar, loaded up plates, passed out plates, and then finally settled around the table, Kent was so hungry he could eat a bear. He picked up his fork, but small fingers on his hand stopped him. He looked over at what was turning out to be his nemesis—one pint-sized little girl.

"Cowboy Daddy gives thanks, doesn't he?" she asked.

He locked gazes with Lauren, who gave him another encouraging smile. He set down his fork. "Okay. Thanks for good vittles and good family."

He picked up his fork, but that soft, little hand stopped him again. This time he just set down his fork and waited for her. Hannah was nothing if not determined that things be done to her satisfaction.

"What about horses?" Hannah asked.

"Okay. We're all mighty thankful for horses, cattle, buffalo, and all the critters out on the plains."

"Amen," Hannah said. "That was real good."

He glanced over and was rewarded with a serious nod of appreciation. He looked across the table at Lauren, who appeared as if she was about to break out in laughter or tears. He hoped she was happy. He was doing his best. He picked up his fork and dug into the potato salad. About the time he raised the fork to his mouth, he felt a rub against his leg. He looked down. Temple was staring up at him with pale-blue eyes, trying to appear as if he hadn't eaten in a month of Sundays.

"Ruby, did you feed your cat?" He pointed down with one hand while he held onto his fork with the other.

"Is he begging?" Ruby asked.

"No. He's demanding."

Hedy chuckled as she pushed food around on her plate. "Better feed him. Temple can be one determined cat."

Kent reluctantly set down his fork, cut off a piece of beef, and chucked it toward the blue bowl. Temple started eating the moment the meat touched down. And Kent finally followed his example with a big bite of delicious potato salad.

"Cowboy Daddy, would you please cut up my meat for me? Mommy's across the table."

"Hannah," Lauren said. "You've been handling your own food for some time now."

"But that was before Cowboy Daddy got here."

Kent wasn't about to argue. No doubt about it. You fed kids and critters first. He just reached over and cut up Hannah's meat, beginning to feel like the cowboy daddy she'd named him.

"Thank you." Hannah forked up a piece of meat. "You did that real good."

"Well, I wouldn't want to disappoint the li'l dogie." He couldn't keep from chuckling at her compliment, feeling a mite on the proud side for no good reason except he'd made a little girl happy.

As he chewed, he looked across the table at Lauren. She definitely had tears in her eyes. He glanced at Hedy. She probably hadn't eaten a bite. He looked out of the corner of his eye at Hannah. She was staring at him instead of eating her food. Finally, he focused on Ruby. She was the only one who was totally into the barbeque. She raised her fork in a slight salute.

He returned the gesture even though he felt a little like he'd fallen down the rabbit hole behind Alice into Wonderland. Maybe that's what kids did to you. They turned your life upside down and you ended up not wanting it any other way.

Guess that's how they finagled their way into your heart.

Chapter 13

Lauren watched the others eat at Ruby's table, thinking that they truly felt like a family. Even Kent had gotten over his initial surprise and taken Hannah's neediness for a father in stride and been wonderful to her. They were so cute together, although she'd never say that to either of them.

Beyond that, Hannah was making it so clear how much she wanted and needed a father figure in her life. Lauren hadn't realized just how desperately Hannah had missed her own dad. From now on, she'd simply need to make sure Hannah had time with Slade, Trey, and others along with Kent. She felt sure that once Hannah realized there were dependable guys in her life to take the place of her father, she'd regain her self-confidence. At least, she hoped that'd be the case.

For now, Lauren simply enjoyed the cozy family gathering, not the least of which reminded her of those long-ago days when she'd sit at this table with Jake and Gladys, along with Ruby, Hedy, Kent, and whoever happened to be around in time for supper. Maybe Lauren should've stayed back East so Hannah could've enjoyed her Grandma and Grandpa, but Texas had been a big draw. Now she could understand why. And she wouldn't be a bit surprised if her parents moved back to Wildcat Bluff when they retired from their jobs.

She glanced over her shoulder out the window. Night had already fallen. When she looked across the table, she noticed that Hannah's eyes had begun to droop. Her daughter needed to get to bed early before she got fussy from being too tired after her long, exciting day. She was feeling a little tired, too, but maybe she was also simply feeling relaxed among friends.

"I cleaned my plate. Almost," Hannah said. "Now sweets."

"You did real well," Ruby agreed as she got up. She returned with Slade's pie and set it on top of the table. "Who wants a piece?"

"It's about time you asked," Hedy mock-complained. "I've been waiting forever."

"Me too," Hannah agreed.

Ruby expertly cut the pie, quickly set one piece after another on vintage Frankoma dessert plates, and passed them around the group.

Lauren cut through the flaky pie crust and put a piece into her mouth. Wonderful flavor exploded and she moaned in delight. "Delicious!"

"Yum," Hedy agreed, quickly eating several bites until her plate was empty. "Slade sure knows how to bake pies."

Hannah finished off her small piece and then patted her stomach.

"If Slade keeps this up, he might win a blue ribbon at the next county fair." Kent said as he set down his fork.

"If he enters," Hedy chuckled, "he'll put every county fair pie-winner's nose out of joint. Our local ladies won't take kindly if they're shown up by a bull rider turned pie baker."

"True enough," Kent said. "Maybe he won't enter his pies."

Hedy laughed louder. "As if he's not a born competitor."

"Cookies, Aunt Ruby," Hannah said. "Bet we make blue-ribbon cookies."

"Okay," Ruby agreed. "When county fair time comes around, we'll enter our cookies to win."

"Yay!" Hannah grinned from ear to ear. "Cowboy Daddy can help, can't he?"

"Why not?" Ruby said. "The more the merrier."

Kent simply shrugged, shaking his head but saying nothing.

"Folks, I'd better be on my way. I like to be home close to dark." Hedy rolled back her wheelchair. "Lauren, are you sure you don't want to stay with me?"

Lauren leaned forward and pressed a kiss to her aunt's soft cheek. "Thanks for the offer, but Hannah can be a handful. Besides, I'm sure you've got more than enough on your plate without adding guests."

"You're family, not guests," Hedy said. "But I'll give you a chance to get settled in before we make plans for you and Hannah to come out and see the old homestead. Call me tomorrow."

"I will." Lauren stood up and started stacking dishes.

"I'll wrap up the rest of the pie so you can take it home." Ruby got to her feet and hurried into the kitchen.

"I'd better be on my way, too." Kent stood up and stepped back from the table. "First, what can I do to help clean up?"

"Cowboy Daddy, you're going?" Hannah jumped and threw her arms around his legs again.

Lauren watched him freeze, not knowing how to

handle her daughter. "Hannah, we'll see Kent later. Right now he has to go home."

"And take care of horses?" Hannah looked up at him.

"That's right." Ruby handed a sealed plastic container to Hedy. "For the road."

"Thanks." Hedy smiled up at her.

"Great-auntie, you're going, too?" Hannah left Kent and threw her arms around Hedy. "Can't you stay?"

Hedy gave Hannah a big hug, then stroked her long, blond hair. "You're in Wildcat Bluff now. None of us ever goes anywhere for long."

"For sure?" Hannah stepped back to look at Hedy's face.

"Cross my heart." Hedy used two fingers to cross her heart.

"Okay." Hannah glanced up at all the faces above her. "We're family."

"That's right." Ruby flipped on the outside porch light, then she took hold of Hannah's hand. "Why don't we go upstairs? I've got a special bubble bath for you to try. And then I'll read you to sleep in your very own little rollaway in your mom's room. Sound like a plan?"

Hannah looked at Lauren. "Mommy?"

"Good idea. Y'all go ahead and have fun."

"Yeah," Kent agreed. "We've got it covered down here."

Hannah turned toward Kent. "Don't forget to take your cookies."

"I'll get your mom to bag them up for me."

She grinned, hugged his legs hard, then grabbed Ruby's hand and tugged her toward the stairs. Temple quickly ran around them and led them up with his tail held high.

Lauren watched them disappear to the top level before she looked back. "Ruby's a gem, isn't she?"

"Sure is." Hedy headed toward the door.

"Kent, if you'll wait a moment, I'll walk Aunt Hedy outside."

"I'll get started cleaning up the leftovers." Kent gave her a warm smile before he stepped up to the bar.

Lauren grinned, feeling more lighthearted now that she knew Hannah was enjoying herself with Ruby. "Eat the leftovers more likely."

He laughed, revealing his dimples. "Might at that."

She turned away and followed Hedy outside. She felt full of good food, but she felt even fuller of love and home and happiness.

At Hedy's van, she reached down and hugged her aunt. "I'm so glad to be here. I really think it's good for Hannah."

Hedy nodded thoughtfully. "I'm glad you're here, too. As much as I'd like you with me, I can see Ruby's got the energy to keep up with a little girl."

"That never slowed you down before."

"Water under the bridge." Hedy slid open her van's door. "To tell you the truth, I just don't have the oomph I had in younger years."

"Are you in pain?"

"No more than usual." Hedy sighed. "But time's running out for me and it's coming home to me plain as day that I'll never get on the back of a horse again. I'm not complaining. I had a good run. I'm proud of all you kids. And now you've brought little Hannah back home. I want to see her ride a horse. She's obviously got it in her blood."

"She does want to be a cowgirl."

"And I want to see you settled here. And happy."

"I'm here now. And we'll see how it goes."

"It'll go fine if you give it, and I mean everybody, a chance." Hedy squeezed the arms of her wheelchair.

"I will."

"Promise?"

"Yes." She kissed her aunt's cheek again.

"Guess I can't ask for more." Hedy hesitated again, then looked up at Lauren. "It's just that sometimes I think that if I could get back on a horse again—well, it'd be like having my legs under me. I could ride across the land and feel like I was young and strong."

"Oh, Aunt Hedy—" Finally Lauren understood what was going on with her beloved aunt. She was giving up on life. If Lauren didn't find a way to intervene, she didn't know how long Hedy would last before she gave up.

"Shhh now. I'm just getting to be a maudlin old lady thinking back on her glory days."

"You're not nearly old and I don't want to hear it."

"Maybe not yet, but I'm staring seventy in the face." Hedy gave Lauren a thoughtful look. "Let's face it, every day I spend in this wheelchair I shrink a little bit more. Still, I'm not going to complain, but when I rode horses I was strong and agile."

Lauren felt tears sting her eyes as heaviness entered her heart, because she knew her aunt was right. She'd had enough experience as a physical therapist to know the end game. And she wasn't going to let it happen to her beloved aunt, not if she could do anything about it.

"Got to be on my way," Hedy said in a crisp voice. "I'm putting a downer on your return, and I don't mean to do it. But I'm glad you're here."

"Wait! I'm not letting you off that easy."

"What do you mean?"

"You know I'm a physical therapist, don't you?" Lauren stepped closer to her aunt as unexpected possibilities whirled through her mind.

"Yes. But I've been through all of that. I've got upper body exercises. I know the drill and I take care of myself."

"When I came here, I didn't know what I was going to do. I'd lost my job and I was at loose ends." Lauren felt excitement race through her as an idea to help Hedy and others began to form in her mind.

"You can find work here or over in Sherman or even down in Dallas."

"I'd like to stay in Wildcat Bluff, if it's possible."

"I can always use your help at Adelia's Delights. I'm behind in buying new products and stocking shelves. And the store will be yours eventually anyway."

"I'll be happy to help. But I'm hoping to use my skills here, too."

"That'd be good." Hedy backed toward her van. "Let me know what I can do to help."

"As soon as I've got a workable plan, you'll be the first to know." Lauren hugged her aunt, feeling the fragileness of her body but also the strength of determination that had always been at Hedy's core.

"Now that you're home, I think all will be well in Wildcat Bluff. You remind me of our Christmas angel."

"What Christmas angel?"

"Misty Reynolds. She arrived here last Christmas as a troubleshooter and saved us from dangerous fires. Now she's engaged to Trey Duval."

"Somebody finally snagged him?"

"It took our Christmas angel to do it." Hedy squeezed Lauren's hand. "And now you've returned to us. And brought Hannah. You make me proud."

Lauren grinned at her aunt. "Just you wait. I'm going to make you even prouder now that I'm back in Wildcat Bluff."

Chapter 14

Lauren watched Hedy drive away, feeling relieved and worried at the same time. As far as she knew now, her aunt had no dread disease, but she was wasting away a little at a time. She looked up at Big John. He'd come back from a lightning-blast to his core and regrown new limbs with vibrant green leaves. He was a good symbol of what needed to be accomplished with Hedy, healing and growing stronger every single day. Like Big John, her aunt was a survivor.

Lauren felt inspired, not simply by the resilience of nature, but by the possibilities of life. She glanced toward the lights of Wildcat Bluff. If there was anywhere in the world with outstretched hands to help her, she'd find them in the people of her hometown. She felt a sudden sense of peace, as well as energy, flow through her.

When she heard a squeak from the screen door to the kitchen, she glanced up. Kent stood silhouetted in the open doorway, a strong, dark shape against the cozy light of indoors. Her feeling of peace merged with a surge of heat that radiated outward from her molten core to completely engulf her. Had she never stopped wanting him?

"Lauren?" He spoke softly, as if not wanting to disturb the tranquility of the night.

Yet she was so attuned to his presence that she heard his voice as if he spoke right next to her ear. Only now did she realize how she'd missed his deep, seductive

Texas drawl that reminded her of the famous outlaw country singers such as Waylon and Willie.

She figured Kent couldn't see her since she stood in the shadow of the porch. For a moment she didn't respond so she could simply observe him from afar. Everything about him seemed bigger than life, or maybe he'd always represented life at its biggest to her. In any case, his sheer presence set her heart to beating faster, and she felt that old zing of heightened awareness.

He stepped outside, letting the screen door shut behind him.

She couldn't help but notice once more how he'd muscled up over the years, taking on a man's body where she'd known a boy's thinner frame. She wanted to feel his heat and strength surrounding her, binding her, and exciting her as only he could do. Still, she'd made a promise to herself that she wouldn't trust a man's glib words again. And she must put her daughter's welfare first. She still felt surprised that Hannah's response to Kent had been so unexpectedly strong and positive. She was glad to see her daughter reach out to others, so she'd be careful to nurture Hannah's feelings of empowerment and yet protect her emotions at the same time.

Kent walked quietly down the redbrick stairs on the opposite side of the wheelchair ramp. "Lauren?"

"I'm over here."

He stopped beside her. "I cleaned up stuff except the Frankoma. I'm not sure, but I don't think that pottery ought to go in the dishwasher."

"You're right."

"Good. I've got it soaking in the sink."

"Thanks."

"For what?"

"Everything."

"That's pretty broad in scope." He clasped her hand and traced her palm with his rough thumb.

She felt his touch like wildfire straight to her heart. She swallowed hard to tamp down her growing feelings. "I talked with Hedy—"

"What did she say?"

Lauren hesitated as she glanced up at the light glowing in the top-floor window where she knew Ruby was reading to Hannah. "Let's discuss this matter somewhere more private."

He followed her gaze upward and then nodded in understanding. "Let's finish up in the kitchen. After that we can go out by the spring to talk. There's nobody to overhear us out there."

"Do you have time?"

He squeezed her hand. "Where you're concerned, I've got all the time in the world."

She pressed his fingers in return, then reluctantly headed for the kitchen. When she reached the screen door, he leaned in close and opened it for her. She felt the heat of his body and caught his scent, but she resisted the urge to lean back against him. She had to stay focused on what was important in her life, not succumb to unnecessary feelings.

She resolutely stepped into the kitchen and noticed that he'd already cleaned everything off the table except the Frankoma orange cornucopia filled with brightly wrapped candy that Ruby kept in the center of the table. She walked over to the sink while he shut and locked the door behind them.

"You wash while I dry?" He picked up a big dish towel and moved to the left of the sink where there was plenty of room on the wide breakfast bar.

"Suits me."

"I just don't trust my big hands with slippery pottery."

"If there's breakage, you want me to be the one in trouble with Ruby, don't you?" She chuckled as she lightly teased him.

"You caught me." He joined her laughter.

"Okay. I can take the heat."

"I don't doubt that for a minute."

She glanced up at him, saw the double meaning in his intent gaze, and then quickly sunk her hands into the warm dishwater. She was glad to know she wasn't the only one feeling the heat between them, but she wasn't following up on his direction. Instead, she started washing Ruby's beautiful pottery.

As she shared the task with Kent, she realized this familiar household chore had never before been so pleasant. She washed, rinsed, set aside several plates, and glanced up at him as he picked up one and dried it. When their gazes caught, he smiled, and she felt as if she'd stepped inside a dream world where a perfect little family moment held sway. But she knew better. Jeffrey had never had time for family, and he'd particularly disdained family chores. She quickly went back to washing dishes. She was well past that togetherness fantasy like the Musketeers with their "all for one and one for all," no matter how enticing Kent looked drying dishes.

"I'm anxious to know about Hedy." Kent stacked a dry dish onto the growing pile of Frankoma. "Anything you can share now?"

Lauren stopped and bowed her head over the sink for a moment, feeling determination rise to envelop her. "She's going to be okay. I'll make sure of it."

"*We'll* make sure of it. Whether you believe it or not yet, you're not alone. Not anymore."

She watched in stunned silence as he reached into the soapy water and clasped her hand, melding their fingers together, as if making a firm commitment.

"Hear me?" He gripped her hand, then withdrew and dried his fingers on his dish towel. "Believe me?"

She slowly raised her head and glanced over at him. She saw nothing but sincerity in his hazel eyes gone dark.

"Hedy belongs to all of us," he continued in his deep voice. "We won't let you go this alone. And if you need help with Hannah, I'll do my best, though I can't promise I'm at the top of my game with kids."

She smiled, feeling his words go straight to her heart. "I do need your help. I hate to ask, but—"

"Don't go any farther with that thought. All you have to do is ask and everybody in Wildcat Bluff will roll over backwards to assist you."

"And you?"

He threw down the dish towel, then pulled her wet hands out of the water and placed them around his neck. "I was a fool not to come after you. Connecticut or Houston or anyplace shouldn't have mattered one bit."

He put his arms around her waist and tugged her close to his hot body.

"We were too young."

"Hell if we were."

And when she opened her mouth to say more, she forgot all her words in the heat of the moment as his mouth descended on her lips. Passion shimmered between them as he teased her with small nips and quick kisses until she felt like a rosebud blooming under his touch. When he deepened their kiss, she twined her hands around his neck, not caring about the water that cascaded down his back as she pulled him closer so she could stroke across his broad, muscular shoulders. When she felt his large hands caress her back until he reached her hips and pulled her against his hot hardness, she moaned deep in her throat.

How had she lived without his touch? She was aching and burning and needing him with all of her being. She pushed her fingers deep into his thick hair, cradling his head as their kiss turned molten with unquenched desire. He raised her T-shirt and stroked hot fingers across the bare flesh of her back, and she wanted more of what only he could give her.

As she forgot all time and place, a loud sound came from the top floor, as if something had been dropped on the floor. Reality came flooding back, and she quickly raised her head and pushed at his chest.

"Hannah. Ruby. What are we doing?" she asked in alarm. "They could be down here any moment."

Kent quickly stepped back. "Not thinking straight. To hell with the dishes. Let's go down to the spring."

She looked at his beloved face with whisker shadow darkening his jawline and desire darkening his eyes. And she knew she didn't want to be anywhere except in his arms. And yet she had responsibilities. If a problem had occurred upstairs, Ruby would have come down to get her. She'd probably just dropped a book or hairbrush or something.

Kent held up his hands, as if in surrender. "Do you still want to go to the spring?"

"Two more plates." She felt anxious now to be out of the house. "I'll let them air dry. Why don't you grab the pitcher of tea? I'll bring two glasses."

"Do you really think we're going to drink tea?"

"I need to talk with you."

He nodded before he turned away and opened the refrigerator.

She quickly finished washing the dishes and set them in the drainer to dry. She grabbed two clean glasses that he'd dried earlier and she was ready to go.

"Okay, we talk. And drink." He held up the pitcher. "But I get a reward."

"What kind of reward?"

He grinned, looking hungry as he revealed his dimples. "You'll do just fine."

Chapter 15

LAUREN COULD ONLY CHUCKLE AT KENT'S WORDS. HE sounded so much like a Texas male, perfectly comfortable with teasing and flattering and flirting with a touch of humor that made it all go down easy. Not that he wasn't serious. He was telling her right up front that the choice was hers to make because he was obviously more than ready to take it to the next step.

"Come on." He motioned toward the stairs with the pitcher of tea. "I want to hear what you've got to say."

"And then?"

He gave her a little half-smile while his eyes turned dark. "We'll see if I've earned my reward."

She grinned, shaking her head at his determination but liking it at the same time, even if he was making her question her own resolve.

She quickly walked down the steps, across the living room, and out into the garden room with him right behind her. At the sliding glass door in back, she hesitated, knowing she was getting set to make major changes in her life and wondering if she was doing the right thing.

Kent put a large hand on her shoulder, squeezed lightly, and reached around her to slide open the door.

At his touch, she felt ignited with renewed purpose. She didn't have to do anything alone, not here in Wildcat Bluff.

She stepped out into the early spring night that was just on the edge of too cool but still warm enough not to need a jacket. She took a deep breath as she walked along the redbrick path, enjoying the scent of pine and dry grass. Just the smell alone propelled her back in time to those heady days of her youth. And with Kent right behind her, she was reminded of the power of friends, family, and love.

She walked past Big Bertha, noticing how one wall of the redbrick, enclosed gazebo with a slate-gray roof and green trim had been built around the ancient oak to accommodate the wide trunk. She crunched across a few dried oak leaves left from the fall. Small solar lights illuminated the path as she headed toward the spring out back.

Jake had really outdone himself when he'd set to work on the natural spring. He'd designed and built another gazebo, only this one was open-air with redbrick Roman arches that enclosed a large area with a terra-cotta tile floor and a see-through, aqua-tint roof. Spring water bubbled up from a round, beaten-copper basin to cascade downward into an adjacent big, blue pool.

She silently thanked Jake for creating this little piece of heaven on Earth and Ruby for faithfully maintaining it. As far as Lauren could tell, nothing had much changed in the time she'd been gone. Black wrought-iron outdoor furniture sported plush aqua cushions for comfort. An open fire pit nestled between two luxurious lounge chairs. The black barrel smoker was big enough to handle food for a large group. She remembered enjoying parties out here, smelling hamburgers and hot dogs sizzling on the grill and listening to the splashes and laughter of friends and family.

She stepped under the gazebo's roof, walked to the

edge of the pool, and glanced upward. White fairy lights twinkled across the ceiling, adding a mystical touch to the evening. A gentle breeze carried the scent of pine from the rows of green trees not far away. An owl hooted, an eerie sound followed by the whoosh of wings as the bird flew deeper into the pine forest.

A round table surrounded by four chairs with aqua-and-white-striped cushions looked inviting, but so did the water. She hesitated between the two before she set the Frankoma glasses on the table.

A moment later, Kent carefully set the matching tea pitcher beside the glasses. "Do you want a drink?"

"I'm torn between sitting by the pool and sitting by the table."

"How can you resist the pool?"

"Yeah. After all this time, it's pretty irresistible."

"You could roll up your jeans and put your feet in the warm water. I'd even bring you a glass of tea."

"That sounds good. Thanks." She didn't have a swimsuit, but at least she could put her feet in the warm water. She kicked off her flip-flops, rolled up her jeans to her knees, then sat down on the edge of the pool. She glanced around at Kent with a contented smile on her lips.

He filled two glasses, then handed one to her. He pulled a chair over beside her, sat down, and took a long drink of his tea.

"Join me?"

"Another time I'll get in the pool with you like the old days, but I need to go home soon, so not tonight."

"I'll take a rain check." She smiled, feeling content to just sit and enjoy the ambiance of Twin Oaks.

"Now that we're comfy, what's on your mind?"

She sipped sweet-tart tea and then kicked out with her right foot, splashing water up and out so she could watch the fan of liquid sparkle in the soft light. Felt wonderful. Still, she was procrastinating and knew it. As much as she wanted to trust Kent, did she dare bare her soul? No, she didn't think she could, not anymore. After Jeffrey, she'd been protecting herself for a long time.

"I'm happy to help any way I can, even if you only need a sounding board." Kent paused as he drank tea. "I'd like to hear about Hedy."

She nodded, coming to a decision. If there was anyone in the world she could trust besides Hedy, Hannah, and her parents, it'd be Kent. She set her glass on the edge of the pool and turned toward him. He looked strong, solid, and relaxed in the soft light. She felt her heartbeat speed up at the sight of him, just like in the old days.

"Lauren?" he asked in his deep drawl. "Are you okay?"

"I was just thinking how we used to come here."

He gave her a thoughtful look. "Ruby'd run interference so we could snatch a few moments alone. I miss those days. I didn't even know how much till you walked back into my life this morning."

"We shared good times, didn't we?"

"We shared a lot more than that."

She nodded as she felt his longing gaze as if he were almost touching her. She understood, maybe too much. She wanted those simple days. And him. But they couldn't go back. They could only go forward. She stiffened her spine. "I talked with Aunt Hedy."

"And?" He leaned forward, resting his elbows on his knee while he held his glass in one hand.

"The good news is that she's basically healthy."

"That's a relief."

"The bad news is that she's dispirited, depressed, whatever you want to call a loss of interest in life."

"How can that be possible? She's always been so upbeat and full of life. And yet, I've thought for some time that she has a secret eating at her. Maybe that's it?"

"I don't know about a secret. I don't see how. Everybody knows everything about Hedy."

Kent shrugged as he looked off into the distance. "I guess so. But as much as we know folks, sometimes we don't know them at all."

Lauren nodded in agreement, well aware that she preferred to keep her true feelings about Jeffrey a secret. "You may be right, but I doubt it. From what Hedy said, I think she's feeling down because she's turning seventy this year. She's getting weaker due to her injury. Age doesn't help her condition. She's looking at being able to do less and less. In particular, she believes she'll never ride a horse again."

"But that's not new. Hedy's known she can't ride for years. Besides, everybody ages. It's natural. And she's got lots of friends and interests that don't require physical strength or riding a horse."

"But what is the great love of her life?" Lauren reached down, cupped water in her palm, then opened her fingers and let the water run out.

"Horses. Rodeo." He exhaled sharply as he nodded in understanding.

“She’s losing her core strength. She knows it. And we can see it.”

“I hate to think about her being unhappy, or for that matter completely losing her. She’s always been there for us.” Kent groaned, shaking his head.

“I agree. So, it’s our time to be there for her. And I have an idea.”

“What is it?”

“I need help putting it into play.”

“Tell me what you need and you’ve got it.” He leaned farther toward her, watching her with an intense expression in his hazel eyes.

“Do you know anything about equine-assisted therapy, or hippotherapy?”

“Not much. I’ve heard it can help certain people. But Hedy can’t ride.”

“I’m trained as a physical therapist.”

“Can you help her?”

“Not me alone. Aunt Hedy needs more than a strengthened body. She needs a strengthened will, too.”

“If you’re thinking of getting her up on a horse again—well, that’s a tall, damn order. And dangerous.”

“It’s not. At least it’s not with the proper equipment, certified horse, and a hippotherapist.”

“How the hell, excuse my language, will you put that package together?”

“That’s where I need your help.”

“Oh, Lauren, you’re heading down a heartbreaking path.”

“Hear me out.” She glanced up at him, determined to get him to believe in her vision. “I know equine-assisted therapy really works wonders—especially for people who've tried everything else and given up hope. Horses are so sensitive that they pick up humans' emotions just like that," she said, snapping her fingers. "They heal folks, body and mind. It's been proven."

"After all this time, do you think you can actually heal Hedy?"

"I can't repair my aunt's old injury, but I can help her develop core muscle strength again. And more important, she'll feel as if she has her legs and mobility back when she rides a horse. It'll be almost like walking for her."

"What I wouldn't give to see her on horseback."

"Me too." Lauren pulled her feet out of the water and twisted around to face him. "I don't need too much equipment, and I can buy it online. I have some training in hippotherapy and I can get certified. Most important is the right horse."

He nodded, as if considering her idea. "If anybody has a trained horse or one that can be trained, it'd be in Sure-Shot."

"Billye Jo would know."

"Listen to me." He groaned. "You've got me believing that Hedy can actually ride a horse again."

Lauren grasped his hand. "I don't know anything for sure, but I'd like to try my best. If we can make this work, think of all the other people we could help with equine-assisted therapy."

"You'd stay in Wildcat Bluff if we started a hippotherapy center, wouldn't you?"

"Yes! We're right in the middle of horse and cattle country. What could be better?"

"True enough."

She quickly stood up and picked up her glass. She set it on the table, stalling so she wouldn't have to face the lack of faith she might see in his face or acknowledge the daunting reality of her idea. "But I've got nothing. No trained horses. No barn. No land."

"You've got the will and the knowledge. I've got everything else. And we can get horses." He stood up and set his glass on the table beside hers. He quietly walked over, put an arm around her shoulders, and turned her to face him. "Besides all that, don't you know that all you have to do is ask and Wildcat Bluff will get behind you?"

"Do you really think this might work?"

He nodded, smiling. "I didn't at first, but it could turn out to be a great idea for the whole county."

She glanced up at his face. She saw nothing but support, and that made her feel even stronger. "I've got a little money saved up, but Hannah's needs still come first."

He tilted her chin up with the tip of one finger. "Do you need or want a partner?"

Oh, how she'd love to have a partner, somebody to share the ups and downs of life, as well as her hippotherapy center. But how could she put her trust in a man again? "I'm not sure. I mean—"

"Please don't turn down my help."

"You've got your own business to run."

"We're talking about Hedy. And we're talking about you." He grasped her shoulders and tugged her toward him. "You know I'd walk to the ends of the Earth for both of you."

She stepped back, forfeiting the comfort of his touch

for the practicality of life. "I won't turn down your help, or anybody else's help, but it'll need to be all business."

"Oh, Lauren, you're not making this easy."

"In or out?"

"I'm in, but I'm not agreeing to anything else." He gave her his dimpled grin. "We take this one step at a time."

She smiled back, having never been able to resist his dimples. "You're just holding out for your reward, aren't you?"

"Maybe you deserve one, too."

She felt her breath catch in her throat. Maybe he wasn't far off the mark. She'd been good for a very long time. She'd been practical. Responsible. Could she safely throw caution to the wind and let her heart and dreams fly free?

Chapter 16

Kent felt a surge of relief at the news regarding Hedy, even if he wasn't so sure about Lauren's plan. He didn't say that because he wanted to believe her and he'd assist her in any way possible to make her dream happen, but he couldn't help but feel a little skeptical about the results. For the life of him, he didn't see how Hedy could ride again, but he hoped it was the truth.

He also wondered if his skepticism about Hedy's health was a substitute for his own renewed feelings for Lauren. He didn't know how he could believe in a loving relationship after Charlene. Bottom line, he was a practical man. A fast track to health and love were simply not within the realm of believability for him. And yet, Lauren had swept back into his life, and she was making impossibilities seem possible. That alone should scare the hell out of him, because it meant major changes in his life.

And yet, this was Lauren. They'd picked up right where they'd left off in high school. That alone amazed him. They'd both been through major changes in their lives, but maybe at their core they were still the same two people who'd once shared love. And as far as wanting Lauren—physically and in every other way—he realized now that she was his ultimate dream turned reality.

Maybe he should deep-six his doubts. She'd always been sharp as a tack, quick on her feet, and generous with others. If anybody could light the way for Hedy, it'd be

Lauren. And if anybody could heal his wounded heart, it'd be Lauren, too. And yet, life had taught him to be cautious, so he'd go forward with both eyes wide open.

Mind made up, he grasped Lauren's hand, entwined their fingers, and tugged her toward the table. "Come on. Let's sit down and talk."

"My head is reeling. I haven't even been in town twenty-four hours and my life has turned upside down."

"What do you think has happened to me?" He stopped, raised their hands, and placed them over his heart. Maybe she had doubts, too, but she was going forward anyway. Could he do any less?

She glanced into the distance at the pine trees, then back up at him. "Am I biting off more than I can chew?"

"You can chew on me any time you like." He chuckled, intentionally twisting her words to suit him.

"You always did know how to lighten my mood."

He tugged her over to the table and pulled out a chair.

She sat down and then poured more tea into each glass. She stroked the side of the pitcher. "I've always loved this pottery."

"Ruby swears by it."

"That's partly because it has family meaning for her."

"For all of us."

"True." Lauren smiled at him. "Kent, I want you to know how much I appreciate your kindness and patience with Hannah. I knew she missed her father, but I had no idea she was in that much need of a male figure in her life. I hope she didn't put you on the spot and—"

"Stop right there." He felt as if she'd punched him in the gut. "Are you telling me that just any man would do as a father figure, so she had no real interest in me? If not that, maybe you're trying to say that I'm mean to kids and completely insensitive to their emotions. If neither of those, perhaps you think I couldn't feel anything for an adorable little girl who reached out to me with a big, open heart?"

"Oh." Lauren sounded subdued with that one word. "You know the last thing I'd do is insult you, particularly about my daughter."

"That's what you just did."

"I'm sorry. Please believe me that was my last intention."

He felt some of his anger dissipate in light of her stricken look. "I believe you, but still—"

"Forgive me?"

"No forgiveness needed since that wasn't your intent."

"I was actually trying to compliment you."

"You have a funny way of going about it."

She sighed as she shook her head. "I guess so. Maybe I'm out of practice."

"Hannah's a doll." Kent leaned toward Lauren to emphasize his point. "She reminds me so much of you. And I'm honored she'd feel comfortable enough with me to start bossing me about."

Lauren laughed, cradling her head in her hands. "Sometimes kids can so embarrass their parents."

"Not a word of it. I'd much prefer to see her bold instead of shy."

"But that's just it." She raised her head to look at him. "Hannah has been shy, just not herself, since she lost her father."

"But not tonight?"

"You saw her. She took to you like a duck on a June bug."

"Guess it was my cowboy hat." He laughed at Lauren's turn of phrase, realizing she'd never left her country roots behind. He guessed you could take the gal out of the country but not the country out of the gal. He was glad for a lot of reasons.

Lauren joined his laughter. "She latched on to Ruby's red one pretty quick."

"I do believe I'd better buy Hannah one of her own."

"I'll do that. We'll go shopping in Old Town."

"I'd like to surprise her." He realized in that moment how much he wanted to make Lauren's daughter happy because that'd make him happy, too. It was a new sensation, wanting to please a child, and it felt good.

"Really?"

"How often do I get to do something nice for a little girl?"

She chuckled as she smiled at him. "Stick with me, kid, and you can do it all the time."

He returned her smile, but for some reason he felt more sad than glad inside. Maybe he felt a little jealous, too. She had an adorable daughter. He had, well—herds of cattle and buffalo. Horses. Dogs. Cats. He'd been satisfied that his life was full enough till now. For some reason, he suddenly felt emptiness in his heart. And he didn't like it one bit.

"That's partly the reason I brought Hannah back to Wildcat Bluff."

"Why?"

"I didn't know how it'd work out, but I thought I'd give her a chance to be around friends, guys and gals, who'd help bring her out of her shell."

"Looks like your idea already started working fine."

"She adores Ruby. Now you."

"And she'll love Hedy once she has the chance to spend time with her." He set his tea to one side and leaned his elbows on top of the table. "You did the right thing bringing Hannah home."

"Thanks. I'm already encouraged by her response to this new environment." She set aside her glass, too. "I hate to ask this of you, but do you think you could spend a little time with her and maybe even show her a little about riding a horse?"

"Why would you hate to ask that of me?"

"Hannah can be a handful, and I know you're busy."

He clasped Lauren's wrist and felt the pulse beat strong, picking up speed as they stayed connected with that single touch. "I'd like nothing better than to spend time with you and Hannah."

"I'd like that. I know Hannah will, too."

"Good."

She pulled her hand away and quickly stood up. "Now I've taken up enough of your time. At the rate I'm going, you'll think I'm a clinging vine."

He simply sat there watching her, knowing she was feeling too dependent, maybe even cornered, and she wasn't used to it. He understood because he'd been on his own a long time, too. "It's okay to lean on others sometimes."

She walked over to the spring and cupped the water with one hand as it flowed out of the basin. "I'm starting over here. And there's just so much to do."

He got up, walked over to her, put his arms around her small waist, and felt her lean back against his chest just like the good old days. "You're not starting over. You're picking up where you left off."

"Good point."

"Bet you're tired." He stroked across her flat stomach, feeling her muscles respond to his touch. He kissed the top of her head, drawing in the flowery scent of her shampoo. She felt soft and strong and right in his arms. He squeezed, drawing her against him as he grew hot and hard. He wanted her in his bed right this moment. And yet she was a mother and a widow still mourning the loss of her great love. How could he presume to take the place of the perfect man in her life?

She twisted around in his arms and stroked his face with a hand still wet with springwater. "How could I be tired? You energize me. All the ideas and love and friendship that I've experienced this day have me stoked with excitement and hope and expectations."

He grinned, feeling his own energy and expectations rise with her words. When she tickled his dimples with her fingertip, he chuckled because she'd done the very same thing years ago.

"How many hearts have you slayed with your cute dimples?"

"They're not cute."

"Right. Manly dimples."

He laughed, remembering how they'd said those same words so long ago. "You're the only one who ever said they were cute."

She chuckled as she twined her arms around his shoulders and pulled him closer.

He splayed his hands across her back as he fitted her against the length of him, getting hotter and harder by the moment. "Tell me what you need." He heard the huskiness in his voice as his mind turned toward his king-size bed where he could satisfy both their needs.

"A horse. Barn. Equipment."

He appreciated her practicality, but he wanted her to want more. "That's all?"

"Not enough?"

"What about me?"

"Do you want to be on my list of needs?"

"What do you think?"

"Maybe it's time for your reward."

And that was it for him. He was burning up with his need for her. He clasped her with both hands and held her close so she knew in no uncertain terms how much he wanted to be on her to-do list.

When she pushed her fingers into his hair, drawing his head down, he didn't wait for a second invitation. He quickly covered her mouth, nibbling and licking across her plump, soft lips till she moaned and tugged at his hair for more. He delved into her mouth, tasting her sweetness with just the hint of tea, and groaned as he felt their heat catch fire.

He quickly picked her up and carried her to a chaise lounge where he gently set her down. When she held out her arms, he sat down and she tugged him on top of her. She felt so right, all soft and warm with the perfect amount of curves. How had he ever thought anyone could take her place?

When he eased over so they were lying on their sides facing each other, she lifted his T-shirt and ran her soft palms over the hard contours of his chest. He felt heat blaze almost out of control in the wake of her touch as she stroked down to the edge of his jeans. He groaned, knowing she couldn't go any farther or he'd lose complete control. But he could pleasure her—and give himself pleasure at the same time.

With one hand, he captured her wrists and raised her hands above her head so she was spread before him like the finest of feasts. He stroked her breasts through her T-shirt. She was bigger, more fully rounded, than she had been when she was younger. He thought motherhood and a little weight gain had simply added to her allure. He gently squeezed and was rewarded with a soft moan, so he raised her shirt and saw pink tips beneath a sheer white bra.

If he'd been hot before, now he was on fire with a lust that had obviously lingered, gathering steam, for too many long years. He kissed each taut, rosy tip to a hard peak, savoring her sweet taste and the rasp of silken fabric with each stroke of his tongue. When she moaned again, he continued downward across the smoothness of her bare flesh, teasing and tormenting till he reached her delectable belly button. He hesitated there, wondering how far she wanted him to go or if it was wise to tempt fate when everything had gone so well so far today. And yet, how could he resist the passion that was urging him to stoke the flames into fire at the very heart of her?

He wasn't one to question his actions for long, not when he could feel Lauren's heat and smell her sweet scent. When she thrust her hips up toward him, he had the only answer he needed for action.

He quickly undid the button of her jeans and zipped down to expose more of her tantalizing skin. Now nothing could stop him from giving her what she so obviously wanted, and what he craved, too. He stroked across her silky flesh with long fingers to the very core of her. He felt liquid heat, as if she were on fire from the inside out.

He swallowed hard to control his urgent need to possess her in every possible way. Yet this was about her, so he couldn't let his own desire run amuck and chance sending her spiraling away from him. He must be tender when he wanted to be tough. He must be sensitive to her when he wanted to think only about himself. He must remember love when he wanted unbridled lust. Because this was Lauren, the first—and he was beginning to think the only—love of his life.

She moved restlessly against his hand, as if urging him to delve deeper and harder while he drove her senses into overload so that he could bring her to full and final completion.

"Kent, I need you," she whispered in a husky voice.

"I'm here." He didn't have the wit to say more, not with his mind lost in her lusciousness while his body ached to drive into her hot depths so that they became one in ecstasy.

He captured her mouth and thrust his tongue inside even as he thrust deep with his fingers below, titillating her sensitive flesh, reveling in her hot satin core, giving her everything he could give until she shuddered and moaned as she reached her own pinnacle of pleasure. And he drank in her pleasure as if it were his own.

He gave her a final kiss before he raised his head and looked at her flushed face in the soft light. She looked even more beautiful, if that were possible, as she rode her wave of passion. And still he wanted, needed so much more from her. He took a deep breath to control his own growing urgency as he slid his palm back up her smooth stomach, treasuring the feel of her bare flesh as he started to zip up her jeans.

On a ragged breath, she stilled his hand with her own long fingers. "What about you?"

"Not tonight." He hated to say those words, but they were necessary. He glanced up at the house where Ruby and Hannah were probably asleep. Even so, he didn't want to put Lauren in an even more awkward position, particularly on her first day back. No matter what he wanted or needed, he could wait for the perfect moment. He quickly buttoned the waistband of her jeans, and then gently slipped her T-shirt back in place, noticing that his hands trembled with barely leashed desire.

She pressed a soft kiss to his lips. "What about your reward?"

"That was my reward, but I'll take a rain check for more." He smiled at her, wondering how she could think touching her wasn't a reward for him. After so long a time, she had quickly transported him back to those heady days when they'd made wishes on falling stars in the back of his pickup. He couldn't see the stars right now, but he knew they were there. And he wished on a falling star for Lauren's love again.

He quickly stood up, knowing he had to leave while his good intentions held sway. He held out his hand, she clasped his fingers, and he helped her to her feet. He didn't touch her except to respond to an irresistible urge to tuck a strand of honey-blond hair behind her ear.

"Stay here. I'll find my own way out." He sounded gruff and knew it, but he was on the far edge of control.

"That wouldn't be very polite of me."

“If I stay here a minute longer, I won’t be able to leave.” He took a few steps away, then turned back. “I’ll call you tomorrow.”

And he took off down the redbrick path as if he could outrun the fire that blazed inside him.

Chapter 17

LAUREN JUMPED TO HER FEET, FEELING A SUDDEN LOSS much like the one she'd felt when her parents had taken her from Wildcat Bluff to Connecticut. In just a short time, Kent had made her feel so much that she'd thought lost or no longer relevant in her life. Maybe nothing with him was perfect or even in the cards, but she couldn't live with herself if she didn't reach out to him. She couldn't help but wonder if their feelings had lain dormant all these years just waiting for them to get back together.

She ran to catch up to him because he was covering ground with his long legs as if he was outrunning a fire. She grasped his elbow and tugged to stop him. Not that she had the physical strength to make him do anything he didn't want to do, so he had to be willing to respond to her. He turned to look at her, and she experienced the heat of his gaze like a live spark that could set her on fire. As she held on to him, she felt his muscles contract under her fingertips, as if he were exerting great control over his response to her.

"Just a minute." She forced the words out of a dry throat, suddenly feeling as if her brain had taken a hiatus. She didn't know quite how to reach him, not when he appeared hell-bent on getting away. But she didn't want them to part with so little settled between them.

He placed a strong hand over her fingers and gently

moved her hand away from his arm. "Lauren, I've got work tomorrow and you've got a daughter to see about." He spoke in a low, urgent, husky tone, as if forcing himself to say words that he didn't want to get past his lips. "We can pick up where we left off later."

She had no intention of taking no for an answer. She stood on tiptoe, wrapped her arms around his broad shoulders, and planted a kiss on his warm lips as she pressed against his hard chest.

"You're ruining my good intentions," he murmured as he cradled the back of her head with one hand. He wrapped a strong arm around her waist and hauled her abruptly against the long length of his body. He returned her kiss—hot, hard, hungry—and took them well past the point where they'd been before as he nipped and licked and tasted her as if she was the most delicious of candies.

She couldn't get enough of him either as she thrust deep into his mouth, warring as to who could get closer faster while their heat mingled, growing hotter as if they were swimming in legendary Tabasco sauce or paint-stripping chili. When he clasped her hips in both hands and pulled her against his hardness, she shivered from the chill that came from extraordinary heat.

A moment later, Kent's phone loudly played Johnny Cash's "Ring of Fire." He dropped his hands and stepped back from her, breathing hard. "I've got to take this. Fire-rescue."

She nodded, understanding even if she didn't want critical work to destroy their time together. She slowed her breath as she tried to put her raging hormones in a box and nail shut the lid. She took a few steps toward the house to give him a little privacy.

"How bad?" Kent asked with urgency in his voice. "You mean that old barn on the McGuire place?"

Lauren shamelessly listened to his end of the conversation, but she couldn't have done much else since his voice was getting louder by the moment.

"Okay. I got you. I'm at Ruby's, so I'm close. I'll check out the situation and let you know what rigs we may need."

Lauren moved back to Kent, suddenly feeling alarmed at his words. "Fire?"

"You heard?"

She nodded, not even trying to pretend that she hadn't heard him.

"That was Hedy. Somebody drove by the old McGuire place and thought they saw a reddish glow."

"Folks aren't living there anymore, are they?"

"Right. The old farmhouse is long gone. If it's anything, it's got to be the barn. It's just down from here on Cougar Lane. I'll run over there and check it out."

"I'm coming with you."

He shook his head in denial. "There's no need. It's probably nothing, but—"

"Let's get going." She pulled her phone out of her pocket. "I'll let Ruby know. The McGuire place is too close for comfort."

"You've already helped more than anybody'd expect today."

"I'm not about to let all that high school training go to waste." She tried for a light tone, but her effort fell flat. "Besides, you may need a second pair of hands."

"True enough. But as soon as we see what's what, I'm bringing you right back here. I can call in volunteers."

She didn't say it, but she had no intention of being shoved to one side, not when she could help, and not when Hannah might be in danger. Instead, she headed around the side of the house and hit speed dial for Ruby.

"Lauren?" Ruby quickly answered her phone. "Is everything okay?"

"Not exactly. Kent got a call about a possible fire at the old McGuire farm. I'm going to tag along while he takes a look and see if I can help."

"That's not far away. I don't like it." Ruby said with unease in her voice.

"That's another reason I want to go and see for myself. Maybe it's nothing to worry about, but if the wind comes up and whips fire this way—"

"We'll be in real trouble," Ruby finished for her.

"If you'll take care of Hannah, I'll let you know about the fire." Lauren rounded the side of the house with Kent right behind her.

"I read to Hannah and she's sound asleep now," Ruby said softly. "I'm sure she's tuckered out from her long day."

Lauren reached Kent's truck and he opened the door for her. "And she's met so many new people today."

"She wished sweet dreams to you, me, Hedy, and Cowboy Daddy before she fell fast asleep."

"Kent, too?"

"She's taken a shine to him." Ruby said. "Don't worry. I'll just read this new mystery while I sit in the rocking chair beside her till you get back. Take care now and let me know as soon as you know something."

"Will do. And thanks." Lauren quickly tucked her phone back in her pocket, thinking about Ruby's words.

She didn't want her daughter to become attached to someone like Kent who might not always be there for her. On the other hand, she couldn't stand in the way of Hannah's happiness either.

"Just to warn you"—Kent cleared his throat—"I didn't have time to clean out my truck."

"I thought you washed it."

"Yeah. But that's all."

She stepped up and dislodged empty soda cans, water bottles, and fast food sacks. She had to push a horse bridle, a cowboy hat, and a pair of leather gloves aside before she could sit down. He sure wasn't kidding about the junk in his truck, but she never let a little mess bother her.

"Okay?" Kent asked, hovering with one hand on the door.

"Sure. It's fine."

He slammed the door shut, quickly walked around the front of the truck, sat down beside her, and revved the engine.

As he backed out of the driveway, she turned to look at him. "Two fires in one day. Isn't that unusual? What's going on around here?"

"Good question."

She noticed he hesitated before he answered her concern, and that made her wonder even more. As she waited for his reply, he drove quickly down the road, moving in and out of illumination from mercury-sodium lights attached to tall creosote-painted telephone-type poles. She remembered when all this land had been deep in darkness at night, but folks had built houses on the land and installed security lights.

When she saw red-orange flames against the darkness of the night, she forgot all about her concern in the face of the immediate problem. She remembered the old wooden barn that was set back on acreage. She hated the sight of the structure enveloped in flames.

Kent eased off onto the shoulder of the road before he got to the fire and stopped on the side across from it. He cut the engine. "Doubt there's anything we can do to save the barn. What we don't want is for this fire to spread across the pasture and to other structures."

"Like Twin Oaks."

"Right." He pulled his phone out of a pocket as he stepped down from the pickup, leaving the door open behind him. "I'm calling in fire-rescue."

Lauren scrambled out her side and ran over to the ditch. She looked across the barbwire fence that separated the pasture from Cougar Lane. A chill ran up her spine at the sight of the growing blaze as the fire gathered strength. She glanced back toward Twin Oaks, thinking about the vulnerability of Hannah and Ruby.

She hurried over to Kent. "Maybe I'd better call Ruby and ask her to get Hannah to safety."

"Not yet. This looks containable. Rigs are on their way."

"I'll at least let her know what's happening here." She pulled out her phone and hit speed dial for Ruby again.

"What's the situation?" Ruby whispered.

"The barn is ablaze and Kent's called in fire-rescue. Rigs should be here soon."

"Do I need to take a drive?"

Lauren could tell Ruby was choosing her words carefully so as not to alarm Hannah if she woke up to the sound of Ruby's voice. Lauren appreciated the caution. "No need to get out yet. Kent thinks the fire is containable."

"Okay. If there's the slightest chance of a change, you let me know right away. Hear?"

"You bet I will."

"Take care now."

"Bye." Lauren slipped her phone back in her pocket, wishing Hannah was far away from the fire. Maybe she should get Kent to take her back to Twin Oaks so she could drive her daughter into town where it was safe. But she didn't want to alarm Hannah when there was no need for it. She particularly didn't want her daughter to start fearing the countryside on her first day in Wildcat Bluff.

"Do you smell that accelerant?" Kent asked. "I've got little doubt that somebody set this fire with gasoline." He wrapped an arm around Lauren's waist and tugged her close to his side.

"But that's terrible." She felt his warmth and strength give her renewed courage and confidence in the face of so many doubts.

"I suspect it's the only way this old structure would go up so fast."

"I can smell gasoline, too. But who would do such a thing?"

"Hate to say it, but this isn't the first time empty buildings have gone up in smoke."

"Something like in Sure-Shot?"

"Maybe that firebug's moved over here, but maybe not. We've had our own problem for some time now."

"How so?" She leaned into him, feeling safe and secure despite the fire. She'd been taking care of herself and her daughter for a long time, but sometimes it felt good to find support in another person.

"Do you remember the Holloway family?"

"Sure. Bert Two was a little ahead of us in school, wasn't he?"

"Right."

"If memory serves me, wasn't his dad some kind of mover and shaker in real estate?"

"Yep. Somebody'll need to notify Bertram Holloway. He bought this acreage not too long ago. The barn's not worth much, I wouldn't think, not unless Bert has been making improvements."

"What are you trying to say?"

"I'm not saying anything except Bert's had an odd string of bad luck. A number of his insured buildings have gone up in flames. And he's never around when it happens. He's off fishing or hunting up in Southeast Oklahoma. Bert insists somebody's got a vendetta against him and is causing him trouble."

"I can't imagine somebody around here doing something like that."

"It's possible. Rumor has it Bert's made enemies because he's a tough businessman. Nobody has been caught setting fires or leaving incriminating evidence, so there's no way to prove what's going on."

"Either way, these fires put the community at risk." She caught a strong whiff of smoke and grew worried again. How long would it take for the rigs to get here?

"Wind's sprung up." Kent glanced down the road toward Twin Oaks. "Not good."

"I'm getting concerned about Hannah and Ruby." Lauren heard the snap, crackle, and pop of fire as sparks, like lightning bugs, rained down around the barn then winked out.

"Hedy's on the job. Boosters will be here soon. If that wind doesn't start a brush fire, I don't think we'll need more than a couple of rigs. Sydney and Trey will bring one. Dune will get the other, and I'll help him pump and roll."

"Who's Dune?"

"You don't know him." Kent stepped back from the fire and tugged her with him. "Dune Barrett has been here a couple of months. He's my new ranch hand. We toured the rodeo circuit a few times together back in the day. He won enough buckles, saddles, horse trailers, and money to outfit a ranch. I hadn't talked with him in years when he called me out of the blue. Between us, and don't tell anybody else, he asked me to let him work on my ranch so he can keep his head down for a while."

"He's got trouble?" She quickly thought of Hannah and didn't want her daughter around a less than stand-up guy.

"Maybe. Maybe not. For sure, he's got a secret he hasn't shared with me. I figure he's probably got gal trouble. Not that he'd say or I'd ask. A rodeo star, even a former one, always has a trail of cowgirls bird-dogging him."

"And that's unlike cowboys bird-dogging cowgirls, how?" she asked, teasing Kent a little bit.

"You got me there." He chuckled as he glanced down at her.

"Is Dune from Texas?"

"Hill Country. His family's got a big spread down around Fredericksburg. He's a good, experienced hand.

I'm glad to help him out and have him help me out. Dune's not wild about being a volunteer firefighter, but I told him that came with the job. Turns out, he's a natural at it."

"I take it you trust him."

"Sure do. We've been through some tough times together, and that gives you a sense of a man's core."

"Dune sounds interesting." She was starting to feel better about Kent's ranch hand.

"He is that." Kent squeezed her waist. "Just don't go finding him too interesting."

She smiled at Kent's words, wondering if he might get a tad jealous if she showed interest in another guy. She realized she liked the idea that Kent might still be protective of her. And she had to admit she felt a little jealous of his former fiancée, even if that gal had already moved along.

"Hear me?" he asked, pushing his earlier words.

"Is he that good-looking?" She couldn't resist teasing Kent.

"I'm not going there," he said with a chuckle.

"Tell you what, I'll let you know."

"Please, spare me."

She laughed and then turned serious as part of the barn's roof caved and sent red-orange sparks flying outward. "What can I do to help here?"

"When the rigs arrive, stay on the road and by the phone in case we need more assistance."

"Okay. But I sure wish they'd get here. I'm about ready to roll up my sleeves and start fighting that fire with my bare hands."

"I know. But safety comes first. They'll be here soon.

We'll quickly set up a perimeter with water to contain the fire and let the barn burn out."

"You're sure Hannah and Ruby are okay?"

"So far so good. I'll be the first to get them out of the area if that fire looks like it's getting away from us." He squeezed her waist as he looked down at her. "Trust me?"

She wanted to say, "Always," but could she really put her complete faith in a man again, even if his name was Kent Duval? She wasn't sure, so she gave a noncommittal nod, hoping she could learn to trust him in the way she had when she was young.

Chapter 18

When Kent saw the headlights of two vehicles coming down Cougar Lane from the direction of the fire station, he gave a big, ole Texas-size sigh of relief. He hadn't said anything to Lauren because he didn't want to worry her, but he'd been about to go to his backup plan. He had a couple of fire extinguishers in his truck that he could use to help keep stray sparks under control, but that was only a stopgap measure. Now that the big guns were here, he'd save his alternate plan for another day.

They were lucky they had some illumination from a couple of security lights on nearby properties. And they were even luckier that so far the fire was mostly staying confined to the barn. On the bad luck side, the wind had picked up and was sending smoke gusting in one direction and then another. Hot sparks were carried on the breeze and could easily turn the surrounding pastures into blazing infernos. He could smell the acrid scent of burning wood and hear the spitting, crackling sound of leaping flames. Now was the time to get the blaze under control.

"Those are the boosters, aren't they?" Lauren pointed at the vehicles coming down the road toward them.

"Got to be."

"What a relief."

"You know it." Now that the rigs were almost here,

he needed to get ready to fight fire. "Come on to the truck. I've got some stuff back there." He clasped her hand, threaded their fingers together, and realized how right it felt. As they walked quickly to his pickup, he knew without a doubt that she belonged in Wildcat Bluff. Now if he could just convince her of that fact.

"I'd like to help."

"I understand, but you can do more another time." He jerked open the back door of his truck. "We won't enter the barn, so we won't need full turnout gear or breathing apparatus."

He reached inside his pickup, moved aside the fire extinguishers, and pulled out a high-visibility orange-and-yellow parka. He pulled on the jacket and tucked leather gloves into his pocket. He reached for his cowboy hat, remembered he'd left it in Ruby's kitchen, so he dug around till he found a battered tan felt one that was better for a dirty job anyway. His scuffed cowboy boots would do to protect his feet.

Lauren watched him get ready to fight fire and realized again that he was a professional at it now, unlike the days when they were learning the ropes.

"I'm here if anybody needs me." She felt for her phone in her pocket to make sure she was ready to call for help at a moment's notice.

"Thanks." He slammed shut the door of his pickup and glanced up as the boosters came to a halt, one in front of the other, across from the fire.

"Kent!" Sydney stepped out of the front booster and gestured past him. "Is that Lauren with you?"

"Yes," Lauren called back. "He's got me staying by his truck out of the way, but I'm ready to help."

Sydney put her hands on her hips, looked at the fire, and then back at Lauren. "I think we can manage on our own, but we'll let you know if we need you."

"Okay!" Lauren called as she stepped back to Kent's truck.

As she watched from her safe distance, Lauren saw a tall, familiar-looking guy with dark hair leap down from the other side of the booster. Like Sydney, he wore a high-viz yellow jacket, pants, boots, and carried a yellow fire helmet in one hand. Thick leather gloves protruded from one pocket.

Sydney pointed at him. "Trey here is fit to be tied because most everybody's seen Lauren but him."

"Looks like you're back in town for a day and Kent's already got you into trouble," Trey teased in a deep, melodic voice as he quickly walked down the road toward Lauren.

Everybody laughed at his words.

"I'm doing my best here." Kent shook his head, grinning at them. "But you know how she's a magnet for trouble."

"Cuz, I thought that was you." Trey chuckled as he grabbed Lauren in a big bear hug. "It's about time you got back in town to keep Kent in line."

Lauren laughed, hugging him back. "I thought that was your job."

"Nothing keeps those two guys in line," Sydney complained with a mock pout.

"Pot calling the kettle black." Trey said as he stepped back. "Come on, let's set this fire back on its heels."

"Okay." Kent tried to keep down the spurt of jealousy that burned through him at the sight of Lauren in his cousin's arms. He knew better than to think there could be anything between them. Trey was newly engaged and happy as a calf in clover with his new love, smart city gal Misty Reynolds, who'd come to town last Christmas. She'd found love, not just with Trey but with the town itself, and she was already an important part of Wildcat Bluff County.

Kent stuffed his jealousy away as he focused on the efficient boosters. He doubted they'd need the big engine that night.

A tall guy stepped out of the second booster and walked over to Kent. "Hey, partner, let's get this show on the road."

"Lauren, I'd like you to meet Dune Barrett. He's our newest fire-rescue volunteer. Dune, this is Lauren Sheridan. She grew up in Wildcat Bluff and just got back today."

"Good to meet you," Dune said in a deep, gravelly voice that suggested dark nights in old-time dance venues like the Hill Country's Gruene Hall where the liquor flowed and the country-western bands played like they had for over a hundred years. He was about six-three or so and built muscle upon muscle, with shaggy dark-blond hair that made him look as if he'd just returned from a long cattle drive.

Kent felt that flicker of jealousy again when Lauren shook Dune's hand. By now Kent had figured out that he didn't want any other man touching her in any way. He'd better get a grip before he did something stupid that'd get him laughed out of town. Besides, the only thing that mattered right now was containing the fire.

"Dune, I'll work with you on Booster 2," Kent said,

getting back to the business at hand, although he'd rarely taken his eyes off the burning barn since he'd arrived at the site.

"You sure?" Dune turned from Lauren and gave Sydney a long look. "Hey, Syd, why don't you work with me?"

"I told you not to call me 'Syd,' and I already have a partner." She turned a cold shoulder to him and walked back to Trey.

Dune just shook his head, then followed right along behind her.

"History with those two?" Lauren asked quietly.

"She's not looking to hook up, and he's not looking to give up."

"Recipe for disaster?"

"Nah. She'll read him the riot act one of the days and that'll be that."

"I'm not so sure," Lauren said, shaking her head.

Kent shrugged, wanting to leave that volatile situation alone. He took off after the firefighters, opened wide the gate in front of the barn, and joined the others on the road as they prepared to control the blaze.

"Anybody else smell gasoline?" Trey asked as he walked over to Booster 1.

"Sure do," Dune agreed.

"Didn't Bert buy this property?" Sydney asked, turning to look at Kent.

"Yep. This is another of his buildings going up in flames."

"Bet he's up in Oklahoma fishing or some such," Trey said.

"That's not a bet I'd cover." Sydney joined Trey

at Booster 1. "Let's just make sure nobody else loses property around here."

Kent joined Dune at Booster 2. They'd worked together before, so they were a pretty good team. Tonight, Kent wasn't wearing much firefighter gear, so he'd pump water and roll out the hose while Dune drug the nozzle near the fire and kept up a steady flow of water as he wet a perimeter around the barn. Sydney took a position to pump while Trey sprayed the other side of the ground around the barn. Kent watched as they turned streams of water on the blazing structure and steam rose along with smoke as the water fought to bring the fire under control.

Even so, the fire quickly expanded in size as it ate up oxygen. Soon the wooden structure was fully engaged and pumping smoke from every crevice and open doorway. Flames and smoke surged higher into the sky.

Trey and Dune kept up the water barrage, catching stray sparks as the wind whipped the fire into sudden bursts. They were beating back the blaze, despite the orange-and-yellow flames spitting and licking and clawing to take back what they gave up. Every fire had its own personality. This one reminded Kent of a dangerous wild bull.

And just when he thought they had the fire contained, it erupted when a piece of shake-shingle roof was ripped off by the wind and whipped across Trey's head to land in the adjacent pasture. Flames immediately set the dry grass ablaze, and a line of fire headed straight for Twin Oaks.

Kent immediately rolled out more hose and upped the pressure on the pump so Dune could go after the expanding blaze, while Trey kept a stream of water on the barn. But it didn't work out like Kent had planned because the wind whipped back around and Dune had to return to spraying the barn.

"Sydney, watch my pump." When he got her nod of understanding, he took off running, hoping he could stomp out the fire with his boots before it took hold and swept away from them.

He got ahead of the blaze, but the flames were moving fast, consuming the grass at an unbelievable rate. He pulled on his gloves as he stomped, making a little headway, but he quickly realized that he wasn't going to be able to do enough quick enough. And the others couldn't leave the barn. He'd have to call for backup, but he feared the engine couldn't get there in time.

Just as he pulled his cell out of his pocket to make the call, he heard Lauren hollering his name. He glanced up. She'd crossed the road, dragging a heavy fire extinguisher in each hand, up to the barbwire fence. He could've cheered because she might just have saved the day.

He pocketed his cell, ran over to her, grabbed the extinguishers, and set them down on his side of the fence.

"Hold up the barbwire and I'll crawl under," she said as she went down on her knees.

"Lauren, I don't want you in danger."

"I'm not letting that fire get anywhere near my daughter." She lay down and started to crawl on her stomach under the fence.

He quickly raised the bottom strand of wire so she wouldn't tear her clothes or scratch her back.

Once she was on the other side, she grabbed an extinguisher and dragged it toward the leading edge of the blaze.

He used the black strap to hang the other fire extinguisher over his shoulder and caught up to her. He tried to take the other extinguisher from her, but she gave him a dark look.

"Two of us are faster than one," she said. "I remember how to use these cans, so let's get to it."

He grinned, loving her sassiness even as he wanted to keep her safe. He knew better. This was his Lauren, and she didn't back down for nothing or nobody. "Let's do it."

Together, they got out in front of the fire and started spraying the potent chemical on the blaze, leaving a trail of yellow. They continued to douse the flames till nothing was left except charred grass. When their cans were empty, they tossed them aside, and then stomped on the crisp grass to make sure there were no hot embers left that might reignite.

Finally, Kent picked up one empty canister and hung it from his shoulder by the strap before he put the other strap over his free shoulder. He couldn't resist leaning down and giving Lauren a quick kiss on her plump lips.

"Don't you know I'm too hot to handle?" she teased, laughing with a sound caught somewhere between delight and relief.

"Guess I'm looking to get burned."

"I think we're both a little on the scorched side." She laughed harder, pointing toward the barn. "But that building took the brunt of it."

He looked in that direction. He felt a vast sense of relief when he saw that the old barn was nothing more than a pile of black rubble with a red-orange glow of banked embers here and there. He glanced back at the blackened patch of pasture. He'd been cocky tonight, maybe because being with Lauren had made him feel like Superman, and he knew better. You could never count on a fire doing what it was supposed to do, and particularly not when it was a raging bull of a blaze.

He clasped Lauren's hand and threaded their fingers together again. "Guess you're a Wildcat Bluff volunteer firefighter all over again."

She squeezed his hand. "I feel like I've never been gone."

"Let's get you home."

"Twin Oaks will look mighty good."

But Kent hadn't been thinking about Ruby's place. He'd been thinking about his own farmhouse on Cougar Ranch.

Chapter 19

High and dry in Kent's truck, Lauren completed her text to Ruby so her friend would know all was now safe and sound in the area. She slipped her phone back into her pocket as she turned to look at Kent. He drove in the easy, controlled manner that volunteer firefighters were trained to use as he headed toward Twin Oaks. She felt a warm contentment with him, just like the old days.

She also smelled like smoke, but he did, too. Fact of the matter, the entire cab reeked of the bitter, pungent scent of burnt wood, mostly emanating from their clothes. But that didn't matter, not when lives and property had been saved by their help. She was proud of her friends who'd dedicated their lives to Wildcat Bluff, their families, and each other. She felt a little guilty that she hadn't returned sooner so that she could lend a hand to the folks who had made this county so special. But life had thrown her a curve ball, and she was just now stepping up to the plate back home.

They'd left the other volunteers in charge of making sure there were no stray embers to ignite the pasture and wreak more havoc. She'd like to have spent time catching up with her friends, but there'd be plenty of opportunity to do that later.

Illumination from the dashboard cast the strong planes of Kent's handsome face in light and shadow. Maybe that's what life was all about—some light, some shadow, some in between. She felt as if a spotlight had been shining on her life since she'd set foot in Wildcat Bluff that morning. With so much that had happened today, she felt a little contemplative. Maybe the shadows of uncertainty were giving way to the certainty of hope. She smiled at the idea, feeling as if Kent were making her poetic, or at least thoughtful, since he was a major factor in her fast transformation from city gal back to country gal.

He pulled up to Twin Oaks and stopped in front of the three-car garage, letting the engine idle as he switched off the headlights. For a moment, she sat perfectly still because she felt a little disoriented, as if he were leaving her at the wrong place instead of taking her home with him. But Hannah was here at Ruby's cozy B&B, and Kent's house was not Lauren's home. Still, she couldn't help her feeling of not wanting to be separated from him, not after all they'd shared during this long, special day.

Kent cleared his throat, drumming his fingertips on the steering wheel as he looked over at her. "If you don't mind me saying so, I hate to leave you here."

"Why?" She unbuckled her seat belt and turned to face him. "Twin Oaks is safe now."

"Doesn't seem right," he said in a voice gone deep and husky with repressed emotion.

"I don't have any other place, not yet anyway."

"You could come home with me."

She felt his words go straight to her heart as heat flushed her body, along with longing for what might have been if they'd remained sweethearts. He was also voicing her own thoughts and putting them right out in the open so there was no mistake about what he wanted from her. She felt a little giddy, in a good way, at the thought of them being together again.

"I'm coming on too strong, too fast, aren't I?" He gripped the steering wheel with both hands as if to keep from reaching for her.

"Kent, I'm not the carefree girl I used to be. There's Hannah to think about and—"

"She's a doll. And she's part of you, so I care about her, too."

"Thank you." She felt deeply touched by his words. Could he really still care about her after all this time? She reached over and squeezed the hard muscles of his forearm to make her point. "I want you to understand that my daughter comes first in my life."

"That's only right." He covered her fingers with his big, strong hand. "But there can be more than one right in life."

"True." She felt the power of his strength in their simple touch. "But for now, Hannah *is* my right."

He squeezed her hand, and then gripped the steering wheel again. "You'll bring her out to the ranch?"

"We've got plans. Remember?" She reluctantly let go of his arm and immediately felt the loss of their connection. And yet, she'd been on her own a long time and didn't need a man to make her feel complete. Maybe she needed Kent to help her feel happy and content. She was beginning to think she wanted more in life than what she'd allowed herself to experience in a long time.

He turned toward her, reached out, and massaged the back of her neck in gentle spirals. "We'll find a way to make everything right."

She wanted very much to believe him, particularly as

she responded so strongly to the sensuality of his touch. Waves of heat cascaded outward from the erotic caress of his rough fingertips, setting her entire body ablaze and turning her core molten. When he tugged her toward him, angling his head in the way he'd done so long ago, she eagerly leaned into his kiss, wanting nothing more than to lose herself in this shared moment.

He stroked her lower lip with the tip of his hot tongue, sending shivers chasing through her, then kissed the corner of her mouth as he easily upped the sizzle between them. Soon she needed more, much more, and she nipped his lower lip in return, letting him know how intently she wanted his kiss, his touch, his nearness. And with that encouragement, he deepened the kiss as she eagerly opened her mouth to explore the depth of their shared passion. And still nothing in all the intervening years had diminished their spark one bit. Instead, a hot core of desire like nothing she'd felt when she was younger exploded into a raging inferno of blatant sexual need.

Kent must have been ignited by their kiss as well because they quickly reached a boiling point that called for much, much more than a single kiss. And as he shifted to draw her against his chest, the outdoor lights of Twin Oaks snapped on and illuminated the pickup.

He groaned in obvious frustration, and she echoed the sound. And yet they ended the kiss and pulled away from each other as their breath came fast.

"Ruby's not letting us get away with anything, is she?" he said in a rough, husky voice.

Lauren took a deep breath, trying to slow her racing heart as she clasped the door handle. "Has she ever?"

"Nope." He smiled as he gently rubbed the pad of his thumb back and forth across her lower lip. "Guess I'd better let you go. I'll get out and open your door."

"Just stay where you are. If you get out, no telling how long it'll take me to say good night and reach the front door."

He chuckled, but the sound came out in a strained rasp. "Yeah. Trouble is—I just want to take you home."

"And I'd like to be there." As she opened the door and the interior lights came on, she glanced down at her borrowed jeans. "I'll wash these and get them back to the station."

"Reminds me." He reached behind him, grabbed her sundress off the backseat, and thrust it into her hands.

"Thanks. Your hat's still inside."

"I'll get it later."

She hesitated as silence fell between them, along with a reluctance to separate. She took another deep breath, knowing she had to go or she'd never leave him. "Well, thanks for everything."

She quickly stepped out of the truck and slammed the door behind her. She walked under the covered porch before she turned back for a last, irresistible look at him. She realized that there'd never been anyone else like him in her life, no matter where she'd gone, no matter what she'd done.

He switched on his truck's headlights, blinked them once in good-bye, backed out, and headed down Cougar Lane.

She watched him drive away, trying to slow her heartbeat and cool her overheated body. She'd never dreamed that he could still make her feel like a giddy girl in his arms. Surely she was made of stronger stuff after all these years. Hannah needed her. Hedy needed her. She needed to build a new life. And yet, surely she deserved a few stolen kisses or even a luscious roll in the hay with the man who knew how to make all her sensual dreams come true.

But she determinedly thrust those thoughts aside and walked up the brick stairs, opened the door, and stepped into Twin Oak's warm and cozy kitchen.

Ruby stood there with a big grin on her face, shaking her head. She held out a steaming mug of hot cider. "Land's sake. When you come back to town, you come back like a herd of horses."

"Not my doing." Lauren chuckled as she clasped the beautiful Frankoma mug with one hand.

"I doubt Kent knows what's hit him."

"I'm not sure I do either."

"You two always were the cat's meow." Ruby leaned back against the counter and picked up her own steaming mug.

"He wanted to take me home."

"I don't doubt it for a minute."

"I'm not sure I'm ready to get involved with anyone again. I've got too much to do. And there's Hannah. She always comes first." Lauren took a sip of the sweet-tart brew and felt the liquid slide down easy.

"Don't look a gift horse in the mouth."

"You think?"

"I knew you and Kent were always a special couple, even if you were young. Anybody could see it." Ruby nodded toward where Kent had been before he drove away. "Far as I can tell, you still are."

"I'm not sure I can ever trust a guy again."

"Give it time." Ruby set her mug in the sink. "And get some sleep. Life always looks more doable in the morning."

"You're right." She drank more cider before she set her mug beside Ruby's. "Thanks for the cider. And everything." She put her arms around her friend and gave her a big hug.

"Welcome home," Ruby said as she returned the hug, then stepped back. "The Sun Room is at the end of the hall, so you have the most privacy on the top floor." She quickly headed down the stairs, then glanced back. "Sleep late if you like in the morning."

"I might do that, but I bet Hannah will be up and raring to go."

"I don't doubt it." Ruby chuckled in her alto voice. "Just let her come downstairs. We'll make blueberry muffins for breakfast."

"Thanks."

Lauren glanced downstairs where Temple jumped down from his cozy seat in a chair to lead Ruby into her suite.

When the door closed behind them, she looked up the staircase, thoughts turning to her daughter asleep in their suite. After being in Wildcat Bluff a single day, she felt sure she had done the right thing in bringing Hannah home. Of course, time would tell, but she hadn't felt so surrounded by love since she'd left her parents' home in Connecticut. And love of all kinds was exactly what she wanted for her daughter.

She quickly washed the mugs, always careful with the Frankoma pottery, and left them out to dry. She noticed Kent's cowboy hat on the counter and picked it up. She held it near her face and inhaled the scent of him, reminding her of the clean, heady smell of sage and leather. Somehow just holding his hat made him seem closer to her again. She'd just hold on to his hat till he asked for it.

She walked up the stairs to the top floor and quietly opened the door to her suite. She stepped inside and locked the door behind her. For a moment, she simply stood very still and looked at the small shape snugged beneath the vibrant-orange spread in the center of a queen-size bed, having abandoned the foldout bed. She felt love as big and hot as the sun envelope her. Hannah was simply the love and light of her life. She was glad her daughter felt safe enough at Twin Oaks to be sleeping so soundly in a strange environment, but Hannah also had to be completely tuckered out after such a big, long day.

Lauren walked over to the bed, then pulled the cover up and over her daughter's small shoulders. She placed a kiss on Hannah's soft hair and felt the inner glow that she'd felt since the moment she'd nestled her daughter's tiny body against her breast. Whatever it took, she'd do the right thing by Hannah.

She stepped back and glanced around the cheerful room that had been painted with peach walls and bright-white trim. Contemporary furniture with straight, elegant lines in cherry wood made up the headboard, dresser, desk, chair, and settee. Colorful purple and apple-green throw pillows that probably belonged on the bed now filled the settee. A rocking chair with a floor lamp beside it looked like a cozy place to read or rock a little girl.

Lauren yawned, feeling the day catch up with her. She'd take a quick shower, brush her teeth, and join her daughter in deep sleep.

She set Kent's cowboy hat on top of her sundress on the desk, smiling at that bit of togetherness. She pulled out her phone, sent a quick text to her parents to let them know all was well, and checked for messages. She felt her breath catch in her throat when she read a text from Kent. "I'm in bed thinking of you."

Heat flashed through her at the thought and she couldn't resist a reply. "I'm thinking of Lovers Leap."

And with that, she set her phone on the desk, resisting the urge to check for an answer. She quickly walked into the bathroom with its gleaming white tile, chrome fixtures, and orange bath towels.

Her new life in Wildcat Bluff had begun.

Chapter 20

KENT STEPPED OUT THE OPEN FRONT DOOR OF HIS farmhouse onto the covered porch after he'd done his ranch chores early that morning. He held a cup of coffee in one hand and his phone to his ear with the other.

"Yes, Mom, I know you're glad Lauren's back in town."

"And I'll throw a big party to welcome her back," Mimi Duval said in an excited voice. "I always did like that girl."

"Let me run it by her first. She might not want the hubbub."

"Of course she'll love a party in her honor."

"She's got a little girl now." Kent wedged his cell between his ear and his shoulder so he had a free hand to shut the door behind him.

"Perfect! I can't wait to meet her."

"I mean Lauren might be protective of Hannah and not want her around a bunch of strangers."

"We're not strangers. We're almost family. In fact, we would be family if not for—"

"Please don't go there."

"No need to get cantankerous. I heard you spent most of the day with Lauren yesterday, so naturally I assumed that—"

"Don't assume anything. We're just friends." Kent hated that his mom sounded hopeful because he didn't want to disappoint her on the wife front. *Again.* "She asked for my help."

"That sounds interesting. What kind of help?"

"Hedy." He looked out across the ranch and watched a small herd of black cattle contentedly grazing on hay. His mom was getting more desperate by the year for a grandchild of her own. No two ways about it, Charlene had been a disaster.

"Of course Lauren would want to help her aunt, but we all know that's just not possible," Mimi said in a hushed tone, as if the matter was almost too painful to discuss.

"Lauren's got some ideas. She needs my help to get there, and that means I need your help, as well as Dad's."

"I'll throw that party so she can get reintroduced to the folks of Wildcat Bluff County. That ought to do it."

"Not what I mean."

"Then what?"

"Okay, here goes. I want you to keep an open mind."

"When have I ever not been open to your ideas?"

"I know, but this may surprise you." He was glad his parents had always been supportive of what he chose to do in life, but Lauren was a different matter. He felt overly protective of her.

"Just give it to me straight."

"Okay, Mom." He took a deep breath, hoping against hope that this went well. "Lauren is a physical therapist, and she came up with the idea to use equine-assisted therapy to get Hedy back on a horse and help her get stronger."

"Hippotherapy," Mimi said in voice filled with wonder. "Is that even safe for Hedy?"

"If it'll work, it'll be worth the chance, won't it?"

"Maybe, but still—"

"And Hannah wants to be a cowgirl."

"How delightful!" Mimi sounded excited at that idea. "I'd love to help Lauren's daughter any way I can. Hedy, too."

Kent gulped coffee, knowing his mom was imagining helping her own grandchild become a cowgirl. But that wasn't in the cards, at least not right away. "I might need a little time off from doing my part in running the ranch."

"And you want your father and me to take over?"

"Just for a bit. I'd like to help Lauren get her idea up and running as quickly as possible to help Hedy. And Hannah."

"How involved are you in this project?" Mimi sounded cautious, as if evaluating the extent of the situation.

"Lauren's staying with Ruby right now, so she doesn't have a place of her own. First off, she needs horses, a barn to house them, and an arena."

"Kent, dearest, I don't want to see you hurt again."

"I'm not putting my heart out there." He gripped his coffee mug, hoping that was true. "What I'm doing is helping friends."

"That's admirable, but—"

"I've got the old horse stables, the arena, and the pasture out here. They're not in use since y'all built the fancy new barn up by your house. I thought it'd be a good place for Lauren to start."

"What about horses?"

"I figure we can find something right in Sure-Shot." He knew he could depend on the horse breeders and trainers there.

"Most likely so."

"What do you say?"

"I say you've got a big heart."

"Mom, I mean about me taking some time off to help Lauren start her new project."

"Are you saying this is more than just for Hedy?"

"I think Lauren's the one with a big heart." He paced across the wooden floor, then back again as he realized how important his mom's reaction to Lauren's idea would be for getting her hippotherapy center off the ground.

"It's a wonderful idea," Mimi finally said with warmth in her voice. "In fact, I believe it's something Wildcat Bluff could get behind in a big way."

"You're sure?" He tried not to sound relieved, but he felt like a huge weight had been lifted off his shoulders.

"Absolutely."

"She just wants to start with Hannah and Hedy."

"I've heard hippotherapy can help with a lot of medical issues, but I've always been too busy with the ranch to learn very much about it."

He smiled, knowing his mom was almost always ahead of the game.

"Think about it," she said. "In this county alone, we've got experienced riders and horses. We could also get official training as volunteers like our firefighters do."

"Do you mean certification programs?"

"Yes. I understand programs can be coordinated with physicians, psychologists, and—"

"Physical therapists like Lauren." Kent paced back across the porch as he realized the idea was quickly getting out of hand—or maybe Lauren was already thinking big.

"I guess if she started an equine-assisted therapy program, she could eventually provide local jobs."

"Folks who love horses always need work, volunteer or otherwise," Mimi said with determination in her voice. "It's a terrific concept for our community. But first we need to get Lauren's idea off the ground. We might want to turn our party into a hippotherapy benefit."

"You're way ahead of me. And Lauren. I don't know how she'll feel if we get too many cooks in the kitchen."

Mimi chuckled. "So true. If she's as independent as the rest of us, she'll want to be in charge."

"I like the way you're thinking. Let me feel her out about it as we go along. First, I wanted to run the idea by you and Dad before I focused on getting her set up."

"I'll tell your father. In the meantime, let me know what we can do to help. And please, call me when Lauren's at your place so I can come over to welcome her home and meet Hannah."

"Will do." He smiled at the phone, once more glad his parents were his parents. "And thanks."

"Anything for my favorite son."

"I'm your only son." He gave the much-used response to their old standing joke.

She laughed in a low tone as she dropped her voice to a whisper. "And remember, roses are always good, particularly yellow ones for Texas." She disconnected.

Kent groaned as he tucked his phone in the back pocket of his jeans. He should've known this would somehow turn out to be all about getting him a wife. His mom was probably planning the wedding, or more likely, pulling out her original plans. Nothing he could do about it. Moms would be moms. And he'd lucked out with one of the best, so he couldn't complain, or at least not where she could hear him.

He paced over to the railing and leaned against it, feeling as if his get-up-and-go had got-up-and-went straight to Lauren Sheridan. He hadn't been able to get her off his mind or out of his bed, if only in the metaphorical sense. He had a hot ache that was burning a hole in his jeans, and he wasn't sure he liked it one bit. How the hell had she come back to town and gotten under his skin in only one day?

He liked relationships simple anymore. He'd built his life around simple. He was dedicated to simple. Sure as shootin', Lauren was anything but simple.

He took another swig of coffee out of his porcelain mug shaped like a much-worn cowboy boot. He used it because he didn't have the heart to tell his mom, who'd given it to him, all proud-like, that it was a pain in the neck to clean and tended to spill out the uneven top if he didn't hold it just right.

He sighed and glanced over at the glossy front door of the hundred-year-old farmhouse. *Pink.* Not bright pink or even an acceptable red, but pale pink. He didn't complain about it either, or change the color, because his mom had put her heart and soul into decorating their family's original house on Cougar Ranch. Not that his parents lived there anymore. They'd built a comfy, stone ranch house on the highest point, and he'd taken over the farmhouse.

He squinted, trying to get the pink to change color. No dice. His mom insisted the color was a tribute to former First Lady Mamie Eisenhower's love of pink. As she'd explained, that was why so many houses built in the 1950s had pink bathrooms and other stuff. Pink was considered a neutral color instead of a feminine shade back then.

He shook his head. Who knew from First Ladies or pink tile? Anyway, the farmhouse wasn't built in the fifties. Still, he never said what was really on his mind. He just endured the annoying pink door along with his boot mug. Sometimes you had to pay a steep price for those you loved, particularly women and their cockamamie notions.

He walked past two white rocking chairs with pale-pink cushions and sat down on a pink cushion that covered the seat of a white porch swing that hung from the ceiling. The wooden house was painted bright white from top to bottom except for the gray porch floor and the silver metal covering its peaked roof. He liked being surrounded by wood and age and heritage. He took another slug of coffee, careful not to spill brown sludge onto the pink chintz.

For some no-good reason, he felt lonely. And that wasn't like him at all, not with his kinfolk and friends running in and out of his life. Maybe his brain was on the fritz. His hormones sure as hell were in overdrive, thanks to the arrival of his first sweetheart.

He might as well just go ahead and admit it. He'd been courtin' Lauren since the moment he'd stepped outside the firehouse wearing nothing but his jeans and a big grin and seen her standing there like a dream come true. Bottom line, he could twist every which way but Sunday, and he'd still end up bird-dogging her.

And then there was that little chip off the old block named Hannah. Lauren's adorable little girl took him right back in time to when he'd grown up with Lauren. Hannah was sugar and spice all rolled into one smart cookie. And yet, there was a loneliness and wistfulness to her that tugged at his heart. He wanted her to be whole and happy, just like he'd want for his own child. If he could help set her on the right path, he'd do it in a minute.

In his world, the right path almost always included the healing power of horses. Kids loved and trusted ponies. They were right to do so. The four-legged animals were smart, intuitive, and generous with their affections. He'd seen it time and time again that folks who were unable to trust other people or communicate with them on an emotional level could do both with horses. Far as he was concerned, horses were a great gift to everyone from leathery-skinned codgers to rosy-cheeked kiddos.

Still and all, the right horse had to be placed with the right person. Sometimes that placement could come fast, but other times it could take a while to find the perfect mount. Hannah was correct to want a pony of her own. She'd make a fine cowgirl. He wished he'd thought of equine-assisted therapy for Hedy, but he hadn't even considered going there. He hoped Lauren was right about changing Hedy's life with therapeutic riding.

He was willing to help find the right horses and provide the space for them. In his book, loved ones came first. And he couldn't tolerate seeing somebody in emotional or physical distress, not when he had the ability to help solve the problem.

As he finished off his coffee, he set the swing in motion, creaking back and forth like it had for over a hundred years. *Time.* It had a way of getting away from you if you didn't catch it and ride it like a bucking horse. Maybe you'd stay on. Maybe you wouldn't. But it wasn't the count that mattered in the long run. It was the act itself. If he didn't take action, he might be sitting here on this same porch in this same swing fifty years from now with not much to show for it. At least, he wouldn't have much to show for it in the way of family.

He could see now that he'd been blaming Charlene for not being what he wanted her to be. She had as much right to her own way of life as anybody else. But if he gave up the thorns he'd woven around his heart for protection, where did that leave him? He'd be about as vulnerable as a turtle without its shell. On the other hand, he could take a chance again.

He pushed off with his right foot and swung higher, harder, realizing that his head was gonna follow his heart with or without his rational consent.

Chapter 21

About midmorning, Lauren turned off Wildcat Road at an open gate. A sign overhead read "Welcome to Cougar Ranch" studded with a lone star in a circle on either side of the words. The ranch sign stretched from tall post to tall post, and it was made of powder-coated, heavy-gauge steel in a dark-blue finish that was typical of the area. She really liked Cougar Ranch's traditional sign, particularly since it hadn't changed in all these years.

She drove slowly across the cattle guard. It had an old wagon wheel on either side of a row of horizontal metal pipes that kept cattle from straying off the property but let wheeled traffic move easily in and out. She headed up the graded gravel road that led to the old farmhouse, feeling as if she were moving back in time to those long-ago happy days.

When they'd made plans on the phone earlier, Kent had told her that he now lived at the farmhouse, while his parents had built a new home with all the modern conveniences and open floor plan. Yet the original home site would always have a special place in her heart. She'd played there as a child and sat on the porch swing when she was older. She vividly remembered sharing the turn of the seasons with Kent and his family. They'd made and eaten caramel apples in the fall, creamy divinity candy at Christmas, fresh peach ice cream in the spring, and deviled eggs dyed red, white, and blue then arranged on a platter in the shape of a United States flag for the Fourth of July.

She couldn't help but feel nostalgic for those innocent days that had seemed endless at the time. Now she knew they were fleeting from one moment to the next. If she could go back in time, she'd savor every single minute, knowing that her special world of love, laughter, and friendship was an endangered creation. And yet, as with all of life, she could only live in the present and take it as it came—one precious moment after another.

She glanced at her daughter, strapped into a booster seat in the passenger seat of their SUV. All those years ago she couldn't have imagined sharing her current life with Hannah. She smiled as she thought of that very morning. Hannah had awakened her with giggles and tickles. Pretty quick, they'd gotten into a tickle-fest across the bed that had left them both with big grins on their faces. That fleeting experience would last as a bright jewel in her memory forever.

So far, she was relieved that Hannah appeared to be adjusting remarkably fast and well to her new environment. In just a day, she'd bonded with new friends and family. Right now Hannah couldn't seem to get enough of the North Texas scenery. And yes, it was as beautiful as ever.

A few fluffy white clouds highlighted the clear, azure sky, casting shadows across the wide plains with rolling hills that extended as far as the eye could see. Cottonwood trees grew along meandering streams while live oaks shaded black cattle. She couldn't see the Red River below the bluff to the north, but she knew the water moved sluggishly in a winding red slash between Oklahoma and Texas as it made its way to Louisiana before turning south for the Gulf of Mexico.

As she wound her way up to an elevated spot on the ranch, she saw the farmhouse. And sighed. She hadn't realized how much she'd missed this one special place on Earth till this very moment.

Ancient oaks with spreading limbs trimmed upward made a canopy over the front yard, and when their leaves fully sprouted would shade the peaked roof of the house. She'd almost forgotten how the simple farmhouse had touches of Victorian gingerbread along the roofline of the octagonal room that jutted out from the front with a covered porch to one side. Three narrow posts held up the porch roof, while a simple wood railing of vertical slats enclosed the floor. A stone walkway meandered up to three stone steps that made the entrance look warm and cozy.

When had Kent painted the front door, a barn type with eight glass panes, pale pink? She couldn't imagine why he'd selected that color, but it made her grin in delight because it was so against a rugged, cowboy type that it was simply fun. Then again, maybe his former fiancée had decorated and he hadn't had the heart to change her improvements to his home. She felt a little deflated at that thought, but then pushed it from her mind. No matter, the pink door contrasting with the white house and silver roof worked well for her.

She felt her breath catch in her throat and her heart speed up when she saw Kent rise from the swing and walk to the edge of the porch. Somehow, he might still hold the key to her heart. She wasn't sure how she felt about that fact, but she realized she might like it very much despite her past with Jeffrey.

Kent looked good in a crisp blue cowboy shirt, faded jeans, and brown boots. He raised a hand in greeting. She waved in return before she drove around and parked on the cement drive at the side of the house beside Kent's blue truck. She turned off the engine, glanced at Hannah, and was rewarded with a big grin.

"I like that house." Hannah grinned even bigger. "Is my pony inside?"

Lauren chuckled, shaking her head. "That's a people-house. There's a barn in back that's a horse-house."

"Yay! Let's go see the horses."

"Let's talk with Kent first."

Hannah turned big brown eyes on Lauren. "I like Cowboy Daddy, and I like his house."

"Me too."

Lauren chuckled in happiness as she stepped out of the SUV, leaving her handbag on the floorboard. She slipped her cell phone into the front pocket of her well-fitting jeans and smoothed down her crimson long-sleeve T-shirt before she walked around to the passenger side. She helped Hannah out of her booster seat, then watched her daughter dance impatiently in place. She proudly wore her favorite pink long-sleeve T-shirt—studded with rhinestones in the shape of a horse's head—with blue jeans and yellow athletic shoes.

As they rounded the corner of the house, Kent walked down the steps with his easy, long-legged stride to meet them.

Lauren felt her heart speed up even faster this close

to him. Maybe she was excited because she was back at the old home place, but she guessed the feeling had more to do with Kent than anything else.

"Mornin'." Kent gave them a lazy smile that revealed his dimples.

"Hi Cowboy Daddy," Hannah said shyly, grasping Lauren's fingers and swinging their hands back and forth.

"Hey there, little one," he replied.

"I'm not so little."

"That's right," he quickly agreed, smiling at her.

"We're not intruding or keeping you from work, are we?" Lauren asked even though they'd made plans earlier. She didn't want to put anybody out just to meet her needs.

"Remember, you're back in Wildcat Bluff now. We take care of our own." Kent's hazel eyes lit with inner fire as his gaze swept over her.

"I'm not used to small-town Texas anymore."

"Better get used to it. You know everybody'll be up in your business whether you want it or not."

"Guess you're right. And it's all with the best of intentions."

"You know we're like the old-time ranchers and farmers around here. We all depend on family, friends, and community to make life safe and good." He gave her a big grin before he took a sip of coffee from his cowboy boot mug.

"I appreciate everyone being so generous already."

"You'll return the favor someday."

She nodded in agreement. "Fine mug you've got there." She couldn't help teasing him. "Real cute."

He grimaced, looked down at the mug, and shook his

head. "Don't say a word. Mom found it someplace and decided it suited me."

Lauren chuckled, appreciating Kent's love for his mother. She squeezed Hannah's hand, completely understanding the power of a mother's love for her child. "I was going to bring your hat, but Hannah's taken a liking to it and if you don't mind—"

"She can keep it as long as she likes. I've got plenty."

"Thanks. Once she has her own cowgirl hat, I'm sure she'll be willing to let it go."

"No worry."

Hannah suddenly jerked her hand free of Lauren's fingers and pointed at the front porch. "Look!" She ran down the stone walkway, up the steps, and flattened herself against the pink front door, arms outstretched as if caressing the door.

Lauren exchanged a puzzled look with Kent, then glanced back at her child. "What is it?"

"It's the best door ever!" Hannah hollered. "We match!"

Kent chuckled, taking hold of Lauren's hand, entwining their fingers, and leading her up the walkway. "She's a doll."

"Thanks. She can be a mess, too."

"That's good. Real good," Kent said, smiling.

When they reached the stairs, Hannah whipped around and flattened her body against the door with her arms outstretched again. "Mommy, will you take my picture? I bet I disappear into this door."

Lauren laughed as she stepped up to the porch, pulled out her phone, and snapped several quick shots.

"Thanks!" Hannah twirled around before she bounded over to Lauren. "Let's see."

Lauren held out her phone so all three of them could see Hannah in pink against pink. "You look adorable."

Hannah pushed back her long, blond hair and grinned at Kent. "Your door is the best."

"Thanks." Kent smiled at her. "You and that door are quite the sight for sore eyes."

Hannah appeared puzzled, cocking her head to one side. "Do your eyes hurt?"

Kent chuckled. "No. That's an old-fashioned saying that means you and the door look good together."

She rolled her big, brown eyes, and then she nodded with a great deal of skepticism.

Lauren couldn't help but laugh. "You'll be learning lots of new, colorful sayings now that we're in Wildcat Bluff."

Hannah glanced from Lauren to Kent then back again as if judging if they were funning her or not.

"She's right. Scout's honor." Kent quickly held up two fingers in a Scout's honor salute, then crossed his heart with the same two fingers.

"Okay." Hannah obviously lost interest. "Mommy, can we have a pink door when we get our new home?"

"I don't know. We'll see." Lauren hated to disappoint her daughter, but she never made promises she couldn't keep.

"You can use my pink door any time you like," Kent said.

Hannah grinned, revealing small, white teeth. "I like this place!"

"I've always loved it here," Lauren said wistfully. "Only I don't remember the pink front door."

Kent laughed and held up his boot mug. "Goes

with the mug. Not my choice, but I'm learning to live with it."

Lauren felt a sudden heaviness in her heart. She couldn't imagine him letting anybody paint that door pink unless it was somebody he loved like his former fiancée. But she couldn't let that get in the way of Hannah's happiness—or her own, for that matter. They just needed to move forward from here.

"A swing!" Hannah launched herself across the porch and leaped onto the swing. She lay flat on her back and kicked her legs into the air, setting the swing to rocking back and forth. "Best house in the whole, wide world!"

When Kent put an arm around Lauren's shoulders and pulled her close, she leaned into him just like old times.

"Remember how we used to swing there after school?" he asked.

"And neck—isn't that the old-fashioned term—at night?"

"That's right. Only now I don't have to get you home by ten on weeknights." He tightened his grip on her shoulder. "You could stay all night every night."

Lauren shivered as chills swept through her. What would it be like to be out here on the ranch alone with Kent in his big bed as she'd imagined so many times when she was sweet sixteen? Only now there were no parents, no school, no curfews, and she knew exactly how delicious a night in his arms could be. When a wicked blaze swept through her at the thought of joining Kent under his covers, she felt her skin ignite in moist heat.

Kent squeezed her shoulder as he pressed a soft kiss to her cheek. "Think Ruby would watch Hannah if you came out here one evening? I grill a mean steak."

If Lauren had been hot before, now she was on fire. It was as if he'd read her mind, or maybe he'd always imagined her in his bed out here, too.

"Kisses!" Hannah leaped off the swing and raced over to them. She held up her face toward Kent. "I love kisses as much as I love pink doors."

"I love little girls more than pink doors." Kent leaned down and gave Hannah's cheek a gentle kiss.

"You do?" Hannah beamed from Kent to Lauren. "Pink door. Kisses. Only thing better is a pony."

Lauren chuckled, shaking her head. "Incorrigible."

Hannah grinned, looking mischievous. "I need cowgirl boots to go with my pony. I wanted red ones to match Aunt Hedy's, but not now. They've got to be pink!"

When Kent burst out laughing, Lauren joined him.

Hannah looked back and forth between them, appearing concerned. "You like red better?"

Lauren laughed even harder. "I think pink is just perfect for you." She glanced up at Kent and felt an upwelling of love like she hadn't felt in so many years. She took a deep breath. If she wasn't careful, she was going to lose complete control around him.

Kent smiled at her, warmth shinning in his eyes. "Pink's starting to be my favorite color."

"Good." Hannah clapped her hands together. "Now we've settled on pink, let's go get my pony."

Chapter 22

"I'd invite you inside, but I think if I did we might have a mutiny on our hands." Kent gestured toward Hannah, who was hanging over the porch railing with both hands as she tried to peer around the house toward the barn. He hoped his words didn't sound rude, because they were the best he could come up with on the spur of the moment. His place was a mess. No telling where he'd thrown his clothes or pizza boxes or whatever. He wished he could hose out the inside like he'd hosed off his truck, but it wouldn't be that easy. Whatever had to do with animals or business, he kept top notch, but he always let things for himself slide because he didn't figure it made much difference. Now he might have to rethink that habit.

Lauren nodded as she walked over to Hannah, eased her daughter back from possible danger, and turned to Kent. "Looks like you've been decorating. I'd love to see all the changes you've made inside."

"Pony. Pony. Pony," Hannah chanted as she twirled around on tiptoes.

"I'll be happy to show you later." Much later, if he had anything to say about it. As a distraction, he leaned forward, ready to catch Hannah if she overbalanced and started to fall. He suddenly realized he'd need to keep an eye on her near horses or anything else. "Were we that full of energy at her age?"

Lauren chuckled, nodding. "I bet. She'll run out of steam later. For now, we'd better just get this show on the road."

"Okay. While she's still full of get-up-and-go, let's look at the facilities." He gestured down the stairs. "Mom and Dad moved the horses and tack to the new barn by their place. That means my barn and arena aren't in use. Why don't we take a look and see if they'll suit what you have in mind."

"That's generous." Lauren frowned slightly as she looked at him. "But are you sure you don't mind? It could be a lot of trouble."

"Pony. Pony. Pony." Hannah danced down the stairs and over to the big oak tree in front. She leaned back against the trunk and crossed her arm as if impatiently waiting for them.

Kent chuckled at the sight. "She reminds me more of you all the time."

Lauren smiled at her daughter. "Hannah's fitting in quicker than I could've hoped for around here."

"Chip off the old block." He caught Lauren's hand and squeezed her fingers. "I talked with Mom, and she's anxious to see you and meet Hannah."

"She was always great. I can't wait to see her again, too."

"I'll set something up later." He tugged Lauren closer, feeling the heat of her body against him. "She likes your idea about horse-assisted therapy and wants to help any way she can."

Lauren eased away and gave him a hard stare. "You told her?"

"I thought it best since you may be working here."

"But I don't know anything yet. I mean, I don't know if it'll be possible, if we can get horses, if—"

"Let's count on everything working out just fine." He pulled her back to him, fitting her body to the long length of his own. She was creating a wildfire in him that was building all the time. "And we can start right here on Cougar Ranch."

She put her hands against his chest, splayed her fingers against his hard muscles, and tilted her head back. "I'll pay you rent."

He shook his head. "No way in hell."

"Yes, I will. And I'll buy horses and equipment and—"

He lifted one of her hands and kissed each fingertip. "Lauren, I'm taking some time off to help you."

She jerked her hand away and stepped back, shaking her head negatively in concern.

He saw tears brim her eyes and couldn't figure out what he'd done or said wrong to upset her. "What?"

She turned away and clasped the railing with both hands. "We're not a couple anymore. You don't owe me anything." She glanced back over her shoulder. "And I don't want to owe you anything."

He felt a cold chill race down his spine followed by a hot burn that spread outward to engulf his entire body. He wanted to grab her and shake some sense into her, but that wasn't the answer. She had to come to his reasoning on her own. "Did you forget we're friends? Did you forget how friends help each other in Wildcat Bluff? Did you forget we'd all do just about anything to make Hedy better?"

He stepped toward her, holding down his frustration by force of will. "You're trying to throw away all of us in this county who'd consider it an honor, as well as a duty, to get your idea off the ground. You might even end up providing jobs for some down-on-their-luck horse folks."

She groaned and put her face in her hands. "No more, please." She raised her head and looked at him, tears shining in her dark eyes. "I'm not used to so much kindness and generosity."

"You better get used to it. Nobody's letting you make a go of it on your own. All you have to do is let us do what we know how to do."

"And what is that?" She sniffed back her tears as she gave him a tentative smile.

"Whatever is needed." He returned her smile, feeling so much lust and love rolled into one big ball of hope that he thought he'd fair burst with it. He'd promised himself that he'd protect his heart, but he was going to have one hell of a time keeping that promise. He could see now that Lauren was everything he'd ever wanted in a woman. But she'd been hurt, just like him, and she'd need to be eased back into country life so she could believe in family and friends and community again.

"Mommy! Cowboy Daddy!" Hannah called as she stepped away from the tree and planted her hands on her hips, looking all sassy.

"Come on." Kent placed a gentle kiss on Lauren's forehead. "I bet the barn looks about like it did the last time you saw it."

"Just so you know, I'm not making any promises, but I can use help. Hedy and Hannah come first. I'm willing to do whatever needs to be done for them."

"It seems to me as if you've been putting yourself last for too long. That works for a while, but after a time it backs up on you." He smiled to ease the sting of his words and encourage her. "As long as I'm around, nobody's putting you last. You deserve better, and you're going to get it."

She appeared a little surprised by his words, but nodded anyway. "I've given that same advice to my patients on occasion. You're right. It's the strong ones that need to hear it before they collapse from good intentions."

"I'm here to catch you if you fall, but you're not going to need it. You just need a little help carrying the load. And that's what friends are for." He held out his hand. "Let's shake on it."

"Still, Hannah and Hedy—"

"Trust me."

When Lauren put her small, soft hand into his big, rough one, he felt as if they were committing to much more than getting her hippotherapy center off the ground. He looked into her chocolate-brown eyes and felt himself melt like a candy bar on a hot summer day.

"Now?" Hannah ran up to the porch and whirled in a circle.

Lauren smiled a rueful twist of her lips. "And that's being a parent."

"All I can do today is show you both where horses can live, so don't get your hopes too high." Kent chuckled in a raspy tone. "At least, Hannah knows what's important in life."

Lauren joined his laughter. "Horses!"

As they all tromped around the side of the house toward the barn, Kent felt a deep sense of satisfaction. He hadn't known being part of a family like this would be so much fun. And then a cold dose of reality hit him. Lauren and

Hannah weren't his family, even if he was starting to think of them that way. He'd better get his head screwed on straight or wrap barbwire around his heart if he was going to stay out of trouble. Fact of the matter, he was simply helping out friends, nothing more and nothing less.

That point set in his mind, he lead the gals through a gate in a fence that was constructed of white-painted pipe that wouldn't hurt horses. The original wooden barn had collapsed long ago. It'd been replaced in the seventies with a simple structure built of concrete blocks that had a peaked tin roof for ventilation and a gated entry on each end of the structure.

Hannah ran ahead of them, reached the barn, and patted the cement blocks lovingly as she looked through the metal bars of the gate.

Kent opened the gate and she ran ahead of them into the cool, shadowy interior that had a packed dirt floor so as to ease the strain on horses. On one side were several metal gates made of vertical bars that opened into horse stalls with empty water troughs. Each stall had another gate in back that led into an enclosed arena for exercise and training. On the other side of the wide center aisle were a couple of large horse stalls and a big tack and feed storage room. He liked this basic, efficient horse stable even though it couldn't compare in design, size, or function to the new one his parents had built.

He smelled the lingering scent of hay, oats, and horse as he watched Hannah run down the center aisle and peek into one horse stall after another. Finally, she stopped, put her hands on her hips, and looked back.

"I know." Kent threw wide his hands. "No horses."

Hannah vigorously nodded in agreement.

"First thing," Kent said, "I need to know if you and Lauren think this place will do to start."

"Oh, Kent, it's wonderful." Lauren wandered down the center aisle. "I remember when we used to saddle horses here and ride out over the ranch."

"Good days." He watched her repeat Hannah's movements as she walked from stall to stall and looked inside each as if reliving memories.

"It's a pity this place isn't in use." Lauren glanced back at him.

"Yep. But it was best to consolidate business at the new headquarters."

"I'm very lucky. This is absolutely as perfect as I remember."

"Glad you think so. It'll easily handle six horses, but we can start with two."

Lauren nodded in agreement. "One for Hedy and—"

"One for me!" Hannah danced up to them and clapped her hands.

"Besides horses," Lauren continued, "I'll need equipment, tack, feed, and who knows what all."

"We're not starting from scratch. We can borrow stuff from Mom and Dad."

"I hate to impose. I've got some savings."

"No need to go there yet. Let's start simple with two horses and see how it progresses from there." He gestured around the barn. "You've got a place here if you want it."

"Oh, I do! Thank you."

"Maybe later you'll want to get your own headquarters. But right now, isn't this all about Hedy and Hannah?"

"Absolutely. I'm grateful to borrow at first. Later,

we'll see." She looked toward Hannah. "What do you say about your own pony?"

"I need pink cowgirl boots." Hannah ran over, grabbed Kent's hand, and swung back and forth. "Right?"

"Sure do." He couldn't resist picking Hannah up, swinging her high, and setting her on his shoulder. "How does the world look now?" He was surprised at his own actions, but he was enjoying his gals too much to resist.

Hannah shrieked in delight and patted the top of his head. "Go, horsey, go!"

"Now you've done it." Lauren laughed as she watched them. "Once she likes something, there's never an end to it."

"Come on." He set a rocking-horse gait as he headed for the exit. "Let's go get the real deal in Sure-Shot."

He set a ground-eating pace back to his pickup with Lauren by his side. Hannah remained perched on his shoulders, giggling and patting the top of his head. He'd never dreamed he could become so fond of a child so fast, but Hannah was stealing his heart. She was making him feel younger and happier like the days he'd thought long gone.

Soon he stopped by his pickup and eased Hannah to the ground. "Why don't I drive us over to Sure-Shot? We could pick up lunch at the Bluebonnet Café."

"I only now realized that I haven't discussed any of this with Hedy," Lauren said. "We've just decided what's best for her without including her in the discussion."

"You're right." He felt uneasiness sweep over him. "And we know better than to do something like that, particularly with an independent lady like Hedy."

"I feel kind of bad about it now. I haven't even

been to see her today, and that's why I came back to Wildcat Bluff."

"We can put our trip to Sure-Shot on hold till you talk to her about your idea. I'm sure she'll love it."

"What about my pony?" Hannah clasped Kent's hand and tugged on him.

He looked down at her and saw tears glistening in her eyes. He felt like the lowest form of snake. They'd gotten a little girl's hopes up only to dash them. He glanced back at Lauren. "What does Mommy say in situations like this?"

"I'm going to get my pony!" Hannah dropped his hand and ran around the house toward the road.

"We can't let her out near traffic." Kent took off after Hannah, who was running as fast as her short legs could take her.

"I don't know what got into her," Lauren called right behind him.

When he reached Hannah, he hurried in front of her, knelt down, and held out his arms. "I'll make sure you get your pony."

Hannah threw herself into his arms, clasped him around his neck, and sobbed against his shoulder.

He glanced up at Lauren in confusion. He had no idea how to handle the situation, but he patted Hannah on the back before he gave her a gentle hug until her tears slowly gave way to hiccups.

"Hannah, come here," Lauren said gently as she knelt beside the two of them. "We need to talk."

"Thanks, Cowboy Daddy." Hannah patted his shoulder and then slowly walked over to her mother with her head down.

"Is that any way to act?" Lauren asked as she clasped Hannah's small hands.

"No, Mommy. But I'm afraid I'll never get my pony."

"I understand, but you scared us by running off like that. Now what do you say?"

Hannah raised her head and looked from Lauren to Kent. "I'm sorry I worried you."

"That's okay." Kent hated to see Hannah unhappy as much as he'd feared her running into the road. "We just want you to be safe."

"I know." She hung her head again. "Does this mean I don't get my pony?"

"Nope." Kent chuckled as he reached out and tickled Hannah under her chin. "This means we better go get your pony before he gets away."

"Really?" Hannah looked up at him with eyes gone wide. "Truly?"

"Kent, I need to talk with Hedy first," Lauren said.

"How about I take Hannah with me to Sure-Shot while you get Hedy and meet us there?"

"Are you sure?"

"If you'll trust me with her, I'll do my utmost."

"She can be a handful."

"If I can go with Cowboy Daddy in his big blue truck, I'll be a good girl." Hannah leaped up and down, spun around, and then quickly grew still and solemn. "I won't run or make noise or anything."

Kent didn't know what had made him volunteer to take care of a four-year-old girl for a few hours. He didn't know the first thing about it, but he couldn't stand to see her disappointment. Anyway, could it be much harder than managing a frisky colt? Maybe he could put her on a lead so he wouldn't worry about her running away again. No, that probably wouldn't do.

"Okay, I guess," Lauren said as she looked uneasily at him. "I'm not used to letting her out of my sight, but we're in Wildcat Bluff now. And she'll be with you."

"Yay!" Hannah spun around several times, then abruptly stopped and stood still. "I'm good."

Kent chuckled, shaking his head. "She'll be safe. I'll call Billye Jo. She'll know if there's a pony right for Hannah in Sure-Shot. And if I run into trouble on the parenting front, she'll know what to do."

Lauren nodded. "Yeah. You know horse people. They raise their kids like they raise their horses. And they get all the respect."

"Sure do."

When he felt a small hand clasp his own, he glanced down at Hannah's upturned face.

"Can, I mean, may we go now, Cowboy Daddy?"

He felt his heart melt a little more at the look into her big, brown eyes. He hated to think about the hearts she was going to break when she turned sweet sixteen, just like her mother had done with all the local cowboys.

"Go ahead," Lauren agreed, pulling her cell phone out of her front pocket. "But be careful and stay in touch."

Hannah wheeled around and raced over to Kent's truck where she hugged the front bumper.

Kent put a hand on Lauren's shoulder. "You okay with this? If not, we can wait."

"It's okay. I need to talk with Hedy alone. Maybe by the time we get to Sure-Shot, you'll have found the perfect pony."

"I hope it's that easy."

"Cowboy Daddy, let's go!"

"How quickly they grow up." Lauren shook her head as she smiled at him. "Let's move her booster seat from my SUV to your truck so she'll be safe."

"Good idea." He quickly removed the booster seat, installed it in the passenger seat of his pickup, and check to make sure it was secure.

"That looks good," Lauren said. "Hannah is tall for her age, so this size seat suits her fine."

"Let's go, Cowboy Daddy!"

"Now, you be a good girl." Lauren lifted Hannah into the booster seat, strapped her into place, and shut the door. She turned to Kent with a smile.

He pressed a kiss to her soft lips. "Promise we'll have time for each other later?"

She nodded with eyes as dark as melted chocolate. "Didn't you promise me a tour of your home?"

He grinned, feeling heat spiral outward at the idea of being alone with her again. "I think you'll like the changes, such as my king-size bed."

"If you're in it, I'm sure I'll like it."

"I can definitely be there." He felt hotter at her suggestion, so he gave her another quick kiss before he walked over to her SUV and opened the door. "You best get in here and get gone before that house tour starts here and now."

She chuckled as she gave him a sensual pout before she walked over and put a hand on his chest. "Hang on to that idea, cowboy." And then she disappeared inside her vehicle.

He reluctantly shut the door and turned his mind to the safer subject of ponies.

Chapter 23

As Lauren drove down Wildcat Road, she felt as if a part of her had gone with Kent and Hannah. She wanted to be with them, finding a pony, grabbing a burger, and exploring Sure-Shot's equine-centered shops. Yet she felt guilty for wanting to have fun when Hedy needed her.

She kept making assumptions about her aunt. She knew better than to create plans for other people without consulting them. She didn't normally do it. Maybe being back in Wildcat Bluff and worried about Hedy was causing her to act too quickly. In any case, she needed to talk with her aunt before she made any more plans that involved her.

With that thought in mind, Lauren pulled off to the side of the road, picked up her phone from the center console, and hit speed dial for her aunt.

"Morning, Lauren," Hedy said in a warm voice. "How'd you sleep last night in Wildcat Bluff?"

"Good. It's great to be back."

"Not any better than having you back."

"Thanks." Lauren cleared her throat. "If you don't mind, I thought I'd stop by your house and chat a bit."

"That'd be wonderful, except I'm not at home."

"Maybe later?"

"I'm at the store. Why don't you come over here? We can enjoy a cup of tea together like the old days."

"Perfect."

"You'll bring Hannah, won't you?"

Lauren thought fast, wondering how to explain that her daughter was with Kent. She supposed there was no help for it except the unvarnished truth. "She couldn't wait to get a pony. Kent's taken her to Sure-Shot."

"Kent? Pony? Sure-Shot?" Hedy chuckled, a deep, rumbling sound of pleasure. "That cowboy sure works fast, doesn't he?"

Lauren smiled, remembering once more how supportive Hedy had always been of them. "Hannah's taken a real shine to him. I'm going to meet them later, but I wanted to spend time with you first."

"Thanks. But don't you think a pony for Hannah comes before me?"

"Not today. Right now, you're first on my list."

"I'll be here."

"See you soon." Lauren clicked off, set down her phone, and got back onto the road.

As she drove toward Wildcat Bluff, she felt nostalgic. She'd helped Hedy in Adelia's Delights many an afternoon after school while Kent worked down the street in his family's Chuckwagon Café. They'd been part of close-knit family and community. Now she hoped she could build that type of life for Hannah.

She arrived in Old Town and parked on Main Street just down from the Wildcat Bluff Hotel. Next door to the hotel she heard the sound of boot-scooting country music floating through old batwing-style wooden doors coming from the Lone Star Saloon. She felt a little burst of excitement. Now she was old enough to go inside the Lone Star and enjoy dancing to live bands on weekends.

Maybe she could wrangle Kent into taking her there like she'd wanted him to in high school. That'd be fun later.

Next door to the Lone Star was Gene's Boot Hospital with the big, neon boot in the front window. Gene's dated back to the days when Texas cowboys drove their cattle herds north to Kansas. They'd needed tough boots, so Gene had hand-made them to order and repaired them as well. She could hardly wait to take Hannah in there to buy her fancy new cowgirl boots. Pink, of course.

Finally, she turned her gaze on Adelia's Delights and felt warm memories bubble up. She'd spent many happy hours helping her aunt run her store. Once more, Rosie made a pretty picture of a contented cat in the Bluebird of Happiness display.

She watched a few people walk up and down the wooden boardwalk as they entered and exited businesses. Several vehicles were parked in front, but the area was fairly quiet since it was a weekday. She knew she was stalling since she wasn't sure how her aunt would respond to her suggestion. But surely Hedy would be thrilled at the idea of getting back on a horse again.

Now or never. Lauren slipped her phone into her handbag, stepped out of her SUV, and locked the door behind her. She caught the scent of lavender piped out of Morning's Glory, the store next to Adelia's. Lauren smiled as she thought of the business owner, a flower child firmly stuck in the sixties and proud of it. As far as Lauren could tell, Morning Glory had hardly aged a day, so maybe there was something to be said for indulging in her handmade soaps, creams, lotions, incense, and positive affirmation cards decorated with watercolors and calligraphy.

Lauren opened the door to Adelia's, heard the

sound of chimes announcing her entrance, and shut the door behind her. She felt as if she'd been transported back in time when she read "Established 1883" on a sign attached to a wall near the entrance. She admired the mellow oak floor to the high ceiling of intricately designed pressed tin and the tall glass containers of old-fashioned hard candy on the counter next to the ancient black-and-gold cash register.

She'd always loved this store. Knickknacks in all shapes, sizes, colors, and prices filled deep shelves and glass cabinets. Western-themed gifts for bathrooms, bedrooms, and kitchens dominated one wall. Another section contained pickles, jams, and other edible items in canning jars with an Adelia's Delights label. All of the items were a definite temptation. She only wished the shelves were stocked as fully as in the past.

She gave Rosie a gentle stroke across the top of her head and was rewarded with a soft, welcoming meow. "I'll see you later, pretty kitty."

Lauren walked farther into the store and glanced over at the tearoom area where small, round ice cream tables with matching chairs were tucked into a corner near the front window. She quickly decided that was the perfect spot for a quiet conversation with Hedy.

"Lauren, is that you?" Hedy called from one side of the store.

"Yes!"

"I'm over here with MG."

Lauren walked toward the open archway that connected Adelia's with Morning's Glory. She smiled in delight to see her aunt and her friend standing under the arch. Hedy appeared a little slumped in her wheelchair, but she gave

Lauren a big grin. Morning Glory gave a little wave. She was still a tall, slim woman with a riot of long, curly ginger hair. She wore a bright-aqua blouse with a long, swirling skirt in many colors and turquoise cowgirl boots. At least half a dozen necklaces hung down to her small waist.

"Now do you believe me?" Morning Glory glanced down at Hedy. "I told you I had a premonition that Lauren was coming back to Wildcat Bluff, and here she is in living color."

"You've said that for years." Hedy tossed her head, a bit like a horse, as she teased her friend.

"Vibes!" Morning Glory raised two fingers in the peace sign. "I've had good, strong vibes about it for a week now."

Hedy rolled her eyes at Lauren, chuckling to show she was in a teasing frame of mind. "Good thing you're back or I'd have to hear all about MG's vibes for another umpteen years."

"Come here and give me a hug," Morning Glory commanded. "I've needed one from you for years."

Lauren was happy to comply, feeling the strength and agility in Morning Glory's body, but she was also almost overwhelmed by a familiar scent. "Are you wearing patchouli again?"

"Glad you remember your scents." Morning Glory set Lauren back, looked her up and down, and nodded in approval.

"You taught me well." She'd never say it out loud, but patchouli was her least favorite scent, and she avoided it whenever possible. She just hoped she wouldn't sneeze from the cloying odor and have one of Morning Glory's herbal remedies thrust upon her.

"Good." Morning Glory cocked her head to one side. "I believe you're in need of a little extra power right about now."

"Lauren's obviously fine," Hedy said. "She's hardly back in town and you're already messing with her aura or whatever."

Morning Glory glanced to the side of Lauren, squinted her eyes as if trying to bring something into focus, and then nodded in approval again. "Her aura's fine and dandy, thank you very much. Appears to me she's just starting out on a grand adventure and needs a little extra fire power and protection to get her where she wants to go."

Lauren smiled, feeling warm all over with Morning Glory's concern. She never knew half of what her friend was talking about, but she was usually right or her concern just made a person feel better.

Morning Glory fumbled with the jewelry around her neck, selected a necklace, pulled it over her head, and held it out to Lauren. "This one must be for you. I just made it yesterday."

"Are you sure? It's gorgeous."

"Of course I'm sure." Morning Glory thrust it at Lauren. "That's a macramé cord I knotted myself. I got a hankering to make them long about last Christmas. I guess it was because I found a cache of brass horse harness hardware that I'd lost track of back in the seventies. They make fine necklaces."

"She teaching Misty to macramé," Hedy said.

"Misty?" Lauren raised an eyebrow in query. "Isn't that—"

"Right. Trey's fiancée," Morning Glory said. "You'll

love her. She's from Dallas, but you can't hold that against her. She fits right in here."

"I'm looking forward to meeting her." Lauren slipped the smooth knotted macramé necklace over her head and centered the brass piece over her sternum. She stroked the pendant.

"Looks good," Morning Glory said. "Horse harness hardware works perfectly for pendants since it comes in all sorts of designs like swans, animals, and such. That phoenix rising is perfect for you. Back in the day, a shiny row of those sewed on leather looked pretty on horses pulling conveyances."

"Thank you." Lauren knew the necklace probably wouldn't be right for Houston, but it was perfect in Wildcat Bluff.

"Now, what's this about Kent taking off with Hannah when I wanted a chance to meet her?" Morning Glory asked.

"She's determined to be a cowgirl." Lauren felt proud of her daughter for being so willing to spread her wings. "They're looking for a pony."

"But where are you going to put a horse?" Morning Glory looked from Lauren to Hedy and back again. "That's not a small item like a Bluebird of Happiness."

"I've got an idea." Hedy looked like the cat that ate the cream. "Kent's got an empty barn, doesn't he?"

Lauren couldn't keep from chuckling at her aunt the matchmaker. "As a matter of fact, he does indeed, and he volunteered it. I think we'll start there till we see how everything goes in Wildcat Bluff."

"Everything will go just fine," Morning Glory said

with finality. "But don't you dare start using that place till you clean it first."

"I saw it this morning and it looks fine."

Morning Glory narrowed her bright eyes. "That's not what I mean and you know it. Stay right there and I'll get what you need to move forward with that place." She quickly turned and disappeared into her store.

Lauren glanced down at her aunt. "I don't think she's changed a bit since I left here."

"I agree." Hedy smiled fondly. "She's got more energy than a two-year-old and enough ideas to float a fleet."

"Here you go!" Morning Glory popped back through the open doorway and held out two items. "These are for you."

"Thanks. What do I owe you?" Lauren felt skeptical as she accepted what looked like a roll of dried leaves wrapped and tied with a red cord along with a long, braided section of grass.

"Not a thing. You'll do something for me sometime and it'll all come out in the wash," Morning Glory said. "Now, that's sage and sweetgrass. You remember, don't you? Once you light them, they'll burn slow and steady. You want to smudge by swirling the smoke around inside the barn. That'll remove any lingering odors or negative vibrations."

"Oh yes." Now Lauren remembered the ancient Comanche and other native nation cleansing system that Morning Glory recommended for all new enterprises. It couldn't hurt to try it. "I'm sure this will do the trick."

"Groovy," Morning Glory agreed.

Listening to her, Lauren couldn't help but remember

how Wildcat Bluff was built by strong, independent settlers who had minds of their own when it came to life and happiness. They came west so nobody could tell them how to live their lives. They fit right in to the former Comancheria that had been created by the fiercely protective Comanche. Wildcat Bluff's descendants were of that same strong persuasion. And Lauren was glad to be back amongst her people.

"What about that cup of tea?" Hedy gestured toward the tearoom. "I've got pomegranate green tea steeping for us."

"Sounds delicious," Lauren said. "Morning Glory, do you want to join us?"

"Wish I could, but I've got work to do." She waved a languid hand toward her store. "We'll have plenty of time to chat later."

"Bye for now." Lauren watched Morning Glory hurry away before she smiled down at her aunt. Fish or cut bait. She hoped this chat went well. Still, she didn't see how Hedy couldn't love her idea.

"Come along." Hedy zipped toward the tearoom.

"I hope you've got my favorite blueberry muffins, too." Lauren followed her aunt, feeling as if she'd truly stepped back in time.

"Blueberry?" Hedy stopped, and then gave a big smile. "Of course, blueberry muffins. I'd almost forgotten. Those were good days, weren't they?"

Lauren returned Hedy's smile, but she could tell her aunt hadn't remembered the muffins. She felt uneasiness spread like a chill up her spine.

Chapter 24

LAUREN SAT ACROSS THE SMALL TABLE FROM HEDY IN the tearoom area of Adelia's Delights. She took a sip of tea from the to-go container, remembering nostalgically when they'd enjoyed drinking tea from pretty, delicate china. Earlier she'd carefully put her sage and sweetgrass in her purse and hung her bag over the back of her chair.

"I bet I know what you're thinking about the cups. I never thought I'd do it, but I've changed with the times." Hedy held up her tea. "I miss the old days when we drank from beautiful china, but that time is long gone for me. I even use paper plates at home. It's just not worth the bother to wash and dry anymore."

"I understand," Lauren agreed, even as she knew the old Hedy would never have resorted to paper products. "I use plenty of paper, too. And don't even get me started on the trouble with the new dishwashers."

"Mine's twenty years old and still chugging away." Hedy chuckled. "It'll probably last me forever since I don't use it much anymore."

"That's the legacy I want from you." Lauren smiled, thinking of all the problems she'd heard from friends about their new, flaky appliances. "Vintage dishwasher, range, washer and dryer, freezer. Those are like gold."

Hedy laughed harder. "You don't want my beautiful china and silver?"

"If you insist, I'll eventually take that, too—only it all gets washed by hand."

"Good choice. I've already packed those away for you since I'm not using them nowadays."

"But don't you want to keep enjoying your fine things?"

"No 'buts' about it. You're the child of my heart as well as my family. I want to pass my heritage, meaning my stuff while it's in good shape, down to you. You can keep it, use it, or pass it along to someone who'll enjoy it."

"Aunt Hedy, please don't talk like that. You're much too young to think about the distant future."

"Not a bit of it. Seventy is about the right age to get your affairs in order." Hedy glanced around the store, then back at Lauren. "I'm working on it, but it's going to take some time."

"You've got too much going on in your life to start planning on how to limit it now."

"Truth of the matter"—Hedy leaned forward—"I'm not feeling as spry as I used to when I was younger."

"There's not a medical reason, is there?" Lauren held her breath, not wanting to hear some devastating news.

"No. I'm the same-ole, same-ole, but I'm feeling more like a sourpuss every day."

"That doesn't sound like my Aunt Hedy."

"Not the old me, but the new me."

"Let's back up here. You're too important to Wildcat Bluff, what with the fire station, Adelia's, and everything else you do to even think about—"

"I'm going to cut back. Let the younger ones step up to the plate."

"They won't know what to do."

"I'll train them." Hedy set down her cup and looked

down at her motorized wheelchair. "I've been meaning to talk to you about—"

"I want to talk to you about—" Lauren stopped once she realized they were about to speak over each other. "Excuse me. Go ahead."

Hedy leaned back, picked up her tea, and cradled the cup in both hands. "No, you're just back in town. I want to hear what's on your mind besides a certain good-looking cowboy firefighter."

Lauren couldn't help but smile. "I admit he is that." Now was the time to take the plunge with Hedy before she got cold feet, particularly since she was more concerned than ever by the way her aunt was feeling and thinking about life. No wonder she appeared so dispirited to everyone.

"Even Hannah adores him," Hedy said.

"True. I'm thrilled she's reaching out to others here."

"Wildcat Bluff folks have a way about them, don't they?"

"Just like you." Lauren set her cup on the table. "Aunt Hedy, all this talk about horses and barns has given me an idea."

"Really?"

"I'm beginning to think I can make Wildcat Bluff work for me, as well as Hannah."

"Well, of course it'll work for you."

"I mean, I'm thinking about starting a business here."

Hedy appeared puzzled, frowning as she stared at Lauren. "But I thought now that you're back you could help me in the store. That'd just be for a start. Didn't I mention that you'll be inheriting and running Adelia's when I'm gone?"

Lauren's breath caught in her throat as she realized that she and her aunt were going in different directions for her future. "Truthfully, I never thought about you being gone. And I still can't, or won't, go there."

"Darlin', as much as I love you, I simply will not be here forever. Your mom and I are discussing plans for your future, and Hannah's too, but not ours anymore."

Lauren couldn't stand the idea. It went against everything she had in mind for her aunt. She stood up, paced toward the Bluebird of Happiness display, glared at the happy-looking bluebirds, and turned back.

"I didn't mean to upset you." Hedy gestured toward the table. "Please come back and talk to me."

Lauren sat down, feeling weighed down by the past and the future, then she sat up straight. She wasn't going to borrow trouble. She'd deal with the present. Everything else could take care of itself. "Okay. You know I'll always help you in the store. Hannah will love it, too. But I'm a physical therapist. I have a passion to help others be the best they can be no matter their circumstances or physical ability. I can make a difference in folks' lives. I *have* made a difference, and I want to continue doing it."

"That's wonderful. I had no idea you were so passionate about it. I've always felt the same way. It must run in the family, what with your mother being such a wonderful nurse."

"Thank you. But you and Mom are the ones who've made such a big difference in the lives of others. I'm just getting started now."

"I think it's a great idea." Hedy leaned forward with bright interest in her dark eyes. "We have a clinic here, but folks must travel to Sherman, Denison, or Bonham for physical therapy. Some even drive to Dallas or Fort Worth."

"I want to do more than that." Lauren took a deep breath, hoping against hope that her aunt would support her idea. "We're in horse and cattle country here."

"Right. Horse riders and rodeo folks can get pretty stove up."

"I'd like to take my skills in that direction."

"Sounds good."

"You've heard of equine-assisted therapy, haven't you?"

"Yes." Hedy looked away from Lauren and down at her legs. "I hope you're not thinking about me."

"I can get you up on horseback. You'll feel like you're walking again. We can build up your core strength. Hippotherapy works."

Hedy shook her head as she glanced up at Lauren with tears filling her eyes. "And to think I was so happy you'd come home."

"Aunt Hedy, I didn't mean to upset you. I only want to help you and others."

"Don't you think every day of my life I've yearned to ride again?"

"We can make this work."

"Do you really think I haven't researched every which way but Sunday to come up with a better way of life?" Hedy backed away from the table. "But I've never, not even for one moment, deluded myself that I could ever get on the back of a horse once more."

Lauren felt her jaw drop in astonishment, and then quickly closed her mouth with a snap of her teeth.

"You go right ahead and teach Hannah to ride, start

your equine-assisted therapy. I wish you the best of luck. I'm sure you'll help many people."

"But I want to help you."

Hedy backed farther away. "I don't need help. I want peace and quiet in my final years. I want to leave my legacy to you, but if you don't want it—"

"Of course I want it." Lauren jumped to her feet. She didn't know how this could have gone so wrong. "Your heritage is my heritage. Hannah's, too. But we can have more many good, long years together right here in Wildcat Bluff."

"I may be strong and I may be courageous, but there's nothing on this good, green Earth that could get me back on a horse again. I've got what I've got and I'm thankful for it. I've lived a good, long life and I'm thankful for that, too."

"I'm thankful for you in my life." Tears blurred Lauren's vision as she stood helplessly looking at Hedy, one of the strongest, smartest, and bravest people she'd ever known. Suddenly she was struck by the terrible realization that her aunt was terrified of change. Hedy was afraid of losing what she'd built in life. She'd rather slowly slip into the sunset than risk what could make her whole in body and spirit once more.

"Go now." Hedy spoke in a clipped tone, as if she was barely holding her emotions together. "We'll talk more later. You're the child of my heart, but right now you've deeply wounded me. I always thought you respected me and my choices even if I'm confined to a wheelchair. Now I wonder about that fact."

"I do respect you. Perhaps more than you can ever realize. But I want more for you. I want to help."

"Go to your daughter. Show her what it's like to ride like the wind. I'll never know it again. And that's okay. I had my day, and it was a good one."

"But Aunt Hedy—"

"Please, leave me now." Hedy turned away and zipped toward the back of her store.

Lauren simply stood there, not knowing what to do. She felt tears slip down her cheeks, then wiped them off with the back of her hand. She straightened her shoulders, picked up her handbag, slung the strap over her shoulder, and marched toward the front door. When she reached the Bluebird of Happiness display, she stopped and looked at the cat curled peacefully amongst the beautiful glass birds.

Rosie raised her face, cocked her head, and twitched her ears.

"Take care of Aunt Hedy for me, will you?"

Rosie meowed, stood up, stretched, leaped down, and headed for the back of the store.

"Aunt Hedy," Lauren called, putting steel in her voice. "We're not nearly done here. Right now I'm headed to Sure-Shot to pick out a pony—and a therapy horse."

She waited a moment, but got no reply. "Okay. I'll see you later."

When she opened the front door and stepped outside, she caught the scent of pine and cedar drifting on the breeze. She inhaled deeply, as if drawing in the strength of Wildcat Bluff's founders and the powerful Comanche who'd made this land their home.

She walked over to her SUV and looked back at Adelia's Delights. Birds of blue glass flickered in the sunlight, reminding her that courage came in many forms, from tiny sparrows defending their babies to eagles soaring above the clouds.

Somehow or other, she wouldn't give up till she'd found the key to unlocking the courage that Hedy had shown throughout her life.

Chapter 25

KENT SAT ON A WOODEN BENCH IN FRONT OF THE Bluebonnet Café in Sure-Shot. He ate his butter pecan ice cream cone and felt like a kid again. Hannah sat beside him busily licking her strawberry ice cream and humming happily to herself. He enjoyed the companionable silence as he watched a faded red pickup hauling a horse trailer drive past on Main Street.

Hannah was opening up his life in a way he never could have imagined, no matter how many times Sydney had told him Storm was the best thing that had ever happened to her. Now he was beginning to understand the charm of a child adding so much to a person's life.

"Do we need to tell Mommy we had ice cream for breakfast?" Hannah asked in her sweet, high voice.

"Technically, it's not breakfast."

"It's morning." She licked her ice cream and left a smudge of pink on the tip of her nose. "I never get ice cream mornings."

"You do today." He picked up a napkin from the mound he'd set between them. "Lean over and let me get that ice cream off your nose."

She crossed her eyes as she tried to see strawberry on the end of her nose, tossing her head one way and then the other.

He couldn't keep from chuckling because she

appeared so adorably comical, but he laughed out loud when she stuck out her tongue to lick at the ice cream.

"Did I get it?"

"Not even close."

"I hate to waste ice cream." She looked down at his napkin, then back at his face. "I guess you better clean me up. Pink on my nose is a mommy no-no."

"Yep, it is." He quickly rubbed the little smudge clean. Last thing he wanted was for Lauren to think he'd let her daughter get as messy as his truck.

"Cowboy Daddy," Hannah said in a solemn voice, "you did that good. It didn't hurt a bit."

With those few appreciative words and the admiration in her big, brown eyes, Kent felt as if she'd captured his heart. First her mommy. And now her. He hadn't gotten that barbwire in place nearly fast enough if he still wanted to protect his heart. He wasn't so sure he did anymore.

As he finished off his ice cream and crunched down on the cone, he realized Hannah wasn't able to keep up with the melt. Pink was oozing down her hand and dripping onto her arm. She changed hands to lick the liquid off and smeared pink across her cheek while she accidentally tipped the cone and ice cream oozed out, over, and off onto her lap.

"Oh no, big mess!" She looked up at him with panic in her eyes.

He felt the same sense of panic. What was he going to do? She obviously expected him to fix the mess. He grabbed a bunch of napkins, but he didn't think that was the answer. He needed to turn a hose on her. A trip to the car wash would be about right. But he was sure those weren't the right choices, not when he'd have to explain his actions to Lauren.

He glanced outward, as if he could pull the right answer out of the sky. And low and behold, that's about what greeted him. He saw Lauren turn off the street in her SUV and park in front of the café.

"Hey, there!" She stepped out of her vehicle, smiling at them.

"Hi, Mommy," Hannah said in a small voice, glancing down at her lap and up again.

"You arrived just in the nick of time." Kent stood and gestured toward Hannah. "We had an accident."

"Mess!" Hannah smeared ice cream into her long, blond hair as she tried to clean her face.

Lauren chuckled and quickly walked over to them. "I can't tell you how much you both just lifted my spirits."

"That was my line," Kent said. "I'm clueless about how to clean up Hannah."

"It's a mommy secret." Lauren winked.

"Want a lick?" Hannah held out her cone with ice cream oozing down her hand. "Cowboy Daddy says it's not breakfast."

"Does he now?" Lauren glanced at Kent, obviously holding back a laugh at the situation.

"Yes, I do." He smiled, taking in Lauren's beauty like a brilliant sun rising at daybreak. "Morning ice cream. I'll treat you, too. What flavor do you want?"

"This morning absolutely screams for ice cream," Lauren said with a heartfelt sigh.

"Screams for ice cream!" Hannah giggled, shaking in mirth and sending ice cream droplets flying outward.

"I'd better take over here," Lauren said in a

humorous tone. "You get the ice cream while I do the cleanup."

"You got it."

"I'll take a double mocha chocolate."

"Good choice." Kent would've bought her a whole gallon in appreciation for her timely arrival, but he figured that might only cause more trouble.

"I bet some wet paper towels in the restroom will get the sticky off. A pass of her clothes through the washer later will do the rest." She took Hannah's cone out of her small hand. "Done with it?"

Hannah nodded, appearing relieved at Lauren taking over. "Cowboy Daddy got me a double."

Lauren smiled at Kent. "She's still on the small side for a double cone."

"Yeah, I can see that now."

Lauren tossed the messy cone in a nearby trash before she led Hannah by her sticky hand into the café.

Kent sat down with a sigh of relief. He wasn't ordering any more ice cream till Lauren got back. Who knew how long it took to clean up a little girl. Last thing he needed was another melting mess. If he wasn't careful, Lauren was going to think he didn't know how to take care of his life, or at least keep it in order. What with his messy pickup and all. Thankfully, he hadn't let her see the inside of his house.

He took a deep breath and leaned back against the bench, feeling the sun warm on his face. He was beginning to think raising a child might not be quite as easy as Lauren made it look. One thing was for sure, ice cream cones could be dangerous. He'd better stick with cups from now on out.

When Lauren returned a little later, Hannah looked a bit damp around the edges but perfectly happy.

"Where's my ice cream cone?" Lauren asked, putting a hand on her hip as if taking a tough stance.

He threw up his hands. "I wasn't taking any chances on melting ice cream."

She laughed as she shook her head.

"I'll get it and be right back." He almost opened the door, then stopped and looked back. "Cup okay?"

"Don't you dare! I want a waffle cone."

"Think you can handle it?" he teased, enjoying the challenge in her eyes.

"Maybe if you help me."

He rolled his eyes, feeling a surge of heat at the idea of sharing ice cream licks with her. He quickly opened the door. He heard her teasing laughter as he stepped into the Bluebonnet, knowing she was thinking just what he was thinking. At this rate, they both probably needed cold ice cream to cool their hot bodies.

Fortunately, there was no waiting because Elsie, the owner and server, was behind the old-fashioned soda bar. He placed his order, got his double-dip cone, and headed back. When he stepped outside, Lauren was waiting for him, a naughty smile on her lips. Hannah had returned to the bench and was swinging her legs back and forth as if there'd been no mess at all.

He walked over to Lauren and held out the cone, but when she reached for it, he pulled it back and took a big bite.

"Oh, you're bad," she said in a breathy voice.

"Want some?" he asked, teasing her.

"I do!" Hannah leaped up and held high her chin.

Lauren burst out laughing and he joined her. He quickly held down the cone and let Hannah take a big lick.

She gave him a grin, then plopped back onto the bench and watched traffic again.

"Are you two going to leave me any ice cream?" Lauren mock complained as she looked at Kent.

He held out the cone to her, wanting to see her eat it even as he knew that was going to make him hotter still.

"Thanks." She took the cone, suggestively stroking across his hand with her long fingers, then turned the ice cream and licked right over the spot where he'd taken a bite. She looked up at him, eyes dark with mischief and building heat, as she let her pink tongue slid up the side of the ice cream scoop and back into her mouth.

"I think I'd better thank you, too, for that fine visual."

She threw back her head and laughed at his underlying message. "Any time, cowboy."

"I'll take you up on those words later."

She simply grinned, then set about enjoying her ice cream as she tormented him with one lick after another.

When Kent couldn't take the torture anymore, he looked away and down the street toward the old Sinclair station. "I talked with Billye Jo about a pony for Hannah."

"Yay!" Hannah glanced up at him and grinned wide enough to show most of her white teeth.

He smiled down at her, enjoying her happiness. "Billye Jo said she had a paint pony—half-Shetland—that she thought would be perfect."

"Really?" Lauren finished her ice cream by popping the tip into her mouth and crunching down. "That's wonderful news. But will this horse suit my daughter?"

"Pony. Pony. Pony." Hannah jumped to her feet and danced up and down the boardwalk.

"Billye Jo said the pony is a mare of ten hands and doesn't buck, bite, or kick. She's been ridden by a six-year-old girl on trail rides and play days until she graduated to a bigger horse."

"Sounds perfect. When can we see the pony?"

"Billye Jo was coming to the Sure-Shot rodeo arena today, so she said she'd bring the pony with her."

"That's great. It'll save us a drive out to her ranch."

"That's what Billye Jo thought, too," Kent agreed.

"When is she going to get here?"

"Pretty soon. She said to meet her at the Sinclair station." He glanced down the street, but he didn't see anybody there yet.

"Okay," Lauren agreed. "Why don't we go ahead and wait for her down there."

"Suits me."

"Sweetie, come along with me now." Lauren held out her hand to her daughter.

Hannah stomped her foot. "I want to ride with Cowboy Daddy."

"You've already ridden with him," Lauren said. "You don't want to wear out your welcome, do you?"

Hannah shook her head and trudged over to the SUV.

Kent didn't want the little girl to feel rejected, but he didn't want to go against her mother's word either. "Hannah, you can ride with me some other time."

She glanced up at him, hope shinning in her big eyes. "For sure?"

"Sure enough." He opened the passenger door of his pickup, pulled out the booster seat, and carried it over to

Lauren's SUV. As soon as he had it correctly installed, he gestured for Hannah.

"Thanks." Lauren steered her daughter over to her SUV, buckled Hannah inside, and returned to Kent. "You've got a good way with children."

"I do my best." He smiled, deciding that if he hauled Hannah around much more he ought to get a booster seat to keep in his truck. A little red seat was a lot less than what he used to haul horses and cattle, so it wouldn't be much trouble. And its occupant would be a lot more fun. "Come on. Let's get down to the station."

"I'm right behind you."

Kent got into his pickup, backed out, made sure Lauren was behind him, and drove the short distance to the station. It didn't look much different than it had yesterday. Then again, he figured there hadn't been enough time to make many changes. He hoped the beauty salon worked out for Billye Jo's daughter. It was a good idea, and they could always use new businesses in Wildcat Bluff County.

He parked in front and stepped outside. Lauren pulled in beside him, so he walked around to her side of the SUV. She lowered her window and looked up at him.

"Any sign of Billye Jo?" she asked.

"Guess she could've ridden over since the arena is across the field behind the station. Let me go look."

She nodded, then raised her window again.

He checked the Sinclair station as he walked around the side of the building to make sure there was no sign of vandalism like they'd seen the day before. Wildcat Bluff Fire-Rescue hadn't gotten a call about any more fires, but he still felt uneasy that the firebug hadn't been caught yet. If some kids were simply letting off steam, then the fires might stop as quickly as they'd started and they'd never know who'd caused them. That'd be okay by him, if that's the way it turned out, just so long as the fires didn't escalate or do more damage.

As he walked around to the back of the structure, he smelled smoke. He quickly glanced around the area but didn't see anything suspicious. Maybe somebody was burning trash or had a fireplace going and the wind had whipped the smoke in his direction. But he didn't think that was likely, not with the trouble Sure-Shot was having with fires. Worst of all, Lauren and Hannah were sitting out front in a vulnerable position.

And then he saw smoke curling out around the edges of the back door. He ran over there. The door had been jimmied open before being shut tight again. An old building like this one would draw in oxygen like a bellows and feed the flames fast and furious. Far as he could tell, he'd gotten to the scene pretty quick after the fire had started, but a dry building like this would go up fast.

No time to call in help. He was it. One lone firefighter to beat back the flames and try to save Sure-Shot.

But first, he had to make sure Lauren and Hannah got to safety.

Chapter 26

Kent ran around the side of the building, hoping against hope that he'd be in time to control the blaze. He slid to a stop beside Lauren's SUV, saw her talking with Hannah, and pounded on her window with the flat of his hand to get her attention.

She quickly lowered the window, looking at him in concern.

"We've got a fire out back!"

"Oh no! What can I do to help?"

"Take Hannah to safety first." He glanced back at the structure and smelled smoke even stronger now. "I've got fire extinguishers in my truck. Good thing I had time to refill them after we used them at Bert's barn. Maybe they'll be enough. For now, get down to the Bluebonnet and tell Elsie to spread the word to the other business owners. If they've got extra fire extinguishers, maybe Elsie or somebody could bring them to me real quick."

"And I'll alert Wildcat Bluff Fire-Rescue."

"Good. A rig can't get here in time for the Sinclair station, but volunteers need to know in case the fire gets out of hand." He leaned down and pressed a fierce kiss to Lauren's lips. "Now get the hell out of here."

She nodded, then backed up and headed toward downtown.

With Lauren and Hannah safely on their way, Kent's mind returned to the fire. He jogged over to his pickup and jerked open the back door. He quickly pulled on his fire-resistant yellow parka and made sure gloves were in one pocket. He pulled a face mask out of another pocket, jerked the mask over his head, and left it to dangle below his chin. He zipped his parka up to his jaw and pulled up the hood to protect his head.

Now he wore as much protection as he had with him, so he leaned back into his truck, grabbed the two professional fire extinguishers, and slung them over his shoulders by the straps. He selected a military-type spade, snapped up the handle, and tucked it under a canister strap. He didn't have a hose attached to a water source since the building was still closed, but he might make do with dirt to smother the flames if he ran out of juice.

He glanced down the street where Lauren had parked her SUV in front of the café and was just running inside. Perfect. He quickly walked over to the station and checked the front. So far, so good. The structure wasn't pumping smoke out of the cracks around the bay doors. Yet it was only a matter of time before a building so dry and drafty with such an oxygen-rich interior would feed the flames till there was no saving it. Far as he could tell, the structure hadn't reached that point yet.

He jogged around the side of the building, checking out the corrugated tin that lined the roof and sides. Metal would help stop the flames outside, but he figured the inside would be mostly flammable wood. When he reached the back door, he felt the heat of the blaze as more smoke oozed out around the door and windows.

He coughed from the smoke, then quickly pulled up his face mask and eased on his thick leather gloves. He eyed the back door. He hoped there'd be no blowback when he opened the door and introduced extra oxygen into the structure. He had to be fast, whatever he did now. He stood to one side so he'd be behind the door for a little protection. He wrapped his gloved hand around the old metal handle and jerked open the door. No flames rushed out at him, so he looked inside. Fortunately, sunlight and firelight illuminated the room enough so he could see what was going on.

Greasy rags—maybe gasoline soaked from the smell—had been stuffed into three old oil cans and placed underneath an old schoolhouse-type wooden desk that was built solid as a rock. If the desk had been made of pressboard or other flammable material, the fire would already have consumed the desk and leaped to other combustibles. As it stood at the moment, the desk was only now catching fire and sending up swirls of dark smoke.

He slipped one fire extinguisher off his shoulder, along with the shovel, and set them down on a bare dirt patch. He stepped up into the structure, shrugged the other canister off his shoulder, and aimed the nozzle. He started to lay down a chemical containment around the outer edge of the fire, working as quickly as possible against the hissing and spitting of a blaze that fought back. Soon a finger of fire escaped and leaped up toward the wall. He caught his breath, knowing that a single stray spark could end in disaster. He turned the nozzle upward and sprayed the blaze repeatedly until it gave out. He felt sweat trickle down his face as he exhaled in relief. If he hadn't been there at that very moment, the building most likely would have been lost to the fire.

But that extra spurt of chemical had emptied the can. He quickly moved outside, set the canister down, and picked up the full one. He glanced around to make sure no other flames were in evidence before he walked back into the building. He checked his surroundings again, but the fire hadn't spread from the original area. He sprayed a complete containment field around the desk to limit the fire's ability to jump to other parts of the structure. He worked fast until he quickly emptied the fire extinguisher. He needed another canister, but he didn't have one, so he'd have to go with his backup plan.

He stepped outside, set the empty can next to other one, then grabbed the spade and dug deep into the clumpy, black soil. When he had the shovel piled high with dirt, he carried it back into the building. He was relieved to see the containment area was holding back the blaze. He dumped dirt on top of each oil can until the fires sputtered, gained strength, then sputtered and went out, sending up dark, acrid-smelling smoke. He sighed in relief. The desk was smoldering, but he couldn't see any more flames.

He stepped outside again, jerked off his mask, and tucked it in his pocket. He stuck his shovel in the ground beside the canisters and bent over with his hands on his knees as he sucked in a deep lungful of clean air.

"Kent!" Lauren shouted as she ran over to him with a fire extinguisher hanging from a strap on each shoulder. "Are you okay?"

He stood up, shocked to see her. "What are you doing here? I thought you were safely away with Hannah."

"I was. But you needed help. Sure-Shot needed help." She set the canisters on the ground. "I brought more fire extinguishers."

He grabbed her around the waist, lifted her off the

ground, spun her around in a circle, and held her tight as he set her back on her feet. "I don't know what I'd do if anything happened to you."

"I'm fine." She pushed back from him. "You're the one who has been in danger. Are you okay?"

"Yeah. I'm just catching my breath."

"That's a relief." She looked over at the station where smoke slowly curled out the back door. "What about the fire?"

"I caught it in time." He picked up one of the canisters she'd brought. "But I'm glad you brought more cans. We can use them."

"I'll help." She picked up the other full fire extinguisher.

"Come on." He quickly stepped back into the station and made room for her to join him.

"Looks like you did a good job with limited supplies." She walked over and examined the blackened area.

"I did my best." He pointed the nozzle of his can and sprayed chemicals over the dirt covering the oil cans. When he'd emptied the canister, he motioned for her to finish up the job.

She resprayed the containment area, slowly extinguishing the last of the glowing embers and putting a stop to the rising smoke.

He walked around the mostly empty interior of the structure to make sure he hadn't missed any wayward sparks that might later burst into flames. Everything looked okay.

"Thanks to your quick thinking, this Sinclair station still stands," Lauren said quietly, putting the empty can's strap over her shoulder.

"I'm glad we were here at the right time." He walked

back to where she stood just inside the open door. "You helped, too. Thanks."

"Odd, isn't it? This building has been hit twice."

He nodded, not liking what her words suggested about the trouble in Sure-Shot. "The fires may be random, but it's beginning to look like somebody might have it in for this station or the family."

Lauren nodded in agreement, eyes dark with concern.

"Come on. Let's get out of here." He wanted her safely away from the stench and the destruction.

She quickly stepped outside and set her canister beside his empty fire extinguishers.

He followed her actions, keeping an eye out for anything that looked like it didn't belong or that might help solve the mystery of the fire.

"I don't know how you had time to take Hannah to Wildcat Bluff and get back here so fast," he said with a puzzled lilt to his voice.

She appeared a little guilty. "Hannah's drinking lemonade at the Bluebonnet."

"What?"

"She's safe there. I didn't want to scare or worry her by rushing her out of the area in a panic. And I knew you'd get the fire under control. It couldn't have been a big one or we'd have seen more indication."

"True, but you never know about a fire." He frowned at her, wishing she'd done what he'd asked and yet glad she'd returned with the extra canisters.

"Besides, I wasn't going to leave you here alone, not when Hannah could be safe at the café and I could retrieve her in a matter of minutes." Lauren stepped closer and smiled sweetly up at him. "I grabbed Elsie's extra cans and slipped away while all the business owners were pulling out water hoses and fire extinguishers in case they needed them."

He couldn't help but respond to her luring him out of his worry. "You know I appreciate it, but next time—"

"I'll be better prepared as a Wildcat Bluff volunteer firefighter, won't I?" She chuckled as she leaned in close to him.

"You bet." He put an arm around her slim body and pulled her close, giving her a hard hug as much in relief that they were all okay as in a promise for more later. She also sounded like she meant to get more involved in Wildcat Bluff, and that set his heart to beating fast in anticipation of their future.

She snuggled against his body. "Guess I always wanted a cowboy firefighter of my own." She glanced up at him with a teasing light in her brown eyes.

"Guess you got one." He placed a kiss against her forehead, wanting to follow up on her words but knowing the time wasn't right. "For now, we'd better let folks know all is well here."

She sighed and moved back from him.

He pulled his cell phone out of his back pocket. "I'll call Sheriff Calhoun so he can come out and have a look. I'll also call Dune and ask him to come babysit the station till he's sure there's not going to be a flare-up. Plus, he's pretty good at spotting evidence."

"Good. Will Dune let Aunt Hedy know?"

"Sure. But don't you want to call her?"

Lauren shook her head, glancing away. "I'll call Elsie and she can tell the others that their businesses are no longer in danger."

"Okay." Kent wondered why Lauren didn't want to call Hedy, but he didn't figure it was any of his business. Anyway, the fewer calls they made the quicker they'd be done. He hit speed dial, reported the situation to the sheriff, and got Dune on the line while Lauren talked with Elsie.

When they were both done, he slipped his cell back into his pocket. As much as he wanted to stay close to Lauren, he needed to take photos and get a quick look around in case anything got disturbed later.

"Did you talk to Billye Jo?" Lauren looked at her phone, a puzzled frown on her face. "I tried earlier, but she didn't answer her cell."

"She'll probably be here any minute."

"I'll try again." Lauren punched in a number, listened a moment, then shook her head. "Still no answer."

"When she gets here, she won't like what she sees one little bit."

"But she'll like it a lot better than if she'd lost the building."

"True enough. Wait here a minute while I get my camera out of the truck." He quickly picked up the canisters along with the spade, then hurried out to his truck. He stowed the equipment away, jerked off the mask, and tossed it on the backseat. Finally, he picked up his camera and walked to the back of the building.

He searched the ground for something that didn't fit, but nothing caught his eye. He could see the area wouldn't be easy to investigate due to old detritus like rusted car parts, leaky cans, and shredded red work rags, but Sheriff Calhoun would need a report since the fire appeared to be arson. He took photos outside, then finished up inside.

"All done?" Lauren asked.

"Yep. I doubt there's much that will help us identify the firebug, but maybe something will give us a clue."

"I hope so."

A moment later, he heard the sound of a horse. He glanced up and saw a woman riding a bay across the field toward him. She led a brown-and-white paint pony.

"Now there's a welcome sight." He pointed toward the rider. "Looks like Billye Jo decided to ride instead of drive to meet us."

"Is that Hannah's pony?"

"I'd guess so."

"I'm so excited for my daughter."

"So am I."

She turned toward him, gave him a hug, and then ran to meet Billye Jo and the horses.

He couldn't help but smile at her happiness. No doubt about it, Lauren belonged in Wildcat Bluff County.

Chapter 27

Lauren could hardly contain her excitement. She was about to complete a promise to her daughter. Back in Houston, this moment had appeared almost impossible. But in Wildcat Bluff County, just about everything appeared possible. She took a deep breath to control her emotions. With the danger of the fire and the sight of Hannah's pony, she was bouncing between extremes. If she wasn't careful, she'd appear to be riding a sugar wave like Hannah probably was at this very moment in the Bluebonnet Café.

She stopped her headlong rush and looked back at Kent just to savor the moment. They were doing this together, another something she wouldn't have been able to imagine in Houston. She simply couldn't ask for a better friend in Wildcat Bluff, or a friend so hot he set her internal thermostat on constant high. But thoughts like that were for later. Right now, she wanted nothing but horses on her mind.

She watched as Billye Jo set her mount to a trot, quickly swept across the open field, and pulled her bay—a reddish-brown horse with dark mane and tail—to a stop. She tossed a leg over her saddle horn, leaped to the ground, dropped the reins in a ground-tie, and strode over to them with a big grin on her face.

"Did somebody order up a paint pony?" Billye Jo gestured toward the brown-and-white pony that now stood beside the bay. "Meet Spot. She's a good little pony for a good little girl."

"Oh, she's beautiful!" Lauren exclaimed as she hurried over to the pony with a long white mane and tail.

"Spot doesn't bite, buck, or kick."

"Perfect," Lauren said.

Kent walked over and ran a hand down the white blaze on Spot's long nose. "Fine-looking animal."

"Thanks," Billye Jo said. "Spot belonged to a little girl who hated to give up her pony, but she'd grown big enough to need a horse. Now she just wants Spot to have a good home and a loving rider."

"I think Hannah fits the bill." Lauren felt more excited than ever as she looked over the pony.

"I hope so," Billye Jo said. "Spot won't stay on the market long, so I wanted you to have first chance to snap her up."

"She suits me fine, but Hannah will have the final say." Lauren reached out and stroked Spot's thick, full mane.

"Spot's a pony who likes her apples and oats, don't you?" Billye Jo asked.

Lauren looked into Spot's dark-brown eyes that were much the same color as Hannah's. "If I don't miss my guess, my daughter will love you and give you lots of special treats."

Spot gave a soft nicker, lifted her head, and nuzzled Lauren's shoulder with her thick lips in a grooming gesture that revealed her acceptance.

"Looks like you've already made a friend." Billye Jo gave everybody a big smile.

"I notice you've got a blanket, saddle, and halter on

her." Kent gestured toward the tack. "Do those come with her?"

"Sure do." Billye Jo patted the empty saddle seat made of natural leather and decorated with fancy leather trim around the rim. "Spot's used to this saddle and it's a child's saddle, so it'll perfectly fit Hannah. We can adjust the stirrups for your daughter's height."

"She's tall for her age," Lauren said, "so I think we'll need to let out the stirrups."

"Easy to do," Kent said. "I can take care of it."

"Good," Billye Jo agreed. "Just make sure they're comfortable for Hannah."

"Will do." Kent reached over and stroked down the bay's nose. "What a beauty."

"Thanks." Billye Jo walked over and gave the horse a pat on his wide jaw. "Rowdy here is my daughter Serena's baby. They've run many a barrel together. I'm just giving Rowdy some exercise to keep him in shape till Serena gets home."

Kent reached under Rowdy's head and felt the gelding's throat behind his jaws. "Good size. He can draw plenty of wind when he runs, can't he?"

"You know it," Billye Jo agreed. "When Serena gets her business up and running, she plans to rodeo again."

"I'd like to see her compete," Kent said.

"And I'm sure Hannah will as well." Lauren stroked down Rowdy's long nose. "You're a handsome horse."

"Even better," Billye Jo said, "he's fast."

Lauren nodded in understanding, feeling happy to be around horses and equestrians again. She could hardly wait for Hannah to meet Spot.

Kent cleared his throat, glanced at the Sinclair station,

then back at Billye Jo. "I hate to be the bearer of bad news, particularly on such a happy occasion, but—"

"But what?" Billye Jo's smile turned into a frown. "Go ahead and spit it out. I can take it."

"You had a break-in and fire in your building." Kent pointed back toward the Sinclair station.

Billye Jo whipped her head around, gave a frustrated groan, and stomped over to the building's back door. She peered inside, checked the busted lock, and put her hands on her hips. "Well, I'll be hornswoggled."

"I'm so sorry." Lauren hurried to Billye Jo with Kent on her heels. "Fortunately, you'd planned to meet us here, so we arrived in time to save the structure. There's not too much damage."

"Thank you." Billye Jo shook her head as she looked around. "That old desk isn't much of a loss. We're fortunate Serena hadn't stored any of her vintage Sinclair items here."

"You're fortunate all the way around," Kent added. "But it's odd. Who stuffs old oil cans with greasy rags and sets them on fire? It's almost as if the firebug wanted a contained fire instead of a whole building fire."

"It is odd," Lauren agreed. "But that fire still could've burned down the station."

"All's well that ends well." Billye Jo turned to look at them. "I can't thank you enough for saving Serena's dream. She would've been brokenhearted if she'd lost this building."

"Glad we could help," Kent said.

"You know," Billye Jo continued, "somebody went to a lot of trouble to break the lock and start a fire inside.

I have to wonder if that dad-burned varmint came back to finish the job."

Kent nodded in agreement. "Do you have any ideas? Maybe somebody wants to cause you, your family, or Sure-Shot trouble?"

Billye Jo sighed as she looked out across the empty field in back. "I hate to say it, but I saw a tall, gangly guy wearing jeans and a blue sweatshirt walk across the field away from here when I was riding up."

"Did you recognize him?" Kent asked. "Firebugs like to hang around and see their handiwork go up in flames. I wonder if he was here watching when Lauren and I were putting out the fire."

"That's a chilling thought." Lauren felt a shiver run up her spine.

"Sure is," Billye Jo agreed. "Wish I could say for sure, but the guy was at a distance and I wasn't paying close attention. Still, he had a gait kind of like Moore Chatham."

"What do you mean?" Lauren asked.

Billye Jo gestured toward the horses. "You get real attuned to a horse's gait. You're watching for a rock in a hoof, a strain in a tendon, or a particular way a horse moves. Guess I naturally watch a person's gait, too."

"Makes sense." Lauren cocked her head to one side, looking at the horses and thinking about the importance of gaits.

"Who is this guy?" Kent glanced out toward the pasture in back.

"Remember River Ranch?" Billye Jo asked.

"Sure." Kent nodded. "Wasn't the owner about a hundred years old?"

"Something like that," Billye Jo agreed. "Anyway, he

up and died a few years back. His granddaughter and her son moved from Dallas back into the old ranch house. I guess they've been fixing it up, because it'd sure need it."

"Ranchers?"

"Don't seem to be." Billye Jo raised her shoulders in a shrug. "They don't seem to fit in real well here, or at least they've never returned friendly overtures by local folks."

"You think Moore might be up to mischief?"

"Maybe. Maybe not." Billye Jo looked back at the station. "You know, Moore was in Serena's class. I always thought he was sweet on her, but you never know about kids. Anyhow, they graduated a couple of years ago and went their separate ways."

"That's interesting." Lauren couldn't help but wonder if this was the key to the problem. Unrequited love could take unexpected turns.

"Any problems with him?" Kent asked.

"Not as far as I know," Billye Jo said. "Serena hasn't mentioned him, but she's totally focused on getting her business up and running."

"Sounds like she's got a good head on her shoulders." Lauren wished she could think of a way to ease Billye Jo's concern, but she'd done all she could for the moment.

"She does," Billye Jo agreed. "Look, I'm not putting this fire on Moore. He might have been in the wrong place at the wrong time, or that might not have been him at all."

"Don't worry. Nothing goes forward without proof. But a few questions might be in order," Kent said.

"I agree." Billye Jo walked over to Rowdy. "Heaven knows, this goes beyond vandalism. We better call the sheriff."

"Already done," Kent said. "And I let Wildcat Bluff Fire-Rescue know about the situation. Dune will be here soon. He'll keep an eye on the structure till Sheriff Calhoun gets here."

"Thanks." Billye Jo sighed as she glanced around the area. "I don't like to take chances, not with family, horses, or Sure-Shot. Guess we better start a local patrol in town."

"Bet the sheriff will have some recommendations, too," Kent said.

"I'll ask him about it." Billye Jo reached out and patted Spot's saddle. "Now, let's turn our minds to happier thoughts. Where's Hannah?"

"I left her at the Bluebonnet, so she'd be safe while we put out the fire," Lauren explained.

"Well then, let's don't keep a girl from her horse. That'd be plain cruel. And we don't do mean in Sure-Shot." Billye Jo grinned as she picked up Rowdy's reins.

"Suits me." Lauren was more than ready to introduce Hannah to Spot and see her daughter's reaction.

"Okay," Kent agreed. "Let's go around front. Dune ought to be here soon because he drives like a bat out of hell."

Billye Jo laughed. "That'd be like nobody else in Wildcat Bluff County, how?"

Kent joined her laughter. "Guess we're all guilty of pushing the speed limit sometimes."

"But not when we've got a child in our vehicles." Lauren clasped Kent's hand to make her point.

"You know it." He squeezed her fingers in response. "In Wildcat Bluff County, we take care of our own."

Chapter 28

LAUREN FELT AS IF SHE COULD DROWN IN KENT'S smoldering gaze. Everything about him, from his hazel eyes to his dimples, set her ablaze with a yearning so deep, so heartfelt that she wanted nothing more than to drag him off to the woods and have her way with him.

She swallowed hard, forcing her eyes away from him. She had to be realistic and do what mommies did best, and that was to take care of their babies. She'd brought Hannah to Sure-Shot to find a pony. The fire had interfered, but Kent had saved the day and all was well. Now was the time to refocus on her daughter rather than break out in a damp glow—as the term had long been used in Texas by ladies who preferred not to use the more descriptive term of sweat—because a hot guy had set her hormones on too hot to handle.

"Sounds like Dune just pulled up in front," Kent said. "He's got that big motor in his truck."

"Got a way with engines, does he?" Billye Jo asked in a teasing lilt.

"And gals," Kent added, glancing down at Lauren as if to warn her off a player.

She chuckled as they all headed around the side of the building with Billye Jo leading the horses. She kind of liked the idea that Kent might be a little jealous. She hadn't felt that way about a guy in a long time. Fact of the matter, she hadn't felt that way since she'd last been with Kent. Maybe some things never changed or died or got left behind through all the twists and turns of life. Like Kent. He just might be the one who stayed a lifetime.

When Lauren rounded the corner of the Sinclair station, she saw Dune—hot by anyone's standards with his shaggy, dark-blond hair and sky-blue eyes—step down from his white dually with the red-and-yellow racing stripes. He wore a tan cowboy hat with his starched and pressed blue shirt and jeans. With the extra tires, his truck looked like it could pull any heavy load.

She glanced from Dune's pristine pickup to Kent's blue truck that was already dirty despite being washed yesterday. Somehow Kent tended to attract dust like Peanuts' perfectly happy Pigpen, a cartoon character who traveled in his own cloud of dust. Lauren wouldn't tell Kent, but she found that trait just as endearing as always because it made him so very human in a world that too often sought perfection over connection.

"Glad to see y'all did my job for me," Dune said in his deep, gravelly voice as he closed his door behind him.

"You bet," Kent said, following up on the Texan's understated humor in a crisis situation. "Appreciate you coming over to keep an eye on the building for us." Kent gestured toward Billye Jo. "I'd like you to meet Billye Jo Simmons. Her daughter Serena is repurposing the old Sinclair station. Billye Jo, this is Dune Barrett. He's working out at Cougar Ranch and volunteering as a firefighter."

"Good to meet you, ma'am." Dune respectfully tipped his cowboy hat.

"Likewise," Billye Jo agreed. "I'm always glad to see a new face around here."

"Good-looking horses you got there." Dune cast an obviously practiced eye over the animals.

"Thanks." Billye Jo stroked down the nose of her bay. "I'm right fond of them myself."

Dune glanced toward the back of the building. "Do I smell gasoline?"

"Yep," Kent agreed.

"Another case of arson?"

"Looks like it."

"Got any ideas on the firebug's identity?" Dune's straight brows came together in a puzzled frown.

"Billye Jo saw somebody crossing the field away from the structure after the start of the fire," Kent explained.

"I can't be sure," Billye Jo said. "I saw him at a distance, but he did remind me of Moore Chatham."

"Sheriff will be wanting to talk with you," Dune said.

"He's on his way." Kent glanced toward Wildcat Bluff as if looking for the sheriff's vehicle.

"Would you let him know I'm down at the Bluebonnet when he gets here?" Billye Jo asked. "Right now I'm taking this pony down to Lauren's daughter."

"Don't let me stop you or slow you down." Dune patted the pony's head. "I'll be here, so y'all go ahead and make a little girl happy."

Billye Jo mounted her horse, waved good-bye, and led the pony toward the Bluebonnet.

"We'll see you in a bit." Kent nodded in farewell.

Dune doffed his cowboy hat to Lauren, gave her a big grin, and then ambled his lanky six-five frame toward the back of the station.

"Tall drink of water, isn't he?" Lauren couldn't help but watch the hunk, knowing he could easily star in a gal's favorite dream.

"Too tall, I'd say," Kent growled.

She glanced over at him and saw the jealousy in his eyes. She stepped close to him, lifted up on her toes, and placed a kiss on his lips. "Way too tall. You're just right."

"I better be." He gave her a sizzling kiss before he stepped back. "I hate to say it, but we better go. Hannah's waiting."

She smiled as she wiped away the hint of lip gloss she'd left on his mouth, thinking how much she liked a man who put her child first. "Let's see how she likes her new pony."

Lauren quickly got into her SUV and glanced at the empty booster seat. She wasn't used to being separated from her daughter, but Hannah needed to grow and develop friendships so that she felt comfortable in a larger world. If not for the fires, Lauren would think Wildcat Bluff was the perfect safe place for that to happen. But the fires gave her pause, so until the firebug was caught she'd stay cautious.

She drove to the Bluebonnet with Kent right behind her. She parked in front and he nestled his pickup beside her. She got out of her SUV, not bothering to lock it as she was relearning to do in Wildcat Bluff County. Kent joined her in front of the café and clasped her hand as Billye Jo rode up with Spot.

"I can't wait to see Hannah's face," Kent said in a low voice, squeezing Lauren's hand.

"Me too. I'm so excited to make her dream a reality."

She let go of his hand and opened the door to the café. "If y'all will wait here, I'll get Hannah."

She took a deep breath before she stepped inside the Bluebonnet, feeling concerned that Hannah wouldn't like her pony. Maybe the pony would appear too small or not the right color or some other reason she couldn't imagine right now. She shut down those thoughts. She'd come all the way from Houston to give Hannah the opportunity to expand and grow and experience a bigger world. And that included becoming a cowgirl.

Lauren glanced around to see if anything had changed while she'd been gone from the county. Earlier she'd been too distracted with Hannah to notice. Now she was happy to see the café looked much the same as when it'd been updated and upgraded in the fifties. The interior was still all chrome, red vinyl booths and barstools, gray linoleum floor, and rough wood walls decorated with framed photos of veterans and rodeo winners, both considered defenders of Sure-Shot values.

A few folks sat at several of the chrome-framed tables with laminate surfaces and matching chrome chairs with red vinyl seats. A glossy black-and-white poster of Annie Oakley in a fancy cowgirl costume with a smoking Colt .45 in each hand graced the wall behind the long counter. On a round stool with a tall glass in front of her sat Hannah gazing up at the photo in rapt attention.

Lauren smiled at the sight of her contented daughter and nodded at Elsie, who stood with her hip cocked at one table while she took an order on a pad with a pencil. She wore cat-eye, rhinestone eyeglasses and her bright-red hair was pulled back in a curly ponytail. She'd squeezed her long-limbed body into a lilac tunic matched with hot-pink leggings and purple cowgirl boots.

Elsie grinned at Lauren, revealing bright-white teeth. “Your little darlin’ is still sitting safely right where you left her.” She laughed in a deep, husky tone. “All that sugar today and she probably won’t sleep for a week. Just warning you.”

“Thanks, Elsie. I’ll take over now.”

“Bring her back any time. We’ve talked cowgirls nonstop.”

“Mommy,” Hannah called as she swiveled around on the barstool. “Look at that lady!” She pointed at Annie Oakley. “She can ride standing on the back of a horse and shoot targets at the same time.”

“That’s right,” Elsie agreed. “Annie wasn’t called ‘Little Miss Sure Shot’ for nothing. She wowed the Queen of England and others in Europe back in her day.”

Hannah giggled at Elsie’s words.

Elsie gave a sharp nod. “One look at Annie’s can-do American spirit and those folks knew they’d met a real, honest-to-goodness queen of the Wild West.”

“That’s me!” Hannah clapped her small hands together. “Only, may I be a princess?”

Elsie adjusted her snazzy glasses. “Darlin’, you’re a United States of America citizen, and that means you can be anything you want to be. Princess. Queen. President. You name it.”

When Elsie received a round of applause from her diners, she raised her chin. “That goes for all of you. I’m here in Sure-Shot because it’s the best place in the world for me. And I’m putting my MBA to work by running my very own business.”

"And we're mighty grateful for that fact," one of diners called, "but do you think we could get our burgers and fries anytime soon?"

Elsie threw back her head and laughed till she wiped tears from her eyes. "Now that's one of the things I love about Sure-Shot. Nobody's allowed to get the big head around here."

Lauren couldn't keep from chuckling along with Elsie, smelling onions and fries and grilled meat in a place that might be considered small on a bigger stage but was as big as the heart of Texas. She knew she'd done exactly right to come home as she looked at her adorable daughter. Hannah was perfectly content sitting at a counter with strangers all around her while drinking lemonade and deciding to be a princess.

She'd been worried for so long that Hannah would never come out of her shell from the loss of her father. Now that worry was slowly but surely being put to rest. Her daughter was blossoming in Wildcat Bluff. And nothing could suit her better.

"Mommy, do you want some lemonade? Elsie makes the very best."

"That's right," Elsie agreed, walking behind the counter. "And I'm serving Slade Steele pies made special for the Bluebonnet Café."

"How'd you manage that?" Lauren walked over, leaned down, and kissed Hannah's soft cheek. "I thought he was strictly working for Granny at the Chuckwagon Café."

Elsie flipped her long ponytail with one hand. "I have my ways."

"I'm sure you do," Lauren said with a smile.

"Honestly." Elsie turned serious. "Slade's reputation

for pie-baking is growing far and wide. If he doesn't watch it, he's going to have a business take off out from under him."

"Likc a mad bull?"

"If he can ride a bull, and that cowboy surely can, he can ride a business." Elsie picked up Hannah's empty glass. "I've already told him I'll help him any way I can to get his biz off the ground. You know, there's overnight shipping all over this great country. I might even be willing to throw in with him and add some items of my own."

"Sounds wonderful," Lauren said to encourage her.

"Truth of the matter, I want us to cater to the hipster market."

"What is that?"

"Hip millennials like quality over quantity. They'll pay extra for craft beer, gin, and vodka. Organic food and drinks."

"They aren't the only ones who like all that," Lauren agreed. "Folks such as Morning Glory got that ball rolling, didn't they?"

"Sure. But hipsters are expanding it now." She set down Hannah's glass behind the counter. "Slade's already making muscadine wine from his vineyard. We've been talking about him expanding his product and marketing it as craft. What do you think?"

"Sounds great."

"Thanks. We're just getting started here. Serena is going to get the Sure-Shot Beauty Station up and running pretty quick. It'll be fun for all of us."

"I'm thinking of starting something in our county, too."

"Really!" Elsie grinned in delight. "Great minds think alike. What are you going to do?"

"I'll let you know later." She glanced down at Hannah who was beginning to squirm impatiently. "Right now I've got a little girl who wants to see her first pony."

"All right!" Elsie leaned down and looked into Hannah's eyes. "Now, once you get your pony, you'd better get a tiara since you're going to be a cowgirl princess."

"Yeah!" Hannah leaped off the stool.

"Stop by and see me soon so we can talk business," Elsie said. "Folks used to leave our county to find work. Now we're creating it in our own backyard."

"That's great to hear. I'll be back to chat."

"See you later."

Lauren gave Elsie a warm smile, then took hold of Hannah's small hand and led her toward the front door.

Chapter 29

When Lauren stepped outside the Bluebonnet Café, she waved at Kent and Billye Jo, who looked to be impatiently waiting for Hannah.

"Mommy! Is that a real, live pony?" Hannah screamed in delight, ran toward Spot, stopped in indecision, and danced back toward Lauren.

"That's Spot, a fine paint pony."

"Spot! That's the best name in the whole, wide world. And she's the most beautiful pony in the whole, wide world." Hannah twirled around in excitement, eyes wide with wonder. "May I touch her?"

"Come on." Lauren clasped her daughter's small hand, feeling as if her heart might burst with so much love and happiness. "It's time for you to meet your new friend."

"Spot. Spot. Spot." Hannah danced beside Lauren, bouncing up and down in excitement.

"Billye Jo, this is my daughter. And Hannah, this is the horse trainer who brought you Spot."

Hannah stuck out her small hand, shyly ducking her head. "I'm pleased to meet you."

Billye Jo reached down and shook Hannah's hand. "I'm delighted to know you, too."

"Thank you." Hannah raised her head to look at Spot. "Do you think she'll like me? I'm not a cowgirl."

"I think she'll like you very much." Billye Jo squatted

to be on the same eye level as Hannah. "You see, Spot lost her cowgirl when that girl grew too big for a pony, so now Spot needs another little girl who'll love her and ride her and give her treats."

"I bet Spot's sad, isn't she?" Hannah straightened to her full height with determination in her brown eyes. "I may not be as good as Spot's cowgirl. I don't know how to ride and I don't have treats, but I'll love her with all my heart. And I'll do my best to keep her from feeling sad." She gave Lauren a worried look. "Mommy, isn't that right?"

"Oh, yes. And love is the most important part of all." Lauren glanced from her daughter to Kent and was rewarded with a slow, tender smile. If her heart had been full before, now it was overflowing with love. She felt proud of Hannah, who'd been sad for so long and now recognized how another could feel that same emotion. In reaching out to this pony with compassion, Hannah was also reaching out to herself as she moved into the healing process.

"I agree," Kent said in a voice gone deep and husky. "And soon, Hannah, you'll be the best cowgirl in the whole, wide world."

"Yay!" Hannah clapped her hands together, throwing off concern for excitement as she seesawed between the two emotions.

Billye Jo stood up, clasped Spot's halter, and led her forward. "Spot, meet Hannah. She's promised to love you and take care of you."

Hannah reached up and put her hand on Spot's velvety nose. She was rewarded with a burst of soft breath and an even softer nicker. "Oh, you're the best pony ever!" She threw her arms around Spot's neck and hugged while Spot turned her head, leaned down, and hugged Hannah back in that special way that horses show affection.

Lauren sniffed back tears of happiness. With so much love in Hannah's life, she would surely now leave her sad past behind and embrace her happy future in Wildcat Bluff. Lauren glanced at Kent, realizing that her daughter wasn't the only one discovering how much difference love could make in life.

"Horses heal." Kent put an arm around Lauren's waist and gently tugged her to his side. "Think how much good you're going to do with your equine-assisted therapy."

"What's that?" Billye Jo turned toward them. "Did you say something about hippotherapy?"

"Yes," Lauren agreed as she watched Hannah stroked Spot's long mane and murmur endearments. "I'm a physical therapist. I've had some training in equine-assisted therapy, but I intend to get a special certification."

"Lauren's got an idea to help folks in Wildcat Bluff County. I bet others will come here, too," Kent added with a touch of pride in his voice.

Billye Jo's eyes grew wide with admiration. "That's wonderful news. In Sure-Shot, we've been talking about training horses in equine-assisted therapy for some time, but we needed a therapist to bring our plan together."

"You've got her now." Kent dimpled as he gave them a big grin.

"That's terrific news." Billye Jo looked left and right, then leaned in close. "Nobody but a few of us know this, but I've got a hippotherapy-certified horse right now."

"Really? I'm thrilled to hear it." Lauren felt her heart speed up with excitement. Hedy wouldn't need to wait for an appropriate horse.

"You're a sly one." Kent chuckled with good humor.

"Well, I wanted to see if I could do it. And I did." Billye Jo grinned, looking pleased with her accomplishment.

"Is your certified horse for sale?" Lauren asked, hoping she could afford the probably steep price.

"Nope."

Lauren felt deflated, realizing she might not be able to get Hedy help as quickly as she'd thought.

"But he can be borrowed."

"That'll work, too." Lauren felt a great sense of relief, not only for Hedy but for Hannah, who was now pressing kisses down Spot's long nose.

"Where are you going to be setting up shop?" Billye Jo asked.

"My place," Kent said. "At least for now. I've got that empty barn just waiting to be used again."

Billye Jo nodded in agreement. "Tell you what, let me know when you're ready to start and I'll bring my horse over."

"Do you trust us to take care of him?" Kent asked, obviously serious about the responsibility.

"Sure do." Billye Jo put her hands on her hips. "Besides, I plan to be there plenty to learn and help out."

"Thank you." Lauren felt almost overwhelmed by everyone's generosity, but she still didn't want impose on them. "I don't want you to feel obligated to volunteer so much. I'm happy to pay you for the use of your horse and your expertise."

"Won't hear a word of it." Billye Jo shook her head.

"We're all learning at this stage. If we get this up and running, there'll be plenty to keep us going and help others at the same time. There are always horse folks, along with their horses, who can use work."

"Thanks." Lauren glanced over at Hannah, who was hugging Spot again. "But I'm definitely paying you for Spot."

"That's a deal because the money goes to a little cowgirl's college fund. I'm just handling the sale for her family."

"Be sure to let her know how happy Hannah is with Spot." Lauren had a sudden thought. "And let her know she's welcome to come and visit her former pony anytime she'd like."

"That's right generous," Billye Jo said, smiling. "I'll let her family know."

Kent gestured toward Hannah. "Maybe she'd like to take her first ride as a cowgirl."

Lauren grinned with happiness. "Hannah, would you like to sit in the saddle?"

Hannah stepped back and whirled around. "Now?"

"Sure," Lauren agreed.

"But how will I get up there?"

Kent walked over to her. "If you'll allow me, I'll lift you up and set you in the saddle."

Hannah's eyes grew big. "She won't run away with me, will she?"

"No," Billye Jo said. "I'll hold her halter."

"And I'll keep my hands on the saddle," Kent added. "When you want to get down, just let me know."

"Mommy?"

"I'll be right here." Lauren walked over and gave her

daughter a hug. "You're a big girl now that you've got your very own pony friend."

"Okay." Hannah held up her arms to Kent. "Cowboy Daddy, I'm ready to ride."

Lauren watched while Billye Jo took hold of Spot's bridle. Kent gently lifted Hannah and set her in the saddle with her feet hanging well below the stirrups. She grabbed the saddle horn and held on as if for dear life. Lauren suppressed a chuckle at her daughter's reaction, wondering if she'd reacted the same way when she'd first been put on the back of a horse. Probably so.

"Mommy! I'm riding a horse."

"You look just like a cowgirl."

"I am a cowgirl!"

"That's right," Kent quickly agreed.

"You look mighty fine," Billye Jo added.

"Hold still and I'll get your photo." Lauren pulled out her phone and snapped several quick shots. Now she'd have a photo of this miraculous moment to keep and to share. She quickly texted a copy to her parents so they could share in this wonderful moment.

About that time, several people pushed open the front door of the Bluebonnet Café and stepped outside. They waved at Hannah, laughing in enjoyment at the sight.

Hannah waved back. "I'm a cowgirl!"

One of the diners gave Hannah a thumbs-up before the group walked toward a pickup and got inside.

Lauren felt tears sting her eyes. Her daughter—who'd been so withdrawn for so long—was actually talking to strangers. And she was even proclaiming herself to be exactly what she'd wanted to be for so long. Life in Wildcat Bluff was definitely going in the right direction.

"Guess we'd better save more horseback riding for the arena at home," Kent said. "Pretty quick, we'll be putting on a show for the whole town."

Billye Jo laughed. "I kind of doubt it. If they've seen one horseback rider, they've seen a million."

"But they haven't seen me!" Hannah exclaimed, raising her fist in the air. "Look, Cowboy Daddy, I'm the best cowgirl ever."

"That's right," Lauren agreed. "But for now, let's go home so Billye Jo can bring Spot to the ranch later."

"Now?" Hannah looked downcast.

"Don't you want to have Spot at home?" Kent asked, stroking her long hair with one hand.

Hannah nodded, then reached down and patted Spot's mane. "Now you be a good pony till you come home. I'll get you some—" She stopped and looked at Lauren. "Mommy, may we get treats?"

"I'll bring some with Spot," Billye Jo said. "Is tomorrow okay? I think there's a cowgirl in town who'd like to say good-bye to her former pony."

Hannah suddenly looked contrite. "Tell her, please, not to be sad. I'll take good care of Spot."

"I'll be happy to tell her," Billye Joe agreed.

"Come on, let's get down." Kent lifted Hannah out of the saddle and set her on the ground.

She ran around and gave Spot a loud smack of a kiss on her long nose. "Don't be lonely now. You've got a good home."

Billye Jo held out her hand to Lauren. "Thanks. I'm excited to be working with you. Equine-assisted therapy. Just think about it."

"I'm thrilled to be working with you, too." Lauren

shook her hand. "And I've got someone in mind who'll greatly benefit from our services."

"Who is it, if you don't mind me asking?"

"I'll be happy to tell you later." Lauren hoped against hope that somehow she could get Hedy to change her mind. "First, let's just get everything in working order."

"Fine by me." Billye Jo picked up Spot's lead, then easily leaped up on the back of Rowdy. "Let's talk tomorrow and set up a time to bring the horses to your place."

"Sounds good," Kent agreed. "You know I'm living at the old farmhouse, don't you?"

"Sure do."

"Need directions?"

"Nope. It's been awhile, but I've been there."

"Good. See you tomorrow." Kent raised a hand in good-bye.

Billye Jo nodded, clicked to her horses, and started back toward the Sinclair station where Dune's truck was still parked in front.

Lauren glanced at Kent. "I'm amazed at how quickly and easily everything is coming together."

"That's because it's right." He clasped her hand with a gentle squeeze. "Like we are." He held out his other fingers to Hannah, and she trustingly grabbed his hand as she grinned up at him.

And Lauren felt as if she'd truly come home.

Chapter 30

Kent felt an almost overwhelming sense of protectiveness as he held hands with Lauren on one side and Hannah on the other. He'd had no idea he could become a family man so fast or want it so much. He guessed he'd put a family of his own on the back burner after Lauren had left Wildcat Bluff. Now he realized he'd wandered in a whole lot of directions till he'd come back to the one that felt most like home.

He supposed pride and youth could get in the way of a lot of sound decisions. He'd felt rejected by Lauren when she'd left, he realized now, even if the move hadn't been her fault. He'd run hard to fill in the space she'd left in his heart. He'd even tried to fill that gap with Charlene, but she hadn't belonged in Wildcat Bluff any more than he belonged in Dallas.

He knew he shouldn't rush Lauren, but it didn't feel like rushing her. He felt like he'd been waiting forever for her to come home. Now they both had baggage from their lives. He was willing to put his false starts behind him, but could she move on from losing her husband for a second chance? He didn't know, but he was willing to put everything on the line to find out.

"Ladies," he said, glancing from one to the other, "we've worn the morning away. How about getting some lunch, or dinner as we say around here?"

"Yay!" Hannah kicked up her feet. "Ice cream!"

Lauren chuckled as she shook her head. "I'm starving, but it's time for some real food."

"Stick to our ribs?" He smiled down at her.

"Perfect."

"Chicken strips?" Hannah asked, swinging Kent's arm back and forth. "Yummy!"

"Let's see what Elsie's got on the menu." Lauren pointed at the front door of the café.

As Kent started to open the door, he heard the loud rumble of a truck's engine as it came to a stop in the parking lot. He glanced over and saw a King Ranch pickup painted smoky gray with embossed, black leather seats inside. A couple of rifles stretched in holders across the back window.

Kent would recognize that fancy, one-of-a-kind, clean-as-a-whistle truck anywhere. The Holloway family lived in high clover. Not that Kent was against anybody living life high on the hog, not when they'd earned it fair and square. What concerned him, as a volunteer firefighter, was the string of fires associated with Holloway buildings. All in all, he gave the family a wide berth while remaining on friendly terms.

Kent hesitated, wanting to go inside and avoid the Holloways but knowing it'd be rude to ignore them. Besides, he'd been raised to be friendly the Texas way.

He stepped back from the door, angling Lauren and Hannah toward the pickup.

"What's up?" Lauren asked.

"Looks like we've got company. It's probably a good idea to say hello."

"Friends of yours?"

"The Holloways."

"I'll be happy to say hello."

Kent heard truck doors slam simultaneously as two tall men stepped down from the pickup. Both were good-looking guys wearing Western-cut suits—one in navy and the other in charcoal—with Zuni inlay silver-and-turquoise bolo ties, expensive ostrich cowboy boots, and rancher-style gray cowboy hats. Bert had thick, dark hair streaked with silver while Bert Two's hair was still dark brown. They both had tanned skin from time spent golfing and hunting in the sun.

"Kent Duval!" Bert called jovially. "You're just the man I want to see."

"Really?"

"Yep." Bert quickly walked over and held out his hand. "I can't thank you and our firefighters enough for putting out that blaze on our property."

Bert Two stepped beside his dad and held out his hand, too. "Fine job. Thanks."

Kent shook both their hands, quick, hard, get-it-done movements.

Bert Two tipped his hat. "And who are these two lovely ladies?"

"Looks like you've come up in the world," Bert quickly agreed, tipping his own hat.

Hannah tugged on Kent's hand and when he looked down, she raised her arms to be picked up. As Morning Glory would say, she must not like the vibes. He quickly raised her and she wrapped her arms around his neck and laid her face against his chest. He patted her back, comforting her in a way he hadn't even known he could do.

"Now that's real sweet." Bert Two gave a big smile at the sight.

"Bert Two," Lauren said, drawing the Holloways' attention away from her daughter, "don't you remember me?"

Bert looked her over, frowning, before his face eased into a grin. "You've got Hedy's eyes! Darn tooting I remember you. Lauren, isn't it?"

"That's right! You grew up real fine." Bert Two grabbed Lauren in a tight embrace, hugged her hard, then set her back as he looked her over top to bottom again. "Real fine."

"You've got to admit Wildcat Bluff County has the most beautiful ladies on this green Earth," Bert said.

"That's the truth of it," Bert Two agreed.

"What are you doing in our neck of the woods?" Bert asked.

"She's visiting her aunt." Kent gave Lauren a look to let her know he wasn't willing to let the Holloways know about their venture yet.

"That's right," Lauren quickly agreed. "I wanted my daughter Hannah to spend some time with Aunt Hedy."

"That's good." Bert looked at Hannah. "Beautiful little girl. She looks just like her mother and aunt."

Hannah glanced up at him, then buried her face against Kent's shoulder again.

"Shy little thing, isn't she?" Bert Two asked.

"Sometimes." Lauren stroked a hand down Hannah's back. "She's not used to a lot of strangers."

"That's the way of children," Bert agreed.

"What brings you to Sure-Shot?" Kent protectively moved the conversation away from Lauren and Hannah. "Are you buying horses?"

"Not exactly." Bert pointed past the Sinclair station. "That old drive-in theater beyond the station came up for sale. Not much to it anymore, but—"

"We kind of like the location. And the vintage buildings," Bert Two finished. "And Sure-Shot appears to be getting its feet under it."

"So why not invest in a growing part of our county?" Bert asked. "A little bit of land, a few buildings, and who knows what we might do with it."

Kent felt a chill run up his spine. Two fires at the former filling station and a few fires in trash bins behind the downtown buildings occurred just down the street from Holloway property. He eyed the two guys with renewed interest. There'd been too many suspicious fires in their buildings while they were off fishing in Southeast Oklahoma.

"I heard there'd been a few small fires around here," Bert Two said casually. "Sounds like unruly kids to me."

Bert sighed, as if in exasperation. "I know what folks are saying about us, but I swear somebody's got it in for the Holloway family. I've told Sheriff Calhoun, but it doesn't do a bit of good."

"The fire department and the sheriff are doing all that's possible. So far, there's just not enough evidence to prove anything beyond arson." Kent hesitated, trying to smooth over the situation because he could feel Hannah tensing and snuggling harder against him. "I'm sorry for your losses."

"Thank you." Bert took off his hat, ran a hand through his thick hair, and set his hat back in place. "It's frustrating as all get-out, but I do appreciate your help and concern."

"Double that," Bert Two added. "Let's hope that local firebug doesn't get a mind to light up our new Sure-Shot property."

"Aren't they going to set up a watch?" Lauren glanced at Kent with an understanding glint in her eyes.

"That right?" Bert asked.

"Sounds like it," Kent agreed. "I hope they follow up."

"Good idea." Bert Two agreed. "Dad, we ought to ask them if they'll keep an eye on our property, too."

"We'll do it," Bert said. "Fact of the matter, we ought to get right on it as soon as we eat dinner. You'll excuse us if don't stay to chat longer, but you've got me worried about that old drive-in now."

"Don't blame you one bit. We were just on our way back to Wildcat Bluff." Kent gave Lauren a look to go along with him as he turned away from the café.

Bert tipped his hat to Lauren. "Now don't be a stranger while you're in town. And tell your aunt I'm always ready to squire her about town or any place she may take a fancy to go."

Lauren smiled as she shook her head. "I doubt I have to tell her. It seems you've been trying to get her to go out with you forever."

Bert chuckled. "Little lady, it *has* been forever, but I'm not a man who ever gives up—not when the prize is Hedy Murray."

"And Lauren, now that you're back in town," Bert Two said, "let's get together and talk about old times or new ones. Please give me a call when you get settled in. I'd be happy to take you and your adorable daughter to supper." He pulled a business card from his coat pocket and held it out to her.

Kent felt like growling and giving Bert Two what-for, but he held his peace because he had a little girl in his arms that he didn't want to alarm. Later he'd better not hear that Bert Two was trying to make time with his gal. Jealousy hadn't reared its head in a long time, but Lauren brought out all Kent's possessive and protective instincts.

Lauren smiled sweetly as she accepted Bert Two's card and put it in her front pocket. "Good to see you both again. Right now, I've got a sleepy child who needs a nap."

Bert Two nodded, tipped his hat, and opened the door to the Bluebonnet Café. "Now don't forget to call."

"And be sure to tell Hedy I asked after her," Bert added.

As the men disappeared into the Bluebonnet, Kent clasped Lauren's elbow and steered her toward their vehicles. He opened the door to Lauren's SUV, then gently set Hannah in her booster seat and fastened the seat belt.

She looked up at him sleepily. "Cowboy Daddy, what about my chicken strips?"

"We'll get you something to eat later." He leaned forward and pressed a gentle kiss to her forehead before he backed away and shut the door.

"Thanks." Lauren stood in front of her SUV with her arms crossed over her stomach. "You really have a way with her."

"She's exhausted and sleepy." He held out his hand. "Hungry, too."

"Same goes for me." She clasped his fingers. "I was looking forward to lunch, but I didn't want to sit down at a table with Bert and Bert Two. They're nice enough, but Hannah didn't need any more strangers today."

"I got that." He walked with her around to the driver's side. "Do you want to get food someplace else?"

She shook her head. "It'd be pushing Hannah too far. She's had a great day. I think I'll just take her back to Ruby's. We can get something to eat there."

"I understand." He did but he didn't. He wanted more from Lauren, and he wanted it now. "Look, could I pick you up later?"

She smiled, happiness lighting up her brown eyes. "Do you mean like a date?"

"That's exactly what I mean."

"Barbeque from the Chuckwagon Café?"

"And a trip up to Lovers Leap." He felt a scorching blaze rush through him at the thought of being alone with her in their favorite place again.

"Are we up to that much fun?"

"Why don't we find out?"

"I'm willing if you're willing." She squeezed his hand, smiling up at him, then glanced down the street. "Look, the sheriff's car is in front of the Sinclair station."

"Glad to hear it."

"Are you going down to talk with him?"

"I'd better. And I'll stop by the fire station, download the photos, and pick up new fire extinguishers."

"You'd best get on your way then." She hesitated, glanced back at the café, then at him again. "Funny how there've been fires near the Holloway's new property, isn't it?"

"That's my exact thought. I'll talk to Sheriff Calhoun about it again."

"Still, let's don't jump to conclusions."

"Wouldn't think of it, but it's something to keep in mind."

She rose up, pressed a quick kiss to his lips, and

then stepped back. "Now, be on your way before I kidnap you."

He laughed, pushing fingers into her thick hair to cradle her head as he gazed down at her. "If you want to kidnap me, I won't fight you."

She covered his hand with her fingers and leaned her face in and kissed his palm. "If I'm going to kidnap you, better bring your sleeping bag tonight."

He chuckled, feeling hotter at her words. "Guess a well-prepared cowboy firefighter's equipment should include a sleeping bag."

"That's right. I'd expect him to always be ready to fight a fire or satisfy a gal in need."

"Are you in need?"

She pressed her face to his cheek so she could whisper in his ear. "I've been in need since the first moment I saw you at the fire station."

He felt her body tremble down the entire length of him, making him feel even wilder for her. "Tonight, be ready for me to meet all your needs."

She eased away from him, tossing an enticing glance his way before she opened the door to her SUV and slipped inside.

He quickly shut her door and stepped back, knowing he'd be counting the minutes till that evening.

Chapter 31

LAUREN SAT IN THE GARDEN ROOM AT TWIN OAKS, swinging back and forth, as she waited for Kent to pick her up. *For their date.* How many years had it been since she'd waited with this same sense of expectation? How much water had gone under the bridge for both of them? How many disappointments had they overcome and how many victories had they won to be here in this time and place? *Together again.*

She felt as if she'd been given a second chance at life. Kent was a big part of that second chance, but Wildcat Bluff and Sure-Shot with Hedy, Morning Glory, Ruby, Billye Jo, Elsie, Slade, Sydney, Dune, Trey, and so many more had welcomed her and Hannah with open arms and loving hearts. She felt truly blessed with her family and friendships.

She'd talked with her parents earlier, catching them up on her exciting news. They'd loved the photo of Hannah on horseback. Hannah had told them all about ice cream and pony experiences. Everybody had laughed together, sharing their lives even though they were separated by many miles. She hadn't told her parents about her disagreement with Hedy regarding hippotherapy because she hoped to have that resolved in a positive way soon.

After hearing all the good news, her mom and dad were talking about coming for a visit soon and about how much they missed Hedy, as well as their old friends. Lauren hoped that if everything worked out here maybe her parents would eventually move back. Wildcat Bluff could be a great place to retire. Yet that was for the future. For now, she wanted to focus on the present.

Hannah had pouted that she couldn't go tonight, but Ruby had promised they'd bake brownies and read a new book. Lauren felt a little guilty since she hadn't been separated often from Hannah in her short life. Yet Ruby had encouraged Lauren to go ahead and take advantage of a ready babysitter, particularly since it meant getting out and having fun with her former sweetheart.

So here Lauren sat wearing soft jeans, long-sleeve crimson T-shirt, jean jacket, and red moccasins. Most likely the weather would turn cooler later, but she doubted that she'd get very cold with Kent nearby. That image set a smile to her lips and she leaned forward to look out the sliding glass doors at Cougar Lane in hopes of seeing Kent's pickup. But the road was still empty.

She sank back against the wooden swing, taking a moment to catch her breath and collect her thoughts. Ruby was giving Hannah a bath upstairs, so her daughter was happy, and that always came first.

She hadn't let any grass grow under her feet since she'd returned to Twin Oaks that afternoon. While Hannah had napped, she'd gone online and ordered hippotherapy equipment to be shipped overnight to Kent's farmhouse. Billye Jo would bring the horse and pony to Kent's barn in the morning. With the horse, equipment, and so much local support, Lauren would be ready for equine-assisted therapy tomorrow. Well, she'd be ready except for Hedy. That was her one big disappointment.

She opened her red purse on the seat beside her, pulled out her phone, and hit Hedy's number. She hoped her aunt would pick up this time, although she'd tried several times earlier to no avail.

"Lauren," Hedy said, sounding tired and listless. "I believe we said all we needed to say to each other earlier today."

She flinched at her aunt's tone of voice, having never heard it before that day. "Aunt Hedy, you know I love you—"

"I love you, too. That's not what this is about."

Lauren took a deep breath to control her surging emotions. "I just called to keep you up with my hippotherapy plans."

"Why would you think—"

"Billye Jo has already trained and certified a horse. She's bringing him over to Kent's barn tomorrow."

"I'm not getting on a horse's back. Didn't I make myself clear?" Hedy said politely but firmly.

"Don't you want to come over and see Hannah's new pony?"

"You found one for her already?" Hedy's voice took on a sudden surge of interest and energy.

"Yes! Hannah is in love with Spot, a beautiful paint pony."

"Is Spot trained for a little girl?"

"Yes again. A girl just outgrew Spot, so the pony needed a new rider and home."

"That's wonderful." Hedy hesitated, as if thinking

through her next words. "Of course, I'd love to see Hannah ride her first horse."

"I know she'd want you to see her, too." Lauren hoped she could lure her aunt to Kent's barn with the new pony. "Billye Jo is bringing both horses over tomorrow."

"Well, I'll see. I'm pretty busy at the store and station."

"I know you are, but maybe you can make time. I'll let you know when they're at the barn."

"You don't need to—"

"Wait!" Lauren smiled as she saw Kent's blue truck pull up and stop in front of the house. "Kent's here. Gotta run."

"Kent?"

"We're getting Chuckwagon barbeque and going to our favorite spot."

"Bet I know where that is." Hedy gave a slow chuckle, as if remembering better times.

Lauren laughed, too, feeling a deep relief that her aunt was sounding more her usual self. "I bet you know the exact location of Lovers Leap."

"I wouldn't say yes and I wouldn't say no."

"By the way, I saw Bert in Sure-Shot today. He said to tell you hello and he'd be the happiest of men if you'd ever say yes."

"That Bert! He's been after me since high school. You'd think he'd grow up and give up."

Lauren laughed harder. "I don't think that's ever going to happen. He's sure got an eye for you."

"Go on now. He probably can't half see nowadays."

"I wouldn't count on it. And don't be surprised if he stops in at the store tomorrow."

"Please. That man must have the biggest collection

of bluebirds in the county. I can't think what he's doing with them."

Lauren grinned, shaking her head at her aunt's denseness. "He's trying to get you to go out with him."

"By buying bluebirds?" Hedy sounded sincerely puzzled at the idea. "That'd sure be a roundabout way of going about it."

Lauren glanced up when she heard a tap on the sliding glass door. Kent stood outside, looking good in crisp, pressed jeans, blue-and-white-striped pearl-snap shirt, and buff cowboy boots. She gave him a big grin while holding up one finger to wait a moment. "Aunt Hedy, why don't you cut Bert some slack?"

Hedy chuckled. "He gets on my last nerve, but I'll sell him another bluebird if he's so inclined to want one."

"There you go. As for me, I've got a good-looking cowboy firefighter standing outside looking ready, willing, and able to take me out."

"I'd say," Hedy lowered her voice to a whisper, "let him take you to the moon."

Lauren burst out in laughter, feeling relieved that she and Hedy were beginning to return to their old comradery.

"For now, I'm going to take these poor, old, tired bones to bed. You have fun." And Hedy quickly hung up.

"See you tomorrow," Lauren said to empty air, but she hoped against hope that her words came true. She felt sure if she could get her aunt back on a horse, she wouldn't hear any more about "poor, old, tired bones." Still, that was for another day. Tonight was reserved for Kent alone.

She quickly clicked off her cell, slipped it back in her purse, slung her bag over her shoulder, and stood up. A trip to the moon didn't sound half bad. And she figured Kent was just the guy to take her there.

When she slid open the door and stepped outside, he snagged her around the waist and pulled her close. She caught his fresh scent of citrus shampoo with a hint of leather and sage. Yum. He smelled good enough to lick all over and come back for more. Surprisingly, she giggled like a teenager at the thought.

"Want to share your humor?" He nuzzled her hair. "You sure do smell good."

She chuckled again. "That's what I was thinking about you. Mine's lavender. What's yours?"

"Who knows? Morning Glory mixes up a batch when she takes a notion and thrusts it on me. Wouldn't dare not use it."

Lauren laughed harder. "She's got you hornswoggled, doesn't she?"

"Me? I'm not alone. That goes for the whole town. No, make that the whole county."

"I hope she blends something special for me."

"Somehow I don't think that'll be a problem."

"Great!" Lauren hugged him, glancing out at his pickup. "Did you wash your truck again?"

He draped an arm over her shoulders and led her toward his pickup. "Yep. I cleaned it inside and out. I've got the comfort of my favorite gals to think about, don't I?"

"Thanks. It looks good."

He opened the front passenger door. "Take a gander at the backseat."

"Oh, Kent! You got a booster seat for Hannah." She whirled around and hugged him again.

"I thought it'd be easier than transferring your seat back and forth."

She put a hand to her lips, holding back strong emotions. He'd thought about them while they were separated during the afternoon, going so far as to find a way to make their lives better. And even more, he'd thought about their future and spending more time together. Maybe he wasn't so attached to his former fiancée after all if he could think about another woman, one with a child.

"What is it?"

"Here I was wanting you for your manly body and you go and make me think about wanting—"

"Wait. Back up. What was that about my manly body?"

She chuckled, rolling her eyes at him. "I'm not saying another word or you'll get the big head."

"With you on my arm tonight, I can't help but be the proudest cowboy in Wildcat Bluff County."

"I bet you say that to all the gals." She tried for lighthearted since his hazel eyes had turned dark with intent. Now was not the time or place to pursue what was obviously on both their minds, no matter how much she was willing to go there.

He pushed her hair back behind one ear, then leaned down and placed a soft kiss on her cheekbone. "No other gals. There's only ever truly been one for me. I know that now that you're back in town."

"Oh," she said on a breathy note. She wanted to say more, but he'd stopped her thoughts in their tracks with those words. Could he be feeling what she was feeling, as if nothing between them had changed in the years apart?

"Is that all you've got to say?" he murmured against

her ear, and then gently nibbled the outer edge of the delicate shell with his teeth.

She shivered in response, feeling heat burn outward from her inner core to set her entire body on fire. "I wish we could step back in time."

"Tonight." He kissed her forehead, groaned with suppressed need, and backed up. "Tonight we'll make the lonely years go away. It'll be as if they never happened to us."

She sighed, wanting it to be so. "But what about our former—"

"Tonight it's the two of us. Okay?"

She nodded, tamping down her questions and concerns as her body continued to burn hotter with every soft word he spoke and every intent look he gave her.

He took a deep breath, as if to control his rising emotions, and dropped his hands to his sides. "Come on. Let's go get barbeque. It'll be dark before you know it."

"That's right. We always liked to watch the sun set over the Red River." She stepped up into his truck and sat down in an amazingly clean space.

He leaned in and gave her a brash, brazen look. "But it's what we do after the sun goes down that's got me in a rush to get to Lovers Leap." He quickly shut the door and walked around the front of his pickup.

As if time had melted away, Lauren took a deep breath, feeling all safe and snuggly and excited in Kent's truck.

When he sat down beside her, started his pickup, and gave her a big grin, revealing his adorable dimples, she felt like a piece of chocolate on steamy summer days—a soft, gooey, hot mess.

Chapter 32

A little later, Kent stepped out of the Chuckwagon Café carrying a bag of barbeque and fixings in one hand and two big drinks nestled in a container in the other. He frowned when he saw Lauren talking with Morning Glory on the boardwalk in front of his pickup. He'd asked her to stay in his truck so they wouldn't get hung up on their way out of town with folks in the café wanting to say hello, but he might as well have saved his breath because she'd been caught in Old Town anyway.

As he walked up to them, he saw Morning Glory point at the closed sign on the front door of Adelia's Delights, then point at Lauren. He'd never seen Morning Glory act so intense because she was always laid-back. He perked up his ears to hear their conversation.

"I don't care if you have to drag Hedy to Kent's barn kicking and screaming, you find a way to do it," Morning Glory said in a decisive voice.

Kent blinked in shock at those words, hardly able to imagine Morning Glory being so upset. He stopped beside them, looking from one to the other. "Ladies, don't let me interrupt, but sounds like somebody's got a burr under their saddle about something. Any way I can help?"

"Hedy!" Morning Glory grumped. "I swear that gal's got her head on backward. I'm counting on you two to set her straight."

"What'd she do?" he asked.

"It's not what she did," Morning Glory explained. "It's what she won't do."

"You lost me there." He held up his sack and shook it. "At the moment, all I know about is barbeque."

Lauren sighed as she looked heavenward. "I haven't told him yet."

"Why not?" Morning Glory demanded.

"There just hasn't been time."

"More likely you were putting your head in the sand." Morning Glory shook her finger at Lauren.

"You want to enlighten me?" Kent pushed for an answer.

"Hedy got all riled up when Lauren suggested she try hippotherapy, so Hedy came complaining to me that she wasn't going to do it." Morning Glory put her hand on her hips, necklaces jingling and jangling. "Like I was gonna support her malingering if she had an option to get better, even if it is a long shot. Quick as a duck on a June bug, I gave her a piece of my mind."

"How'd that go over?" Kent asked, shaking his head.

"About like you'd expect," Morning Glory said. "Made her madder than a wet hen. She stormed out of my store, closed her place early, and went home." Morning Glory clasped her necklaces in a fist. "Maybe I should've kept my mouth shut. I haven't walked a mile in her moccasins, so what do I know?"

"You know what we all know," Kent said. "We love Hedy and we want her back to her old cantankerous self."

"Maybe there's a better way to help her, but if there is, I don't know about it." Lauren gave a big sigh. "This is something I know how to do, and I've seen equine-assisted therapy heal others. Body and mind."

"Well, it sure as shootin' is worth a try," Morning Glory agreed. "Right now, Hedy's got her tail in a crack and she's not pulling it out."

"Not on her lonesome." Kent gave Lauren a sharp look. "I wish you'd told me sooner that Hedy had cold feet about hippotherapy. I would've talked to her about it today. Maybe I could've turned her head in the right direction."

"I didn't say anything because I was hoping she'd come around by tomorrow," Lauren explained with a shrug of her shoulders.

"Hah!" Morning Glory let go of her necklaces and flung wide her arms. "When has that gal ever come around after she got her mind set on a course of action?" She snorted indelicately. "That's why Hedy was a champion barrel racer. Nothing, and I mean nothing, got in between her and her win."

"If we could get her to bring that attitude to hippotherapy, she'd be a winner again," Lauren said.

Morning Glory slumped as she glanced toward Adelia's Delights. "Tell you the truth, I'm worried sick about Hedy. What would I do without her? Even worse, what would the town do without her? It just don't bear thinking on."

Lauren reached out and squeezed Morning Glory's hand. "Don't fret. I'm working on a way to get Aunt Hedy up on a horse again. We're not going to lose her, not anytime soon."

"I guess I need some of my own medicine," Morning Glory said. "I need to trust that all will be as it should be. And that includes my dear friend Hedy's future." She looked through the necklaces hanging around her neck, selected one, pulled it over her head, and handed it to Lauren. "See if you can get Hedy to wear this one. I imagine she's too mad to accept anything from me."

"She's mad at me, too." Lauren looked at the pendant. "A soaring eagle piece of horse harness hardware is just perfect." She looked up at Kent. "But you'd better be the one to give it to her."

"I'll try, but I doubt she'll set a wheel inside my barn now." He frowned at Lauren, feeling renewed frustration. "If you'd told me sooner, I'd have made a special trip to her place today."

"Water under the bridge now," Morning Glory said. "Let's go forward from here and see what we can do to persuade Hedy."

"Okay," Lauren agreed.

Morning Glory glanced at Kent's food and shook her head. "Regret I've kept y'all from your meal. It'll be cold now."

"No matter," Lauren said. "Barbeque's good hot or cold."

"True enough." Morning Glory glanced back and forth between them as a sly smile came to her lips. "Better get on your way. You want to get up on Lovers Leap before the sun sets."

"How'd you know that's where we're going?" Lauren asked.

Morning Glory chuckled. "Let's just say a little bluebird whispered in my ear." She whirled around in a flurry of colorful skirts, opened the door to her store, and glanced back. "Now don't be a stranger." And then she stepped into Morning's Glory and was gone.

Lauren turned toward Kent, smiling. "She almost disappeared in a cloud of smoke, didn't she?"

"That's our gal. You never know what she's going to get up to next." He walked over to his truck, opened the passenger door, and glanced up at the sky. "Come on. If the sun gets any lower, we'll be out of luck."

"We're never going to be out of luck." Lauren walked over and sat down inside. "Don't you know that?"

"That's exactly right now that you're back in town." He grinned as he handed her the sack and drinks.

As he settled behind the wheel, he noticed Lauren quickly set the two drinks in the cupholder in the center console. She put the sack between her feet, glanced over at him, and raised a shoulder.

"You aren't mad at me, are you? I mean about Hedy." She slipped the smoothly knotted macramé cord back and forth between her fingers before she draped it over the rearview mirror, where the eagle hung like a good luck talisman.

"No." He gave a big sigh as he backed out of the parking place. "I just wished you'd trusted me enough to share that bit of information."

"I do trust you. It's just there was so much going on, what with the fire and the horses and Hannah and well, I apologize that I didn't tell you sooner."

"No apology necessary." He reached over and quickly squeezed her hand. "I thought we were in this together, so any information about Hedy is vital in making plans for her."

"We *are* in this together, but I'm used to working alone, so you'll need to give me a little catch-up time."

"You've got all the time you want, just so it's today." He chuckled, gave her hand another squeeze, and gripped the steering wheel with both hands.

She joined his laughter. “I’ll tell you what, that barbeque smells so good I’m about ready to tear into the sack and start chowing down.”

“You’d start without me?” He glanced over at her sitting in the shotgun seat as pretty as you please and generating enough heat in him so that he might need to flip on the AC.

“You know I’d never start without you.” She said with a little bit of a growl as she gave him a smoldering look.

“Better put the straws in the drinks. I’m starting to need something cold.”

She laughed as she bent over, dug two straws out of the brown paper bag, unwrapped them, and stuck them through the plastic lids on the drinks. “What’d you get us?”

“Traditional Texas.”

“Sweet tea or Dr Pepper?”

“Which do you want? I got one of each to make sure you had your choice.”

“Don’t you remember what I used to drink?”

“DP. But I thought you might’ve grown up and want tea.”

She laughed again, then quickly slurped from each cup. “Yum! Maybe I’ll have both.”

“You’ve made them both sweeter now.”

She laughed even harder. “Sweet-talking man, you’re getting in bigger trouble by the moment.”

“I hope so.” He glanced over at her and they shared a hot, lingering look before he settled his gaze back on the road.

He left Main Street and drove back lanes till he hit the twists and turns of No-Name Road that gradually turned from asphalt to gravel to rutted dirt until it played out on the bluff overlooking the Red River.

Kent saw the familiar line of daffodils that always heralded the return of spring sporting their early yellow blossoms along the edge of the cliff. No one knew anymore who'd planted the daffodils, but they suspected an early Republic of Texas pioneer had brought a touch of home to join the native bluebonnet and Indian paintbrush of the Comancheria.

"Do you remember our favorite tree?" He drove across the dry, clumped grass of the flat land.

"How could I forget?" She pointed at an ancient oak near the edge of the tall cliff. "Our oak is still there!"

"It's just been waiting for us."

With a quick turn of the steering wheel, Kent backed up under their tree. Its spreading limbs cast long fingers of shadow from the slanting rays of the sun across the golden grass that spread out around them. He cut the engine, and silence enveloped them in the cocoon of his truck.

"Alone at last." He unbuckled his seat belt and glanced over at her. "Does this feel like old times?"

She looked all around, then back at him. "Old times, but new times, too."

"Hungry?"

"Starving."

"If you'll get the food, I'll get the yoga mats and sleeping bags for the bed of the pickup."

"Yoga mats? Sounds like we're getting fancy."

He chuckled as he opened his door. "Comfy, that's all."

"I never complain about comfort."

He stepped outside, opened the back door of his truck,

and slid out two yoga mats, two sleeping bags, four pillows, and several towels. He carried the pile to the back of his pickup, tossed them in the open flatbed, and lowered the tailgate. He went back and picked up an ice chest that he'd loaded with bottles of water and Dr Pepper.

Lauren walked around the truck, carrying the barbeque. She set the sack in the back of the pickup, then moved to the edge of the cliff. She looked down, then back at him. "It's beautiful here."

He joined her and put an arm around her waist to hold her close. "Peaceful and quiet, too, except for the sounds of nature. Just listen to the frogs singing their nightly song down by the river."

"I've missed it all." She snuggled close to him, leaning her head against his chest.

He stroked up and down her upper arm, feeling her slender yet strong shape under her T-shirt's soft fabric. He looked out over the Red River Valley with her once more as they had so many years ago.

With Lauren by his side, he felt renewed in body and spirit while he watched the rust-colored water sluggishly slide around sandbars in the twists and turns of the river meandering its way east. Across the river, the red cliffs rose up in Oklahoma, meaning Red People, a name chosen from the Choctaw Nation when their vast land in the Indian Territory was confiscated and turned into a state, much as Kent's own Comanche ancestors had lost their huge track of territory. But the Choctaw, like the Comanche, still watched over and protected their ancestral land and people just as they had always done, so that in the end nothing had changed except the names.

As Kent watched, he felt as if he'd stepped back

in time not only with Lauren but with his ancestors as well. The sun cast one last ray of brilliant light across the river until a snake of glowing crimson connected the old Indian Territory with the older Comancheria.

And then the light went out and they were enveloped in darkness.

Chapter 33

Lauren felt as if a cape had been cast over the land as the sun disappeared and they were blanketed in darkness. And in that moment, all around her turned silent as frogs stopped singing, birds on their nighttime perches went still, and the rustle of insects and small critters in the grass stopped all movement. She shivered at the coolness in the air along with the lack of sight and sound.

Suddenly, soft light spread slowly across the Red River, turning the water into a bright, burnished ribbon of orange. Surprised at the sight, Lauren looked to her right, along the path of illumination, and saw the huge, round, orange moon rising on the eastern horizon.

As if the Earth had rested for the briefest of seconds after the sun set in the west, life suddenly burst forth again when the river shimmered from orange to silver as the moon rose in the sky. Frogs resumed their songs, night birds trilled together, coyotes yipped in harmony, and cattle mooed as moonlight spread across the Red River Valley.

"Ah, beautiful, enchanting muea." Kent squeezed Lauren's waist as he dipped his head in respect toward the rising moon.

"Muea?"

"*Muea* is Comanche for *moon*. Don't you remember?"

"I'd forgotten so many people in our county still speak a little Comanche."

"It'll always be our heritage." He leaned down and pressed a soft kiss to her lips.

She shivered again, but this time from his nearness and all he was saying without words.

He glanced over at the moon again. "Hope the cattle don't spook."

"Why would they?"

"A big, orange moon on the horizon can scare cattle. In old times, cowboys on a trail drive always kept an eye out for the moon. The last thing they wanted was a stampede, particularly after dark."

"Do you need to be back at the ranch?"

"Not tonight. Extra ranch hands are on duty on a night like this one."

"Good."

He gestured toward the moon. "Reminds me of the Comanche legend about how the moon got spots. Do you remember it?"

Lauren shook her head. "I don't think so."

"It's a long story."

"And it's a long night. I'd like to hear it. I bet Hannah would love to hear Comanche legends, too."

"Any time." Kent cleared his throat as he prepared to tell his story. "Once upon a time, Coyote warned the children to be very quiet when they walked through the territory of Peah Moopit, the monster of a giant owl. A little girl—named Hannah—did her best, but her baby brother cried and cried. Peah Moopit flew down from the tallest tree and kidnapped them. Hannah managed to escape with her brother. Yet Peah Moopit came after them. On a full moon night, the children ran and ran across the plains until they were worn out. Baby Buffalo found them and stepped in front of the little ones to protect them. Peah Moopit just laughed at the sight. 'A baby to protect babies. I will get you now!' When Peah Moopit lunged, Baby Buffalo charged and knocked Peah Moopit high into the sky, up and up toward the bright moon. Soon dark spots appeared across the white surface. And that is how spots came to be on the moon."

"Oh, Kent, that's a wonderful story."

"There's a reason for it."

"What?"

"Did you know the Comanche taught their babies never to cry or make loud sounds because their noise could endanger the entire village? Comanche children were always quiet so as not to draw attention to their people."

"Unlike kids today."

"True. But nowadays, noise isn't a matter of life and death."

"I'm glad we live in a world where our children are safe."

"The Comanche were willing to pay whatever price it took to keep their families safe." He pulled Lauren into a tight embrace. "That's the world I want for Hannah. And my children."

Lauren leaned into him, feeling his warmth and strength and determination. "I'm so glad I came home."

"We need you here." He tightened his grip. "I need you."

She reached up and wound her arms around his neck, tugging his face toward her. "No more than I need you."

He kissed her, a light touch rather than hard heat, and raised his head. "If I'm moving too fast, tell me. I can slow down. Well, I think I can."

She felt warmth spread from her heart, radiating outward until her entire body felt ablaze. “If you slow down, I may just have to knock you to the moon where you can join that big, bad owl.”

Kent chuckled, captured her face with both hands, and pressed his lips to her mouth. But again, he didn’t go further. “You want to go to the moon?”

“Only if it’s with you.”

He nodded, eyes shimmering like the river, then stepped back, clasped her hand, and tugged her toward his truck. “If we’re going to make a long trip like that, it’s time we got comfortable.”

“And maybe filled our bellies.”

“That, too.”

As they walked back to Kent’s truck, she dropped his hand and headed toward the passenger door. “I just remembered I left my phone in my purse. I’d better get it. With a child as young as Hannah, you just never know.”

“Good idea. You should be available.”

She tossed him a grin, once more glad that he so understood the needs of her daughter. She quickly opened the door, pulled out her phone, and tucked it into her front pocket.

“Grab the drinks while you’re up there, will you?”

She picked up the drinks, now sloshy from melting ice, and closed the door with her hip. “I’m guessing they’ll be kind of weak by now.”

“If you want, we can toss them and start with fresh ones from my cooler.”

“Let’s try these first.” When she walked to the back of the truck, Kent had already laid the yoga mats flat with the unzipped sleeping bags on top. “Looks comfy.”

"Better be." He leaned over the side of the truck, took the drinks from her hands, walked back to the cab, and set both drinks in the open ice chest. He looked back at her and gestured for her to join him.

She hesitated a moment at the down tailgate, thinking back to all those times they'd come out here when they were young. Somehow or other, she just didn't feel that much different, particularly not when she was with Kent.

"Need some help?"

"Maybe in fifty years, but not tonight." She turned around, used her palms to brace her arms, leveraged up, and sat down. "How was that?"

"Looks like you're as spry as ever." He sat down and leaned back against the cab.

"This is cozy." She walked back to where he'd piled pillows against the cab and sat down beside him.

"Best I could do on short notice." He tossed a towel in her lap from the pile beside the cooler on his right side. "That's just in case the barbeque gets messy."

"Thanks. It always does." She rubbed her fingers absently across the rough fabric. "I remember when you'd throw a few old quilts back here, along with some cans of Dr Pepper, and we'd be as happy as if we were rodeo winners." She adjusted the pillows behind her back and snuggled against him so that their bodies were touching all the way down to their feet.

"We were winners. And we didn't need any old rodeo to make us that way."

She felt her spirits lift at his words, and so much emotion flooded her that she didn't feel capable of responding with words. Instead, she clasped his hand and felt the rough calluses that hadn't been on his skin when they were so much younger. She rubbed her thumb back and forth across his palm, getting to know this small part of his body again.

"If you don't stop that," Kent growled in a deep, rough voice, "we're never getting to the barbeque."

She picked up the towel from her lap, slid it around his neck, and pulled him toward her by holding both ends of the fabric. "Do you care?"

"Hell, no. I was trying to be a gentleman."

"Don't." She tugged harder and was rewarded when he wrapped his arms around her and pulled her onto his lap.

She dropped the ends of the towel and snuggled into the warmth of his body, feeling a close connection like she hadn't since the last time she'd been with him on Lovers Leap. There'd been Jeffrey, but now she realized he'd only been a poor substitute for Kent Duval. And with that realization came the thought—rather the desire—that he feel the same about her.

"You've gone far away," Kent murmured against her hair as he gently stroked a palm up and down her arm in a comforting gesture. "What are you thinking about?"

"Me. You. Us."

"And?"

"You were engaged to a beauty queen, I heard."

"Flashy model."

"Same thing." She almost shrank in on herself at his words. "I'm not pretty like that."

"Shhh." He put a fingertip to her lips. "You're beautiful, both inside and out."

"But—"

He gave a big, heartfelt sigh, set Lauren back, and

looked into her eyes by the light of the moon. "I don't like to talk about it. But you ought to know. Charlene wasn't the love of my life. I guess she filled the emptiness for a moment—too damn long, if you want my opinion—and then she rode off into the sunset with a diamond rock on her finger big enough to choke a mule. Maybe that's all she ever wanted from me, but she couldn't stand the country either. I guess, in the end, she couldn't stand either of us."

"Oh, I'm so sorry." Lauren felt small for having pushed him into this confession. "You don't have to tell me about her. It's just that—"

"It's okay. People want different things in life. She wanted city. I wanted country."

"That's so true."

"Now, I want to know about your husband. Were you desperately in love with him and mourn him still?"

She buried her face against Kent's warm chest, feeling his muscles contract under her as if he were willing himself to stillness. "I guess my tale is sort of like yours. Jeffrey flew off into the sunset in a single-engine plane, plummeted to the ground, and never returned to us."

"That's not what I asked you," Kent said in a steely voice.

"Did I love him?"

"Yeah."

"Yes and no." She sat back up, holding their connection as if onto a lifeline, and looked into his eyes again. "We got married because I was pregnant with Hannah. I loved him for giving me what is best in my life—my daughter. But I hated him—maybe that's too strong a word but it's not far off—because he wasn't there for Hannah and she loved and missed him so much. Jeffrey was a player, as I found out later, and our little family was never enough for him. I guess, like your situation, we wanted different things in life."

Kent wrapped his arms around Lauren and held her tight, as if he could squeeze away all the old, hurtful memories.

"Hannah deserved better. I deserved better." Lauren realized that in Kent's arms she no longer felt her old despair over her failed marriage. "I'd already talked with an attorney about divorce when the news came about Jeffrey's death."

"Did you feel guilty?" Kent pressed a tender kiss to her temple.

"Yes. And I mourned what never was and never would be."

"And now?"

"I realize Jeffrey had to live on the wild side. He couldn't settle down to married life. It simply wasn't in his nature."

"Sounds like Charlene."

"Did she hurt you very badly?"

"She hurt my ego more than anything."

"Mine took a beating, too." She rubbed her face against Kent's chest, listening to the strong beat of his heart. "But I've worried most for Hannah. She needs love, family, friends, and community."

"She's got those here."

"That's why I brought her home. I wasn't sure it'd work, but I've seen her blossom in Wildcat Bluff."

"She reminds me of you."

"Now, maybe, but we were both sort of lost in

Houston. I don't know. Maybe it's something in the water or the land or the people. But for me, and now Hannah, this is the very best place on Earth."

Chapter 34

Kent gazed out into the night, realizing how much he'd changed since Lauren came back to town. "Now I agree, but not a few days ago."

"What do you mean?" Lauren lifted her head from his chest to look at him with eyes turned mysterious dark pools of silvery moonlight.

He tucked a soft strand of hair behind her ear, taking a deep breath as he considered his next words. "I guess I was pretty dense for a long time, or maybe just too young."

"You're confusing me."

"Once you left, Wildcat Bluff was never the same. I kept twisting and turning to make it right, but it just wasn't."

"But—"

"Wait. What I'm trying to say is that I realize now that you're home with Hannah that this *is* the very best place on Earth."

"Oh, Kent, that's so sweet." She pressed a hot kiss to his mouth before nibbling across his lower lip.

"It's true." He groaned as he felt a rush of heat spiral outward in a blaze of desire. "One thing for sure, I'm not feeling one damn bit sweet."

"Good. I'm not either. Or hungry."

"I'm hungry all right, but not for barbeque." He licked across her lips, tasting her tangerine lip gloss that made him want her even more.

"Oh, Kent, I just wish, I wish—" She clasped his shoulders and tugged him closer, as if she would never let him go.

"I know. I wish this was our first time. It could've been. It should've been."

"But we were waiting for—"

"We waited too damn long." He pressed hot, hard kisses across her jaw to her ear, where he traced the intricate scrolls with the tip of his tongue.

"But how could we have known Daddy would get that great job and I'd be gone in a week?"

"Just another year. That's all it would've taken. You'd have been out of high school and we would've gotten married right here in Wildcat Bluff."

"I know. And then—"

"I should've come after you."

"No. It wouldn't have worked, not after I'd been in Connecticut a year and we'd both moved on with our lives."

"I figured you'd taken to city life and wouldn't want a country guy anymore."

"Silly." She lightly bit the tip of his nose in a rebuking tease. "You're twice the man of any guy I ever met."

"And you're the love of my life."

"Oh, Kent, really?"

"Can you doubt it?"

"I love you so much. I've always loved you." She held his face with both hands and looked deeply into his eyes, blinking back tears of happiness. "Forget the past. Let's make this our very first time."

He crushed her to him, feeling his heart thud hard at her words. He'd never thought to have her love again.

Now that they'd given each other their hearts once more, he'd do everything within his power to make her happy. He couldn't go back in time, but he could make the intervening years a distant memory that no longer mattered to either of them.

"I want to see you," he said in a voice gone deep and husky with emotion.

She gently traced the contours of his face. "Don't you remember? You already did see me naked as a jaybird."

He chuckled, pressing a kiss to her palm. "That was skinny-dipping years ago."

"I'm plumper now." She pulled back and walked her fingers down his chest, grabbed a fistful of fabric, and jerked the shirttail out of his jeans.

"Good. More to love." He groaned at her actions, realizing she'd learned a thing or two over the years. Maybe he didn't want her to forget everything after all.

"You skinny-dipped, too."

"Did you look?"

"I'll never tell." She chuckled as she gave him a mischievous wink. "But now I definitely want my eye candy." She stroked her palms across his broad chest. "I bet you packed on more muscle since that time."

"Wrangling horses'll do that to you."

"Uh-huh." She gave a little, low growl as she walked her fingertips back to the top button of his pearl-snap shirt. "You know, they say these snaps were invented so shirts could easily be ripped off when tangled on barbed wire to save cowboy life and limb. But I don't think so."

"No?"

"Well, yeah, on one hand." She jerked hard and all the snaps popped open to reveal his bare chest. "But on the other, women were making clothes at home back then, so I've got an idea they made snap shirts so they could get their hands on their favorite cowboy faster." And she leaned down, hair cascading around her face, to press kisses across the hard muscles of his chest while she moved lower to toy with his belly button.

"Lauren," he groaned, unable to say more as he dug his fingers into her soft hair while she continued to explore his bare flesh.

If he'd been hot before, now he was on fire. He sat up abruptly, taking her with him, and shucked off his shirt. He tossed it toward the end of the truck bed and turned toward her. She was hungrily looking at his chest, shoulders, arms. He clinched his fists not to grab her and quickly ease the ache that was trapped behind his zipper. Yet he'd promised her this would be good, and he'd hold back till he kept that promise. But it wouldn't be easy.

"My turn." He reached out and tugged at the shoulder of her jean jacket.

"It's too cool to skinny-dip," she teased as she shrugged off her jacket and tossed it beside his shirt.

"I'll keep you warm." He grinned, thinking how much he wanted her, how much he'd missed her, how much he needed her. And more than any of that, now she belonged to him. And he'd treasure her. Forever. "Come here."

She shook her head, moonlight turning her blond hair a silvery hue, as she smiled mischievously and scooted back from him. She quickly pulled her red T-shirt over her head and lobbed it at their growing pile of clothes.

He caught his breath at the sight of the lacy red bra

that barely covered her generous breasts. If she'd been a handful when she was younger, now she was big enough to make a guy give thanks to the great goddess of women. As he watched, growing harder by the moment, she toed off one soft moccasin then the other to reveal long, slender feet. She glanced over at him, looking all soft and silvery in the moonlight. He couldn't wait a moment longer.

He lunged for her, caught her around her hips, pulled her toward him, and unzipped her jeans. "We better get these off you before I tear them to shreds."

She chuckled as she lifted her hips and allowed him to tug them down, down, all the way down to her slim ankles. He jerked the jeans completely off and tossed them behind him, breathing hard as he looked at her nearly nude body. She wore nothing but a little red lace that accented more than it hid from sight.

"Lauren, I—" He caught his breath as he sat back on his heels and simply looked at her one inch at a time. "I'm on my knees to you."

She gave him a slow smile as she reached behind her back, unhooked her bra, and tossed it on top of the pile of clothes.

He groaned, all control snapping at the sight of her pink-tipped breasts, and nudged her backward as he positioned his body between her legs.

She moaned in reply as he teased and tormented one round globe then the other, kissing each tip to a hard peak. When he felt her fingernails raking across the hard planes of his back, urging him harder and faster, he slipped his hand into her panties and stroked her hot, moist center, causing her to writhe up against him, as if begging for more.

He exhaled hard like he'd been running a mile. He unzipped his jeans, then remembered he had a phone in his pocket but no condom. He groaned in frustration and sat up.

"What is it?" She rose slightly and leaned against one elbow, a slow smile tilting up one corner of her full lips. "Please don't stop now."

"I've got condoms in the glove compartment, I think."

"Aren't firefighters always prepared to do their duty?"

"If it involves fire extinguishers, I'm ready."

She chuckled, a low, tantalizing sound. "I've got a better idea as to how to put out your fire."

He groaned in response, shaking his head. "Not funny."

"Yes, it is."

"Hold that position while I get down from here and—"

"Kent, do you really want to use protection?"

He felt everything within him go still, not daring to believe what she might be implying. If anything, he got harder at the thought of creating a baby between them. But surely she couldn't mean right now.

"We were always meant to have a child of our own." She held out her hand to him, palm upward. "Is now too soon to try?"

He went down on his knees before her again. "I'd like nothing better, but I don't want to rush you."

"Hannah needs a little brother or sister to make her world complete."

"I'll be happy to adopt Hannah, if you'd like or she'd want." He lifted Lauren's hand and kissed her palm, lingering over the softness. "But I don't want to rush you or her or anything. This is too precious to me."

"Me too." She tugged his hand to her mouth and

kissed the rough calluses. "I love your offer about Hannah, but let's wait for her to reach out."

"I'm willing to wait a lifetime."

And with those words, he had nothing left to lose and everything to gain. He gathered Lauren into his arms, pressing kisses over her face, down her body to her hot, soft core where he lingered, tasting and titillating until she gasped out her building pleasure and spread her legs for him.

He quickly unzipped his jeans, and then as gently and tenderly as possible, he thrust deeply into her. He felt, after all these years and all the twists and turns of life, as if he had finally come home. She moaned and clutched his shoulders as he set a rhythm, building their connection, their love, their commitment as they both reached higher and higher for fulfillment, then slipped over the edge into bliss together as moonlight bathed them in a pearly glow.

He lay down beside her, breathing hard, tugged her against the length of his body, and covered them with a sleeping bag.

She rose up on one arm and pressed a tender kiss to his cheek. "For me, that was the very first time. I've never felt anything close to what I experienced with you."

"After all these years, yes, this is our very first time." He swept Lauren closer, hardly able to believe the love of his life was in his arms in the bed of his pickup on Lovers Leap. And yet, he felt as if this was exactly the way his life was meant to be.

She snuggled against him and then shrugged her shoulders. "You know what, I'm really hungry."

He grinned, pushing her damp hair back from her face. "Ready again?"

"Food." She laughed and sat up. "Where's that barbeque when a gal needs it?"

He groaned and sat up, too. "Is there no satisfying you?"

She shook her head. "Not if that little session is what you've got in store for my future."

"I've got that for you. And a whole lot more."

"Good. I want to try out your big bed next."

"You got it." He leaned over, picked up the sack of barbeque, and handed it to her. "For now, this'll have to do."

She pulled two Styrofoam containers out of the sack, gave one to him, and opened the other for herself. "Oh yum, this looks good."

"Simple chopped brisket sandwich and fries so it wouldn't be too messy." He watched as she took a big bite of her sandwich and moaned in pleasure. That simple act sent his mind to imagining other pleasures. But he set that thought aside for later, pulled out his sandwich, and bit into it. She was right. It hit the spot.

They ate silently, except for a few moans and groans of pleasure, until the food was all gone. He quickly slipped the containers back into the sack, set it aside, and pulled the drinks out of the cooler. While they slurped from straws, he glanced around the area. They were as alone here as if they were at the top of the world. Maybe they could stay the night. He'd always wanted to spend long hours with her, and this was just the beginning of building a treasured life.

Lauren handed her mostly empty drink back to him, giving him a come hither smile that beckoned him closer. And that was more than fine with him. He set their cups back in the cooler and turned to her.

"I think it's time we got those jeans off you," she said in a husky voice. "I'd like a little show."

He chuckled as he realized her mind had gone exactly where his thoughts had gone a moment earlier. She wanted to be here with him all night long, too. He reached for the waistband of his jeans. He'd be happy to shuck them for her.

As he stood up so she'd get the full effect, the sound of chirping crickets filled the air. Startled, he glanced around to see if a cricket had leaped from the oak tree down onto the truck.

Lauren sat up fast, appearing alarmed as she looked toward their pile of clothes.

"What is it?"

"That's my phone. I can't help but worry something might have happened to Hannah."

He quickly turned serious and zipped up his jeans, looking about at the same time for her phone. He walked over to the clothes and tossed each piece aside until he found Lauren's jeans. He pulled out her cell and carried it over to her.

She grabbed the phone and swiped it open. "Hello." She listened for a moment, appearing more and more concerned, and then nodded. "I'll be right there. Yes, Ruby, I'll bring Kent."

"Is Hannah okay?" He felt suddenly cold with dread at the thought that something could have happened to her.

"She's okay, I think. Ruby said Hannah awoke from a bad dream. She's crying and won't stop." Lauren started putting on her clothes. "I thought maybe now that she's here those nightmares would stop."

"Nightmares?"

Lauren jerked her T-shirt over her head. "She dreams her daddy is gone and she can't find him."

"That's terrible."

Lauren nodded, sighing. "It's my fault. I shouldn't have left her alone with only Ruby tonight."

Kent enfolded Lauren in his arms. "Don't blame yourself. Blame me. I lured you up here. I didn't know about Hannah's nightmares."

"How could you?" She hugged him hard. "Listen, let's don't blame ourselves. Let's just go home and comfort her."

"How do you get her past her fear?"

"So far, nothing works. She'll eventually wear herself out and fall asleep. All I can do is hold her and be there for her."

"Then let's go home and comfort *our* daughter."

Chapter 35

When Kent cut the engine of his truck in front of Twin Oaks, Lauren felt a great sense of relief, as well as a sense of loss. She'd be able to comfort Hannah, but she worried that what she'd just shared with Kent might slip away. They'd confessed their love years ago and still they'd lost each other. She didn't want to think that could happen again, but their reconnection was still so fresh that it felt fragile. But she mustn't let that possibility weigh on her mind, not when Hannah needed her.

"Do you want me to go on home?" Kent asked in a voice tinged with concern. "I don't want to intrude or cause problems."

She gazed at the warm lights glowing inside the house, but she felt no answering warmth, only chills. To feel so helpless to stop her daughter's emotional pain was almost more than she could bear, but she must be strong for Hannah.

"Lauren?" Kent squeezed her hand. "I'll support you any way I can."

She shook her head to clear out the cobwebs. "Normally, I wouldn't want to chance upsetting Hannah with extra people in the house."

"That's fine. I understand. She hasn't been around me very much. I'm still a stranger to her."

"That's just it. Hannah doesn't view you as a stranger. And Ruby asked for you to come in the house."

"Okay. I'll come inside, but I'll hang back till we get a lay of the land. If it looks like my presence causes more trouble, I'll quietly slip back out the door and go home."

"Thanks."

"But if that happens, please call me as soon as she's settled down so I'll know she's okay."

"Of course, I will." She squeezed his hand in return, feeling the welcome power of his warmth and strength, then opened her door.

She was down, out, and headed for the kitchen door before Kent had a chance to round the front of his pickup. She jogged up the brick steps and paused with her hand on the doorknob. She took a deep breath and gave him a quick nod before she opened the door. She stepped inside and smelled the tantalizing aroma of fresh-baked brownies, so she knew Hannah had been having fun earlier in the day. She glanced downstairs and saw Ruby sitting in her recliner with Hannah curled in her lap, softly sobbing.

"Hannah, sweetie, I'm here," Lauren called as she quickly walked across the kitchen.

"Mommy!" Hannah cried as she leaped out of Ruby's lap.

Lauren descended the steps, dropped to her knees, and held out her arms. Hannah launched her small body forward and Lauren caught her, holding her tight as her daughter sobbed against her shoulder. She patted Hannah's back, noticing she wore her favorite teddy bear fleece pajama onesie with feet. She stroked her daughter's long hair, trying to dislodge the mats, but gave up for the moment.

"Did you have a bad dream again?" Lauren asked as she heard Kent quietly enter the kitchen and close the door behind him.

"We read her favorite book before she went to sleep." Ruby sighed and leaned forward, patting her lap. Temple jumped up, kneaded his paws, and settled down in her lap. "We tried to comfort her, but she wasn't having any of it."

"It's okay." Lauren hugged her daughter closer. "I thought maybe once she was here she wouldn't have her nightmare about losing her father."

"Her father?" Ruby asked, sounding puzzled as she glanced up toward Kent in the kitchen.

Hannah raised her tear-streaked face. "Cowboy Daddy! I dreamed he's gone and never coming back."

Lauren felt shock reverberate through her. "You're worried about Cowboy Daddy?"

"Yes!" Hannah nodded vigorously. "He fell off a horse like Aunt Hedy, but he never got up."

Lauren sighed. So much for little ears. She hadn't been careful enough discussing Hedy and hippotherapy and horses. But what amazed her more than anything was her daughter's concern about Kent. Could she be that attached to him already? And if so, what if—somehow—Lauren's relationship with Kent didn't work out? She must protect her daughter's emotional well-being.

"Hannah," Kent called softly, gently as he walked across the kitchen, down the steps, and stopped beside Lauren.

"Cowboy Daddy!" Hannah's head jerked up and her eyes grew wide. She pulled away from Lauren and launched herself at Kent.

"I'm here. All's well." He easily caught Hannah and swung her up into his arms in a big bear hug.

She encircled his neck and buried her face against his chest, sobbing more softly as she clung to him.

He looked from Lauren to Ruby and raised his eyebrows, appearing like a deer caught in headlights.

"Looks like we've got a daddy's girl on our hands." Ruby chuckled, shaking her head. "I thought he was what she needed for reassurance."

Lauren stood up, more surprised than anyone, but also grateful that Kent was handling her daughter so well.

"What do I do?" Kent asked.

Ruby pointed toward a big rocking chair with soft cushions in front of the fireplace. "If Lauren agrees, I suggest you sit right down there and rock Hannah to sleep."

Kent queried Lauren with raised eyebrows.

She nodded in agreement as she remembered his words up on Lovers Leap. "Let's go home and comfort *our* daughter." Why had she suddenly doubted him or his commitment? He was rock-solid, and Hannah must instinctively know it.

Kent carefully sat down in the rocker, eased Hannah into a comfortable position on his lap, and gently began to rock.

Lauren pulled tissues from her front pocket and wiped her daughter's eyes and nose before she settled on the edge of the sofa.

Hannah leaned against Kent, rubbed her eyes with the back of one hand, and gave a big sigh as her tears slowly subsided into quiet calm. "Cowboy Daddy, will you tell me a story?"

"A story?" Kent glanced from Lauren to Ruby and back again. "I'm not sure if I know any bedtime stories."

"Story, Cowboy Daddy. Story!" Hannah insisted in her high, sweet voice as she wriggled to get more comfortable.

"Why don't you tell her a Comanche myth?" Lauren leaned forward so she could quickly help her daughter if she started to cry again.

Hannah reached up and patted Kent's cheek with her small, dimpled hand. "Cowboy Daddy tells the best stories."

Ruby chuckled as she stroked Temple's fur and elicited loud rumbles of contentment.

For the first time in a long while, Lauren relaxed as she looked at the cozy domestic scene in front of her and leaned back against the sofa. If she could trust Kent with her child, she could trust him with her heart.

"Well, let's see," Kent said, glancing down at the top of Hannah's head. "Long ago, when darkness and coldness enveloped the Earth, all the animals called a council to discuss the situation. They gathered at a large tepee, one with a framework of four poles in the Comanche way. Soon they went inside to sit in a circle around a bright blaze in a fire pit made with smooth river stones."

"What's a tepee?" Hannah asked, cocking her head.

Kent chuckled as he looked at Lauren. "Guess she hasn't had much chance to hear Comanche legends."

"Just goes to show it's a good thing she's back in Wildcat Bluff," Ruby said as she continued to stroke Temple's back.

"Tepee?" Hannah patted Kent's chest.

"It's a big, warm tent."

"For camping?" Hannah asked.

"Yep."

"Will you take me and Mommy camping?"

"Sure. We'll do it sometime."

Lauren caught Kent's gaze and smiled as he nodded at her. He certainly had a way with children.

"More animals," Hannah said.

"Okay," Kent agreed. "Coyote took the lead because he always gets into some mess or other."

Hannah giggled. "That's me."

Kent pressed a kiss to the top of her head. "Coyote asked the other animals if they were sure they wanted to change from living in darkness and coldness. Bear agreed, along with Hummingbird, who wanted light, and Turtle, who wanted heat. Coyote warned them that change could be dangerous."

As Lauren listened to Kent's deep voice weave a spell around her, she knew exactly what the Comanche meant by "change is dangerous" because you never knew how it would turn out. In Hannah's case, change was turning out to be the absolute best of all possible worlds.

"Opossum piped up that she liked the dark," Kent continued. "Raccoon agreed because his fur coat kept him warm. But Bear growled that she wanted change. And she usually gets her way because she is so big and strong."

"I like Bear," Hannah murmured in a soft, sleepy voice.

"So as to be fair in their decision, Coyote suggested that they play a hand game to decide on change or no change. Everyone agreed. Bear, Turtle, Hummingbird, and others who wanted light and warmth formed a group. Coyote, Raccoon, Opossum, and others who didn't want change made up the opposing group."

Hannah exhaled on a sigh, then went completely still in Kent's strong arms as she fell into a contented sleep.

Lauren smiled, feeling as happy and satisfied as her daughter. She didn't think Hannah would have the nightmare again, not now that she had Cowboy Daddy to comfort her. Lauren looked up at Kent's face and nodded to keep him telling the story because his voice obviously soothed Hannah and would lull her into a deeper sleep.

"Tricky Coyote started the game," Kent continued. "Bear, Turtle, Hummingbird, and their group lost right away. No matter how hard they tried, they couldn't win. Bear was suspicious of Coyote, so she went outside and made strong medicine. When she returned, Coyote's medicine was broken and his group couldn't win."

When Kent paused in his story, Lauren leaned forward, wanting to hear more even if Hannah was fast asleep.

"Finally, Bear stood up, thrust aside the tepee flap, and gestured outside. 'Watch,' Bear said, 'Dawn comes to bring us daylight and warmth.' Coyote wanted one more game, but Hummingbird insisted their group had won."

Hannah shifted in her sleep, peacefully burying her head in the crook of Kent's arm.

He looked down at the little girl in his arms. "Bear pointed at her big snout and said, 'Watch my mouth at the break of day. You will see a yellow streak that represents dawn.' Hummingbird chimed in, 'Look in my mouth, too. I will show you six tongues to represent warm weather for half the year and cold for the other half.' As dawn broke, all the animals looked in Bear's mouth and saw a yellow streak. Hummingbird shouted in triumph and the animals counted six tongues.

"And on this new beginning," Kent said, "Bear, Turtle, and their group happily followed Hummingbird out into the light of day. Coyote, Raccoon, Opossum, and their group huddled in the tepee, too frightened by change to go outside." Kent paused, smiling at Lauren. "And that is how day and night, winter and summer came into the Comanche world."

Lauren returned his smile. "And that is also how change can be so very good for us all." She stood up and held out her hand. "Come on, Cowboy Daddy. Let's put our daughter to bed."

Chapter 36

Lauren arrived at Cougar Ranch the next day in the early afternoon. Hannah sat in her booster seat proudly wearing her new cowgirl outfit. They'd shopped in Old Town and fortunately found everything that suited Hannah's new image. Lauren had even bought a pair of boots with red hearts on blue leather for herself. If there ever was a time for wearing hearts, now was certainly the time.

She drove past Kent's farmhouse with its pretty pink door down to the barn and parked to one side of Billye Jo's truck and empty horse trailer. An empty trailer had to mean that Hannah's pony and Lauren's hippotherapy horse were inside the barn. She felt her heart speed up at the realization that she was really on her way to establishing an equine-assisted therapy center right here and right now. She had many people in the county to thank for helping her get this far, and she'd never forget their generosity and support.

She felt her spirits lift even higher at the thought of seeing Kent again. So much had happened so fast between them that she felt giddy with happiness. What had given her the biggest surprise since returning to Wildcat Bluff was the almost instant connection between Hannah and Kent. Of course, she was thrilled about it, but she was still a little in awe that her daughter had selected her own daddy and he'd chosen her for his daughter as well. Sometimes life was just about perfect.

She'd called Kent earlier about the hippotherapy equipment she'd ordered and had sent to his house. He'd explained that it had arrived and he'd spent the morning getting stuff set up at the barn and arena. She could hardly wait to go forward with her plans now that so much was in place.

If she could just persuade her aunt to try therapeutic riding, all would be well. Surely Hedy couldn't hold out against the lure of seeing her great-niece ride her first pony. With that in mind, Lauren picked up her cell from the center console, decided against a call that might give Hedy a chance to beg off, and sent a text.

"Cougar Ranch. Hannah here. Pony here. Where are you?"

She hoped her message would intrigue her aunt enough to hurry over to Kent's barn.

Lauren tucked her phone into her front pocket and stepped outside, noticing that the chill of the morning had given way to a glorious afternoon with clear, blue skies and a warm breeze from the south. She shucked off her jean jacket and tossed it on the backseat, leaving her wearing a green, long-sleeve T-shirt and blue jeans.

She picked up a bag of apples from the seat, walked around the front of her SUV, and opened the passenger door. Hannah gave a big grin, rocking back and forth in her seat as if she was so anxious for her pony that she couldn't sit still another moment. Lauren quickly unclicked the restraints, lifted Hannah out, and set her on the ground.

"Wait till Cowboy Daddy sees me!" Hannah twirled around in a circle to show off her new clothes.

Lauren heard a squeak as a gate opened and glanced over to see Kent walking out of the barn dressed in crisp jeans and snap shirt.

"Who's that over there?" he called, grinning at Hannah.

"It's me, Cowboy Daddy!" She twirled faster. "I bet you can't tell it's Hannah!"

He chuckled as he walked over to her and stood with his hands on his hips as he surveyed her. "Land's sake, can this cowgirl be our Hannah?"

"Yes!" She threw out her arms, still twirling, and toppled toward him, windmilling her arms to keep from falling over.

He grabbed her, lifted her into the air, spun her around, and set her safely on the ground. "Well, so it is. You look pretty as a picture."

"Thank you." Hannah put her hands on her hips, mimicking his earlier stance, and stood as tall as possible. "I brought Spot apples for a treat. Mommy said best not start him on sugar, but I don't know—"

"Good choice."

Lauren hung back and watched in delight as her once reticent daughter bloomed like a flower in sunshine. Hannah looked adorable, too, in a pink cowgirl hat, blue pearl-snap shirt with a rose pattern, pink belt with a rhinestone buckle, blue jeans, and pink cowgirl boots. For a finishing touch, Hannah had insisted on adding her pink tutu to create the perfect look.

Lauren had taken photos, sent them to her parents, and received excited responses. If they hadn't been planning on coming to Wildcat Bluff, she figured now they couldn't resist the temptation. To encourage Hedy, she'd copied her with photos, too. Now she just needed to wait and see if the plan for her aunt came together as perfectly as Hannah's outfit.

When Kent glanced over, she held up the bag of apples so he'd know she was carrying them to the barn.

"Mornin'." He gave a big grin, revealing dimples, with a gleam in his hazel eyes.

"Hey there." She returned his smile, knowing she had a certain gleam in her own eyes, too. "Looks like you and Billye Jo are already way down the line in getting everything set up."

"We couldn't resist, so it's not our fault if we're getting too far ahead of you."

"No problem. I'm excited, too."

"Good." He glanced beyond her shoulder as if searching for something. "Hedy coming?"

"I hope so. I texted her that we are all here waiting for her."

"Best you can do. She'll come around, if I don't miss my guess."

"I hope so."

"Mommy! Cowboy Daddy!" Hannah jumped up and down. "Pony. Pony. Pony."

"Let's go." Kent snagged her small hand and headed for the barn.

Lauren followed, swinging the bag of apples as she watched her two loved ones go through the barn gate together. She could still hardly believe how quickly and wonderfully her life had changed since she'd returned to her roots. Now she'd simply enjoy going forward as she contributed to the community in her own small way.

Inside the shady barn, Billye Jo waved from where she stood holding the lead on Spot's halter. Lauren stopped beside Kent, and he put an arm around her waist, tugging her close. She caught the scent of sage and sweetgrass, so he must have smudged the barn with the dried herbs she'd left him with per Morning Glory's instructions.

Together, they watched Hannah race down the center aisle and throw her short arms around Spot's neck.

"Hey there, cowgirl," Billye Jo said with a teasing lilt to her voice. "Are you ready to ride this wild, cantankerous brute of a horse?"

Hannah quickly stepped back and put her hands on her hips. "Spot is the very best pony in the whole, wide world." She leaned over and gave Spot a loud kiss on her long nose. "And Spot gets an apple to prove it."

Billye Jo chuckled as she glanced at Lauren. "Looks to me like you've got the makings of a fine cowgirl here."

"Don't you know it," Kent agreed, taking the bag of apples from Lauren's hand. He set the sack in a bin on the wall, selected an apple, and carried it to Hannah. "When you give this apple to Spot, hold out your hand and let the apple lie flat on your palm." He demonstrated with the apple on his own palm as he held out his hand to her.

"Thanks!" She grabbed the apple with a big grin. "You're the very best Cowboy Daddy in the whole, wide world." She whirled around and held the apple out to Spot.

Spot gave an excited whinny and plucked the apple from Hannah's hand in one big bite. Spot promptly set to chewing with a contented look on her face.

"Spot likes apples!" Hannah clapped her hands together in delight.

"That's a particularly sweet one since you held it," Kent said.

Billye Jo laughed out loud as she glanced from Kent to Lauren. "No doubt about it, she's got Kent Duval wrapped around her little finger."

Kent joined her laughter. "Yeah. Just like her mom."

Lauren chuckled, too, as she leaned into Kent's warmth and strength, inhaling the familiar, pleasant aroma of hay and oats and horses. If she hadn't already been convinced that she'd come home, now she knew it for an out-and-out fact.

"Hannah's gonna make a real fine cowgirl," Billye Jo said.

"I'm so happy for her," Lauren agreed as she focused on Billye Jo. "As much as I like seeing Spot, I hope there's another horse here today that I'll get to meet."

Billye Jo grinned, glancing toward the back gate. "Chancy Boy is out in the arena just waiting for the opportunity to strut his stuff."

"Let's go see him," Lauren said.

"Hannah, why don't you ride Spot out to the arena." Kent easily picked her up, set her in the saddle, took the lead rope from Billye Jo, and led Hannah through the back gate.

"I always took him for a family man," Billye Jo said quietly. "He just needed the right gal, didn't he?"

"And the right daughter," Lauren agreed on a sigh of happiness.

"Come on. I want you to see what we've done. Kent already had a mounting ramp, but we adjusted it to better suit challenged riders."

"I'm anxious to get going." Lauren squeezed Billye Jo's strong shoulder. "I want to thank you again for making this possible."

"You're welcome. But don't ever think I'm not getting as much out of this as you are, because it's important to me, too." Billye Jo grinned, nodding toward the arena.

Lauren turned to accompany her when she heard a sound at the other end of the barn. She glanced back and was thrilled to see Hedy in her wheelchair barreling toward them.

"You may not be getting me up on the back of a horse, but I'm sure as shootin' gonna see my great-niece ride her pony."

"Aunt Hedy!" Lauren felt her heart swell with happiness. "I'm so glad you could make it."

"If that pony hadn't lured me here, Hannah's duded-up outfit was sure to do the trick. Right?"

"Yep." Lauren was happy to agree, not caring one bit that her aunt had seen right through her plan.

"Let's get this show on the road." Hedy raced right by them, through the gate, and stopped out by the arena.

Lauren walked outside, feeling the sunshine on her face and hearing sparrows chirping in the trees. She was very thankful for this first big step in returning Hedy to her former sassy self.

"Aunt Hedy!" Hannah called from the back of Spot. "Look at me. I'm a cowgirl!"

"Yes, you surely are," Hedy said in a choked voice. "And as fine a looking cowgirl as I ever saw."

"While you're here," Billye Jo said, gesturing toward the arena. "Why don't you meet Chancy Boy."

"Oh my, he's a beauty," Hedy said in a voice that held nothing but absolute awe as she moved closer to the arena.

Lauren walked over, stopped beside her aunt, and

gazed at the proud palomino with a deep, rich golden coat and full, white mane. Lauren was pleased that Chancy Boy already wore the therapeutic riding fleece bareback pad she'd selected from an online catalog. She preferred this particular riding pad because it had natural lambskin fleece for both horse and rider. The large padded pommel and cantle gave extra support to a rider, too. She particularly liked the fact that the pad could be washed and tumble dried.

Chancy Boy noticed all the attention, trotted across the arena, stopped at the fence, and nickered in greeting.

"Palominos are your favorite, aren't they?" Lauren could hardly believe that piece of good luck, but she was grateful for it.

"Oh, yes," Hedy agreed. "You didn't tell me you'd selected a palomino. If I'd known that—"

"I didn't know till this very moment."

Hedy rolled closer to the fence and held out her hand toward the horse.

Chancy Boy put his head over the fence, sniffed Hedy's hand, and then blew hard against her fingers.

Hedy stroked his long nose with a trembling hand—tentative at first, then with growing strength of purpose.

"We've got a ramp set up by the fence so you can motor up it and get onto Chancy Boy's back while he's still in the arena. Somebody will always be there to help steady you." Kent gestured toward the sturdy-looking ramp that rose to a flat surface to accommodate a wheelchair. "If that doesn't suit you, I'll be happy to lift you and set you in the saddle, but it'd be just at first till you regain your riding strength."

"I trained Chancy Boy," Billye Jo said. "Hedy, please

help us train him to be a better therapy horse. I'm strong enough to do any lifting that needs doing."

When Hedy didn't respond, quiet settled around the arena. Hannah sat quietly on Spot. Lauren held her breath, hoping against hope that this magnificent horse would break through her aunt's self-imposed exile from the world of riding so that she might regain her will to live. But maybe they'd pushed Hedy too far too fast. Now all they could do was wait for her aunt's choice.

Suddenly, as if coming to a decision, Hedy jerked her hand away from Chancy Boy, wheeled around, and rolled back to the group. "You've all made your point. It's a good one. Chancy Boy would make any rider proud." She took a deep breath and bit her lower lip. "Nothing is ever as easy as it seems. Lauren, please come with me and let's talk."

Lauren felt her heart beat fast with apprehensive but renewed hope. She gave Hannah an encouraging smile, knowing Kent and Billye Jo would take care of her while she talked with her aunt.

Hedy led Lauren back into the barn, zipped down to the entry gate, and stopped her motorized wheelchair. She wheeled around and looked Lauren straight in the eyes as she blinked back tears.

Lauren reached out to her aunt, wanting to comfort but not knowing how, then dropped her hand back to her side.

"What I'm about to tell you will be our secret forever," Hedy said in a firm voice as she straightened her shoulders. "Agreed?"

"Yes, Aunt Hedy."

Chapter 37

Lauren sat down on the packed dirt of the barn beside Hedy's wheelchair. She crossed her legs and prepared to listen, as she'd done so often as a child when her aunt had taken the time to explain something to her. They hadn't been in this position for thirteen years, but now it seemed appropriate. Whatever secret her aunt was willing to share must be momentous because Hedy rarely shed tears. Lauren leaned forward, wanting her aunt to see that she had her undivided attention and full support.

Hedy cleared her throat and wiped at her eyes with the back of her hand as she looked down the length of the barn. "You'd think after all these years it'd get easier."

"What, Aunt Hedy?"

"But I guess not." Hedy brushed the flat of her palm across the top of the burgundy fleece throw over her legs. "I wanted to see Hannah ride her pony. At least I thought I wanted to see it."

"Of course you did."

"No." Hedy shook her head in denial. "I wish I'd stayed away. I wish I'd never seen a thing. I wish I'd never responded to your text."

"But—"

"More to the point, if you'd stayed away and kept your daughter away, I wouldn't be here now crying all over the place and embarrassing myself."

"You're not—"

"Please don't make excuses. I'm too damn old for anything but the truth."

"Okay." Lauren felt as if the world was disintegrating in a very confusing way around her. This was her aunt, solid as a rock, salt of the Earth, or at least that's what she'd always believed to be true. But now?

"You're not going to make this easy on me, are you?" Hedy glared at Lauren with painful knowledge in her eyes.

"I'm trying to help."

"You're not going to let me ride off into the sunset of my years with my pride intact, are you?"

"I'm sorry if—"

"Nobody lives forever, no matter how the media tries to spin and hide the truth from humans with their fragile bodies."

"But you've always been so strong."

"Have I?" Hedy shrugged her broad, muscular shoulders. "Denial might be a better word for my actions—or compensation or appeasement or reparations."

"What?" Lauren felt chilled to the bone. She no longer wanted to hear anything her aunt had to say. Whatever it was, maybe Hedy should carry her secret to the grave. And whatever part Lauren had in bringing about this confession, she wished she'd never opened that Pandora's box.

"Guilt."

"Surely not." Lauren wanted to wring her hands in dismay or use them to shove the truth that was about to emerge into the light of day back into the cover of darkness.

"I taught you too well." Hedy sighed, pushing back a strand of silver hair that had come loose from her long, thick braid hanging over one shoulder. "You'll never give up, and you'll never let anybody else give up either."

"I'm just trying to help, but if you—"

"Too late now, isn't it?" Hedy gave a deep, heartfelt sigh. "And there's Hannah. She looks like you. Like your mom. Like me."

"That's good, at least I've always thought so." Suddenly Lauren didn't know what was good or bad or even indifferent. And she desperately wanted to return to her safe and sane world. But she didn't think she was going to be given that choice.

"If *my* little girl had lived, I bet she'd have looked just like Hannah." And Hedy burst into brokenhearted tears as she buried her face in her hands.

"Daughter?" Lauren simply sat there in shock, feeling as if she'd been kicked upside the head by a horse as her aunt's words slowly sank into her mind and became reality.

Hedy nodded as she continued to cry.

Lauren looked anywhere but at her aunt. Yet she saw nothing except the shocked blankness of her own mind.

"She'd have been a cowgirl like Hannah, wouldn't she?" Hedy raised her tearstained face and stared straight at Lauren with eyes gone dark with despair.

"Yes." Lauren barely got out the word from a face that felt frozen. She'd never heard a single thing about Hedy losing a child. She'd simply always been the wonderful woman who'd had time for her and the other kids of Wildcat Bluff. Now Lauren saw how much love her aunt had generously shared with others, never asking anything in return. But what if Hedy had had her own child to lavish with praise and attention? How much would the community have lost or perhaps have gained in that case? Lauren had no answer, but it didn't matter. Not now, not ever. Hedy had been there for her, and now she was here for her aunt.

"Yes," Hedy echoed Lauren's word. "Exactly like Hannah."

"Here." Lauren's mommy-training kicked in, and she fumbled in her pocket for the tissues she always carried for Hannah. She thrust the wad of soft paper toward Hedy as the very least gesture she could make to help soothe her aunt's torment.

Hedy grabbed the tissues and rubbed tears from her eyes as she took deep breaths in an obvious attempt to calm her emotions.

"Good. That's my aunt Hedy." Lauren realized she had to be the strong one now—like she was with Hannah—until her aunt could regain her balance.

"Okay." Hedy sniffed back her tears, straightening her shoulders. "Here's the truth of the matter. I never told anyone before because I didn't want pity. I still don't. But I want you to understand the difficult position you've forced me into with this horse mess."

"I'm sorry if—"

"Shhh. Let me finish while I've got the guts to do it." Hedy hit her legs with both fists. "Useless still. But that's not the worst of it. I was thirty-six when I took that spill from my horse. That's about half a lifetime ago. Yeah, I injured my spine. Yeah, I couldn't walk again. Yeah, I lost the ability to compete in rodeo. But that wasn't the worst of it."

"Not the worst?" Lauren dreaded to hear what more tragedy Hedy could have endured in her life.

"No easy way to say it. I was pregnant. That's when I lost my darling little girl."

Lauren's breath caught in her throat as the extent of her aunt's great loss sank deep into her mind. She quickly reached up and squeezed her aunt's hands to give her a small measure of comfort. "I'm so very sorry."

"And I couldn't have any other children."

"I'm just so, so sorry." Lauren knew her words were completely inadequate, but she had no better ones to express her sorrow.

"Thank you."

"What about your baby's father? How did he take the news?"

Hedy sighed, shaking her head. "Met him on the circuit. Good-looking roper. We loved each other fast and furious, then he was gone. No holding him in one place. He couldn't be confined that way, not after Vietnam—a stupid, useless war that killed off way too many of my generation's guys. Even if our young men made it out of the jungle alive, lots couldn't help but bring the jungle home with them. That was my Sam. Good man who should never have been drafted in the first place, but back then guys didn't have a choice unless their families had money or position or they found some sort of loophole. Bad deal for most of us all the way around. I doubt we'll ever completely recover from it."

"Do you still see him?" Lauren didn't know much about the Vietnam War, but she did know that all war was bad for everyone. And yet it kept coming around every generation, so somebody somewhere must benefit.

"Drink got him years ago." Hedy dabbed at her eyes

again. "He never knew about our little girl. I tried to find him on the circuit, but he'd disappeared, probably down into one of his dark jungle holes."

"I wish things had been different for you." Lauren felt as if her words were inadequate, even though they were the best she had to offer.

"Bottom line"—Hedy leaned back in her chair and straightened her shoulders again—"if I hadn't been riding, I wouldn't have lost my baby. I've lived with that guilt every day since my fall."

"But, Aunt Hedy—"

"And then you come back to Wildcat Bluff bringing your daughter and wanting me to get on horseback. Now I'm having nightmares about falling and losing my baby again." Hedy blinked back tears as she dabbed at her eyes with the tissues. "Maybe it's time I stopped fighting and joined my lost little girl."

"Stop it!" Lauren threw herself against her aunt's knees, hugged them hard, and laid her face against Hedy's lap. She couldn't help but cry now, even though she tried to suppress her emotions for her aunt's sake. First Hannah had nightmares about her lost daddy and now Hedy had nightmares about her lost daughter. She'd had Kent to help Hannah, but she was on her own here. Somehow she must find a way to reach her aunt and free her from her painful past.

"I'm tired, that's all." Hedy's voice was soft now as she patted Lauren's head in comfort. "I just want to rest."

Lauren raised her face, feeling determination rise up in her. "I don't care if you're tired. I don't care if you're hurting. I don't care if you're having nightmares. You know you've overcome much more in your life. You've been an inspiration to all of us, and you can't stop now. In fact, I won't let you."

Hedy raised her eyebrows, appearing completely surprised by Lauren's strong words.

"What I do care about is you being here for Hannah—teaching her how to ride horses and enjoy animals and do math, teaching her how to overcome pain and loneliness and loss, teaching her how to love life and people and happiness. Those are all the important things in life that you taught me."

Hedy took a deep breath and sniffed back tears.

"My daughter needs you. I need you. Wildcat Bluff needs you. And I'll be damned if I let you off easy."

"Oh, Lauren, you are so the child of my heart." Hedy pulled Lauren into her arms and gave her a long, strong hug.

Lauren relished the closeness for a moment, then she leaned back and looked her aunt in the eyes. "Now, am I gonna have to get tough and pull out the big guns to get you back on a horse?"

Hedy gave a tentative smile as she blinked back tears. "And you think you've got big enough guns?"

"Oh yeah. I'm packing two powerful ones." Lauren grinned, feeling her spirits soar with determination. "The first is Kent Duval. You know him, he'll pull out a Comanche myth that'll make you feel lower than a rattlesnake if you don't show the courage of a descendent of Republic of Texas pioneers."

Hedy gave a slow chuckle, shaking her head. "That's a pretty big gun all right. I'd hate to give the impression that a Comanche could best a Republic of Texas pioneer."

"That's what I thought. Now, my second gun is the biggest."

"It better be a thirty ought six."

Lauren nodded as she gave her aunt a knowing smile. "The second is Hannah Sheridan. She needs her great-aunt to show her the ropes of life. And that includes how to ride the barrels when she's big enough."

Hedy inhaled sharply, clutching the arms of her wheelchair. "Lots of folks can teach her about life and rodeo. You and Kent and your folks are at the top of the list."

"But none of us can teach her how to overcome the extreme adversities of life and keep going with an open heart and open hand like you."

Silence filled the barn as Hedy simply looked at Lauren. After a long moment, she exhaled sharply as if accepting her fate. "You got me there."

"Good." Lauren grinned, feeling a vast sense of relief. "Now, go ahead and admit it. Wouldn't you like to be on the back of a gorgeous palomino again?"

"Chancy Boy is one fine horse."

"And you're one fine rider."

"Not anymore." Hedy gave Lauren a sharp look. "Are you sure you want to set us on this path? There'll be no turning back."

"That's exactly what I want from you. You'll inspire the whole county again."

"If I can inspire one little girl, that's enough for me."

"It'll be so much more." Lauren stood up and brushed her palms together as if removing the past. "Once we get you duded-up like Hannah and up on the back of that palomino, you're going to drive Bert Holloway crazier than ever."

Hedy gave a soft laugh. "Bert came in the store and bought another bluebird just this morning."

"What'd I tell you? That guy has got it bad."

"Go on. He's just got a thing for bluebirds."

"Sure he does." Lauren pointed toward the arena, then back at her aunt. "Come on. We've got places to go and things to do."

Hedy grasped Lauren's fingers and squeezed them. "Sometimes the mother becomes the child and the child becomes the mother. Thank you. I needed to be reminded that to win you have to take the first step."

"And that's the step that takes you to a hundred plus years."

"In that case, we better get busy."

Chapter 38

Kent kept an eye on the open gate into the barn, wondering what Hedy and Lauren could be talking about. He hoped they were getting to the root of Hedy's issue or secret or whatever and all would be well now. What he wanted to do was run in there and fix the problem. But he knew better. That was just his male problem-solving instinct coming to the fore. Gals had their own way of working through things, and he'd best leave them alone to do it.

In the meantime, he took a great deal of pleasure in watching Billye Jo lead Hannah around on Spot. Hannah couldn't have been more adorable as she got into the swing of sitting in the saddle by hanging onto the saddle horn. She was as safe and secure as she could get on her first pony ride. And he planned to be there for her when she eventually graduated from pony to horse.

He couldn't be more thankful that Lauren had come back into his life and brought her daughter so that they could be a family, one he hadn't even realized how much he'd wanted and needed until now.

He walked over and stroked Chancy Boy's long nose, appreciating the strong lines and noble head. Like Kent, Chancy Boy kept an eye on the barn as if waiting for Hedy to come back to him. Kent had a feeling those two had already bonded and would make a great team, not only for Hedy's recovery but for the health of other folks, too.

Finally, Hedy motored out of the barn with Lauren beside her. He could tell right away they were different after their talk. And they were good, no doubt about it, because both had identical gleams in their eyes. Steely determination. Hedy was back on track. Kent wanted to jump up with a big cheer, but he restrained his enthusiasm.

Chancy Boy leaned his head over the fence and nickered as he watched Hedy zoom over to him.

"Good boy!" Hedy gave him a pat on his nose, and then she turned to look at Kent. "Lauren has convinced me that it's time I got back on a horse."

Kent smiled at her as he tilted his head toward the ramp. "Sounds like a good plan to me. Do you want to try out the ramp or—"

"Ramp. I may not be as strong as I used to be, but I've still got pretty good upper body strength."

"I don't doubt it one bit." Kent gave her a big grin, feeling like finally they were getting their Hedy back.

Lauren pointed toward the ramp. "Aunt Hedy, please put on that safety helmet I ordered for us to use."

"I'll get it. I set it beside the ramp." Kent quickly walked over and picked up the helmet.

"You just want me to look like a wimp," Hedy grumbled as she eyed the helmet with distaste.

Billye Jo laughed. "That's the last thing you'll ever look like. Just wear it to make us happy."

"Okay. I can see I'm outnumbered around here." Hedy motored over to the base of the ramp, then stopped and looked around at everyone. "Let's rock and roll!"

Kent secured the helmet under Hedy's chin. "There you go. You're all set."

Hedy motored up the ramp to the platform overlooking the arena and gave everyone a thumbs-up.

Kent moved to stand beside her, ready to lend a helping hand any way he could from here on out.

Billye Jo led Spot over to Lauren and handed her the lead. "If it suits everybody, I'd like to hold Chancy Boy's lead since he's used to me while Kent takes care of Hedy."

"Suits me this first time. We're all on a learning curve," Lauren agreed as she patted her daughter's cowgirl boot. "Hannah and I will watch from outside the arena."

Billye Jo picked up the lead she'd left by the fence, opened the gate, and stepped inside the arena. She stroked Chancy Boy's jaw, then reached up and clipped the lead to his halter. She quickly led him over to the platform, looked over at Kent, and gave a nod that she was ready to go.

Kent took a deep breath, hoping against hope that nothing would go wrong. "Hedy, if it's okay with you, I'm going to lift you and set you in Lauren's fancy saddle. And if you think the helmet's wimpy, take a look at that fleece-covered, thick pad."

Hedy chuckled as she reached out and stroked both hands across the lambskin. "Softer than my chair. I may need to wimp-out more often."

Kent smiled as he gently picked up Hedy, thinking she felt almost as light as a bird, and positioned her in the saddle. He could tell her old instincts came right back because she immediately grabbed the pommel with both hands and adjusted her seat. He felt a lump in his throat as he slowly eased his hands back from her. She looked good, as if she had perfect use of her body.

"Oh my," Hedy said in a soft, reverential voice. "I

thought I'd forgotten, but it's like riding a bike in that you never forget how to ride a horse."

"I know you want to go tearing across this arena." Billye Jo glanced up from where she held Chancy Boy. "But please give us all a break. We're just learning what to do here."

Hedy laughed out loud, sounding like her old self. "Are you telling me that I'm your guinea pig?"

"That's about the size of it," Kent agreed, watching like a hawk in case Hedy suddenly lost her balance.

"Cowgirls!" Hannah cried out. "That's me and Aunt Hedy!"

Hedy gave her great-niece a nod of agreement. "Give us both a little time on horseback and we'll be riding all over this ranch."

"Cowgirl power!" Hannah's voice carried across the arena.

As everybody laughed, Kent felt his heart fill with happiness. Life was coming together in perfect harmony.

"I don't want to be a spoilsport," Lauren said, "but I don't want to push our success today too far either."

"I won't fight you. I've got lots of time now." Hedy leaned slightly forward to stroke Clancy Boy's mane, and then she smiled at Lauren. "Thank you. Up here with four legs under me, I feel young again. Oh, like about fifty."

"That's just what we want to hear," Kent agreed as he reached out to her. "Ready to get down, cowgirl?"

"You bet." Hedy put her strong hands on his arms.

He gently lifted her out of the saddle and set her back in her wheelchair where she'd been confined for so many years.

"Thanks." Hedy looked at Chancy Boy. "I'll be seeing you later, and I'll be bringing treats."

"He'll be waiting for you." Billye Jo led Chancy Boy over to the gate. "I'll just get him back in his stall before I put up Spot."

Kent unbuckled Hedy's helmet, set it aside, and followed Hedy off the ramp. He walked over to Hannah, lifted her from her saddle, and set her on the ground. He felt a great sense of satisfaction in their accomplishments this day.

Hannah ran over to Hedy and gave her a big hug. "We're the best cowgirls in the whole, wide world."

"We certainly are." Hedy blinked back the tears as she smiled at her great-niece.

Kent saw Lauren gazing at her daughter and aunt with love in her eyes. He knew how she felt. He was full of love, too. And he couldn't imagine a better day in a better place.

As he picked up Spot's lead and started for the barn, his phone rang, interrupting the perfect moment. He felt a spurt of apprehension as he dug his cell out of his front pocket. He wasn't reassured when he saw he had an incoming call from Sheriff Calhoun. He wondered if his day had just taken a turn for the worse.

"Sheriff, what can I do for you?" he asked, nodding at Lauren as she stared at him in concern.

"Howdy, Kent. Is Billye Jo at your place?"

"Sure is."

"Good. I need her to come over to the Sinclair station in Sure-Shot."

Kent felt his gut clench at the news. "Not another fire, is there?"

"Nope." The sheriff gave a big sigh. "Look, just get Billye Jo over here right away. And why don't you come, too."

"I'll be there. You don't need the booster or anything from fire-rescue?"

"Not today."

"Lauren is with me. Okay if I bring her along?"

"Not a bad idea. I've got a head-scratcher here."

"We'll be along as soon as we put up the horses."

"Alrighty." And the sheriff was gone.

"Trouble?" Lauren asked with a puzzled frown on her face.

"I don't think so. Sheriff Calhoun wants Billye Jo and me at the Sinclair station. I thought you'd want to come along and see what it's all about."

"I do. I'm curious." Lauren glanced at her daughter. "But I can't leave Hannah, and I don't want to take her there."

"Don't fret." Hedy grinned as she settled Hannah onto her lap. "We'll go along to my place where everything is just her height."

"Yay!" Hannah nestled against Hedy and gave a big yawn.

"Maybe we'll bake some cookies, but first I think we'll both take a nap." Hedy kissed the top of Hannah's head.

"You're sure?" Lauren asked.

"It's about time my great-niece spent some time with me, don't you think?" Hedy asked with a warm smile on her lips.

"Hannah?" Lauren said. "Would you like to spend some time with your aunt? I'll come get you later today."

“Yay! We cowgirls got to stick together.” Hannah yawned again as she snuggled against Hedy.

“I guess that settles it.” Lauren gave Kent a positive nod.

“Okay, folks, let’s get on our way.” Kent tugged on Spot’s lead and headed for the barn. “The sheriff’s awaiting us in Sure-Shot.”

Chapter 39

Sure-Shot lazed in the late afternoon sunlight as Kent drove past the Bluebonnet Café toward the Sinclair station. Billye Jo pulled her horse trailer behind her pickup in back of him. Hedy and Hannah had gone off together, happy as two peas in a pod, but he still kept fighting the inclination to look in the backseat to check on Hannah. He realized now that he'd stepped into being Cowboy Daddy without even realizing it, and he couldn't imagine life any other way.

Lauren rode quietly beside him as if deep in thought or just resting from her strenuous day. He could tell she'd cried with Hedy because she'd repaired her makeup as best she could on the drive. Not that she needed makeup, but you didn't bring up a Texas gal's appearance, at least not to her face.

Up ahead, he saw Sheriff Calhoun's cruiser parked in front of the Sinclair station. A beat-up-looking four-wheeler blocked the garage's front double doors. Other than the vehicles, the building looked about like it needed as much repair and paint as the last time he'd seen it.

Kent parked beside the sheriff's cruiser and Billye Jo pulled to one side of the station so she had plenty of room to park her horse trailer. He glanced over at Lauren, and she gave him a tired smile.

"Are you up to a little more today?"

"I feel emotionally wrung out, but I'm really happy, too. Everything went so well that I can still hardly believe it."

"Whatever you said to Hedy did the trick."

Lauren nodded, looking teary, but she didn't say anything.

"Do you want to talk about it?"

She shook her head, smiling a bit. "All's well that ends well."

"That's sure the truth." Out of the corner of his eye, he noticed Sheriff Calhoun exit his cruiser. "Guess it's time we find out what's going on here."

"Let's hope it's good news."

Kent got out of his truck, walked around the front of it, and opened Lauren's door. She stepped down and he gave her a quick hug just as Billye Jo joined them.

"If you're passing out those hugs, Kent, I deserve one, too." Billye Jo winked at Lauren. "I'm proud as punch after our first go-round with Chancy Boy."

Lauren laughed as she hugged Billye Jo. "You can have all the hugs you want after what you just did for Aunt Hedy."

"That was a combined effort," Billye Jo said. "And a good one."

"Absolutely," Lauren agreed. "And it's just the beginning."

Sheriff Calhoun slammed the door of his cruiser. "If y'all will stop jawing and come over here, somebody wants to talk with you."

Kent glanced over to see a tall, gangly guy about twenty or so with thick, tawny hair and beard stubble exit the passenger side of the sheriff's vehicle. The guy wore a gray T-shirt and faded jeans with ripped-out knees. His athletic shoes had seen better days.

"Come on." Kent shrugged as he glanced at Lauren and Billye Jo, then they all walked over to the sheriff.

"Afternoon, folks," Sheriff Calhoun said. "Billye Jo, you know Moore Chatham here, don't you?"

"Yes, I do." Billye Jo nodded at Moore. "You and your mom moved onto River Ranch a few years ago, didn't you?"

"Yes, ma'am. We came back to Granddad's place after he died. We'd have been back sooner, but he and mom didn't get along."

"Be that as it may," Sheriff Calhoun interrupted. "Moore, I want you to meet Kent Duval and Lauren Sheridan, both of Wildcat Bluff. They helped put out that last fire at the station."

"I'm right sorry." Moore hung his head and looked at his feet.

"Speak up, son," Sheriff Calhoun said.

Moore raised his chin and looked at Billye Jo. "Ma'am, I apologize for any damage I may have caused to your station."

"What!" Billye Jo exclaimed. "You set the fires?"

"Yes, ma'am. I can't pay for the damage, but I'd be happy to work it off."

Billye Jo glared at the sheriff. "Is this some kind of joke?"

"No, it's not," Sheriff Calhoun said. "Moore called me and turned himself in for setting the fires in Sure-Shot. But after hearing his story, I'm inclined to go easy on him with community work."

"You may be inclined to go easy on him, but he

endangered this structure and the entire downtown." Kent wasn't so sure he agreed with the sheriff's assessment, but he was willing to listen.

"Like I said, I'm right sorry for the damage and trouble," Moore insisted. "It was stupid of me. If you want to press charges and put me in jail, I'll go willingly, but it'd leave my mom in a pickle."

"You should've thought about that before starting fires." Kent couldn't help but think about all the danger and destruction that as a firefighter he'd help stop in the county.

"Kent, let Moore have his say." Sheriff Calhoun put a restraining hand on Kent's arm. "I'm trying to do what's best for our community."

"I'm willing to listen, but I'm pretty skeptical." Kent narrowed his eyes as he waited for an explanation.

"Understandable." Sheriff Calhoun nodded in agreement. "Now, Moore, go ahead and explain your actions to these good folks."

"I'm not a whiner," Moore said. "And I don't expect a handout. I'm willing to work and work hard. I can do most anything like small engine repair or carpentry or painting or any dirty, nasty job anybody'd like to set me. I'm up for anything as long as it's honest work for a day's pay. And I'll work cheap."

"And free, if it's community work," Sheriff Calhoun said in a stern voice.

"Yeah, I'll do it," Moore quickly agreed.

"I don't understand," Lauren said. "What does working have to do with setting fires?"

Kent wondered the exact same thing, so he waited for a better explanation.

Moore straightened his shoulders. "Like I said, I can do most any manual labor, but I don't know nothing about horses. This is equine territory. Nobody'll hire me. Mom can't live alone, so I can't leave Sure-Shot. I've been picking up odd jobs here and there since I graduated high school, but nothing that makes a dint in her needs."

"Your mother's always been standoffish since she moved back here," Billye Jo said. "We figured she didn't like our community."

"It's not that at all. She can't work. She's got her pride. And we don't accept charity," Moore stated in a flat voice. "I got bummed out, so I set fire in those dumpsters. But I never meant harm to anybody. I just wanted folks to know how it feels to, to—"

"Feel vulnerable?" Lauren asked.

"Yeah." Moore looked down and rubbed the toe of his shoe in the dirt.

"What about the station?" Billye Jo pushed the point.

"Got out of hand. I only meant a little scorch, but I heard somebody coming and took off running." He looked up at her. "I'm sorry, and I'll work off the damages."

Kent wasn't sure if he ought to believe Moore or not, but maybe the guy needed a break. "Sheriff, what do you think?"

"We're a charitable community and we take care of our own." Sheriff Calhoun cleared his throat. "In this case, I think we let a family fall through the cracks."

Kent nodded, beginning to agree.

"If you don't mind me asking, what is your mother's trouble?" Lauren asked, appearing sympathetic.

"RA. Rheumatoid arthritis. Crippled up some. She's

got her good days and her bad days." He stared hard at Billye Jo. "And don't you dare tell her I told you, if you were ever to see her."

"I won't say a word." Billye Jo paused, as if considering the situation. "Sheriff, I do believe you're right in this situation. I'm not going to press charges."

"Really?" Moore looked up at her with hope brightening his eyes. "You won't hold the fires against me?"

"Not if you're true to your word."

"Ma'am, my word is my bond."

"In that case, my daughter and I could use some help around here. We're fixing up the place for her new business."

"I know Serena. She was the prettiest girl in our class." Moore ducked his head, appearing embarrassed by his words.

"She's pretty, all right," Billye Jo agreed. "And she needs help when she comes back to town. If you'll work off what you owe us for the fire, then we'll consider hiring you to help around here."

Moore gazed at her in astonishment. "You'd pay me?"

Billye Jo nodded in agreement. "We could use a strong back and ready hand."

"I'm no good with horses."

Billye Jo chuckled, shaking her head. "We'll see about that in time."

"We're starting a new program in Wildcat Bluff County," Lauren said. "Equine-assisted therapy. Your mother might be a good candidate for it."

"I don't know about that, but she loves horses," Moore said. "She grew up here riding horseback, but I grew up in Dallas so that's not my thing."

Lauren smiled at him. "I'd be happy to discuss the possibility of hippotherapy with her."

"Oh, no." Moore vigorously shook his head. "She's got her pride and she can't afford it."

"We're just getting started, so we're looking for volunteers."

"No charge?" Moore glanced suspiciously from one to the other.

"For volunteers, it'd be free," Lauren said. "I'm not sure how much we could help her, but we could try."

"It'd be good for her to get out of the house," Moore said with relief in his voice.

"No rush." Lauren smiled in encouragement. "When you think the time is right, you might ask her about it."

"I'll do it." Moore gave her a shy smile in return.

"That's settled then." Billye Jo rubbed her hands together. "When would you like to start work?"

"Yesterday."

"Tomorrow morning then," Billye Jo agreed. "Eight sharp."

"I'll be here."

"I like your attitude and your willingness to work, but keep in mind that we'll be watching you." Kent wanted to make sure Moore understood they couldn't take him at his word till he'd proven himself, not after he'd set those dangerous fires.

"I'll be on my best behavior from here on out," Moore agreed.

Kent started to say more, but he saw a fancy King Ranch pickup slow down, then pull in and park beside his truck.

Bert and Bert Two got out and sauntered over to

the group, both wearing spiffy Western suits, boots, and hats.

"Afternoon." Bert tipped his cowboy hat. "We were headed to check on our drive-in theater, saw you jawing, and thought we'd join you."

"Sheriff Calhoun, you're a sight for sore eyes," Bert Two added. "We were hoping to run into you."

"That's right," Bert agreed. "It'd sure help us out if you or a deputy could keep an extra eye on our new purchase. We've been having a hell—pardon me, ladies—of a time with our buildings burning down."

"That's the truth." Bert Two gave a big sigh. "Somebody's got it in for us or they sure do hate vintage buildings."

"Maybe both," Bert agreed. "I've been trying to save our historical structures in the county, but I'm losing them as fast as I buy them."

"We're right proud of that old drive-in built in the fifties," Bert Two added. "But we're afraid it's targeted now just because we bought it."

Kent gave them both a closer look. Could he have been mistaken about the Holloways and their business dealings? Maybe so. Then again, maybe not. He glanced at Moore, wondering if there might be a solution to all their problems.

"What do you plan to do with the drive-in?" Billye Jo cocked her head to one side as she looked at them.

"We're not sure yet," Bert said. "But the place has got lots of possibilities."

"Once we get it cleaned up," Bert Two added. "It's an overgrown trash heap right now."

"What would you say about hiring somebody local

to keep an eye on the place and start cleaning it up?" Kent asked.

"I'd say it'd be a lifesaver." Bert tapped the brim of his hat for emphasis. "But most folks around here have jobs or don't want to do that kind of work."

Kent gestured toward Moore. "I'd like you to meet Moore Chatham. He's a local guy who's looking to fill his time."

"That so?" Bert gave Moore the once over. "You look strong enough. Do you work hard and steady?"

"Yes, sir." Moore grinned from ear to ear. "I can do most anything if it don't mean horses. Dirt and sweat are fine and dandy with me."

"Sounds good," Sheriff Calhoun said. "And Moore here just might save us from another county fire."

"I'll do my best." Moore stood taller and prouder.

"Okay." Bert pointed down the road. "Moore, meet us down at the drive-in so we can show you around the place."

"Suits me," Moore quickly agreed. "But I've got work to do here at the station, too."

"Part time is just fine." Bert glanced at Billye Jo. "If that won't put a crimp in your style."

"It works for me," Billye Jo said. "Pretty quick I think Moore is going to have more business than he can shake a stick at."

"I'll take as much as I can get." Moore gave everybody a big grin. "And it'll keep me out of trouble."

"That's always a plus." Sheriff Calhoun chuckled, then turned toward Bert and Bert Two. "Now don't y'all fret none. It's just a matter of time till that firebug makes a mistake and winds up in my jail."

"Thanks," Bert said. "We appreciate your help."

"Sure do," Bert Two agreed.

They nodded to all around, then quickly got back into their truck and headed down the road.

"I can't thank y'all enough," Moore said. "Not only am I not going to jail, but I've got two jobs. I can't wait to tell Mom."

"That's the way it works in our county," Sheriff Calhoun said. "Friends help friends."

"Let us know if your mom is interested in working with us," Lauren added, giving Moore an encouraging smile.

"I will. And thanks." Moore hurried over to his four-wheeler, climbed on, and took off after the Holloways.

"Looks to me like we saved a good one," Sheriff Calhoun said. "If I can, that's the way I like to handle problems." He raised his cowboy hat before he sauntered over to his cruiser, got inside, and headed toward Wildcat Bluff.

"Good man," Lauren said. "I bet that's why he gets elected sheriff in this county."

"He's the best, all right." Billye Jo glanced up at the Sinclair station. "Now we can finally get started on our renovation."

"We'll throw a big grand opening party for you," Lauren said, "and invite the entire county."

"Perfect," Billye Jo agreed.

"But Mom's throwing the first party." Kent put an arm around Lauren's shoulders and tugged her close. "She wants to encourage the whole county to support our hippotherapy center."

"Can't beat that with a stick." Billye Jo chuckled as she looked from one to the other. "I hear tell it's gonna be real fancy, so we'd all better get duded up."

"I know Hannah will," Lauren agreed, joining her laughter as she glanced at Kent. "I can't wait to see you all spiffy."

Kent suppressed a groan, wondering if he could find anything in his mess of a closet. Maybe it was due for a good cleaning like his pickup. "Guess we better be on our way."

"Thanks for the horses and help." Lauren gave Billye Jo a quick hug.

"Any time," Billye Jo said. "Appears we're on a winning streak."

"Looks like it," Kent agreed, angling Lauren toward his truck. "See you at Cougar Ranch."

Chapter 40

Saturday evening, Lauren stood on the porch of Kent's farmhouse at Cougar Ranch, watching the party that was spread across the front lawn. Daffodils in flower beds here and there gave testimony to spring as their bright-yellow blooms bobbed in a warm breeze. A rosy hue spread across the land as the sun slowly sank in the west.

Country-western music filled the air as a band played favorites from Merle Haggard to Kitty Wells to Willie Nelson. Couples were two-steppin' out on the cement driveway to the strains of heartstring-tugging songs. Dozens of folks chowed down on barbeque and fixings from the Chuckwagon Café, pecan pie by Slade Steele, and vanilla ice cream from the Bluebonnet Café.

Lauren had eaten enough to make the waistband of her skirt feel tight, so she'd taken a break on the front porch. She was wearing pretty, new clothes. Hannah, Hedy, and Ruby had helped her select a rich turquoise blouse with white piping and a matching full skirt that swirled around her new turquoise cowgirl boots stitched with white. She'd finished off her outfit with Morning Glory's white macramé necklace with the phoenix pendant.

As she caught her breath, she thought about the reality of her new life. Everything had moved so fast since she'd returned to Wildcat Bluff that she could hardly believe her own good luck. Of course, it was much more than luck. Folks in this county had a way of making all things possible with a positive attitude and a helping hand. She truly had come home.

She saw Dune had corralled Sydney and was leading her in a complicated two-step that must be leaving her breathless. They made a handsome couple, but she doubted it'd last more than one dance, not with Sydney's dedication to the memory of her long-lost husband. Lauren smiled at the wonderful image of Kent's cousin Trey dancing close with Misty, his talented fiancée, because they obviously had eyes only for each other.

Lauren couldn't keep from chuckling at Storm cutting a rug with her uncle Slade as he shuffled along, compensating for his bull-riding injury. He wasn't letting anything slow him down, but she hoped later she could help his mobility with hippotherapy. She figured a lot of rodeo injuries, or just sheer wear and tear on bodies, could benefit from equine-assisted therapy. At least, she intended to give it a well-deserved try.

Morning Glory stepped in front of the band with a swirl of multicolored skirts and jingling necklaces. She raised her tambourine and led the musicians in Dolly Parton's "Coat of Many Colors," a number that always brought tears to eyes. She segued into Patsy Cline's "Crazy" and "Always," other powerful numbers that made Lauren think of Patsy's tragic death at thirty and what she might have done if she'd lived longer.

Like her aunt now, Lauren intended to enjoy a long life so she could be there for her family and friends. She had a lot of reasons to be grateful this evening. Hedy was already stronger and happier in just a matter of days. Hannah had blossomed like the early daffodils.

And Kent had given her, as well as Hannah, unconditional love. She had a long list of folks who'd helped make her return a success, and she appreciated each and every one of them. For the moment, she simply stood with her hands on the white railing and enjoyed the beauty of the evening.

As she took a deep breath of the sweet-smelling air, she heard the front door open. She glanced around and felt her breath catch in her throat. Kent stood in front of the pink door, smiling at her and looking more handsome than ever. He wore a charcoal-gray Western suit with a crimson snap shirt and a turquoise thunderbird bolo tie with black cowboy boots.

"Miss me?" He gave her a dimpled grin along with a gleam in his bright hazel eyes.

"Were you gone?" she teased, knowing her gaze held the same gleam as his eyes. As much as she was enjoying the party and meeting folks, she really just wanted to be alone with her love.

He chuckled at her words, then walked over and looked across the balcony. "Good party, huh?"

"Wonderful. Your mom is just as amazing as I remember."

"Good thing she took my house in hand and made sure it was presentable."

Lauren laughed as she shook her head. "You never were the neatest boy in town."

He laughed harder. "That's an understatement." He tucked her hand in the crook of his arm. "But I'm willing to reform for you."

"And Hannah. We don't want her learning bad habits, and she'll do exactly what you do."

"I hadn't even thought about how kids learn more from what we do than what we say."

"And you never know what will strike their fancy and stick."

"Lots of good stuff sticks in Wildcat Bluff, doesn't it?"

"So true." She wanted Hannah to learn from the best, so she'd definitely brought her daughter to the right place.

"Where's the little minx?"

"She went off with Billye Jo and Hedy. They were laughing and whispering about some secret." Lauren squeezed Kent's arm as she looked up at him. "What is so wonderful is that my daughter feels perfectly safe and secure with them."

"And she's safe enough for you to let go a bit."

Lauren nodded, thinking about it. "I didn't want to let Hannah out of my sight in Houston. I felt more and more like a hovering helicopter mother. But I still wanted her to grow in strength and independence."

"You couldn't take a chance there." He motioned toward the party. "We won't take chances here either, but Hannah will grow up with a wide circle of supportive friends and relatives."

"Just like we did."

"Yep."

She leaned into his warmth as she continued to watch the party from her vantage point. She saw Bert and Bert Two talking with three strangers as they moved closer to the house. "Who are those guys?" She nodded in their direction.

Kent took a look. "Mom invited them. They must be visiting the Holloways."

"Do you know them?"

"Yeah."

"And?" Lauren couldn't help but appreciate the tall, good-looking guys around her age with dark hair and muscular bodies. They walked with a definite Texas swagger that spoke of confidence and power.

"They're the Tarleton brothers out of East Texas."

"Single? Married? Engaged?" She grew more curious at Kent's reluctance to discuss them.

"Single. And they've got a rep with the ladies."

"No wonder." She leaned forward to get a better look. "Cowboys?"

"Ranchers. They've got a big family spread where they run cattle and horses. But they're into oil and gas, too. Their great-granddaddy was a wildcatter and friends with Dad Joiner. You know Joiner brought in the Daisy Bradford gusher that started the East Texas oil field back in the thirties."

"I didn't know it, but that's interesting."

"Bottom line in dealing with the Tarletons is that they're wildcatters at heart. And that includes their sister."

"Is she here?"

"Doubt it. She's got a popular Western line of clothes that keeps her busy."

"Really?" Lauren grew more interested in the family all the time.

"What I wonder is why they're so far afield," Kent said thoughtfully. "Maybe they've got a business deal going with the Holloways."

"That'd be good for the county, wouldn't it?"

"Remains to be seen." Kent squeezed her hand. "They're volunteer firefighters, so maybe they're giving Bert and Bert Two some pointers about protecting their property."

Lauren chuckled as a funny thought struck her. "Are you saying they're wildcatter cowboy firefighters or just cowboy wildcatters or—"

"Nope." Kent sighed and glanced down at her. "Guess I'm feeling territorial. Fact of the matter, they're Cherokee to our Comanche. Now will you let it go?"

She chuckled at his jealous frown. "Give me a kiss and I'll forget all about them."

He caught her face between his hands and slowly leaned toward her while he traced her face with his gaze as if he would memorize her features to carry with him for always. When his hot mouth touched her lips, she felt an instant sizzle that spread outward to engulf her entire body with flames.

When he raised his head, his eyes were lit with a fire that rivaled the setting sun in brilliance. "Lauren," he said in a voice thick with emotion as he put his right hand in his pocket. "There's something I want—"

"All right, folks!" Morning Glory hollered as the band went silent. "We've got somebody who wants to say a few words." She gestured toward the side of the farmhouse.

"What's going on?" Lauren asked as she leaned over the railing and looked where Morning Glory had pointed with her tambourine.

Three equestrians dressed in bright Western outfits emerged from the long shadow cast by the house. As they walked their horses toward the center of the party, revelers fell back and then surrounded them until the riders were the center of attention.

"Oh my," Lauren whispered as her eyes filled with tears at the sight of Hedy, Hannah, and Billye Jo on horseback.

Kent glanced down at her and grinned big enough to show his dimples.

"You knew?"

"Mom and Dad planned it with them." He clasped her hand and entwined their fingers. "We all wanted to surprise you."

"Me?"

"Just wait." He pointed toward Hedy. "She's wearing Morning Glory's soaring eagle necklace that I finally got around to giving her."

"Looks perfect." Lauren clasped her own macramé necklace, smiling at the thought that pretty soon everybody would be wearing one.

Hedy raised her bright-red cowgirl hat and waved it around in a circle over her head. "It's yeehaw time!" She pointed around the group with a hand in a showy red leather-fringed glove. "Let's hear it!"

As a wave of yeehaws washed over the party, up on the balcony, and around the ranch, Lauren put a hand over her heart, feeling an upsurge of love and appreciation for the folks of Wildcat Bluff.

Hedy put her hat back on her head and the crowd grew quiet in anticipation. "I guess y'all are seeing a sight you never thought you'd see again—namely me riding a horse!"

Again, a wave of yeehaws floated across Cougar Ranch.

"I owe it all to my niece Lauren Sheridan for equine-assisted therapy." She pointed toward Lauren.

Still with her hand over her heart, Lauren bowed her head to the audience, feeling almost overcome with emotion.

"As well as to this magnificent horse named Chancy

Boy who received special training from none other than Sure-Shot's famous horse trainer Billye Jo Simmons." She made a wide gesture toward the horsewoman with one hand while the other remained clutching the pommel.

Billye Jo bowed in her saddle as the crowd went even wilder with enthusiastic yeehaws.

"I'd be remiss if I didn't include my very own grand-niece, Hannah Sheridan, who encourages me as she learns to ride her first pony."

Hannah raised her pink cowgirl hat with a sparkling rhinestone tiara in place of a hatband and grinned from ear to ear.

"We're here tonight," Hedy continued, "to ask your help in funding a center for equine-assisted therapy right here in Wildcat Bluff County. I'm living proof that it works. And we're perfectly positioned in the middle of horse and cattle country to provide the best of the best for those in special need."

Again, a round of yeehaws filled the party with wild clapping and nodding of heads in agreement.

"We're gonna pass the hat, folks, so be generous."

Bert stepped out of the crowd and up to Hedy, grinning big as you please. "If you'll allow me, I'll be pleased to pass my hat and be the first to donate to this excellent cause."

Hedy grinned back at him. "Bert Holloway, you're making this county proud."

Bert quickly took off his silver-gray cowboy hat and held it over his heart. "If you'll allow me to show you my bluebird collection, I'll be the happiest man in the county."

Hedy laughed at his words, nodding her head. "I may just have to take you up on that offer."

"It'd be my honor."

She winked at him before she looked back at the crowd. "Okay, folks! Bert is bringing around his ten-gallon hat, so fill it up for a good cause."

Lauren could hardly believe her eyes, and yet nothing could have made her happier than to see her aunt and daughter together. She looked up at Kent. "Thank you. I want to tell your mom and dad how much this means to me."

"There'll be plenty of time later." He glanced toward the pink door. "Right now I want you to come inside."

"And leave the party?"

"If you don't mind, I'd just as soon the whole county didn't see me down on my knees."

"Are you hurt?"

"Not one bit." He clasped her fingers in a tight grasp, tugged her across the porch's wooden floor, and shut the door behind them.

"This better be good," she said, wondering what had gotten into him. "I want to congratulate our riders before they take their horses back to the barn. I know Hedy and Hannah can't stay on horseback long at this stage of their training, so I need to hurry back."

"They're fine. Billye Jo is watching over them." Kent put his hand in his pocket, dropped to his knee, and looked up at her with a mischievous smile.

"What are you—"

"Lauren, I love you more than ever. I love Hannah as if she were my very own daughter."

Tears of happiness filled Lauren's eyes as she looked down at the man who'd held her heart since she was sweet sixteen.

"Will you marry me?"

"Oh, yes—a million times yes."

He held up his closed hand and opened it to reveal a shiny ring nestled in the center of his palm. "I've kept this ring for you these past thirteen years. It's got a little diamond, but it's all I could afford back then."

"Oh, Kent, I love you so much. And I'd love nothing more than to be your wife and for you to be Hannah's Cowboy Daddy." She put her hands on his shoulders and urged him to stand up. When he did, she held out her left hand, palm down.

"I'll get you something big and shiny, if you want, but in my heart this one has always been yours." He slipped the ring onto her third finger.

"Only this ring will do," she said, smiling happily, "because it represents our love that will last a lifetime."

Acknowledgments

I'd like to extend my appreciation to Jane Archer for her excellent Native American history and mythology book, *Texas Indian Myths and Legends*, for the Comanche information and myths used in writing *Blazing Hot Cowboy*.

Special thanks go to Donna, Darmond, Christina, Brandon, and Buckley for our inspirational research trip deep into the Kiamichi Mountains to visit legendary Medicine Springs and see Gilbert Jones's famous mustangs.

About the Author

Kim Redford is an acclaimed author of Western romance novels. She grew up in Texas with cowboys, cowgirls, horses, cattle, and rodeos for inspiration. She divides her time between homes in Texas and Oklahoma, where she's a rescue cat wrangler and horseback rider—when she takes a break from her keyboard. Visit her at kimredford.com.

Please enjoy this excerpt from bestselling author Kari Lynn Dell's

TANGLED *in* TEXAS

Chapter 1

Delon Sanchez woke up pissed off at the world. No different from every other morning in the past four months. But for Delon—proud owner of the fan-voted *Best Smile in Pro Rodeo*—it was like being trapped inside someone else's skin. And that guy was turning out to be an asshole.

He made a fist and beat on his pillow, as if he could pound the dreams out of it. Those stupid, pointless dreams where he hadn't been hurt right at the end of the best rodeo season of his life, and didn't feel his shot at a world title disintegrate along with the ligaments in his knee. The dreams where he went on to the National Finals Rodeo and walked away with the gold buckle, heavy and warm and so damn real he could still feel the shape of it when he woke up.

Empty-handed.

He jammed his fist into the pillow again. His subconscious was a cruel bastard, and a whiner on top of it. An injury yanked the trapdoor out from under some cowboy's gold buckle dream every year. That was rodeo. Hell, that was life. Delon was no special flower that fate had singled out to trample.

He flopped onto his back. A spider sneered at him from the corner of the ceiling, lounging on its web. He was tempted to reach down, grab a boot, and fling it. The way his luck was running he'd just miss, and it'd bounce off and black his eye. He stuffed his hands behind his head with a gloomy sigh. They should have drawn a chalk outline in the arena where he'd fallen, because the man who'd climbed down into the bucking chute that night was nowhere to be found.

He'd disappeared in the twenty-two seconds from the nod of his head to the moment of impact.

Twenty-two seconds.

He'd timed it on the video out of morbid curiosity. Less than a minute before the paramedics jammed a tube down his throat and reinflated the lung that'd been punctured when the horse trampled him, wiping out his knee and busting two ribs.

In that short time, his entire world had disintegrated.

Either that or it had been an illusion all along. But that was his fault. He'd let himself want too much, dream too big. Other people could reach up, grab the world by the throat, and make demands. Every time Delon tried, he got kicked in the teeth.

Whiner.

He flipped the spider the bird, kicked off the blankets,

and got up. Time to dress for another of the increasingly frustrating therapy sessions that only emphasized his lack of progress. He had plateaued, his therapist kept saying, trying to make it sound like a temporary setback. And now she'd gotten married and run off—to Missouri, of all the damn places, as if there were no good men left in Texas—forcing him to absorb yet another in a barrage of unwelcome changes.

But hey, maybe this new therapist had the magic touch that would give him back his life. Or at least his career.

He slipped down the back stairs, escaping his apartment above the shop at Sanchez Trucking without seeing a soul, but had to stop at the Kwicky Mart for gas. With only two thousand people in Earnest, Texas, the face at the next pump was bound to be familiar.

And it would have to be Hank. At nineteen, the kid was a worse gossip than the old men down at the Corral Café. He hopped out of the family ranch pickup, so nimble Delon wanted to kick him. "Hey, Delon. How's the knee feelin'?"

"Fine." Delon turned his back, hunching his shoulders against the bitter January breeze as he jammed the gas nozzle into the tank of what his big brother jeeringly called his mom car. Well, screw Gil. If the elder Sanchez had paid more attention to safety ratings, he wouldn't have thrown away the brilliant, God-given talent most cowboys—including Delon—could only dream of.

Hank lounged against the side of his dad's one-ton dually while it guzzled four-dollar diesel like sweet tea. "Looks like it's gettin' pretty serious between Violet and Joe. Think they'll get married?"

Delon made a noncommittal noise and mashed harder on the gas nozzle. Short answer? Nope. Joe Cassidy would be gone when the shine wore off, back to Oregon. Bad enough he'd leave Violet in pieces, but there'd be one brokenhearted little boy, too. *Delon's* boy. Until now, Delon had just shrugged and laughed at Violet's dating disasters. She couldn't seem to help herself, so he might as well just let her get it out of her system—but she'd never brought her disasters home to their son before.

Beni worshipped Joe. So did every bull rider in the pro ranks—for good reason. As a bullfighter, Joe's job was to save them from getting stomped, and he was damn good at it. Playing the hero made him hugely popular with the buckle bunnies, and it was no secret that Joe had accepted plenty of what the rodeo groupies offered. So, no. Delon didn't think Joe was the marrying kind.

A red Grand Am whipped around the corner and the little blonde Didsworth girl—Mary Kate?—distracted Hank with a smile and a finger wave. He returned it with a cocky grin. "I hear she's got a thing for bullfighters."

"Don't they all?" Delon muttered.

Even Violet. And she should know better, being a stock contractor's daughter. What was it with women, lusting after men dumb enough to throw their bodies in front of large, pissed-off farm animals? Sure, it was exciting, but the long-term career prospects were not great. *Said the guy who got a knee reconstruction for his twenty-ninth birthday.*

The girl parked down the block, climbed out of her car, and made sure Hank and Delon were watching as she sashayed into the drugstore.

Hank gave a low whistle. "I gotta get me a piece of that."

"She's a human being, not an apple pie," Delon snapped. "And she's still in high school."

"Old enough to know what she wants." Hank turned his smirk on Delon. "And you should talk. Like you've never gone stupid for a hot blonde."

Tori. The memory slammed into Delon. Another of those times he'd made a grab for something *way* out of his reach. And fallen hard. "That was a long time ago," he said stiffly.

"But you were seein' her for, what—five, six months?" Because of course there were no secrets in Earnest, and on the rare occasions that the past died, it was buried in a very shallow grave. Hank shot him a sly grin. "You never brought her around, not even to meet Miz Iris. Sounds like a booty call to me."

Delon had to choke down his fury for fear of sparking the gasoline fumes. Besides—damn it to hell—he couldn't argue.

"Can't blame you. I seen pictures." Hank made a show of wiping his brow with his sleeve. "She was *smokin'*. Melanie and Violet and Shawnee called her Cowgirl Barbie."

Tori might've looked perfect, but she was definitely not made of plastic. Delon would know. He'd examined every inch of her on multiple occasions. Had planned on doing it a whole lot more, until he'd called her that one last time.

We're sorry, the number you have reached is no longer in service...

"Too bad she wasn't the one you knocked up.

Senator Patterson's daughter? Beni would be like royalty around here."

Delon slammed the nozzle back onto the pump and wheeled around, biting off a curse when pain stabbed through his busted knee. "Honest to shit, Hank, why someone hasn't strangled you yet is beyond me."

Hank gazed back in wide-eyed bafflement. "Why? What did I say?"

Only the gas pump between them stopped Delon from running the little bastard down as he drove away. He reached over to the passenger's seat, grabbed a Snickers bar, and ripped it open with his teeth, but even the blast of sugar and chocolate couldn't ward off the memories. Tori, with her long blonde hair sliding like expensive satin between his grease-stained fingers, and eyes as blue as her blood. Whose family spread was a Texas legend, the owners reigning as kings and queens of the Panhandle for well over a century.

Tori, who'd disappeared without so much as a *Kiss my ass, cowboy, we're through.* And *stayed* gone.

He'd been stupid enough to be surprised, even after seeing how being a rich girl's whim had worked out for his brother. Tori and Krista were stamped from the same cookie cutter, sugar-frosted temptation with glittery sprinkles on top. How could a man stop at one bite? Especially Delon, with his sweet tooth. But all he and Tori had in common was mutual lust and the fact that his father trucked loads of cattle, while Richard Patterson served on the United States Senate subcommittee with oversight of the Federal Motor Carrier Safety Administration. The Sanchezes' idea of a big night out was prime rib with all the fixin's at the Lone Steer Saloon. The Pattersons had dined at the White House on multiple occasions during the last Republican presidency.

Yeah, Delon had had a real chance there.

Sometimes he wondered if he'd been following in his brother's footsteps for so long that he couldn't help himself. Little League shortstop—check. Defensive back and punt returner on the Earnest High School football team—check. Bareback rider—check. High class, heart-breaking blonde—check.

Illegitimate son—yep, check that one too.

Except Delon had done his brother one better for a change. The mother of his son was—or had been, pre-Joe—one of his best friends. Having a baby with Violet had made Delon a permanent part of the Jacobs clan, who had folded him in like he was blood-born. But Gil *had* knocked up the rich blonde, and now he waged an endless war against her powerful family to be a significant part of his son's life. At least Delon didn't have to drive clear to Oklahoma to see Beni. He just had to share him with goddamn Joe Cassidy.

Delon crammed the rest of the Snickers into his mouth and punched up the playlist he'd labeled *The Hard Stuff*. The bass notes vibrated clear down into his gonads and he thumped his fist against the steering wheel in time to the beat. He might drive a mom car, but he'd match the custom stereo system against any gangbanger in Amarillo.

When he pulled into the parking lot at the clinic, Delon sat for a moment to delay the upcoming appointment. His new physical therapist was probably competent as hell. Panhandle Orthopedics & Rehabilitation was the best in the region—they wouldn't hire anything less. But he was so damn tired of rolling with the punches—of taking the crumbs he was given and pretending he was satisfied.

Don't kick up a fuss now, Delon. Your mother can't come visit if you're gonna throw such a fit when she leaves.

He scowled, drop-kicking that memory into the distant past as he climbed out of the car. On the worst days along the rodeo trail—beat-up, exhausted, and homesick—he'd always been able to paste on a happy face. He was the guy who could work the crowd, the sponsors, the rodeo committees, trading on the face God had given him to the tune of as much sponsorship money as some of the world champions. Now he could barely manage a smile for the receptionist.

Beth, a faded redhead with tired eyes who didn't have much luck hiding her prematurely gray roots or the hard miles that had put them there, smiled back. She clicked a few times with her computer mouse. "Got you checked in, Delon."

"Thanks. Can I go ahead and warm up?"

She shook her head. "Tori said she wanted to do a full evaluation first thing. She'll be right out."

His heart smacked into his ribs at the name. Then he blew out a dry laugh. Geezus. He'd really let Hank get into his head. Yeah, his—no, scratch that—*the* Tori he'd known had been studying physical therapy. But a Patterson wouldn't work at a general orthopedic clinic. She'd be at a highfalutin research hospital, developing new techniques for treating Parkinson's disease, or at one of those exclusive joints in Houston or Dallas that treated pro football and basketball players.

Besides. Even his luck wasn't *that* bad.

Then the waiting room door opened. A woman stood there—tallish, slender, and almost plain, wearing khakis and a white Panhandle Sports Medicine polo shirt. Her shoulder-length hair was the color of caramel. She was probably wearing makeup, but it was the kind a man never noticed. No jewelry. No glitter. No frosting of any kind on *this* Tori.

Then the voice that had whispered through his memories for almost seven years said, "Hello, Delon."

The floor tilted under his feet. He knew he was gawking, but he couldn't stop himself. She didn't smile. Didn't…anything. Her face was as blank as if they'd never shared more than a cup of coffee. She gestured toward the open door, cool as spring water. "Come on in."

She turned to lead the way without checking to see if he followed. Delon squeezed his eyes shut, taking a moment to steady himself. Here he'd been thinking his life couldn't get much more screwed up than it already was.

That'd teach him.

Chapter 2

DELON WAS STILL GORGEOUS. WHICH, OF COURSE, TORI HAD known. He'd been one of the top bareback riders in the country for years, and fans and sponsors alike swooned over that face, that body, and that way he had of making every person feel like he'd been waiting all day just to smile at them alone.

He wasn't smiling now.

Tori led him through the open gym space immediately adjacent to the waiting room, past patients sweating on stationary bikes, grunting painfully through sets on the weight equipment and stretches on the mat tables. She pointed Delon down the hall toward one of the four private treatment rooms. He walked with the distinctive, slightly duck-footed gait of a bareback rider who'd spent a lifetime turning his toes out to spur bucking horses. From behind, the view was spectacular, despite loose-fitting nylon warm-up pants and a plain navy blue T-shirt. His body was denser, the way men got as they matured. The changes only made him more attractive. More…there.

She'd never seen him in workout clothes. Hell, she'd barely seen him in clothes at all, back in the day. Most of the time they'd spent together had involved the opposite of dressing for the occasion. She poked at the memory, the way her dentist poked her cheek to see if she was numb enough for him to start drilling. *Can you feel that? No? Great. We can go ahead then.*

Ah, the blessed numbness. It had settled around her like thick cotton batting, layer after layer, down the long highway between here and the Wyoming border. By the time she'd crossed into the Panhandle, she hadn't felt anything but the most basic biological urges. Eat. Drink. Pee. Sleep…well, she was working on that one.

Everything else was muted. Grief. Guilt. The gossamer thread of anger that wound through it all. She was aware of their presence, but from a safe distance. An induced coma of the heart, so it could finally rest and heal.

If anyone could penetrate her cocoon, it should have been Delon, but she had looked him straight in the eye and there was…not exactly nothing. But what she felt now was an echo from far in the murky past. Which meant her concerns about whether she could effectively function as his therapist were ungrounded, at least from her perspective. From Delon's…hard to tell, since he had yet to say a word. He hesitated at the treatment room door, as if unsure about being trapped in the confined space with her.

"Climb up on the table," she said. "I want to take some measurements."

He didn't budge. "It's all in my chart."

"I reviewed Margo's notes, but I prefer to form my own opinions." When he still didn't move, she added, "You won't be charged for the evaluation, since it's solely for my benefit."

She held her breath as he stood for a few beats, possibly debating whether or not to turn around, stomp back to reception, and demand to be assigned a different therapist. Being fired by a star patient wasn't quite the impression she wanted to make on her first day. Damn Pepper for insisting that she take over Delon's rehab when she transferred here, but she'd rather hang herself with a cheap rope than explain to her mentor why she shouldn't take the case.

Delon finally moved over to the table. But rather than sit on it, he braced his butt against the edge and faced her, arms and ankles crossed. The pose made all kinds of muscles jump up and beg for attention. A woman would have to be a whole lot more than numb not to notice.

"So, you're back from..."

"Cheyenne," she said, filling in the blank.

He blinked. "Wyoming?"

Was there any other? Probably, but only one that mattered. "Yes. I did my outpatient clinical rotation at Pepper's place and he hired me when I graduated."

"Pepper *Burke*?"

"Yes." Surgeon to the stars of rodeo. The man who'd performed Delon's surgery, also in Cheyenne, where Tori had made damn sure their paths hadn't crossed. "I've worked for him since I graduated."

She watched the wheels turn behind Delon's dark eyes, connections snapping into place. Cowboys traveled from all over the United States and Canada to be treated by Pepper and his staff. "Tough place to get hired on."

"Yes." She gestured toward the table. "If you're satisfied with my credentials..."

He blinked again, then squinted as if he was seeing double, trying to line up his memory of college Tori with the woman who stood in front of him. She could have told him not to bother. She'd shed that girl, layer by superficial layer, until there was barely enough left to recognize in the mirror.

Whatever Delon saw, it convinced him to slide onto the treatment table. She started with girth measurements—calf, knee, thigh—to compare the muscle mass of his injured leg to the uninjured side. As she slid the tape around his thigh, she felt him tense. Glancing up, her gaze caught his and for an instant she saw it all in his eyes. The memories. The heat.

Her pulse skipped ever so slightly, echoing the hitch in his breath. Her emotions might be too anesthetized to react to his proximity, but her body remembered, and with great fondness. A trained response. No more significant than Pavlov's drooling dogs.

"Lie flat," she ordered, and picked up his leg.

Halfway through the series of tests, she knew Pepper's concern was justified. If anything, Delon's injured leg was slightly stronger than the other, testament to how hard he'd worked at his rehab. Four months post surgery, though, he should have had full range of motion. Instead, when she bent the knee, she felt as if she hit a brick wall a few degrees past ninety. She increased the pressure to see how he'd react.

"That's it," he said through gritted teeth.

Well, crap. "How does it feel when I push on it?"

"Like my kneecap is going to explode."

Double crap. She sucked in one corner of her bottom lip and chewed on it as she considered their options.

"Is there any chance it's going to get better?" His voice was quiet, but tension vibrated from every muscle in his body—for good reason. He was asking if his career might be over. It wasn't a question she could, or should, answer.

She stepped back and folded her arms. "I'll give Pepper a call. He'll want new X-rays, possibly an MRI—"

"What will an MRI tell him?" His gaze came up to meet hers, flat, black, daring her to be anything less than honest.

"Whether you've developed an abnormal amount of scar tissue, either inside the joint or in the capsule."

"And if I have?"

"He can go in arthroscopically and clean up inside the joint." But from what she'd felt, she doubted that was the case.

"What about the capsule?"

She kept her eyes on him, steady, unflinching. "You had a contact injury with a lot of trauma. The capsule may have thickened and scarred in response, or adhesions may have formed between folds. There are ways to address the adhesions."

"But not the other kind."

"No. And there are limits to how much we can improve it with therapy. You'll have to learn to live with a deficit."

That would mean a shorter spur stroke with his left compared to his right leg, in an event where symmetry was a huge part of the score. How many points would the lag cost him per ride? Five? Ten? Enough to end his career as he knew it.

"Worst case scenario, we can get you to at least eighty percent of normal. Then we can look at your biomechanics, make adjustments—"

He gave a sharp, impatient shake of his head. "The judges aren't stupid. They'll notice if I try to fake it."

She didn't argue. After the thousands of hours he'd spent training his body to work in a very precise groove, telling Delon he had to change his riding style was no different than informing a pitcher they couldn't stay in the major leagues unless they changed their arm angle, or a golfer that they had to retool their swing.

The tight, angry set to Delon's shoulders suggested it might be a while before he would consider trying. Well, he was in luck. He'd landed a physical therapist who knew all about adapting to loss. One of these days she might even get around to finding *her* new style.

Delon sat up abruptly and swung his legs off the table, forcing her to step aside. She pulled out a business card and scribbled a number on the back.

"For today, stick with your regular exercise program. Between now and your next appointment, I'll decide what changes we need to make. If you want to go ahead with the X-rays and MRI, let Beth know on your way out and she'll make the arrangements." She handed him the card. "That's my direct line if you have any other questions."

He turned the card over and studied the front for a long moment. Then he looked at her, his face a wooden mask. "What does your husband think of living in Texas?"

"I wouldn't know."

His fist curled around the card. "Sorry. Divorced?"

"Dead," she said, and walked out the door before he could join the legions who'd expressed their heartfelt sympathy when they didn't know fuck all about Willy except what they'd heard on the evening news.

A COWBOY FIREFIGHTER FOR CHRISTMAS

First in the Smokin' Hot Cowboys contemporary romance series from author Kim Redford

Trey Duval, a rancher and firefighter in Wildcat Bluff, is out of luck. His ranch has suffered from several "accidental" fires and there is no explanation in sight. All he wants for the upcoming holiday is to get to the bottom of this mystery, but what he gets instead is hotter than any ranch fire when he meets city-girl Misty Reynolds.

"This tale will melt even the iciest heart."

—*Publishers Weekly* Starred Review

RECKLESS IN TEXAS

First in the Texas Rodeo contemporary romance series from author Kari Lynn Dell

Violet Jacobs is trying to get her family's rodeo production company into the big time. When she hires a hotshot rodeo bullfighter, she expected a ruckus—but she never expected her heart to be on the line.

Joe Cassidy is the best bullfighter in the business, but what he finds with Violet is more than just a career opportunity; it's a chance to create a life of his own, if he can let her see him for the man he really is.

"A sexy, engaging romance set in the captivating world of rodeo."

—Kirkus Reviews

For more Kari Lynn Dell, visit:

www.sourcebooks.com

TALK COWBOY TO ME

Bestseller Carolyn Brown brings signature southern quirkiness to this fresh tale of Texas love

Adele O'Donnell is sure the Double Deuce Ranch would be the perfect spot for her and her kids to start a new life. Remington Luckadeau needs the perfect place to raise his orphaned nephews, and he's not going to give up the Double Deuce without a fight.

One cowboy. One cowgirl. One ranch.

Who will win the Double Deuce by the Fourth of July?

"Superb! The vivid characters came to life."

—*Night Owl Reviews* Top Pick for *One Texas Cowboy Too Many*

For more Carolyn Brown, visit:

www.sourcebooks.com

OUTLAW COWBOY

Second in the Big Sky Cowboys series
from author Nicole Helm

Caleb Shaw promised his sister he'd mend his wild ways, and he means to keep his word. He wants nothing to do with his old life...or the gorgeous Delia Rogers.

Delia is the baddest bad girl, and when she finds herself on the run from the law, every door is closed to her but that of the newly reformed Caleb. When help and close quarters turn into more, Delia and Caleb are forced to decide what matters more: their reputations or their hearts...

"A true page-turner."

—Publishers Weekly* for *Rebel Cowboy

For more Nicole Helm, visit:

www.sourcebooks.com